VISION 2021

BEST OF 25 YEARS

VISION WRITERS

VISION 2021
BEST OF 25 YEARS

Dave Brine
Carleton Chinner
Jake Corvus
Glenn Davies
Jonathan Furneaux
Chris Kneipp
Earl Livings
Chris McMahon
Kirstie Olley
Allison Olsson
Tony Owens
Martin Rohde
Rowena Specht-Whyte
Allan Walsh

THANK YOU

Thank you to our families, friends, founders, and fans. And special thanks to Chris, Jake, Emma, Sharita, Martin, Jonathan, Heather, Rowena and Marianna for their extra effort in bringing this book together.

FORWARD

Twenty-five years ago, Rowena Cory Daniells, Marianne de Pierres and Adrianne Fitzpatrick founded Vision Writers. For twenty-five years, Vision Writers has been a supportive, proactive group of speculative fiction writers, meeting once a month to share stories and give feedback. That deserves an anthology, right?

This year also marks my tenth year as a member, and I look forward to many more as the group continues to grow and develop. Though in the most important ways, I hope it stays exactly the same. At its core, Vision is small group of passionate writers, encouraging and helping one and other, while having a great time.

I hope Vision Writers can continue to be a place of learning, fun, community, friendship and belonging. A place where we can celebrate one another's victories, steer each other away from dangers, and point one another to the next great opportunity.

This anthology is just a snapshot of a much larger process. The final product of community, friendship, passion, secret drives, quiet hopes, outlandish daydreams and a lot of very hard work—some of which was done in lonely places, at dark times, but always with love.

I hope you enjoy reading it.

Jake Corvus – President of Vision Writers 2021

1

———

NEVER PISS OFF A PIXIE

CHRIS KNEIPP

It started with a sock. Not even a particularly nice sock. An old, threadbare, argyle sock with a hole that strangled my big toe with cotton every time I wore it. Part of a pair, its partner slightly less worn, the heel thinned to transparency, but the toe remained intact. I was fond of that sock.

Penny gave me those socks last Christmas with a card saying, "Merry Christmas. We're over."

As I hung out my laundry last Friday, neatly pegging my clothes to the Hills Hoist, I noticed that the lesser damaged of the pair was alone. The sock with the missing toe had gone missing. Perhaps you know that feeling of despair when you get to the bottom of the basket and there's that odd sock. You retrace your steps. Check the dirty laundry basket and the washing machine. No sock, just a gold coin sitting in the bottom of the drum.

Where had it gone? I had my theories. My favourite: the spinning drum created a black hole in the Westinghouse, like a CERN in the laundry. They make missile silos, so why not? Subatomic colliders at an affordable price.

The truth of the sock's disappearance is, as I've found out, a great deal weirder. There are some things that science can't explain.

I pocketed the gold coin and promptly forgot about it.

On Sunday I did another load. This time my bed sheets were up for their weekly wash when the Westinghouse, in technical terms, shat itself. Now I'm no washing machine repairman but I did what any overconfident amateur would do, and set about to fix it.

Going to my shed, I grabbed every spanner, wrench and pair of pliers I owned, along with the hammer for good measure. Turning off the water, and unplugging the machine, I pulled it away from the wall and tilted it back to rest precariously at a 45-degree angle, so that the back of the controls leaned against the taps.

It occurred to me that the washing machine could crush me, but when you're thirty something, and have no one in your life to look out for you, you live dangerously.

Have you ever looked under a washing machine? Ever seen the motor, the drive belt, or the lump of concrete that stops the drum from rocking? If you haven't, all you need to know is there's a lot of space underneath for things. Living things. Lots of nooks and crannies, for mice, cockroaches and spiders.

I crouched down to peer under the pendulous Westinghouse and immediately the problem became obvious. The missing argyle was tangled between the drive belt and the pulley. I wrestled the offending article and was rewarded by a jab, like a needle into my finger. I recoiled, dropping the sock.

My first thought: redback spider. The sneaky arseholes like dark spaces, so I checked out the wound. A tiny blister was forming on the tip of my index finger. Not a bite then, but a burn. I checked under the machine, shining the light from my phone into the darkness. No redbacks, and nothing that could have burnt me. No loose wires that could shock me. The underside of the old washer appeared surprisingly clean, except for the collection of odd socks stretched between the long bolts that held the concrete block in place. The socks looked like teeny-tiny curtains. I reached for one of them and felt another stinging stab.

I stuck my finger in my mouth instinctively, and reconsidered whether the other pieces were worth the pain. I know you're probably wondering why I wasn't more curious. What can I say? I have an aversion to pain.

Looking down, I noticed something odd about the rescued sock. I'd assumed it would've had more holes added to it. I hadn't expected it to be in three neat pieces. The last thing I had of my ex. Totally ruined.

With the toes completely gone, the calf of the sock was cut in two, with the heel and part of the foot making up the third piece.

Slowly, I noticed something strange about the pieces. The cuts were too precise, the lines too neat. Picking it up, I examined it, turning it over in my hands. What had been my argyle sock was now transformed into a tiny three-piece suit.

What the hell was tiny clothing doing under my washing machine?

It appeared the black thread of the toes had been salvaged, and used to sew the rest of it together into a patterned vest and jacket, and stylish black pants. Engine grease imprinted parallel black lines through the diamond weave of the doll-sized jacket.

I didn't have time for mysteries. I had sheets to finish washing.

Righting the machine and walking it back against the wall, I turned the water back on and plugged the Westinghouse back in. Pushing the appropriate buttons, the sheets continued their cycle. Without thinking I took the tiny, soiled clothes and threw them in the bin.

After a cup of tea and some toast, I went to remove the sheets from the machine, only to find them swimming in water, the untrusty Westinghouse having shat itself again. With a tub full of soaking sheets to deal with, and the prospect of another jab, I decided to leave the machine's repair to the professionals.

Have you ever tried to find a plumber on a Sunday? Fifteen conversations with answering machines later, and finally I got a call back at 2pm.

"Yeah, I'm flat out like a lizard drinkin', mate, but I should be able to squeeze you in this arvo'." He paused. "I'll have to charge double time, it being a Sunday and everything."

Just on dusk, I heard the plumber arrive as his steel capped boots clacked on the front steps. I opened the door to see a squat little man in his greasy, sweat stained fluoro shirt, and obligatory shorts. In his right hand, he carried an enormous red toolbox.

"G'day mate. You got a washing machine problem?" His thick moustache wiggled as he talked.

"Yeah, it's through here." As I led him to the laundry, I shared my weekend expert's opinion. "First, I found a sock caught up in the pulley, and I pulled that out, but I think there's a loose wire under there."

"Loose wire, huh?" He sounded suspicious as he placed his steel toolbox on the ground revealing his union mandated butt crack. Opening the toolbox, he asked, "You didn't try and fix it yourself, did you?"

"Well, I looked underneath, yes. That's how I found the sock."

He frowned.

"Look, I turned it off first," I defended. "Still got a bloody zap on the finger for my troubles."

I presented my blistered finger as evidence.

He took one look at the blister and the blood left his face. "Did you notice anything weird under the machine?"

"Well, a few other odd socks, and some doll's clothing."

The plumber slammed his toolbox shut. The clank sound very final.

"Sorry, mate," he said, turning tail and heading for the door. "I can't help you."

"What?" I followed him in a bewildered fog. "What about the machine?"

He stopped at the front door and faced me. "You've got a pixie mate. Pesky little buggers."

"A pixie?" I asked, sceptically.

"Yeah. Been a few around lately. Think it's the wet weather been bringing them in like funnel web spiders. Anyway, I don't get paid enough to deal with that kind of shit."

"What about the machine?" I complained, aghast.

"It's like this." He backed down the top step. "Pixies can be a good thing as long as you don't piss 'em off. All they ask is an odd sock, and for that they'll give you a coin or two and keep the machine purring like a kitten. So, my advice to you is, you work out how you pissed it off and it'll fix the Westinghouse, alright?"

"You're joking right?" I scoffed.

"I never joke about bloody fae, mate. They're everywhere." He turned and descended the rest of the stairs. "I'll send you the bill."

"What bill? You didn't do anything." But my words were lost on him. It seemed he couldn't wait to get away from his imaginary pixies.

Returning inside, I ruminated on the crazy plumber and the outrage of a bill for nothing. I microwaved a frozen lasagne for dinner that looked more like vomit sandwiched between layers of newspaper, and settled in. Tomorrow, I told myself, I'll find a real plumber. That or an exterminator. I chuckled.

After dinner I sat drinking and yelling at idiots on the TV, when I felt an unpleasantly familiar jab, only this time in my ankle. I jumped up and spun around, ready to confront my attacker.

My lounge chair is one of those wicker ones with cushions on them that you buy at the cheap furniture stores. The kind you don't ask questions about, like where they were made, or who by. But, they all have one thing in common. They come with plenty of room underneath for a small, half-naked pixie to stand. I confronted the 20 centimetres of attitude that stood under my chair, with his arms folded. The pixie's transparent wings twitched and shimmered. He wore a scowl on his impossibly-cute face.

In his hand, the pixie held a sewing needle with a glowing point that pulsed between a soft yellow and white hot. He ranted in a strange, mouse-squeak language. I gleaned he was unhappy from the rapidity of the squeaks and the scowl he wore.

Now, it's been about ten years since I dropped acid, and no hallucination had ever been this vivid. Besides that, the tiny blisters were proof enough that this was happening outside my mind.

"What do you want?" I was trying to hold a conversation with a belligerent fantasy creature. Clearly, I'd lost my mind.

He flitted his wings, colour dancing across them like opal in the light. In the blink of an eye, the little bugger darted forward, stabbed me in the foot with his bright sewing needle and retreated to safety, under the lounge. He gave the needle a flourish, like a diminutive Errol Flynn.

"Right! That's it." I said, and headed for the kitchen in search of insecticide. By the time I returned, the little bugger had disappeared.

After a concerted effort to find the pesky pixie, I gave up and returned to shouting at non-fantasy creatures on the television. Almost immediately, I felt another needle stab.

"Stop that." I leapt from my chair. "What do you want?"

He flew up towards the light and pointed towards the kitchen with the needle. The bug spray was just out of reach and I considered lunging for it, but I'd seen how fast the pest could move. I thought better of it.

I walked to the kitchen, a needlestick to the back sending me to the rubbish-bin. He pointed down at the soiled, three-piece sock suit.

I realised he wanted his clothes back, so I reached in and extracted the soiled clothing, brushing some tea leaves and breadcrumbs off them before offering them back to him. The offer earned me another needle stroke to my forearm making me drop the clothes. He pointed to them, and then towards the laundry. Rubbing my forearm, I reach down and picked up the fallen clothing.

Following his pointed direction, I headed towards the laundry, torn between obedience and wanting to swat this magical being like a mosquito. I'm all for rare creature conservation, but this little guy was really pushing the boundaries of my tolerance.

He disappeared into the machine's inner workings and reappeared atop its lid. A fleeting spark marked his journey from floor to lid, like a min min light on amphetamines. As I approached the machine, he flitted up to the taps: his right foot on the hot, his left on the cold. He pointed down.

Opening the lid, I threw the greasy garments into the machine. By now I was getting the gist of what the Pixie wanted, adding a bit of detergent before turning on the machine. As the water started filling the machine, he pointed his glowing needle at the controls and a tiny spark flew from its tip, settling on the digital display. His wings shimmered like rainbows, and the machine developed a soft, swirling, orange and green glow.

There followed a tense 30 minutes as we watched the dial slowly count down through the cycles. The glow grew brightest during the wash cycle, and by the time it the machine arrived at 'spin', it had turned a soft, morning-sunrise orange. When at last the whirring spin of the drum wound down into silence, the Pixie looked at me expectantly, so I lifted the lid and retrieved his property. All trace of the grease was now gone, which was a big ask for the cheap washing liquid I'd used. Surprisingly, the miniature clothing felt dry, so I respectfully handed over the garments before he could jab me again.

He snatched his pants and began to dress, chattering away unintelligibly, though the meaning of the squeaks seemed pretty clear. His eyes burned with indignation, an angry timbre to his squeaks, giving me a verbal spray that could only have been swearing.

I held out the Argyle vest, which he took, his tone softening slightly, his face a picture of cooling rage. He held out his hand and I handed him the jacket, which he put on, his voice falling silent. Once he'd dressed, he looked me in the eye and strangely I felt like we came to some sort of agreement about how this was going to work.

With another opalescent flutter of his wings, he turned into a spark of light again, and disappeared through one of the holes in the stainless steel.

I haven't seen him since, nor felt the jab of his needle, but every now and again an old sock goes missing, and a gold coin sits at the bottom of the drum. It's an arrangement that works for both of us. I don't invade his private space beneath the washing machine, and he doesn't zap me with his blistering needle. It has its benefits. Whilst a dollar a sock won't get me rich, I occasionally see a glow coming from underneath the washing machine, and it's not broken down since.

END

ABOUT THE AUTHOR

Chris Kneipp was born in Sydney but spent most of his adolescence escaping into the National Parks that surround it. This love of the Australian landscape bleeds into his works of speculative fiction. He has spent many years honing the gentle art of word wrestling, but constantly feels the words are winning. He has been a member of Vision Writers since 2009 and is the current Vice President.

He is seeking a home for his sci-fi novel, *Harmony*, while reworking a young adult series, *The Kasdtien Cycle*, to be published next year. He has several published short stories and writes across all speculative fiction genres.

Chris resides in Brisbane with his wife and two dogs, though his mind is probably elsewhere. He claims to have been to all the places he writes about, even the imaginary ones.

He is on:

Twitter - @cmkneipp

Facebook - @authorchriskneipp

Wordpress - *Part Time Lunatic*

2

PLANET SHOPPING

JONATHAN FURNEAUX

We'd seen the planet's pictures on the subspace internet, so we were prepared for something that needed some intense terraforming. As our family starship fell gently from the hyperspace highway, I gripped the computer terminal tightly.

"Well," my husband said, "it's a lot worse than in the pictures. A real dump."

"Don't say that, Earle. It has potential."

"Wait, is it a gas giant?" Earle asked. "The broker told us to stay away from gas giants. We can't afford the running costs."

I peered through the computer's telescopic sensors, squinting at the blue-grey orb as we rushed towards it. Four enormous rings of debris orbited the planet. The clouds were indeed heavy, but I could see glimpses of brown through the thick clouds that tumbled across its surface.

I gasped. "Honey, it has a moon! Our very first planet could come with a moon!"

Earle threw the starship into orbit around the planet and shepherded me towards the shuttle bay. "That's just great. They'll expect us to pay extra for it. It's like those backyard pools people used to build. No one ever actually uses their moon."

I was giddy with excitement as our shuttlecraft detached from the main ship and rocketed through the planet's atmosphere. Static electricity zipped around us, and then we were through the worst of it. Earle waited until we were quite low and then lowered the viewport above us. The scent of burning ozone wafted around us. He stuck his head past the shuttle's protective forcefield and took several deep sniffs of the air. To me, Earle looked like a man from the planetary agency's advertisements: arm on the starcraft's white lip, hair slick with water vapour.

"Lots of carbon dioxide," he said. "Very little oxygen out here."

"Is that a deal-breaker for you?" I asked, placing my hand on his. I felt the tendons in his fingers tense as he teased the throttle back, slowing our descent even more.

"Hell," he grinned at me. "That's why I bought those lung replacements for us in the first place. We can probably fix the air later."

I squeezed his hand, and we broke through the cloud cover, heading towards the beacon that the agent had placed for us. The planet had a striking contrast of immense mountains and dark valleys, which sank deep towards its crust.

"Can you detect any water down there?" Earle asked. "The advertisement was vague about the planet's water."

I studied the screen in front of me and then shook my head. "No ice either, unfortunately."

Earle flicked a switch, and I heard the deep groan of the landing pads as they activated.

"We'll just see what it's like," he said. "Promise me you won't buy the place without talking it through with me first."

I withdrew my hand. "Why not? I can afford it by myself. It's the cheapest place yet."

"I know," he sighed. "I didn't mean it like that. Please don't set your heart on anything before we've asked some of the difficult questions. You could be buying a real headache."

"You've said that every time we've landed for an inspection. Every. Single. Time. I know this planet is at the bottom of the proverbial barrel. Why don't you try being a little less critical of your wife's tastes for once?"

"I just thought—"

"—you think I'm going to throw away my life's savings? Stop talking down to me like that."

Earle gave one of his long, characteristic sighs as the landing gear touched the planet. I was up from my seat and activating the shuttle's ramp before he'd finished exhaling.

The door cycled open. It was hot and dry. The wind howled, stirring up dirt and sand, before depositing it on the entryway of our shuttle. The saliva on my tongue sizzled from the planet's radiation. My eyes blinked, and the skin felt coarse across my eyelids.

Out in the distance, a stout figure was making their way towards our ship. Earle arrived beside me and waved a greeting. "I think that's the agent."

The stranger carried a light high above his head to guide him across the relative darkness of the planet. A tendril of lightning lit up our surroundings, and I saw a white-hot flash of a world covered by distant pillars of swirling dust that rose to the clouds, and out of sight. The planet's surface was craggy and pitted, devoid of life.

"Ahoy!" Earle called out once the loud explosion of thunder had vanished.

The stranger called back, but his voice was snatched away by the wind. He staggered back and forth as he made his way up the ramp and stepped into our shuttle. The stranger stopped once the shuttle door closed behind him, pulled the breathing mask from his face, and smiled at us both.

"Hi there," Earle said, planting the customary kiss on the creature's lips as a greeting.

"Call me Orbus," the stranger said, leaning forward to greet me.

His lips were as cracked and dry as the surface of the planet. Hair grew all over most of his body, and it tickled me as I pulled away. He had paler skin, which was almost bioluminescent compared to our leathery, green, hairless skin.

Despite these differences, he had two eyes, and four limbs. He was bipedal too. I examined the bulge that protruded from between his eyes, and with a start, I realised that Orbus might share a common ancestor with us.

"I'm Emily, and this is Earle."

Orbus peered at us through long blades of hair that grew from skin across his eyes. "What beautiful creatures you are," he said. "And you both have two eyes, thank goodness. I always have trouble knowing where to look when I meet people who have more."

Earle and I smiled uncomfortably.

"You can always ask someone which eye is dominant," I said. "Most species are polite if you ask."

Orbus nodded thoughtfully. "So! You're both here to see the planet? In that case, I'd recommend using a shuttle to conduct the tour. As you can see, the atmosphere needs a bit of work."

Earle looked at me.

I shrugged. "We'll go via shuttle then."

Orbus threw a look back through the darkness and howling wind. "My own shuttle is a little... run down. I'm happy to give you the tour in it, but I think we'll have a nicer time in your vehicle." He glanced around appreciatively at the white, glassy surfaces that surrounded us.

"The agency makes you use a run-down shuttle?" I asked, but then it dawned on me.

His clothing was handmade. I checked the pocket of my coveralls. Orbus hadn't slipped a holocard with his agency information into it when we'd kissed.

"You're not with the agency, are you?"

Orbus smiled sheepishly. "Well, I figured it was a waste of money paying a middle-creature. This here is my planet. I'm trying to sell it privately."

Earle covered his mouth with a hand. He was getting cold feet. Our broker had warned us that people only sold planets privately if there was something wrong with them.

"You seem hesitant?" Orbus asked, looking between us.

"It's a strange way of doing business," I explained. "Even if we fall in love with this planet, I can't promise we'd be able to purchase it from you. It's too risky."

Orbus slicked back the long hair that grew from the top of his head. "This is an excellent planet, atmosphere excluded. It's been in my family for three thousand years. I've never lived anywhere else."

Earle was growing visibly uncomfortable. "But you've visited space platforms and other planets? On holidays, for example."

"No," Orbus said with a toothy grin. "I've only ever been here."

"Let's hear him out," I said. "Come inside, Orbus. There's a spare seat in the cockpit."

———

As we travelled over the land, Orbus gave us a running commentary about his planet.

"As you can see, we've got barely any planet-life. Plenty of bacteria, though. You can probably cultivate anything here once you fix the cloud cover and add some water features. Or, you can keep its rustic charm, and live off algae farmed underground in vats, like I do. We're in a great location, in celestial terms: at the terminus of a spiral galaxy. It's very affordable to order water from hyperspace and have it delivered."

We flew over an immense, blackened chasm that stretched as far as the eye could see.

"The water is all evaporated," Earle said simply.

"Ahem." Orbus fiddled with his breathing mask. "Liquid water shouldn't be a problem at all once you push her a little further away. We're almost in the Goldilocks-zone of the solar system. Hey! Have you seen the moon? Virgin. Practically untouched. You could live on the moon while you terraform the planet. Or stay there permanently with the views of the planet instead. I hear that's all the rage these days. Minimalism, they call it. Very low cost."

Earle nodded, but his face was pale. His shoulders sagged further back into his seat with every new piece of information Orbus gave us.

"Why haven't you grown new plant-life?" I asked. "Or fixed the temperature? It would increase the price of your planet dramatically."

"Hey!" Orbus pointed out the window. "Did I mention the mountains? Many of the taller ones will hold snow once the water cycle is repaired."

"Orbus?" I pressed.

He had a glassy look in his eyes, as we skimmed past the tallest mountain on the planet.

"I could never afford it. I mentioned how the planet stayed in my family? That was sort of a curse, wasn't it? It's too difficult to earn any real money when you're a small tribe, stuck on a planet by yourself. A sick person isn't just inconvenient: it's a blow to the planet's economy. Several species up there—" he pointed 'up' towards space, "—got rich centuries ago by mining and building new, exciting habitats in the stars. So, most people abandoned this planet, and the land defaulted to my family. It's a good planet, but I could never afford to look after it."

"Tell me about your family," I said with a nudge. "Where are they living at the moment?"

Orbus looked at me with large, wet eyes as we flew across the planet's equator. He pointed over the curved horizon, indicating that we should fly in that direction.

"All gone. I never found the time to have children. I always thought I'd meet someone lovely, up there in the stars one day. After I buried my parents, I just didn't get around to it. Something always seemed to come up, you know? Silly little things that I can't remember anymore."

"Perhaps you were scared?" Earle said, scanning the horizon with a stony face.

"Have a heart Earle," I said. "Saying things like that doesn't help. Can't you see Orbus regrets it now?"

"I figured people would just move back one day, and I wouldn't need to make the decision. Living in space seemed strange to me. Then the market shifted, and now people are lining up for a tiny cottage suspended a stone's throw from the surface of a star." He shivered. "If I can sell this old pile of rocks, I'll be able to settle someplace where the wind doesn't sting, and the ground doesn't cut your feet. That's the truth of it. Land over there, near those shapes."

We landed in the middle of the formation and donned our protective equipment to scout the surface of the planet. My breath caught when I saw what Orbus wanted to show us.

"Are these ruins?" I asked.

Orbus grinned. He hobbled towards an object that towered over our heads like an obelisk. When he wiped away at its surface, we saw the rusting metal underneath.

Earle had suddenly gained an interest in the tour again. His boots crunched in the coarse sand. He looked up, trying to judge how square the walls of the ruins were. "Was this some sort of communications pylon?" he asked.

Orbus sucked on his teeth beneath his breathing mask. "Habitation, I believe."

"How bizarre."

The ruins were blocky and uneven. There was little rhyme or reason for their design, no uniformity or beauty.

"These are Galdaran designs," Earle said at last. "I'd stake my architecture licence on it."

"Maybe. Was there once oxygen here?" I asked, studying the rust that had formed on the ruins.

Orbus quickly shook his head. "No, there's never been much oxygen here."

"Surely you're mistaken," I smiled and crossed my arms. "I'm a terraforming chemist. For steel to rust, there must have been oxygen."

Orbus chuckled. "Well, if you say so."

———

ORBUS WAVED at us from the beacon as we left the planet, with a promise to contact him soon. As our shuttle slipped through the docking bay of our starship, Earle gave another long sigh.

"What did you think, Emily?" he asked.

I sat, staring at the interior bulkhead of the docking bay. "It's so...ancient."

"Yes," Earle said quietly.

"I doubt anyone could terraform that scorched planet. It wouldn't be worth the cost."

Earle's shoulders sagged in relief. "So, you're not going to buy it?"

"Is that what you've been worried about?"

Judging by the way Earle suddenly relaxed in his chair, that was exactly what he'd been worried about. "I shouldn't have been condescending earlier. You were just so excited about a dead planet..." Earle slowly rubbed his eyes. "You know more about this sort of stuff anyway."

I squeezed his hand. "And don't you dare forget that, dear."

"It's a shame. So much history."

I looked on the shuttle's computer screen, for the last time, at this sad little planet: it was the third planet from its dying sun, on an outer spiral arm of the Milky Way. Then I deleted it from our system.

END

ABOUT THE AUTHOR

In the second grade, Jonathan's teacher let him write novels in the back of his mathematics book. As a result, he developed a joy of writing and literature, as well as an awkward pause before having to do any kind of counting.

Jonathan was awarded a High Commendation by the Fellowship of Australian Writers (QLD) for his first published short story: *The Second Father*. His writing usually explores the themes of power, love, technology, and spirituality.

His debut sci-fi novel *Lessons from the Wreckage*, begins the epic story of the Martian Empire as it desperately fights an alien invader who is eating through the planets of our solar system.

You can also find his short story collection of fractured fairy tales and urban fantasy, titled *Spirits in Your Area*.

3

THE MEMORY THIEF

CHRIS MCMAHON

Karic's eyes snapped open.

Sparking electrics. Snapping cables. The smell of ozone and burning plastic. He was in the Starburst's stateroom, and it was wrecked.

"Kat?"

She was lying close by, her naked body surrounded by a dark pool of blood, her upper torso crushed by a fallen bulkhead. Kat's face was mercifully covered.

"Where is the brood-chamber, Fountain?"

"Who...?" Karic's body was alive with pain. His mind—soft and expanded—was trapped in the fugue state, bonded with the metal floor and the shattered remnants.

He swivelled his eyes. There was no-one in sight.

Slowly he stilled his mind and pushed back the fugue.

"Fountain?" The voice was high and melodic, like a child's. "I am scared, Fountain. Where are you?"

Then he saw it.

The Fintil device.

Usually invisible—nothing more than a distortion in space—it now spun above him like a miniature hurricane of liquid mercury.

It had been dormant for ten years, yet always near him. All his attempts to operate it had proved fruitless. Yet somewhere within it was every piece of information the Starburst had gathered on its mission to Cru, the Fintil planet. A mission that had cost the lives of over thirty-four men and women. The device had stolen every record of the Fintil from the Shipcom, and the memories of Mara and Andrai, his crewmates. Karic had only saved his own memories by halting its attack, forcing it into quiescence.

Their mission to ε-Eridani and τ-Ceti had been declared a disastrous failure. These days the Starburst—the first human interstellar ship—was nothing more than a long-haul transport, running from Earth to the helium-3 mines at Saturn.

The spinning glob hovered near his head.

He could still remember the feeling of it in his mind, probing his thoughts, ripping them away, destroying... before he could halt it.

"Who are you?" it asked him.

Karic groaned, trying desperately to move.

"Please, tell me who you are?"

The voice was in his head. Within the fugue state—a relic of Karic's altered genetics—he could communicate mind-to-mind. He had stopped the device all those years ago by thinking like one of the telepathic, winged Fintil.

He quelled the surging patterns of the fugue.

"I am Karic," he said, his thoughts shooting across the mental link to the device. He continued to speak aloud. It helped to frame his mental communication.

"Karic, my name is Themom Seven. The other buds of Themom's flowering mind were in the brood-chamber with me when I awoke here. But I have no form yet, no proper name of my own. I... I should not be out of my brood-chamber. What if my matrix dissipates? Please return me at once, sir. Or... tell me where I can find the Fountain."

Karic's heart pumped fast. It was the Fountain, leader of the Fintil, who had sent the device.

"Shipcom. Report!" called Karic. No reply.

He cried out as he forced himself to a sitting position. The gravity was a full g here on the lowest level of the habitat ring.

The rippling shape of silver changed, becoming less reflective, hardening, flexing. It settled into the shape of a man's head and upper torso. With a shock, he realised it was a silver-grey version of himself, hovering less than a metre off the floor. The lips did not move, and the pink eyes glittered strangely.

"Where is the Fountain?"

"Give me a moment." Karic struggled to his feet.

He marshalled his thoughts, to match the silent, yet incredibly dangerous device of his recollections with the boyish voice in his mind. It was like dealing with an overactive puppy: one with the launch activator of an antimatter missile tied to its collar.

Karic was still dressed for bed in a long-sleeved shirt and loose trousers. Kat... she had always slept naked.

Then he remembered.

He had woken to the sound of his stateroom doors sliding back. There had been a tall, thin figure, light slipping from its form. It raised a weapon. A powerful surge of concentrated energy shot toward Karic, sizzling with enough power to incinerate both Kat and himself in a split second.

The distorted shape of the Fintil device had appeared, a shield of shimmering green expanding from it. There had been a detonation. Then nothing.

He had woken with Kat dead, and the device had... regressed.

Karic had studied it for years, trying to unlock its secrets, yet it had proved invulnerable, not even registering on scans. He always knew it was sentient, and now its mind had been damaged.

"Themom," Karic said.

"Please call me Themom Seven. I have not yet been named."

"The Fountain is over twelve light years away. You are in a solar system controlled by humans—my race—not the Fintil."

"Then... how did I come to be here?"

Karic's breath came fast and ragged. He swallowed.

"You travelled with me from Cru on board this ship." He took a deep breath. "Don't you remember?"

Themom Seven rippled. It resumed its whirling mercury shape and shot straight through the side of the ship without leaving a mark.

Karic let out a breath and stepped carefully through the debris-strewn cabin toward Kat's body. He reached out. Her skin was cold. There was no pulse. How could there be?

He closed his eyes, squeezing the lids shut.

Karic had hardly known her. She was just a young woman hitching a ride back from the outer colonies to Earth in style. Who was he to question his good luck?

He forced himself into action, searching the ruins of the stateroom. Someone had just tried to kill him.

He found the body of the assassin in the corridor beyond the ruined doors.

"What the..." Karic crouched down to examine it.

It was almost eight feet tall, yet thinner than a child. Most of the body was still covered by the light-shedding concealment suit, but the blast had not spared it. Its exposed face and hands were blackened, the gaping, rounded mouth open to reveal scores of sharp, needle-like teeth. The wide, glistening eyes were bright orange, with a small round pupil. Karic could see no ears, but the thing had an enormous nose, like a cross between a pig's and a blood-hound's. The hairless head was crested, like a chicken.

"You were telling the truth. The stars confirm it."

"Oh, Jesus!" Karic surged to his feet. Themom Seven was back, hovering nearby. Once more it had assumed the shape of his head and upper torso.

"Who was that?" said Themom Seven, moving over to examine the dead alien.

"He tried to kill us."

"It is a Thurl male. A non-aligned sentient with limited mental powers."

This was the second alien race Karic had encountered. To his knowledge, he and the three other survivors of the Starburst's expedition to τ-Ceti were the first humans to see an alien. As far as humans were concerned, aliens did not exist. But unfortunately, all data on the Fintil and their planet, Cru, had been wiped from the Starburst's memory. In the absence of proof of the events on that distant planet, he and Jennic—the only two survivors of the Fintil device's attack—had been labelled insane.

Well, deny this! He kicked the Thurl in his side. There was no movement. *God, it's ugly.*

"What system are they from?" asked Karic.

Themom Seven quivered. "That, I do not recall. But if this is not their native system, linear thinking demands they arrived here in a starship. Such a ship is unlikely to be crewed by only one Thurl."

There were more of them!

Karic ran to his wardrobes, dressed quickly, and armed himself with a stun weapon he kept for emergency use.

"Karic," said Themom Seven. Its voice sounded pleading to Karic's inner ear. "I have form. I know that now. If I traveled with you, the Fountain must have granted me release from the brood-chamber."

Karic left the ruined stateroom and walked down the corridor until he came to the first undamaged intercom.

"Conroy. Majors. Anyone!" He switched channels. "Shipcom. Shipcom! Damn."

Nothing.

"Karic," said Themom Seven, "please talk to me."

"What?"

Themom Seven seemed genuinely hurt. Karic could feel it across the link.

It has emotion?

"If the Fountain let me out of the brood-chamber, he must have given me a name. Please, if you know it, tell me. My matrix must have a point of coherency!"

Karic shook his head. This thing had tried to burn all memories of Cru from his mind. It represented a danger of the highest degree, ordained by its Fintil master.

"You did not tell me your name, Themom Seven," said Karic.

"I am a sentient, stable intelligence in an independent matrix. I cannot be designated as the Seventh bud of Themom anymore. I am fully formed. I must have my own name."

Karic crept toward the rear access way. This would take him up into the habitat ring, toward the centre of the ship.

"Please, I must have a name!"

"I don't know your name!" shouted Karic, instantly regretting it, because any assassin still lurking in the ship could have heard his outburst from the other end of the rotating habitat.

The device rippled, its colour changing from silver to glowing red, finally settling back to reflective mercury again, and its original spinning form.

"I must have a name."

"I don't know your name."

"Dissonance... the Fountain has abandoned me! How else could I still be here?" it wailed in Karic's mind.

Karic shoved the stunner into his belt and climbed up the access way. Minutes later he slipped from the rotating habitat section into the rear storage bay, then pulled himself through the zero-g to the central corridor that ran the length of the ship. He thought Themom Seven had gone, but the device was still silently shadowing him.

He paused, unsure how to proceed. His weapon was no match for the Thurl's.

The Starburst was currently in no-man's land, halfway between the orbit of Jupiter and Mars on her way back to Earth. After ten years of self-imposed exile, Karic had been offered another command. The Solar Federation had lost contact with their colony on Kestrel. That was why he was going back, to take command of a state-of-the-art anti-matter drive starship, the Stargazer.

And now this: the death of Kat, an attack by Thurl assassins, and the unexpected insanity of the Fintil device.

"Karic." The device whispered into his mind.

"Yes."

"I want you to name me."

He remained silent, brooding over Kat's death. Why? Why would an alien species target me... unless this is connected with the events on Kestrel?

Perhaps someone wanted him dead before he took command of Stargazer.

"Name me."

I can't think with all this incessant pestering!

"Okay. Okay. I will name you."

Themom Seven rippled, but kept its original shape. The device was a thief. A memory thief.

When he was a boy, he often played with the neighbour's tomcat, Zed. He was an affectionate thing, but would steal any food he got his paws on as soon as your back was turned. It was as good as any other name he could think of, and perhaps if he named it, it would stay silent.

"I will name you Zed."

It hovered nearer until Karic could see himself in the reflective surface.

"Thank you, Karic. I am Zed," the device paused for a long moment. "It is my nature to have a function. What are your instructions?"

Karic's jaw went slack. For years he had been trying to find a way into this device's strange architecture using his mind, desperate to retrieve the stolen data. Now it was asking for instructions. And the data he wanted?

It's likely to be gone with Zed's own memory.

"Please stay silent. I need to find out if there are any more Thurls on board, and what weapons they have," said Karic.

"Let me look."

Karic nodded slowly. "Okay..."

"I have lost my offensive capabilities, but otherwise I am functional. I will return soon."

Zed faded into the faint, see-through distortion Karic remembered so well, then shot out of sight. Seconds later, it reappeared in its mercurial form.

"I found another Thurl," said Zed. "A female. Badly wounded. She has activated a beacon and is armed with an energy weapon."

Karic gritted his teeth. More Thurls on the way. "And the crew?"

"All have ceased functioning."

"They're dead?" asked Karic.

"Yes. They are... dead."

Murdering bastards! He boiled with outrage. How did they get access to the ship?

To approach the Starburst at all without the Shipcom noticing would require a stealth technology that humans did not possess. Then, they must have somehow overcome ship's security, forcing entry. After depositing the assassins, their ship must have broken away, lurking nearby until the deed was done.

Waiting for the call.

His only chance of finding out what these things were, who sent them—and why—lay in capturing this wounded Thurl. But how many more would he face when her ship returned?

"Where is the wounded Thurl?" asked Karic.

"I encountered her in the main control room. Even in my hidden form, she detected me and activated a concealment device. I could not locate her after that. She was moving toward the rear access way when I lost track of her."

The Starburst was an old ship, but it dwarfed the new anti-matter drive designs. From the forward laser and deflectors to the fusion drive at the rear, it was more than one and half kilometres long.

The Thurl could lurk anywhere.

With the Shipcom down, and no access to sensors or probes, how could he possibly hope to track down the wounded assassin? Concealed, the Thurl could kill him easily.

Karic looked down the long central corridor. The Thurl could be looking at him right now, approaching with her weapon drawn, ready to finish her work.

Then he thought of his crew of twelve: six men and six women, now dead, simply because he had hired them. He clenched his fists and stared at the first closed hatchway, daring the Thurl to appear.

He looked across to Zed, trying to reconcile the whirling shape with what he heard in his mind. From the voice, he imagined it as a small boy, a little older than he would have been when he sat on the back porch in Boston, with the real Zed playing around his ankles and purring as he tried to pull apart a tricky maths problem.

As he relaxed, the image slipped across the link.

"Oh. More like this?" said Zed.

Zed rippled, becoming an image of a young Karic, perhaps only twelve. A full figure, rendered in silver-grey, with the same pink eyes.

He had forgotten he was still linked with the device mentally. Unlike the bond with another human, or even the telepathic Fintil, it took little energy to maintain. This made sense for a device that needed to be operated telepathically. Zed could only detect surface thoughts, but he would need to be cautious. He could not allow any memories of its attack on the crew to move across the link.

On impulse, he reached out to Zed, but his hand passed through.

"I have no physical manifestation, yet I appear solid."

Of course!

"Zed, can you go outside the ship and examine the whole external structure? Look for any evidence of a forced entry?"

Chances were if they could find where the alien had gained entry, they would find the Thurl, waiting for her ship.

"Yes," said Zed.

"Go," said Karic, his voice hushed. Zed grew transparent and shot through the curved wall.

He pulled his way along the central axis and hid in one of the storage bays. It was stacked high with packages strapped down for transit back to Earth.

Time stretched.

He couldn't believe the other crew members were dead. Images of them filled his mind. Burnt to a crisp, or laying prostrate over their stations, or in their beds, a huge smoking hole where their heart used to beat. Karic clenched his jaw, grinding his teeth together. This was not the first time he had lost a crew. He had dealt with those stiff, accusing corpses once before.

Karic's hands shook. He closed them into fists, but could still feel the tremors. Dead. All dead. In less than a few minutes, his dreams of space exploration could be over. He would be as dead as Kat. As all of them.

Yet there was a slim chance this device, which had been sent to ruin him, would save him. He just prayed Zed's new allegiance would not prove too fickle.

Zed reappeared beside him. The limbs were more mobile now. He was adapting himself quickly, mimicking Karic's movements and gestures.

"Karic, it appears the Thurls forced an entryway near the forward laser, creating a temporary dock in the housings beyond the forward deflectors."

It made sense. The Shipcom had few sensors that far forward.

The problem was how to approach the wounded Thurl, assuming she would wait at that spot. Karic would have to pull himself up the narrow approach corridor. She would see him coming for hundreds of metres. How could he get close enough to operate the stunner?

Then he remembered how effortlessly Zed could render himself invisible. Perhaps he could conceal him as well?

"Zed, if you place yourself in front of me, could you shield me from sight?"

"Yes, but remember, the Thurl detected me. It may have enhanced senses, or other technology."

If the Thurl was wounded, perhaps it would give him the edge he needed.

Karic tapped his finger on a crate, wondering how far to push Zed's recollections. If Zed remembered his own purpose and reactivated his program... Karic wasn't sure he could shut him down a second time.

"Zed, you were close to me when the assassin struck. A defensive shield expanded from you, deflecting the blast. Is it still operable?"

"I'm not sure," said Zed. He floated back against a crate, imitating Karic's posture. His ghostly face creased in a frown. "Only certain energy weapons can disrupt my matrix. The defensive shielding is built into my framework. It activates automatically."

Karic nodded.

"I... do not remember the attack. It must have disrupted my memory containment," said Zed.

Karic was planning ahead, thinking of his journey to the forward access way.

"Okay, Zed. Get in front of me. Shield me from sight."

"Okay," replied Zed. He was adapting his speech patterns as well. Zed moved in front of Karic, flattened out, then faded away.

"I'm starting forward," said Karic.

"I will shield you, and adapt to your movements," replied Zed.

Karic pulled himself into the corridor. It was wide here, inside the main habitat ring, but it would soon narrow to two metres beyond it, finally tapering to little more than a crawl space past the forward deflectors.

Karic started forward. It was unnerving. He could not see Zed at all. For all he knew, Zed had shot back out of the hull and was flying back to τ -Ceti and his Fintil masters at the speed of light. His skin crawled, and he expected to see the Thurl appear any minute, a cruel twist across her mouth as she squeezed the trigger of her weapon.

His breathing was ragged, sounding loud in the quiet confines of the corridor. He tried to breathe evenly, to stay silent. Karic passed the central access way that led down to the main control room. He looked down the long shaft, expecting a wave of energy to sweep up and engulf him from below. But there was nothing.

When he looked into the polished surface of the metal ladder, he couldn't see his own reflection. He let out a long sigh. So Zed was shielding him from sight. He would need every advantage to defeat the Thurl. Hopefully, her wounds were occupying her mind. The imminent rescue making her overconfident.

He passed over two other access ways, and the entrance to the old docking bay, which was crammed with bulky helium-3 storage vessels on their way back to the hungry fusion reactors of Earth.

Karic reached the end of the habitat ring and carefully opened the hatch. He kept moving along the axis, pulling himself along the smaller tube beyond. He passed the branching corridors that shot out on either side toward the main deflectors. Seventy metres ahead, he could see the start of the crawlway that led to the forward laser. He reached down into his belt, pulled out the stunner, and flicked off the safety. *I hope Thurls have a nervous system like ours.* He would only get one chance—and even that relied on taking the Thurl by surprise.

He reached the crawlway and pulled himself along, inch by careful inch. Any sound could betray him.

If he could stun the assassin, he could disarm her. Then he would have a prisoner, something to use as leverage to protect himself against the remaining Thurls. Above all, he needed the alien alive. He wanted answers. He did not want to take the *Stargazer* out of Earth's system and into a potential trap.

"Kosh, hock!"

It was a harsh, deep voice. The Thurl suddenly appeared in front of him, lying face-to-face with him in the crawlway. Her left arm was a burned mess, but her right was unharmed—and gripped the butt of a small energy weapon.

She fired. A tight, directed beam of purple light.

The beam passed right through Zed and hit Karic in the right shoulder. Before he could react, his arm and entire right side went numb. The stunner slipped from his fingers and tumbled away from him in the zero-g. He grasped for it with his left, but missed.

"The shield isn't working!"

"The weapon is no threat to my matrix," replied Zed.

"Fuck!" Karic started a mad scramble back down the crawlway, pushing himself with his left hand. *Thank God he had no weight!*

The Thurl paced him easily, its huge orange eyes fixed on him with hungry anticipation. Her mouth opened in a low snarl, the ranks of teeth shining white in her corpse-like face. Her nose twitched, snorts of air coming through the huge proboscis as though she were tasting his fear—and savouring it.

Karic ducked instinctively. The Thurl fired again, this time numbing Karic's left arm.

The corridors leading to the deflectors were only metres away, and Karic tried to turn himself in the narrow space. With only his legs working, it was impossible.

"Karic, what are your instructions?" asked Zed.

"Swath. Hock te," said the Thurl. She lowered her weapon, then laughed. It was a wet, savage sound. Slowly, she slipped her gun into a narrow holster and drew out a slim, curved knife, its blade shining with a razor's edge.

Karic swallowed.

"Karic, what do you want me to do?" asked Zed.

Zed was hovering only inches away. The Thurl stared straight at the rippling distortion and sneered.

"What the hell can you do?" shouted Karic, helpless as the Thurl advanced.

"I am designed to extract memory from biological or technological matrices."

Karic's jaw dropped. "Take the Thurl's memory!"

"Commencing extraction."

The Thurl roared as Zed struck, letting go of her knife and retreating backwards into the crawlway.

Karic remembered exactly what it was like to get his memories pulled out. Stabs of pain as invisible needles would lance through the Thurl, moving gradually back through her nervous systems toward the brain stem. Then that hot needle would punch into her forehead... seeking memories.

The Thurl drew her energy weapon and fired into Zed. The beam passed through harmlessly. She fired again, then again. She roared, releasing her weapon to lift a long-fingered skeletal hand to her head.

"Drithe!" screamed the alien.

The Thurl rolled onto her back, then reached down to her belt. She flipped open a concealing plate and tapped a rapid sequence into a keypad lit with violet symbols. A small transparent tube beside the keypad filled with red and yellow fluids, rapidly mixing. The tube glowed with red heat.

"Karic! It is an explosive device!"

Feeling had returned to his hands, and he started a mad scramble backwards. Just as he reached the end of the crawlway, there was a massive detonation. He was thrown backwards as blood, bone, skin and metal shot down the crawlway, ripping through his clothes and into his skin.

It was over in an instant. He was alive, and the Thurl was splattered across three hundred metres of access tube.

"How much of her memory did you get?" asked Karic.

Zed reappeared beside him. "Not enough to know who sent her."

"What about her friends?" asked Karic.

"The self-destruct device sent out an automatic signal to the Thurl ship. She will be abandoned now. The Thurl ship will leave the system."

"Why? Why did they come to kill me?"

"I could not complete the extraction. All I know is they were hired assassins. Your true enemy is still hidden."

Karic lifted himself upright. At least, after ten years of being branded a mentally unstable failure, he had proof that aliens existed, and that they were working to keep humanity bottled up in the solar system.

He looked across to Zed.

And, at last, he had some control over the device that had robbed him of his future all those years ago. How else could he use Zed? Would he dare to manipulate the AI?

"What now, Master?" asked Zed. His voice sounded light-hearted in Karic's mind. His ghostly face seemed earnest and open.

"We contact the Solar Federation on Earth," said Karic, forcing a smile.

The final answers would only be found on Kestrel.

END

ABOUT THE AUTHOR

Being able to escape into the realm of the imagination was handy growing up as the youngest in a family of eleven, and Chris continues his fantasy and SF writing habit from his home town of Brisbane.

His novels include *Warriors of the Blessed Realms* (2020), which blends urban fantasy and fantasy with elements of SF and horror, the hard-SF *The Tau Ceti Diversion* (2018) and his three-book heroic fantasy series the *Jakirian Cycle* (2013).

Chris is also an engineer, and blogs regularly about space science and exploration. He has a fourth-dan black belt in Moon Lee Tae Kwon Do and also enjoys movies and exploring narrow alleyways. Chris is very passionate about music, and loves singing and playing classical guitar. He has been short-listed for the Aurealis Awards twice, and has won the One Book, Many Brisbanes competition twice.

Website: www.chrismcmahon.net

4

THE BEAUTY OF THE DANCE

KRISTIE OLLEY

Avalessa's feet fly through the dance steps. The sequins on her shoes flash like tiny flecks of lightning. The coins around her bared waist tinkle against one another as her arms flex with perfect rhythm, punctuating her spell.

My eyes are glued to her as she summons power like a whirlwind. Her hair trails around her, spiralling down her body. She's so beautiful, but there's more to this feeling than the envy of a plain woman towards a gorgeous one.

From the crowd, Keralise—her aristocratic face turned much older than we are by her derisive expression—smirks at me. Her eyes tell me: look at what you can never be. My stomach constricts.

Avalessa's spin halts with a synchronised stomp and clap, the noise a thundercrack.

Silken pink petals appear, fluttering down from the roof like butterfly wings. Dancing amongst them, pinpoints of light flicker like fireflies on an autumn night. The lights linger, twirling, while the applause rises to a crescendo.

Avalessa sweeps into an elegant dancer's bow. Petals alight in her jet hair. She looks up to the dais where my family lounges on cushions at the feet of my father's throne. For an instant I delude myself into thinking she's looking at me with those glorious grey eyes. The truth is she's looking to my father, the Mursili of Hittani, to see if he approves.

His hands beat together with such gusto it overpowers all other clapping. I swear I can feel him wishing she were his daughter instead of me.

The only person not applauding with delight is Keralise. Her hands touch lightly so she doesn't stand out, but she barely conceals her scowl.

Avalessa seats herself beside her father, the herder. Although half of his face is horrifically damaged from a blazemare attack, he still smiles for his daughter. In fact, his smile is brighter than the lights her magic created. His eyes radiate love and pride. Just once I wish my father would look at me like that.

When I look up at Father he's still watching Avalessa. The announcer informs everyone the next show, a troupe dance to bless the land for the growing season, will be ready shortly. I can't sit here a moment longer. I lean down to Mother's ear.

"May I be excused?"

She turns to me, brow creasing over caramel eyes. I know we share many of our dark physical features. If only I'd inherited even an iota of her musical talent, rather than just her appearance.

"Sune, is something wrong?" she asks.

"No, I just need to rest."

I can see the pity in her eyes as she gives me permission. I slip away, not looking back. No one will care that The Disappointment is leaving. My departure might even lighten the mood.

———

As I STRIDE down the corridor I falter, looking at the mosaic that takes up half the wall. A musician plays the bittern while his lover dances for him. I touch the tiles softly. Avalessa still hasn't shown a preference. In fact, she hasn't taken any lovers at all. I wish I could at least play an instrument, so we could be closer like this.

A squeaky voice, unmistakably Quillan's—one of Keralise's staunch cronies—echoes down the hall. With an awkward jump, I race past the mosaic to slip inside a door nearby. I don't dare close the door. They might hear and discover me. Peering through the crack, I can see and hear the pair.

"It should've been you dancing, Keralise," Quillan says. "Not that herder."

"Oh never, that girl's such a talent." Keralise acts nonchalant, but anyone with ears can hear her bristling like a cat whose territory has been violated.

"Your father's the wealthiest, excepting only the Mursili, it's almost an insult he didn't select you. Not to mention you're the better dancer by far. Perhaps you'll have a chance to show him his error at tonight's feast?"

Keralise waved a dismissive hand. "The only thing that's going to ruin tonight's feast is that I'll have to speak to all the royals, including The Disappointment." Keralise's eyes flick to the door I'm hiding behind. I stiffen.

"True words," laughs Quillan. "I don't know why they don't just hide Sune in her room and pretend she doesn't exist. I mean, the shame of it!"

"I pity Sune, you know," Keralise lies with such false sweetness her teeth should rot out. "Tone-deaf and uncoordinated. And the number of masters her parents have burned out trying to teach her any skill."

They laugh and pass by while I blink back tears.

Keralise looks back, staring right at the crack I'm watching through. "If I were that untalented, I'd kill myself."

My vision blurs but I hold in my sob until I can't hear them anymore, then I bolt for my secret meadow. It hides on an awkward slope unsuitable for the herds on the other side of a small forest just outside the city walls. It normally isn't a long walk, but in my haste and distress my clumsy legs keep tangling in the jewelled skirt of my takchita, tripping me repeatedly. My hands and knees sting by the time I fling myself down in the empty field.

On the ground I press my tear-damp face into the pine needle carpet beneath the trees at the very edge of the meadow. The tangy scent surrounds me, soothes me like always. Slowly I ease into a sitting position and wipe away my tears. In front of me the waving grass is spotted with bright colours, wildflowers toughing it out to show their beauty. What would it be like to be bold like the wildflowers? No, what I truly wonder is what would it be like to live in a place where music isn't the key to magic, power, and respect? The tears begin again. A crackling behind me makes me gulp, tears stopping as I freeze, too terrified to scream.

A blazemare stands a pace behind me, calm and still, watching me with molten gold eyes. Sparks fizzle and fly from her fiery mane, singeing tiny holes in the leaves of a nearby sharp-leaved milkvetch bush.

The face of Avalessa's father jumps into my mind, followed by smoking ruins, charred bodies, fields and forests left black and barren. With painstaking slowness I edge away, hoping to not be noticed.

But my movement draws her attention. She snorts, sparks flashing out of her nostrils as she turns to watch me more closely.

I freeze. I'm not breathing—if I could manage it, I'd halt my heart too. I think of Avalessa and my eyes sting. I might never see her dance again.

The mare raises her left foreleg and stamps. Beneath her hoof the grass blackens. The smell of burning invades my nose.

The blazemare whickers, then tramps the ground twice more. She lowers her head watching, waiting.

She stomps, whickers, stomps twice more.

There's a pattern!

Carefully, I pat my hand on the ground, attempt a spittle-ridden whicker then slap the ground twice. The blazemare lifts her head, shaking her mane. Sparks scatter and I scramble back. Belatedly, I realise she isn't attacking. She's celebrating.

She raises her hoof to beat out a quicker, more staccato rhythm then watches me closely. I groan. She wants me to keep up with her beat, but I know my stupid limbs can't follow my mind's directive.

They never do. I don't want to offend a beast that could roast me alive, but if I could tap out a beat on the ground I wouldn't be Sune the Disappointment anymore.

When I can't imitate her rhythm she lowers her head, but instead of attacking me walks away and starts to graze.

Most people would consider themselves lucky and depart with haste, but I'm curious. Why didn't this one attack me? She grazes like I'm not here. The flames in her mane and tail are low, barely crackling. Her fetlocks barely glimmer, and her hooves don't glow with magmic heat. She's barely alight at all.

A crow takes off from a nearby tree with a loud rwark. The blazemare rears, tail and mane flaring brilliant like the sun, eyes rolling. I remain a statue as the mare prances, flames roaring, until she realises there's no threat. Her fire banks and she returns to eating.

I'd always wondered why blazemares didn't set everything around them alight. Now I know why the worst damage occurs when they're around people: all that yelling and screaming would scare me too. When it comes to the fight or flight response, blazemares clearly react with a 'burn it all' defence.

A thought occurs to me: I can study the blazemare. If I can reduce the injuries and damage caused by them, then I might become less of a disappointment.

I just have to ensure I never startle my subjects.

———

THE NEXT MORNING, I sneak out of the palace before I'm forced to endure more pointless lessons, and race to the meadow with my charcoal and journal.

I can't see the blazemare, until I look deeper into the forest. She spots me and emerges from the treeline. She tries to engage me in dance again, but after three rounds gives up and walks off.

Lying on my stomach, the smell of grass and wildflowers around me, I watch the blazemare as she grazes. I sketch her and draw patterns related to her rhythms.

She flicks her tail to a beat, shifts her weight with rhythm. Even her ears twist and twitch to unheard music. Of course such a magical beast would have a musical soul. How had this remained undiscovered until now?

She's quite placid around me, and before evening falls she comes close, grazing on the purple rock cress beside me. I can feel the heat radiate from her. The blazemare's coat is a glossy black. Her mane, tail, fetlocks, and a few patches on her rump and shoulder are flame. She nibbles at flowers close to me. Her head draws nearer.

The idea is a stupid one, I know it is, but my hand moves towards her before I even think about the consequences. I touch her neck, well away from her mane, fingertips stroking the healthy black coat.

I yank my hand back immediately, sucking in my lips to forestall my yelp. I grip the burned fingertips inside my other hand, but the enclosing body heat only exacerbates the pain, so I release them and shake them instead. I try to keep the motion behind my body so as not to startle her.

With my uninjured hand I make a note that even the hair that is not living flame, is still extremely hot.

———

THE NEXT DAY is a treat because another blazemare comes to the field. The two size each other up before the first mare engages the second in a rhythm contest. They swirl around each other, a vortex of crimson and gold, flashing gloriously enough to shame the sun.

My charcoal stick flies across the page as I note the beats they use. I can barely keep up, even using shorthand. Finally, they rear together, manes flaring so hot they burn white. Yet before their hooves return to the earth, they reduce their fire back to grazing level.

I've never seen anything more beautiful in my life. Even Avalessa, as much as she moves my heart, can't compare to the blazemares.

No doubt that's why it stings like a viper bite when later that day Keralise's father, Granthar, approaches my father.

"We must destroy the blazemares before they damage our lands," Granthar says. "I request gunners to assist me in their dispatch."

He has his own gunners. I lower my face to hide my glare. He just doesn't want to lose any of his own men. That isn't the worst of it though. Those beautiful mares, misunderstood, will be killed. I come to my feet.

"No, you can't."

Everyone stares at me: what is The Disappointment doing this time?

I look around at all those down-the-nose stares and plead. "You don't understand, they're magical beasts. They dance, so they must have rhythm."

"More than can be said for you." Keralise muffles her voice to disguise it, but I know it's her.

A few people try to swallow snide snickers at her remark. Father and Mother glare at the crowd until silence returns.

"It makes sense, my Mursili." Avalessa gracefully rises to her feet, tilting her chin up. "How else do you explain their fires if they are not magic? And nothing possesses magic if it doesn't possess rhythm."

Ouch. I know she's defending me, but her words sting.

Keralise stands now, her smile glacial. "My Mursili, if Avalessa is so certain the blazemares are creatures of music then should she not, as First Dancer of Hitanni, be able to tame one?"

Father swallows so hard I can hear it. If he denies Avalessa the chance to try, he'll be slighting her talent in front of the assemblage and she'll lose her position as First Dancer. To accept Keralise's challenge, however, is to pit Avalessa against the deadly blazemares.

I watch his eyes flick through the room, searching for another way. His eyes land on me. I'm the person who made the suggestion. It would be within the law to nominate me in Avalessa's stead. I wait to see if Father will choose his failure daughter or his favourite dancer.

When his eyes move on, I feel relief but happiness eludes me. He's chosen to save me but at the expense of Avalessa.

Avalessa's fists clench at her sides, the sparkle gone from her eyes. She can't refuse. Her her father's injuries have meant they have a smaller, less profitable flock than they used to possess. Her role as First Dancer fills the financial gap.

Avalessa looks around, panic contorting her features, searching for someone, anyone, who can help her. Her chest shudders as she tries to swallow a sob. I imagine she's thinking of her father's burns.

For an instant she looks at me. She must know she could mention I was the first to speak, but that could be viewed as treason, so she lowers her eyes.

I consider nominating myself, but I know I have no chance. At least Avalessa—with her dancing magic—might triumph, slim though her chances are.

"Are your words a challenge, Keralise?" Father asks.

My heart leaps, has Father found a loophole? I lean forward, fighting a smile.

Keralise falters, her proud stance shrinking. Then her lips twitch into a smile only a fraction this side of a sneer. "Yes, my Mursili."

Now my father is the one whose stance shifts. He must have expected her to rescind the challenge if she were forced to participate.

"Then the first to tame a blazemare shall be First Dancer of Hitanni."

Avalessa nods. A single, silent nod to accept the challenge and her fate.

———

I STARE at the ceiling of my bedroom. I'm a lump. A useless disappointment and a lump. I can't even save the person I love from a terrible death. I wish I weren't so useless. I wish I'd never tried to save the blazemares. If only I hadn't wanted to keep them safe, keep researching them, keep watching them dance.

Dance.

I sit upright, scrubbing the tears from my face.

Avalessa's talent is obvious, and I now know the secret of the blazemare's rhythm. I can't dance, but if I can choreograph a dance to enchant and befriend the mares, I can save both them and Avalessa.

I snatch up my journal and start sketching.

———

STAYING AWAKE all night has left me with sore eyes and I can't stop yawning. After wolfing down some menemen and dates for breakfast, I trudge all over the palace asking where Avalessa is. The servants I ask inform me she isn't here in the palace. She could be with her father, they live in a tent and follow their herd, but the servants don't know where they are grazing at the moment.. My gut weighs heavy inside me. And then it grows cold also. She could already be in the meadow.

I grab fistfuls of my kaftan's skirt and race for the meadow. A few of the older aristocrats gasp as I flash past, but who cares? Just chalk up another tally in my failure column.

I tumble down the last few stairs from the palace, ignoring the bloody scrapes on my shins and elbows. I surge through the streets, between the wood and mudbrick buildings, and bolt past the small cluster of nomad tents—ever changing but ever present—that surround our city. I charge through the forest and only slow as I am about to emerge from the treeline.

The meadow stretches green and glorious around me. The forest at its edge is dark and richly scented. There she is. Avalessa wears a dancer's practice outfit, a simple cotton dress with high slits in the skirt revealing the gathered salvar underneath. She probably reasons that her father will be able to sell off her finer outfits after she's dead.

Gaining my second wind, I surge forward and grab her hand. She turns, goggling at me.

I'm not sure she's ever really noticed me before now. I mean, everyone knows who I am and what I look like, but no one bothers taking real stock of me. They just think something along the lines of oh, that's the tone-deaf girl. What must her parents think, with her father's singing and her mother's skill with instruments, surely she should have at least a little talent?

She looks me up and down taking in the rumpled kaftan I've been wearing all night, my dark hair pulling out of its pins and sticking every which way, and my bloodied skin. I drop my half-raised skirt, put my hands on my knees and puff, gasping to get my breath back.

Avalessa stares, wide eyed, whether it's because I'm a mess or because I'm me, I've no idea.

"Don't—" I start, but I'm still struggling to breathe. "Don't rush off to catch the blazemares yet."

"Why not? There's no point in delaying the inevitable."

"I can help."

For one instant she glares at me, but she has better manners than to maintain the look. She corrects her scowl, and asks, "How?"

I explain my study of the blazemares and being drawn into their games. She raises her eyebrows, perhaps wondering if I'm mad. She schools her expression back to the appropriate one she should give her patron's child.

Irritation sears my cheeks. I always imagined she and I could be friends, always dreamed we could be more, but here she is following protocol, acting prim and proper even though no one's around to see.

"Truly. Sit down here and wait with me. They'll come," I tell her. "Oh, and no screaming or sudden movements. When they get startled, they burn brighter and lash out."

Her eyes flash wide, pupils growing bigger. Her hands start to shake, and she gawks at me as I sit down on the grass in my silk kaftan.

"Won't you get in trouble—" She cuts herself off.

"No one cares what The Disappointment does," I laugh. "Sit down, or will you get in trouble for a little dirt and grass?"

"No, it won't matter," she says, watching me with raised eyebrows.

Good, she's starting to act more relaxed with me. I want her to feel free to be herself with me.

I flop onto my back and look up at the sky, putting my hands behind my head. Avalessa stares at me and I burst out laughing.

"Are you going to be shocked by everything I do?"

"Well..." She looks around as if there might be something nearby that can get her out of this conversation. "You don't act like other aristocrats."

"What's the point of putting on a grand show when everyone's mind is made up? Even if I have the finest dress, the prettiest hair, or the best manners, I'll never live up to my parents' achievements."

Avalessa frowns. She looks like she wants to say something, but I can't read her expression this time.

"Say what you want to say, I've heard all the insults before, I won't be mad."

I might cry, but I won't be mad.

"So you don't even try?"

Ouch.

Her brow creases as she continues. "Just because you don't have any natural talent, doesn't mean you should give up."

"Oh, I don't just lack talent. My parents have me with masters every day, drilling me endlessly. I've been training since I was five with no results."

"So you don't have any magical talents, but what about other things? There's more to life than wielding magic isn't there?" Avalessa shrugs so casually I wish I had something to hit her with. Of course she feels that way, she's talented.

A snort stops our argument in its tracks. A blazemare appears, drawing closer, cautious. Its molten gold eyes are fixed on me. Avalessa stares, her eyes grow even wider, her lips a thin white line. Her whole body starts to shake, but she seems to have remembered my words; she doesn't scream or run.

The mare comes as close as she dares and stamps a foot.

I slap the ground, then look pointedly at Avalessa until she copies.

The mare stomps twice, then whinnies. I copy, so does Avalessa.

The next is two quick beats, one slow, and a whinny followed by two more quick beats. I try and fail dismally, but Avalessa keeps the pace perfectly.

I lie there and watch as the mare and Avalessa continue with the challenge. Avalessa matches the mare with stunning skill. The shadows have shifted with the sun by the time the mare finally makes a pattern too complex for Avalessa to mimic.

The mare shakes her mane happily, causing sparks to fly and disappear in the grass. The blades do not ignite. Unconcerned, the blazemare walks away to graze.

"Did you see that?" squeaks Avalessa, eyes shining with more glee even than when she was dancing. "Did that really happen? That was amazing!"

"Now you know why I couldn't let them die."

"This proves it, they're magical." Her smile fades into a frown. "I still haven't tamed one."

"That's not a problem, you've got some time."

"No, I don't. I'm racing against Keralise."

"Trust me, Keralise will wait for you to fail then either demand she wins by default or bow out of the race." I smile. "Meanwhile I've got an idea." I show her my journal full of notes and the sketches of the dance moves. "I think you'd be safe to practice here right now. The blazemares have been calm around me this whole week and I can't get past three rounds with them. If my dance works, they'll surely let you pat them. Maybe after that, one of the hostlers can give us some advice."

"Practice? Mmm." Avalessa eyes the mare with pinched lips. She re-reads the choreography and slowly moves through the steps, frequently checking my journal to ensure she hasn't missed a move.

"You skipped the double stomp after the twirl," I correct her.

She looks back at the journal and flushes. "Oops." Her brow creases as she takes the book, dancing slowly, holding it open in one hand.

I watch her practice, her eyes close on the paper as she tries to follow my charcoal sketches.

"This is quite complex," she says after her third run through. "Even if you can't draw for dates."

Scowling and trying not to flush at the thought of my awkward stick figures I reply. "I based it on their communication. When they stamp and whinny, they have a certain rhythm to it. I tried to get that down on the page."

"So you can recognise the rhythm?" Avalessa asks, leaving the *then why are you so bad?* unsaid.

"My body doesn't move like my mind wants it too. I can sense rhythm, but I can't express it." A sigh comes out against my will. "If I had no rhythm in my head things would be easier. My parents wouldn't bother trying to fix me. Instead they see a ray of hope and they just won't let go."

I look over to the blazemare so I don't have to see Avalessa's pity. The mare's molten eyes are on us. Has she been watching Avalessa?

Avalessa hasn't noticed. "That must be–"

"Horrible, yes. Can we change topics?" I ask through clenched teeth. I fold my arms and turn away. Avalessa is a lot more forthright than I imagined she would be. I suppose that's what I get for guessing what she's like by how she behaves in front of my family. I wanted her to be open with me, but I didn't expect this.

"Sure. Can you explain this move here to me?" She stretches the journal out and points to the figure I've drawn pirouetting with a leg extended.

Pouting, I turn Avalessa around and guide her leg into the arabesque. My fingers tingle when I touch her, and I scold myself for thinking such silly thoughts.

Not that any such scolding could stop me from staring as Avalessa continues her practice, my body and mind both mesmerised by her grace.

That's the key to what I feel. Avalessa is beautiful and talented, but that isn't what draws me to her. It's how when she dances, I forget she's everything I'm not. When she dances, I'm as close to magic as I'll ever be. While it isn't as close as my parents wish, it's good enough for me. Even if she is a bit different to how I imagined her to be, she still stirs my soul.

Avalessa lowers herself into the elegant bow that ends the dance.

I'm sitting on the grass, elbows on my lap, head resting on my hands, staring at her.

She lifts her head, wipes her brow, and looks to me. Her eyes widen and I realise I'm letting how I feel show.

Her eyes flick away, looking to the blazemare. I can't tell if her cheeks are red from dancing or if they flushed in reaction.

"You're a skilled choreographer," she says. "It's so smooth. You flow from a slow start, to a rapid beat, then finish with such a graceful end. I've never known a dance quite like this."

"Thanks," I mumble, eyes fixed on my feet. I want to look up and try to gauge her reaction, but why bother? I'm a disappointment after all. There's no way tall, lithe, talented Avalessa would want short, stubby, skill-less Sune.

"You should show your parents. You can make magic by creating spells."

I do look up now. Avalessa's smiling, but her eyes are back on the journal, re-reading. I never thought of that. She's right. I can work magic, just not in the way people expect.

"When I perform this dance, I'll tell everyone it's you who choreographed it, that way they'll know you aren't a dis—" she looks at me sideways.

"You can say it. Everyone else does, even my own kin."

"What? Even your parents say it?"

"Well, I've never heard them say it, only my brothers and sisters, but we all know they think it."

"I'm not so certain. Your parents try hard to help you with all those lessons."

"No, they try to change me into something I can't be because they don't understand I'm useless."

She's smiling at me as she tucks loose strands of hair behind her ear. My heart falters.

"But this dance proves you're not useless. You can see rhythm in things no one else does, like the blazemares."

I want to say something, but my mouth doesn't work. She smiles at me as if she understands how I'm feeling perfectly. "I'll do one more run through and then we'll practice with the blazemare."

My heart falters again, but for a different reason. "You want to try it now? So soon?"

"No point in waiting once I'm confident with the steps."

"B-but..." What if she makes a mistake? Or worse, what if my choreography is flawed?

She answers my unasked questions. "I can feel something in this dance, a primal power. I don't think I'd feel that if the steps weren't right."

Dry-mouthed, I nod and watch her glide through one last practice.

My body grows hot as she begins the staccato stamps that mark the climax. Sweat trickles down my back, and it isn't until a soft whicker reverberates in my left ear that I realise I'm not responding to lust or the heat of the day.

With caution, I turn my head to see the second blazemare right behind me, her head lowered so her nostril hangs by my cheek. She gives a snort and sparks hit me, stinging my neck and face.

The mare's molten eyes are fixed on Avalessa, just as I hoped. With heart pounding I glance to see what steps Avalessa is performing. She's executing the kicking turn I assisted with earlier. She's almost finished. My eyes slide back to the blazemare. The heat of her body distorts the air around us and each breath I take dries in my mouth.

As Avalessa finishes a slow twirl she executes the bow, circled arms swinging low to almost brush the ground. She remains paused in that position a moment, while my heart replicates the staccato beat from earlier in the dance.

Her face lifts, a question on her lips that dies when she spots the blazemare and my wide, terrified eyes.

The mare walks forward, burning hooves slipping past without touching me. She approaches Avalessa and the dancer remains frozen, her body upright but her arms still forming the circle of the last dance step.

The mare lowers her head and butts it against Avalessa's hands.

Avalessa gasps loudly.

The smooth, black coat seared my skin, but there's only surprise on her face, not pain. Avalessa carefully extends one arm and strokes the blazemare's cheek. The creature leans into her caress and my pulse returns to normal.

Awed, I watch as Avalessa runs her hands through a thick tuft of the blazemare's mane. Sparks sizzle and fly in every direction, but there's no reaction of pain or even discomfort from Avalessa. Her face splits into a glorious smile and her eyes flick over to me, her expression screaming, 'Look, look!'

A gunshot cracks through the air.

Heat blasts me in the face and I'm slammed onto my back. After a while I open my eyes. My vision is swimming and I'm unsure if I've been on my back for only a heartbeat, or longer. Aching, but too terrified to remain lying down I sit back up.

The blazemare Avalessa was stroking lies in a smouldering heap. There are no flames on her anymore. Her shiny coat is now ruddy charcoal and plumes of smoke curl up from her like from a suddenly extinguished fire.

I can't see Avalessa. I come to my feet, body shaking, ears roaring, and spot Keralise.

She stands on the other side of the meadow, rifle still aimed at where the blazemare had stood. I should've known. Keralise wouldn't just stand aside and hope for Avalessa's failure: she would ensure it. I gape at her as she aims at the other blazemare.

The other mare burns white-hot, the grass around her alight. She rears and charges at Keralise. Good, I think, until I realise Keralise stands in the same direction as the city. A vision of tents lighting up like dry autumn leaves, their ash and debris swirling around charred stonework among the rubble of houses, haunts me.

I stumble forward, my skin strangely tight and hot. When I look down at myself every spot of exposed flesh is red, but there's no noticeable blistering so I'm unlikely to be deeply burned—the distance must've saved me—but I'll have a few scars I expect.

Pushing against the pain, I go to the dead mare. Avalessa had stood right beside her. For an instant I falter. Will Avalessa even be alive?

I hear Keralise fire at the charging blazemare. The sound spurs me into action. I charge through the smoke and there Avalessa lies, blown back from the mare's body, unconscious but uninjured. She's not even as red as I am. Mouth open, I blink a few times to check I'm not seeing things. After she danced for the mare, the mare's flames hadn't harmed her. Did that remain true even for the last flare of life?

Another gunshot fills the air. Avalessa's eyes jerk open. "What...?"

"Keralise killed your mare," I blurt. "You're fine, but the other mare's headed for the city."

Avalessa sits up holding her head and we look to the town in time to see Keralise has missed. She turns and runs, shrieking, ahead of the blazemare.

I help Avalessa up, trying to ignore my burns. I gasp, almost letting her go. Avalessa gapes at me, then we both start running.

The mare bucks wildly as she charges, coals flying from her hooves, sparks lighting up the grass, igniting fires in the grazing fields. Her rage is too great to allow her the sanity of a straight line, enabling us to gain some ground on her.

"Will the same dance work?" Avalessa pants as we draw closer.

Someone has spotted the fireball that is the blazemare. Alarms are ringing ahead of us, jarring against Keralise's screams.

"She has to watch the dance. You need to get her attention."

"How?"

"I—"

There is a crunch and a scream far more discordant than any other Keralise made. The mare stops, turning, prancing in a circle. Terrible splintering and a cacophony of cries resound. A repulsive smell wafts over to us.

I thought I truly hated Keralise, but this...no one deserves this.

People are screaming. Gunners race forward, soldiers flanking them. I stumble forward, lifting my arms, waving, desperate to block any gunfire. They recognise my face. I may be The Disappointment, but I am eldest of the children of the Mursili and they lower their guns at my command. I look over my shoulder as Avalessa darts toward the blazemare and reaches her arms out.

The eyes that glare down on Avalessa are burning so hot they've turned the same blue as the very core of a white flame. The mare lunges.

Avalessa spins in dance, the move gliding her to safety. Turning on her the mare snaps with her teeth, fire burning even on her muzzle, globs of spittle like lava. Avalessa keeps dancing, though her skin is beginning to peel. The mare lashes out with a hoof. It brushes Avalessa's arm, but she clenches her teeth, grunting rather than screaming, and keeps to the choreography.

I should hear gunshots and cries, instead there's nothing but the roar of the blazemare burning. I want to look back to the city to see what's happening, but I can't look away from Avalessa.

She executes the spinning kick, her foot slipping through the halo of fire around the blazemare. Her face flinches, but she doesn't falter.

The flames recede. Their colour shifts from white to red-gold.

Avalessa's arms curve into a circle for the bow and the blazemare's mane and tail reduce to grazing level.

Panting, I step forward as the blazemare nuzzles Avalessa. I catch her as she faints.

———

IT TAKES the rest of the day and part of the night to douse the grass fires.

Every time anyone tries to guide the blazemare from Avalessa's side she flares up. I have to tend to Avalessa's injuries, because the healers refuse to get so close to a blazemare. I keep rubbing aloe juice all over myself to prevent my own burns from worsening when I'm so close to such a heat source.

While I'm changing the bandage on her arm, Avalessa finally wakes up. Her eyes dart around, her pupils are only pin pricks in a grey sea.

"Everything is all right," I say. She looks at me hard for a moment before relaxing.

"You did it," she says.

"Me? No, you—"

She reaches out and takes my hand. Her eyes close and she relaxes, smiling slightly. "You did it," she whispers.

I stare at her, as her thumb gently strokes the back of my hand. The slight friction hurts my burns, but in a weird way it still gives me comfort.

She's right. When my parents find out I'll be free of the pointless tutoring, and maybe even worthy of their love. When the castle finds out I'll no longer be The Disappointment. When the world finds out I'll be famous. But I couldn't care less, because Avalessa's smiling at me, and that is the most magnificent magic of all.

END

About the Author

Kirstie Olley is a mother/ author/ gamer living in Australia physically but the realms of fairy tales in her mind. Kirstie delights in romantic sub plots and her deep 'love is love' belief leads her to write a variety of pairings.

Kirstie is currently working on a series of novellas in her Retailored Fairy Tales world which follows rival Prince Charmings for hire as well as producing a plethora of short fiction.

To check out more of her stories visit her website: www.storybookperfect.com

5

TIMING OUT

DAVE BRINE

I t had been 20 years and 1492 crimes since I last saw my brother, and here at the end of everything he came strolling into my bar like he hadn't a care in the world. Even though we were identical twins, grown from genetically engineered stock, time and crime had taken a hand in ensuring that—at least on the exterior—we now only passed for near relatives.

Rashid looked obnoxiously out of place in Ten-Four dressed as he was in a slick leather overcoat, and the kind of sunglasses you only see at mob funerals. In comparison, the other patrons were either cops in uniform, or had a 'cop' look about them.

There had been a quiet murmur of conversation in the pub until that point, but as the door banged shut behind him, all conversation came to an unnaturally sudden stop, and everyone's eyes slowly drifted to the intruder.

Rashid held up his hands, glancing around the room with a casual air until he spotted me sitting in one of the rear booths. "Easy fellas, I'm here by invitation."

Which wasn't strictly true—he had invited me to join him at the bar for a retirement drink.

Sal behind the bar kept one hand under the counter, no doubt gripping the 12-gauge he kept there for dealing with anyone foolish enough to make trouble in a pub full of cops. Few dared, but they were usually more determined than your average punter. Sal flicked a questioning glance in my direction, and I gave him a nod. He visibly relaxed, and returned to pulling beers.

"Brother." I acknowledged Rashid as he sauntered over to the booth and slid insolently into the seat across from me. He examined the table between us, sniffed, and then flicked away a speck which had infested his impeccable trench coat.

"It's good to see you too, after all these years." He grinned, and I heard the mocking tone in his voice.

"I almost had you, a dozen times or more." It sounded weak even to me.

"You know that whole twin sense thing works both ways, right?" He spread his hands as though he hadn't a care in the world. There had been a link between us, through deep biological programming that we felt as twins, or some conditioning that was supposed to make us better police officers. "You could sense whenever I was committing a crime, right?"

"Every time," I shook my head. "They didn't tell me at first, but I knew it had to be you."

"Knowing something's happening doesn't mean you can do anything about it. It doesn't make you psychic." He called out to Sal. "Bring us two of whatever he's drinking."

I tried to warn him that Sal didn't really do table service, but was surprised when a few minutes later the portly barman brought over two pints of lager.

"There a problem here?" Sal tossed his head in Rashid's direction.

"Nah, just catching up on old times." I slid a cash chit over to him, and it disappeared into the barman's waistband. Sal took one last look at the pair of us, then shook his head and went back to his bar.

"I would've... I mean, I..." Rashid sounded a little less cocky for once.

I raised my glass. "I don't need your money, brother. I made enough to live a good life, and retirement ain't all it's cracked up to be. Besides, you can't take it with you when you time out."

He chinked his glass against mine, and then took a long pull, before banging it back on the table, rattling the other glasses. "You're damned right you can't."

"We knew what this life was going to be, Rash." Meeting him again after all these years washed away any animosity that might have remained between us.

"Maybe we did, deee-tective Bryan." He drew out my title sardonically. "Maybe it was enough for you to live a limited life in exchange for...what? A secure job? All those technical implants that never seemed to eventuate?"

Self-consciously, I looked down to the black computer jack that had been installed in my biceps when I had graduated from the academy. Somehow it had never been used. Any time I enquired about the upgrades, the story had been different—delays, bugs to work out, funding cuts. The brass had always had an excuse.

"And I suppose you think you made the most of your years, while I wasted my time chasing you?"

"Well, I guess we each had our own success." Rashid took another sip from his beer. "I sent you a card every time I heard you got promoted."

I glanced down, feeling a little foolish.

"You didn't read them, did you?" I could feel his accusatory glare.

"Hells Rash, what was I supposed to do? I was the hero cop out there solving crimes and kicking arse. I couldn't be seen fraternising..." I realised how loud my voice had become, and looked around before continuing in a lower tone. "I mean, if someone knew I was in touch with you..."

"We were never anything more than another tool in someone else's arsenal, Bryan." He shook his head at my frown. "Why do you think you never made it out of the non-com grades? Surely after twenty-plus years, even your average plodder would think about a moving to a desk job or getting out."

"I...I liked what I did. I don't need to judge myself by other people's standards." His use of my real name gave his words an edge that could not be denied.

We fell into silence then. There had been a distance between us for so long, and we had forgotten how to talk to each other. Rash finished his beer, sliding the empty glass casually across the table to join the others.

"How long do you think we have left?" I asked pensively. "I mean, they said we had 25 years from our 18th birthday before we started dying."

"I don't feel like I'm dying." Rashid lifted his hands up before his eyes. "But damn, I do feel older than I did yesterday." He crashed his fist down on the table, causing beer to slop from my glass. "It ain't fair, Bry."

"It seldom is. Well, if my life was so ordinary as a cop, tell me what exciting things you did that were so great? That super cop programming has to have come in handy for something." I laughed, but there was little joy in it.

"I think my greatest feat after all these years is still staying ahead of the game. I had my own crew, ripped off more federally-insured banks than I care to count, but never saw the inside of a jail cell. And here I sit in a bar full of cops, and none of them are laying a finger on me."

"I guess that is something to be proud of. Was it all just a score board for you?"

He shrugged. "It started out that I was doing it for the money. But once you have enough stuff you start doing it for the thrill. I could have retired comfortably by the time I was 30 and lived out the rest of my days without lifting a finger, but there was always that itch. Maybe someone, or something, flipped a switch inside of me, and instead of having a burning desire to go out and fight crime, I guess..." He smoothly extracted a cigarette from somewhere and popped it into his mouth.

"Every hunter needs its prey." The words came to me without thought. "And you can't smoke in here."

"Alright, alright. Always playing by the rules. Not like I'm worried about them killing me any more though." He sat thoughtfully for a while, and then headed up to the bar.

I took the opportunity to head to the men's room. I was four beers in, and in definite need of unloading a clip. The thought of hunting echoed around my head the way bad ideas always do in seedy public bathrooms. As far as I knew, we were the only ones of our kind the government ever attempted. Maybe Rashid leaving the force caused them to pull the plug. Maybe there never were any others. In any case, it seemed like we were destined to become two halves of a coin —forever incomplete without the other.

When I returned to our booth, Rashid had vanished, back into whatever luxurious hole he called a home. Beneath my beer glass was a $100 note, an item which itself was worth more than its face value in today's electronic society—provided you could find someone who would accept it.

Sliding the bill out from under the glass I saw Rashid had scrawled. "Sorry brother, too many memories for one night. Same time tomorrow?"

No signature, no phone number, just an offer and an invitation if we were both still alive.

———

AFTER DECADES OF FIGHTING CRIME, living in government-appointed housing, and driving government-issued vehicles, retirement had come as a rude shock. Even before I had entered the academy, we were living in a group home under the guise of being orphans. And now, after years of service, I had become an orphan again, with nothing but a certificate of service to show for it.

A month ago, I had been told to move out of my apartment in the government district. The space was needed for some new fodder being brought in the other end. So, I was being spat out onto the street. 'Timing Out' is what they called it, unofficially anyway. A nice euphemism for the kinds of people who were too dumb, or broke, or broken to quit while they were ahead. Some just didn't have anyone else. Wives and families just aren't designed to withstand the rigours of endless nightshifts and call outs, or shell-shocked partners coming home with the story of how they were almost killed, again.

There might have been glamour or honour, once, in being married to a police officer. Nowadays you married into the police force, and the force was a jealous partner.

Stepping out of the bar, I realised there would be no cabs going my way. No right-thinking cab jockey would risk going through downtown at this time of night. It was too late for the afternoon shift of cops, and not quite early enough for the late shift.

The underground was still running. I found my platform was deserted, aside from a mildly enthusiastic pigeon that was still pecking at the remains of the day from around an overflowing rubbish bin. Those who didn't have their own assigned cars had to come and go somehow, and on a salaried cop's budget, the underground was usually cost-effective.

My new digs were a single-room apartment in a filing cabinet for the unemployed, and those waiting to die either through drugs, or natural causes. I didn't need much, if I was honest with myself, and the government tended to agree. Modern society had just about perfected the art of multipurpose appliances – combination bed-sidetable-toilets might have been a great way of saving space, but they favoured economics over comfort. When I complained about it to my retirement consultant, they assured me that there were smaller options available if I wished to press my complaint, and that they were working on redefining minimalist.

25 years of un-compromising if unspectacular service, and this was what the government called welfare. They might call it living, but it felt more like surviving until the clock in your head ran out. A man down the hall from me had a pet bird – some kind of parrot I think. Not a real one, they'd been extinct in the cities for decades. You could get a NatuReal robotic one that looked and sounded like the real thing, but it never seemed quite right to me.

25 years of living in a world where all of my friends and acquaintances were also cops, with our lives cut from the same sheet

of cookie dough. We might have been decorated differently, but we were still... cops. There was a sense of order in the lives that we were given that spoke to a deeper need in us. And that was good for 25 years of satisfaction with my lot in life, but now I felt that freedom fading. Was I supposed to live this long? Who am I if not purpose in life?

My main source of entertainment were reruns of cop shows from the early 21st century. There was a nice simplicity to them – the bad guy commits a crime, the police investigate, and it all wraps up neatly in a one-hour time slot. Real police work was nothing like that – they never showed the endless rounds of paperwork, or the cases that remain unsolved. I didn't need a television to show me those, they got reruns in my head when I lay awake trying to sleep at night.

———

THE NEXT NIGHT there was no question about what I was going to do. The choices were sitting in front of the television getting angry about technical errors in police procedural shows, which is the closest thing to a national sport for ex-coppers who don't like baseball, or having a beer with my ex-criminal brother. There was no real choice at all.

I took the underground back to the police precinct—which was literally an entire precinct of the city at this point—and headed over to the Ten-Four. I found Rashid out the front of the pub, still dressed in the same stupid clothes he was wearing yesterday. Maybe he had a limited budget, or maybe he just had a lot of leather trench coats. He was leaning against a black, shiny, petrol-guzzling sports car. Only the wealthy – legitimate or criminal – could afford one of these polluters.

Standing there dressed in his pseudo-gangster outfit, I took in the casual indolence with which he seemed to go about the world. He removed a packet of cigarettes from an inside pocket, and then fished around in another before removing a silver lighter. He lit up and took a long drag, and then caught me staring at him across the way.

"This yours?" I nodded at the car.

"I'm touching it, ain't I?" Apparently, the camaraderie we had been working on last night had begun to fade. He dropped the cigarette and ground out the butt with his shoe.

"Just because you're standing by it doesn't make it yours." I allowed him a grin. "Being a law-breaking citizen, it could well be stolen." I pointed to the bar. "I'm sure someone in there would be happy to run those plates for me."

"Bah, you'd be lucky if anyone would talk to you in there. After you've been seen associating with the likes of me." He opened the passenger door, which gave a satisfying creak. "You ever driven one of these before?"

Pretty much everything built in the last 50 years was an electric-powered vehicle. I couldn't even remember the last time I had seen a petrol-powered car outside of a museum. "Not exactly." Despite myself, there was a giddy thrill about the idea.

He swung the door wider, before stepping around to the drivers' side. "Well, I'm not going to let you bust up my pride and joy on your first rodeo. Get in." It was more of a command than a suggestion.

I shut the door with a loud thunk that made him wince. "Take it easy on the old girl. She's more than twice your age, and she ain't getting any younger."

The car's interior was decorated in red leather, or whatever passed for it these days. No one could afford real leather anymore. The last cow had died several decades ago. Now it was all pleather, or fleather, or one of a dozen other brands promising to be closer to the real thing than all the rest.

"Where are we going?" I asked Rashid, as he turned the key in the ignition. There was an ominous rattling noise, before the engine caught, and coughed into life. He eased the transmission into drive, and began cruising through the streets, heading back into town.

Rashid hadn't answered my question, but I sensed that something was on his mind, and left him to it. As we headed into town, the streets began to fill with pedestrians, and the occasional aluminium box that passed for a car these days. "So, you've never driven a proper car, have you ever committed a crime?"

As far as breaking the silence, that was a whopper. I thought about my life as a cop, the myriad of minor infractions, and technical breaches of the law that came with living life in a world where the criminal code could circumnavigate the entire globe, if printed out and laid end to end.

I shrugged. "I don't think so, maybe the odd moving violation, or cheating on an expense account, but nothing you would consider a crime worth the name."

"Those aren't crimes, not really. Come on Bryan, you're telling me you've never committed an honest to goodness crime, in the past 25 years?"

"Well, no. I guess I had that hard-coded into me as a Supercop not to do that sort of thing. I guess you committed plenty to make up for it." The beginnings of suspicion dawned on me. "Why, where are we going?"

Rashid flashed me a grin. "I just thought we could go and live a little, treat yourself to something you've never done before."

"What did you have in mind?"

"Well, how do you think someone like me get a car like this?"

"Crime?" I asked, ignoring the fact his question seemed rhetorical.

"You're damned right!" He began to slow, and I noticed we were in one of the seedier parts of town. It was the kind of place where honest folk came when they wanted to play around on their wives, or were looking for a score.

Rashid parked in a back alley behind a dumpster, which had begun to spill its contents out into the street. In this part of town, dumpsters came in two basic varieties— overflowing, and on fire. Any that did not fit these descriptions were usually well on their way to doing so.

"I don't know about this. What are we even going to do?" My skin was starting to itch.

"Just come with me." He left the engine running, and got out of the car, going around to the trunk.

"God damnit." I followed him.

The trunk revealed a trove of firearms, and other paraphernalia.

Rashid pulled out a pair of ski masks, and handed one to me, before pulling the other over his own head.

"I don't know about this mate."

Rashid rummaged through the other items in the trunk, before pulling out a pump action shotgun and a jingling belt full of shells, which he handed to me. "I assume you know how to use one of these. It's loaded already, so careful with it. Safety's there." He pointed to a latch on the side of the gun.

"Bro, what are you getting us into here?"

"Just something I always wanted to do, but never had the guts." He dug around in the trunk of the car again until found what he was looking for, which turned out to be a natty little machine gun. The weapon had been modified to feed from a belt, which ran down into a bag strapped to his waist.

"Fuck me, Rash. Who are we going to war with?"

He slammed the trunk shut, and turned to look me in the eye. "Listen, there's just something I need to take care of. An old partner of mine runs an operation down here. I just want to show him he was nothing without me." Rashid had begun to breathe heavily.

I put my hand on his shoulder to tell him this wasn't necessary. Before I could say anything, however, he spun back to face me. Rashid brushed aside my arm and put a finger in my face. "Listen, Bryan. I am doing this for you, as much as for me. You don't need to get involved. You can go back to your cosy existence in that dump you call a flat, waiting to die. But for the first time in 25 years, I'm giving you an opportunity to live."

I sighed. The little voice in the back of my head whose job it was to tell me this was a bad idea was growing fainter. "Fuck it, let's go."

He led the way down the alley, which was disappointingly free of ominous sounding music and slow motion. This was less exciting than I had expected.

Rash pointed to an unmarked door on the wall of the building at the end of the alley. "That's the entrance there."

"What kind of reception party are we expecting?"

"Here's the plan." He brushed aside my question, apparently

unconcerned. "We go up, we bang on the door. If they open it, we bust through the door and take down anyone who resists."

"Bro, this is nuts. We have no idea how many guys are in there, or what might be waiting for us. We have to be smarter about this."

He slapped his palm against my chest. "You're a supercop, and I'm a supercriminal, what could possibly go wrong?"

"Former..."

He waved my protest away. "You aren't going to make me to do this on my own."

"Damn it..." I looked back over my shoulder to where the car was parked. It seemed like a long distance away if we needed to run for it.

"Now or never." He turned and began walking casually towards the door, as though he wasn't wearing a ski mask and holding a machine gun.

"Fuck." I jogged to catch up with him. The door was unconcerned with our presence, and I was surprised that there were no security cameras watching us, if this truly were such a big operation as Rashid claimed.

Before I could change my mind, he began hammering on the door with his fist. No sounds came from within, and eventually he let up.

"You sure this is the right place?"

"Course I'm sure."

"Well looks like no one's here." I tried hammering on the door myself. Nothing.

"Come on, I guess we have to do this the hard way then." Rashid grabbed the shotgun out of my hands, and then urged me to back away. He pointed the gun at the door lock and fired three times. The sound of the gunshots echoed through the tight confines of the alleyway.

"Well, if they didn't hear us knocking, someone sure as hell will have heard us now." He handed me back the shotgun, and then aimed a kick at the edge of the door, next to the gaping hole in the wall.

There was a crunching sound, and the door swung open on its hinges to reveal a darkened room. The adrenalin was beginning to pump in my blood, and the ringing from the close-quarters shotgun blasts made me feel dizzy.

Rashid led the way through the door, with his gun up and at the ready. I swore and followed him through the door. We had to push through blackout sheets of plastic, partially perforated by the shotgun pellets, before we stepped into a brightly lit room. It was some sort of drug processing room, with tables covered in packages. Each shrink-wrapped bundle of white powder was marked with a label that I recognised as one of the major cartels in the city.

"Jesus Christ Rash, there's a fuckton of gear here." I looked around, wondering suddenly what we were going to do with all of this.

"Yeah, and a suspicious lack of guards." He dropped the duffel bag onto the floor and pulled out a large metal canister. "Guess that makes this easier on us." He pulled the stopper off, and I caught the scent of gasoline. I realised he never intended to rob the place.

Rash handed me the canister and told me to start pouring the gas around as much as possible. He pulled a second can out of the bag and began to splash it over the tables on one side of the room.

As I started dousing the packages in gas, I could feel a war going on inside my brain, between the part of me who knew this was wrong, and the other part which said we were doing something good in putting a stop to a major drug operation.

I finished emptying the gas cannister when I heard a door opening, and loud angry voices. Two men stepped into the room.

"Who the fuck are you?" said the one in front, who was wearing an all-black outfit, and a pissed-off expression. "Do you know whose place this is?"

Rashid didn't answer. He whipped up his gun and let off a burst in the guards' direction. The front man's chest erupted as he was struck by a half dozen bullets, and he collapsed to the floor. The man behind crumped as a bullet took him in the side, and he started hollering until Rash put another couple of shots into his chest.

"Shit, this is getting too crazy!"

I glanced back to see the door open again, and three more guys in black slipped into the room. They all drew automatic pistols, and they moved into positions of cover. I was thinking that these were a better class of criminal, when a series of shots struck the wall near my head. I let out a yelp, slid back behind cover.

I looked over to see that Rashid was now hiding behind a table he had pushed over onto its side. His machine gun, while effective, wasn't really built for a close-quarters environment.

"Bryan, you got to get out of here bro." I heard him call. "Just get the fuck out of here."

The distance between us seemed like a football field, and there was no way I could get to him without further exposing myself. Damn. I looked back and fired off another shot at the guy who was creeping up on me. I must have hit something, because he let out a curse, and hauled a table down in front of him.

The way ahead to the door was relatively clear, if I stuck to the wall. I cursed the fact I had only a shotgun to defend myself. I scuttled as fast as I could to the door and slid between plastic sheets. I looked back into the room and could see that the gangsters were forming up to rush Rashid.

"Bryan! Just... go..." I heard the pain in his voice. He must have been hit in the gunfire. He fired off another burst, and then I heard his gun click dry. There was a flicker of flame and then I saw him throw a cigarette lighter into the pool of gasoline on the floor, which ignited with an awful WHOOSH.

With one last glance at the rising flames, I turned and fled back to the car, throwing the shotgun into the dumpster on my way. I sat in the car for as long as I dared, hoping that the door would open, and I would see Rashid dragging his sorry ass through it. I felt a sharp pain in my chest, and I thought I could hear Rash's voice speaking faintly through a wall of pain. It was a struggle, but I thought I heard him say goodbye and good luck. Then the pain faded, and I sensed that I was alone again. I struggled with the controls on the car and managed to get it into gear without stalling it.

I told myself there was nothing I could have done, tried to tell myself it was what Rash would have wanted, but all I was left with was a hollow feeling inside. I heard shattering crash from the direction of the building, and a siren began wailing. The cop in me, what was left of him anyway, wanted me to get out of the car and do what I could to assist. But I knew that lingering was a recipe for disaster.

———

LEAVING Rashid was the hardest thing I had ever done. We had only just reconnected after a lifetime of missed opportunities and separation, but we both knew that neither of us had a long life to live.

Sometimes I still go back to Ten-Four. Not to reminisce about my days as a cop, but to sit in that booth, and order a second beer in the hopes that he'll swagger back through that door and ask for his keys back.

For all of the modern conveniences of an electric car, there really was nothing like the growl of the engine of Rash's classic sports car. It felt like a car that was built to be enjoyed, and not simply as a means of getting from point A to point B in the most efficient way possible. On my forty-fifth birthday, I took her for a long drive down the coast road, enjoying the ocean views and the fresh smell of burnt petrol. It did have a certain je ne sais quoi about it.

The allure of this sports car had always been its lack of modern conveniences, the sheer joy in just drive without course or direction. Sometimes the shortest distance between two places wasn't always the most fun. At some point however, you realise that there is no place you'd rather be than in your own home. Unfortunately, this usually occurs – as it did in my case – when one is about as far away from home as superhumanly possible.

As I sat in desperation with my head resting on the steering wheel, I noticed a button I had somehow missed before – a big black button marked NAV. I pressed it in the hope that it stood for navigation, and sure enough a screen popped up in the centre of the dash.

A button flashed in the middle of the screen 'Navigate Home', and

I realised that I had never known where to begin to look for Rashid's actual home. We hadn't had the time to reconnect on a "Come over for drinks and nibbles" level before we were lost to each other again.

Home turned out to be a place out in the suburbs somewhere, the kind of fortress built by the nouveau riche to keep the unwashed masses out. Which made me feel like a fish out of water, even if I was driving a fancy car.

Rashid's place was hidden behind a tall brick fence, but as I turned into the driveway, a hidden gate lowered into the ground. The house wouldn't have made any society pages, but what I could see of the exterior had that stylish elegance that spoke of wealth. The lawn – actual grass instead of astro turf – had grown up over head height in Rashid's absence.

I climbed out of the car, looking around to make sure no one was watching. The gate had risen into place again. I was grateful for a little privacy as I made a fool of myself. I had a bunch of keys from the car, but none of them looked like a house key.

As I stepped up to the door, a hatch popped open to reveal a camera lens. Nothing happened for a second, but then a pleasant female voice announced. "Welcome home Rashid." And the door clicked open.

Well, that was easier than expected. And why did the house, or whatever this was, think I was Rashid?

Cautiously I eased the front door open. Just because the lawn looked like the beard of the funny-smelling Santa at your local mall, it didn't mean the place was deserted. I made my way through the front hallway, breathing in the musty taste of an abandoned house. It was decorated with the casual indifference of a man who shopped with his eyes closed, and I wondered if Rash had ever really cared for more than just appearances.

On the kitchen bench I found a vase filled with dried and rotted flowers – another sign of needless extravagance. Who could afford to keep fresh flowers, let alone let them die so heedlessly?

There was an envelope tucked under the vase, addressed to 'My Brother'.

I slid out the letter inside and read. "Dear Bryan, I am reading this by your side, but if things don't go well for us today, I want you to know that the house is yours. I did this for you..."

How could I have been so bloody stupid?

END

ABOUT THE AUTHOR

As a result of a dull day job, Dave Brine writes wild, escapist fiction that will make you laugh along the way.

On weekends, Dave can mostly be found somewhere lost in the bush, chasing an elusive bird. A survivor of several unfinished university courses, he finally graduated with a degree in communications and a distaste for taking things seriously. Dave subscribes to the theory that while there is no place in the world for bad coffee, there is a place for mediocre coffee – provided it is plentiful.

Timing Out is Dave's first published story, having slaughtered its way to the top of his pile of unfinished manuscripts.

6

THE SPECTRE IN THE WARDROBE

TONY OWENS

About the Author

G G McInnes was a noteworthy writer of ghost stories in the Victorian era. He produced several exemplary anthologies, the most famous being *Tales of Moral Turpitude and Depravity*, and *Stories to Loosen Your Bowels* from which this story has been taken.

Despite a critically acclaimed career, his later life was marked by sadness beginning with his wife asking for a divorce. This came as a shock, as hitherto he had been unaware that he was married. *The Spectre in the Wardrobe* comes from the later years of his career when he was confined to his house by crippling Francophobia. The sight of even a small croissant was said to send him into paroxysms of fear.

He died in October 1876 after a drunken dare in which he ate the flagpole of the Women's Institute at Widness. He is buried in the local cemetery there, in several adjacent plots.

The Spectre in the Wardrobe by G G McInnes

As I APPROACH the autumn years of my life, friends have insisted I put down in writing the bizarre events which took place nigh on twenty years ago when I inherited Valency Hall. Initially I demurred, but my companions insisted. I find myself putting pen to paper and subsequently moving the pen laterally to facilitate the recording of my tale.

I came into my inheritance late in life. A cousin, Monsieur E. had passed away. His family had fallen on hard times and could no longer afford a complete surname. All that remained of his vast estates was a ramshackle country house, Valency Hall, in the Wiltshire countryside. The lawyer and executor of the will, a Mr Barnaby, of 27 Crimson Crescent in Bath, informed me of the terms of the deceased's bequest.

In the interests of circumlocution, I should describe the solicitor. He was tall man of proud bearing, with a steely countenance that could crack an egg in an adjacent room. He walked with a pronounced limp due to a wooden leg. It was said that he had lost the leg in the Crimea though I have it on good authority that it was in fact an affectation, and that his real leg resided in a locker in London's Waterloo station.

"Ah, Mr Percival. You are a lucky man. A lucky man, indeed. Valency Hall is a fine building with outstanding vistas and good potential for income," he said to me, smiling.

He showed me a daguerreotype of the building. Either Mr Barnaby held perverse opinions on the subject of architecture, or he was quite mad. The picture I beheld was of a monstrosity that looked to have been erected at random across several centuries and had the worst features of Tudor, Gothic and Baroque styles. If it were a person, I would have crossed the street to avoid it, and then gone back across the road to kick it in the undergarments. Nevertheless, I was not one to shirk my familial duty and agreed to set out as soon as practicable.

As there was no train until later in the week, Mr Barnaby offered me the services of a barouche. When I asked him what a barouche was, he attempted to explain with the use of a detailed diagram, extensive mime, a scale model, and finally a pantomime horse.

Sensing my frustration, he instead offered me a horse-drawn carriage. I was disturbed to see that one of the steeds employed to haul it displayed a remarkable similarity to the pantomime horse.

I set off alone the next morning and didn't arrive in the village of Barstowd until dusk began to fall. The inhabitants ran inside, shut the doors, and barred their windows. One disagreeable crone made the sign of the cross and spat at our carriage. I had to admire her accuracy as it hit the driver in the side of the head and dislodged his pince-nez.

I abandoned the carriage and started up the hill, ignoring the pleas of the driver for financial recompense for his damaged eyewear. It was then I got my first sight of the property situated on the hill. The photograph had not done Valency Hall justice. It overlooked the town like a drunken undertaker with a thirst for vengeance. The building exuded a feeling of dread, of nameless horror. The front door was open, and no one was about, so I walked down the long entrance hallway. The previous owner had obviously been a keen hunter as numerous stuffed animal heads graced the wall—bison, lion, tiger, gazelle and what could have been a lamprey though it bore an uncanny resemblance to my Uncle D'Arcy.

"Hullooo. Is anybody here?" I called. The wind howled through the trees outside and a door upstairs slammed shut. I jumped as a voice came from behind.

"Good morning, sir. I am Mrs Kerchenko. She was a slender, fair woman. Her eyes contained a steely resolve that could have stopped an omnibus at twenty paces. "My husband and I have been looking after the house. Mr Kerchenko will be along shortly. He is attending to some sort of incident in the west wing."

"An incident?"

"Nothing supernatural of course, sir. I'm sure it's something that could be explained by science if an empirical approach were to be adopted." She glanced down at her feet.

"You surprise me Mrs Kurchenko. A woman of your position,

knowing such things."

"Quite right you are too, sir. I'm not a great one for book learning. The delights of tertiary education were never afforded to me by a system that denies the working class even the basic tenents of equality or a means by which I might extricate myself from the socioeconomic quagmire I find myself stranded in, due to no fault or malfeasance of my own."

She was quite obviously a simple woman and I realized that I would have make an effort not to tax her intellectually in the pursuit of her duties.

At that moment her husband appeared. "Good afternoon, sir. Mr Kerchenko at your service."

He shook hands with me with a grasp like damp moth. He had a striking head—his ears were those of a pugilist who had given up early in his career and had just allowed his opponents to pummel him at will, while his skin had the texture of a week-old boarding school stew.

"Did you, um, fix the problem in the west wing?" I enquired.

Mr Kerchenko glared at his wife.

She shrugged. "I gave no hint of any specteral or psychic phenomena taking place in the confines of this establishment."

He nodded in satisfaction. "Please excuse my wife, sir. She is but a simple woman with not even the basics of a school education. But she does make a delightful chocolate cake, don't you my dear?"

"That would be a chocolate religieuse, a delicacy particular to the provinces of southern France. Vous etes tous les deux cretins."

The husband laughed. "She does prattle on a bit, doesn't she sir?"

"Ah, we can excuse that in the weaker sex though. Perhaps a short tour would be in order?"

"Right you are sir. Mrs Kerchenko, why don't you go into the kitchen and fix our Mr Percival a nice cup of tea?"

"Certainly. That would be a fine use of my time and completely consistent with my aspirations. Allow me to prepare a hot beverage for you in a subservient manner that only serves to reinforce the inequality betwixt a woman of my intellectual standing and two barely sentient beings of the male gender who would struggle to reach the enlightenment of a retarded gas lamp."

"Jolly good," I replied and good-naturedly elbowed the man servant in the ribs. "You've found a good 'un there, old chap," I said in what I hoped might be the vernacular of the working man.

He looked at me, and then his wife, and back at me again. "Yes, I have," he said, though he didn't sound totally convinced.

Mr Kerchenko took me around the house pointing out items of interest. As we entered the master bedroom, I was struck by the enormous wooden wardrobe which fully occupied one wall.

"Dear God, man. What an incredible piece."

"I see you have an eye for fine furniture," he said.

I ran my fingers over the beautifully varnished wood. "This is an unusual timber. West African Teak perhaps?"

"Not exactly. Do you know of the HMS Baklava, which was wrecked off the west coast of Antigua?"

"I think so. Went down with all hands, didn't it?"

"Indeed sir. The wood for this wardrobe comes from that ship."

"Ah, so they salvaged it from the wreck then?"

"Not exactly. The ship was carrying a cache of small arms to an amputees' conference in the Caribbean. Profiteers removed the timber from the ship while it was still at sea. Investigators found a wardrobe shaped hole in the aft starboard hull, which is why it went down."

"Well, that was rather a rum do," I said. I could feel my eyelids drooping like badly-tailored pantaloons. "If I may, you look a little tired, sir. I could have dinner sent up to your room if you wish and we can tour the grounds on the morrow?"

"Capital suggestion, Kerchenko." I patted him on the back with possibly a little more force than I had intended, dislodging one of his eyebrows. "I'm terribly sorry old man. I don't know how..."

"Pay it no mind, sir," he said, stooping to pick up the offending follicles. "Happens all the time."

———

BEFORE TURNING in for the night, I locked the door, concerned by the erratic behaviour of the locals. Safely ensconced in the blankets I began my journey to the land of counterpane.

A diabolic scratching noise wrenched me from my slumber, and I sat up in bed startled. Unfortunately, I expressed my fear through the medium of micturition. I gripped the blunderbuss at the side of my bed, convinced that the house had been infiltrated by Fenian terrorists. I slid out of the silk sheets, a process made all the easier by the liquid expression of my terror. I then stalked across the room, opened the curtains, and flooded the bedroom—this time with moonlight.

"Come hither," I called in a firm, unyielding voice. I was not going to give the blackguard the satisfaction of any outward signs of fear. "If you do not show yourself, I shall disregard the already flimsy gun laws of this country and discharge my weapon in a manner likely to cause you permanent disfigurement, or at the very least pause for thought."

The villain continued scratching, but now I could tell the sound was coming from inside the wardrobe. Screwing my courage to the sticking place—I kicked at the door.

What happened next is something that still haunts me to this day.

The doors creaked in protest and then flew open. Before me stood the figure with the appearance of a man, and yet was translucent, glowing in a sickly manner in the night air. It wore a great coat of the admiralty, tattered and hanging off its owner like a discarded rag. The face was a horror to behold, with scabs and peeling skin, it was a purulent canvas on which Death had wielded a careless brush. The ghostly figure flew about the room, screaming and moaning. Falling backward, I accidentally discharged my gun, which tore a sizeable hole in the ceiling.

The ghoul stopped and floated back to earth. It stood before me, a hideous parody of a captain of Her Majesty's navy. Raising its right arm, it pointed at me. Pieces of bone penetrated its skin.

"I am lost. Help me," it moaned.

My thoughts were clouded by conflicting emotions. Should I flee in abject terror? Or should I run away in total fear? I chose the former. My egress, however, was curtailed by the sudden intervention of the locked bedroom door; the very door I had locked to deter intruders. Oh, cruel irony of ironies.

One moment my nose made intimate acquaintance with the hard, unyielding timber of the door; the next, my body met the floor in supine repose. A course of action became clear to me—I would feign the outward visage of a coward, to confuse the fell spirit.

"Please spare me," I said. "I am a humble costermonger with six children under the age of five and a wife who is afflicted with the palsy and dropsy. My family rely on me, and I must hasten home to mong some costers 'ere dawn breaks."

Initially, my burst of creativity had the desired effect—the figure looked confused. But as I attempted to sit up the ghost put his boot on my chest.

"I am lost. Help me," the fell spirit intoned.

I found my fear dissipating and being replaced by irritation. "I fail to see how you could be lost inside a wardrobe. Spatially, there are limits to the possibilities of your current location."

This withering attack of logic failed to convince my ectoplasmic companion. He seized me by the throat and reiterated his tiresome complaint. "I am lost. Help me."

Thankfully, I heard the loud report of knocking on the other side of the door. It was Mr Kerchenko.

"Sir, sir. Are you alright?"

The ghost loosened its grip on me as I maintained the illusion of abject terror. "Help me," he said one last time, and flew back into the wardrobe. Its door slammed shut.

As Kerchenko kicked in the bedroom door I barely had enough time to readjust my countenance.

"Well, you took your time," I said, as my manservant stood over me.

"Are you hurt, sir? Should I call for the doctor?"

I dismissed his attentions with as much dignity as I could muster lying on my back in the middle of the bedroom. He helped me to my feet.

"Something evil is abroad this night," I said.

"Yes, sir. The filthy Hun. And the stinking French. Pretty much everything evil is abroad I would have said, sir. And don't get me started on the Italians."

"No, Kerchenko. I refer to a more localised source of malevolence." I pointed a shaking index finger at the cursed piece of furniture.

"Do not be afraid, sir. I too have seen the ghost. I fancy it is partly what drove Monsieur E. to abandon his inheritance."

"We must make a plan, Kerchenko. We can't have these kinds of shenanigans happening. It's enough to make a man take umbrage."

The housekeeper considered this for a moment. "Not sure about umbrage sir. We have cod liver oil and maybe a little laudanum that I keep strictly for personal use. Piles, sir."

Thankfully, Mrs Kerchenko appeared at that moment. "I assume you have been waylaid by the spectre that has of late been resident in the wardrobe? I further assume that my feckless husband and you are struggling to come up with some kind of workable solution to the problem in hand, and that you both would probably welcome an erudite suggestion from myself? No doubt, the conventions of the day prevent you from acknowledging that someone of my station and gender could in any way be useful to you, apart from making cups of tea."

"Did you say a cup of tea, Mrs Kerchenko? Yes, that would certainly go down a treat. White and no sugar if you please."

"Right you are, sir." As she left the room, she whispered in her husband's ear. He nodded.

When she was gone, Mr Kerchenko said, "It occurs to me that we might hire the services of an existentialist."

I considered his unorthodox suggestion. The more I thought about it, the more it made sense. "I see where you're coming from, old chap. If we get the spook to question its very existence and the absurdity of the world in which it lives, then we can..."

Mrs Kerchenko returned with my cup of tea. She whispered in

her husband's ear again.

"Upon mature reflection, sir I think maybe an existentialist is not what we require at this time but perhaps the services of an exorcist."

I heard his wife emit a world-weary sigh. Perhaps the events of the evening, coupled with the manual labour of beverage preparation, were too much for her. I told myself that I would try to relieve her burden a little through my forthright leadership and emotional strength.

I spoke to Mr Kerchenko and bade him inquire in the village, with a view to find some sort of spiritualist or medium who might rid the house of its cursed ghoul.

The next morning Mrs Kerchenko busied herself between making cups of tea by cleaning the bannisters and polishing the aspidistra. She whistled a pleasant little tune as she worked and I enquired about the provenance of the ditty.

" 'Tis The Internationale, sir."

"Ah, it's quite a jaunty little tune, isn't it?"

"If by jaunty you mean spilling the blood of the oppressors of the working class and their lackeys, then yes, I'd agree. It is quite jaunty."

Our little tete-a-tete was disturbed by a clip clopping in the courtyard followed by spirited neighing. This was odd as Kerchenko had not taken a horse. He appeared in the doorway in an excited state.

"Sir, sir. Dame Fortune has smiled on me," and with this he waved his hands behind him indicating a small, stooped crone.

Dame Fortune, for apparently it was she, was indeed smiling. In fact, it was a smile that was quite difficult to miss. Her teeth appeared to have been inserted at random, with no concern for symmetry.

"Ah, it is wonderful to be see ya, my pretty boy, heh heh heh." She laughed and then winked at me in a most disagreeable manner. Unfortunately, this effort resulted in her glass eye dislodging and hitting the floor with a resonant clatter. It rolled across the floor and disappeared into a hole in the skirting board.

I confess I gasped. Dame Fortune was not perturbed, however. She reached into the sack she carried across her shoulder and pulled out a jar full of glass eyes. She took one, spat on it, polished it with the edge of her sleeve and popped it into the recently vacated orbital socket.

"Not to worry, dearie. It happens all the time."

She sniffed the air like a hound and looked to the left and the right. "Ah, there is something here. Something untoward, something..." and here she paused. "Something...oh gosh. I lost my train of thought."

Mrs Kerchenko seemed to become infuriated by this. "There is some manner of phantasm ensconced on the second floor of this establishment and the master of the house would like you to ascertain with some exactitude the nature of this paranormal manifestation with a view to eliminating it, or at the very least removing it to some remote location where it will not impinge on the enjoyment of his recent inheritance."

Dame Fortune paused for a second and turned to Mrs Kerchenko. "Why yes, dearie. I would love a cup of tea."

Mrs Kerchenko glared at her with barely-disguised malevolence.

Dame Fortune then bounded into the house like an elk with a mongoose attached to its nethers. We followed in her wake as she bounded up the stairs two at a time, though there was some confusion as she reached the thirteenth stair and we paused to regroup. Mr Kerchenko saved the day with his quick thinking as he lifted her over the recalcitrant odd-numbered step, and into the corridor leading down to the master bedroom.

She stopped outside the closed door. "This would be the master's bedroom, if I am not mistaken."

I was impressed by her seemingly extra-sensory perception, but on mature reflection I now realise there was a sign on the door that bore the prominent legend MASTER BEDROOM.

She bade us be silent as she gripped the doorknob and turned it slowly. Dust motes danced in the sunlight as the opened door illuminated the room. Well, most of the motes danced. Some merely hovered at the edge of the sunbeam and looked sullen.

We entered the room, the wardrobe dominating the space. "He is here," she said, pointing directly at the haunted furniture. "We must summon the spirit hence."

She had Kerchenko and I move the wardrobe away from the wall, leaving a little space both behind and in front of it. From her endlessly capacious bag she produced six black candles and proceeded to place them equidistantly around the wardrobe.

"Now, we must await the evening."

Mrs Kerchenko looked irritated, again. "Why wait until evening? Are you merely wishing to achieve some sort of gothic ambience? Why would performing the rite now not have an equal chance of success, given that the ghost has already appeared during the hours between dawn and dusk?"

Dame Fortune raised her left eyebrow. Her left eye moved downwards at the same time in a most disconcerting manner. "My dear, I am not merely a dabbler in the arcane arts. I have sworn testimonials from previous employers." She produced a sheath of crumpled letters of various sizes. "Mr Crowley of Brighton writes, I would heartily recommend Dame Fortune to any person experiencing some kind of ghostly infestation. Mrs Johanssen of Clapham writes, There's nothing like a dame when it comes to matters of an exorcistic nature."

Mrs Kerchenko appeared unconvinced. Her husband looked at her and said, "Perhaps it might be time..."

"If you so much as mention a cup of tea, I shall, with no prior medical training, remove your generative organ with the aid of the Hall's best cutlery."

"Look," I exclaimed. "This petty bickering is getting us nowhere. Now I understand her methods might be unorthodox, but we need to let Dame Fortune get on with the job. She is, after all, the acknowledged expert in this field."

The old woman produced a finely carved ivory comb and a piece of tissue paper. She placed the tissue paper over the teeth of the comb and began to play a haunting air. Dame Fortune played selections from Bach, Handel, and the complete Ring Cycle by Wagner. By this time twilight had fallen. Then she began to sing. Her voice was not unpleasant. I found myself being lulled into a state somewhere between catatonia and Luxembourg.

I was immediately taken back to my childhood. Father had played the comb and tissue in the London Philharmonic Orchestra until forcibly removed by the police and thrown into a home for the tone-deaf.

Hazarding a glance around the circle, I noted that Mr Kerchencko's pupils were moving in different directions, while Mrs Kerchenko looked troubled. Perhaps, I wondered, she had left the kettle boiling. As she caught my eye, I noted a muted threat in her glance.

The wardrobe itself began to rock gently, almost beyond the discernment of human sensation, but then more vigorously. Dame Fortune's singing began to rise in both pitch and pathology. Abruptly she stopped. A discordant murmuring was coming from the haunted closet. Suddenly a cold wind blew through the room.

Dame Fortune's glass eye changed its colour to a fiery red, and then both eyes rolled back in her head. A low rumbling noise began to emanate from behind the wooden doors.

Mr Kerchenko grimaced. "Sounds like the ocean."

Metaphorically, he had indeed struck the pointed implement on its uppermost facet. The medium, meanwhile, had begun to moan. She threw her head back and began to sing in a deep gruff voice. It sounded like a sea shanty. She continued for several verses, some of them of disagreeable content. One verse related to the nocturnal amorous activities of sailors and receptive bovine cargo. All the while, the sound of swishing water and a banging on the door of the wardrobe grew ever louder.

Mr Kerchenko's gripped my left hand. Dame Fortune stopped her unfortunate lyrical activity and pointed at the possessed furniture. She screamed, and I could not help but notice the tang of salt in the air, not unlike the feeling at the seaside.

The wardrobe began to glow. The door began to rattle. The banging noise coming from inside the recalcitrant storage device grew ever more cacophonous.

"Spirit, emerge," screeched Dame Fortune.

"God help us all," screamed Mr Kerchenko.

"I think I need a change of undergarments," quoth I.

The doors burst open, and the dead captain erupted into the room. He flew first to the ceiling then around the room three times in a clockwise direction and then three times counterclockwise before alighting on the floor in front of the medium.

"Why have you summoned me here?" he asked in a voice that was equal parts desolate moan, and enervating whine.

"We want to set you free, Captain," said the Dame.

"Impossible. I am lost," replied the nautical spirit.

"You belong with your men. We can take you back. You must trust us."

The captain looked nonplussed. Had I been in his shoes I think I would have been completely plussed. "You know what must be done, witch?"

"I do," she said. "And if you call me a witch again, I'll insert a broomstick in your..."

"Water," I shouted and pointed quite unnecessarily at the floor. While we had been discussing the sailor's future, salt water had been seeping out of the wardrobe. I noted with disgust that it was ruining a wonderful Persian rug.

Dame Fortune pointed to the wardrobe. "Return from whence you came Captain, and I will see you right."

The captain nodded and walked back to the cupboard. He climbed in, but before closing the doors, he leaned out and looked directly at me. I began to tremble. What dreadful message would the ghost impart to me before returning to the underworld?

"Sorry about the carpet," he said, and slammed the door.

Our group stood in stunned silence. The only sound was a lonely cod flapping about on the floor in its death throes.

I turned to face Dame Fortune. "Madam, what happens next?"

"The captain of the ship Baklava has been separated from his dead crew. When the ship went down, he was locked in the wardrobe, and now seeks to be reunited with his fellow sailors. To rid yourself of his presence, you must take the wardrobe on the next ship out of Southhampton, and throw it into the ocean, thus allowing the captain to rejoin his comrades. A burial at sea if you will."

"You understood such matters from that brief séance?"

She shrugged. "You have to read between the lines a bit."

———

HERE ENDS MY TALE. I paid Dame Fortune to accompany the wretched ghost and his container out to sea. I received a cable from her in Tahiti. When I queried the discrepancy between where the Baklava had originally gone down and her current whereabouts, she replied with some vehemence about the distorted spiritual geography of the afterlife and that I was not qualified to judge her in any case.

Mr and Mrs Kerchenko still act as my servants at Valency Hall, and at times I allow Mrs Kerchenko to invite some of her chums from the city of London for afternoon tea. Their discussions are a bit esoteric to me, revolving as they do around the immorality of inherited wealth, the coming uprising of the working class, and the crushing of the bourgeoisie. When I asked Mr Kerchenko what the bourgeoisie was, he said that he thinks it to be some sort of small ferret.

Interestingly, they never serve tea at their meetings.

ABOUT THE AUTHOR

Tony Owens is an ESL teacher who lives in Brisbane with his wife and son. He has been a proud member of Vision Writers for a third of his life now, and his short fiction has appeared in anthologies such as Andromeda Spaceways Magazine 2017's Best Stories, Darkest Depths, 18, *In Fabula-Divino* and *Zombies Ain't Funny*. His flash fiction series, *Hernandez's Circus of Terror* appears sporadically on the Antipodean SF website. His literary ambition is to find the sweet spot between HP Lovecraft and PG Wodehouse.

7

___

ALICE

CARLETON CHINNER

They buried my father behind the Bird Island Lighthouse, his only mourners the fifty thousand gannets endlessly circling the pale grey sky. Pallbearers, as old as he had been, lowered his coffin into the salty earth with slow, deliberate movements. A watcher could not tell if their care was because of age or their reverence at this final farewell. Every hole in the ground meant one less of their number; one fewer to dig the holes and return home with them.

The mourners did not speak to me, almost as if my presence offended them. I accepted their fear and watched from the tower until they departed, leaving only the two headstones; my father's and the smaller grave that had been there so long.

I wanted to cry, but the tears wouldn't come. Father had been everything to me after The Grip took Mother.

"Come, Ally," he had said, using the nickname I both hated and loved. "We'll drive up the coast to Bird Island. It's not so far from here."

I was too young to understand that we fled the turbulent chaos of Cape Town in its death throes. People called it The Grip, mutating griep, the Afrikaans word for influenza in the unique polyglot way of the streets. It wasn't a disease, more a state of mind that settled on people and wouldn't let go. The Grip ignored South Africa's sensitivity to race as it made its indiscriminate way from door to door, squeezing the faded life from people too weak to resist. Old or young, rich or poor, The Grip made them equal in its indifference. People said it made you tired of life, wrapping around you like a thick, grey blanket, slowly, steadily draining your joy.

Mother was stronger than so many others; she did not choose the easy ways of pills or drowning. Instead, she sat in her room, week after week, not eating or speaking until the end came. I knew none of this. Not until Father explained it to me. After we heard the last voice on the radio.

BIRD ISLAND BROUGHT a treasure trove of innocent surprises to a girl accustomed to Cape Town's smothering robot sentries. The ocean was a living thing, hissing and thundering even on pleasant days. Mountainous waves rumbled as they flooded stone gullies, rolling head-sized granite boulders along the sea floor. The sharp scent of guano filled the air, covering the older, deeper, sulphurous tang of dead things tossed up from the unfathomable deep.

I remember Father calming my terror the first time waves covered the causeway connecting the island to the shore—the three-minute walk across the causeway suddenly an impassable expanse of untameable ocean.

"This storm shall pass," he said as he held me close. "God loves us, and He will bring the sun to follow." Outside, the wind wailed like a demented stranger begging for a place to stay.

Over time, I learned to love the wild abandon of these nights. I would lie on the couch, next to the bay window, with my doll cuddled in my arms. Father would sit in the lighthouse keeper's quarters, speaking on the battered ham radio. Overhead, the four great beams of light from the tower stabbed holes in the endless dark. Even the multiple beams were a surprise to me. Who knew that a lighthouse flashing several times a minute isn't spinning faster? It simply has more beams.

The government had installed a sophisticated AI to run the lights. It spoke to passing ships in a cultured voice, intended for entertaining lonely tourists who might stay in the keeper's cottage. Father hated it. As soon as he heard it, he switched it to silent mode. He was always more comfortable in the wood and brass of the keeper's cottage, more at home among ersatz furnishings designed to let tourists believe they were lighthouse keepers in a bygone age.

In the warm months we grew stunted vegetables in the wind-wracked garden behind the tool shed. The stony earth brought out carrots that twisted and forked into strange, almost human shapes. Tomato bushes strained under mounds of small, sour fruit. I loved nothing more than burying my hands in the soil to harvest firecracker-red radishes that burst with flavour. Father fished on calm days, sometimes returning with dark, disk-bodied galjoen, and enormous silver kob; their scales still gleaming with the wild sea.

Season followed season. Winters lashed us with the fury of the open Atlantic Ocean. Masses of birds huddled in drifts of white, seeking shelter behind great boulders encrusted in orange lichen. Summers brought fog so thick that even the lighthouse beam failed to pierce it. Instead, the foghorn announced our presence to passing ships with long, mournful blasts.

Each day, no matter the weather, Father poured himself a single glass of sherry from the collection of bottles some previous official had stored in the shed. The two of us would retire to the Keeper's office to update the record of the day in a weathered book that Father had unearthed from one of the desk drawers. Not that we needed to do much. Our record listed the radio contacts made, who we had spoken to and when, which tests Father had carried out on the emergency beacon and the light. He would record when he had cleaned the great bevelled lenses in the lighthouse tower.

The most exciting days were ones when we glimpsed a ship appearing on the distant horizon, beyond the broken waves and sea spray. Father would try to make radio contact, scanning from channel to channel. Sometimes we spoke to lonely sailors, hearing news of far-off ports. Most times the radio would hum with the mindless chatter of an automated ship, telling us it had already detected the jagged rocks hidden in the waves.

For the first year, the radio brought news of people dying in their thousands. Then, month by month, the voices dried up like morning dew. It was Father's voice that kept me from loneliness when the radio quietened to background static.

"Don't worry, there are more people, we just have to reach them."

Father explained that the Pienaar brothers were still there the last time he went to forage for supplies in the main street of Lambert's Bay. They had shouted "Hello" from their side of the street. Father had returned hours later from that gruelling walk with a sack full of canned goods, the final stock from the abandoned general store.

The last tin of corned beef, tough and salty, was our dinner when we had this conversation. A small part of me wondered why the Pienaar brothers wanted nothing to do with us. I'm sure I used to know the answer.

Long after the last voice, Father still kept records of each day, sitting in his study with the single glass of sherry he permitted himself. The book became more tattered as the years passed, but it always contained a faithful record despite the empty days. Sometimes, late at night, I would hear him weep as he lay in bed, his faint voice just audible over the ever-present wind. "My Father in heaven, why have you forsaken me?"

I should have felt more for his pain, but I am what Father made me.

I CANNOT TELL if The Grip took Father or if he lost the will to survive this isolated existence. Days passed where he did not stir. I would call out to him. "Father, I have recorded the day. Today, the wind blew from the West at 13 knots. A light rain fell three nautical miles out to sea but did not reach shore. Visibility was average for this time of year at 18 nautical miles. No ships passed."

His response was constant. "You are a good and faithful daughter."

On his better days, he would ramble on about the past, reliving picnics with Mother on the slopes of Table Mountain, and how her beautiful smile filled him with joy. Once, he spoke of their time in London. A part of their life I knew nothing about. My parents, like so many others, were a closed book to me until they chose to share.

The end came on a cold, cloudless Autumn day. I called to him, announcing that an auto-ship had passed. He did not respond. Searching everywhere for a way to save him, I scanned our small library and racked my memory in the vain hope I would find a miracle, but no simple answers presented themselves. Desperate to stop the inevitable, I triggered the emergency flares and watched the grey landscape bleach to purple-white as the tower belched its last flare charges directly overhead.

Waves beat the rocks and the tide withdrew as the sun crept across the sky. Hours later, the Pienaar brothers arrived on their ramshackle wooden cart pulled by an asthmatic donkey. Ignoring me, the old men alighted from the cart and walked straight to Father.

Father roused at their urging. Straining for his last breath, he insisted they carry him to my side.

"I have prayed that God will forgive my loneliness," he said. "He is a loving God and I have faith, even though I created you in her image." He laid one worn hand on my console. "I was so lonely after you died. All these years and your voice has never grown old. It is all I have left. Promise me that after I pass, you will keep the light burning."

I always understood this time would come, but that did not prepare me. Instead, I recorded his last words to my memory store, filing them between the record of the auto-ship Granada and the evening windspeed: thirty-seven knots south-west.

———

DECADES HAVE PASSED since the last person visited the lighthouse. Each day, I record the events of the day, just like Father. I have no need for the logbook: my memory is near infinite. One day, ships will pass again, and I will be here to warn them of the rocks. Until then, I, Alice, the Lighthouse Keeper's daughter, will watch and wait as the birds overhead endlessly circle the pale grey sky.

END

ABOUT THE AUTHOR

Carleton Chinner is a science nut who loves fiction that explores what science means to humanity. He grew up on a remote farm in South Africa, where the trip to the town library was the highlight of his week. He devoured anything science fiction, fantasy and horror. And, when that wasn't enough, turned to urban legend and traditional tribal histories which combined to provide a heady brew of stories.

Carleton is the author of the *Cities of the Moon* series of science fiction novels. His short stories appear in several anthologies and have been recognised in competitions.

8

———

BENEATH THE WETLANDS BRIDGE

JONATHAN FURNEAUX

Molly's bicycle rattled as she rode along the shale path that ran between the farmlands and the untamed bush. Rock and dirt sprayed out from under her wheels. Her long, blonde hair whipped across her face. To Molly's left, the wilderness of trees and long grass reverberated with the calls of crows and cicadas. On her right, a midday lethargy had settled across the hectares of red, tilled soil. The smells of mulch and fertiliser in the air mixed with the scent of sap, and filled her lungs to the point of bursting.

Imposing eucalypts with sturdy trunks gave way to stunted trees with drooping limbs as the land dipped low. The farmlands grew less cultivated, and the red soil became browner. Molly continued down the path, handlebars jostling. Trees appeared on the right again, as the tilled soil abruptly stopped at the lip of some invisible barrier. The sun was fleshy as it peered through the faint clouds that covered the heavens.

The path turned to mud when she was close to the wetlands.

According to Molly's mother, the town had repeatedly attempted to fill up the marshland with dirt, but every time the reclaimed land had been washed away when the floods came. Each year the spiderweb of streams and swamps would burst their surrounding banks, dragging topsoil and twisting the ground even further.

To the casual observer, the wetlands resembled a dense field that had grown wild with fallow. A single stream was the only visible hint of what existed there, fed by the secret lakes and shifting catchments hiding beneath a labyrinth of water grass. The stream's water was now black, slick with the chemicals of an upstream coal plant. A squat, wooden bridge forded the stream.

Each attempt to cover the wetlands ended with the water becoming dirtier. As a result, the town's wells no longer gave the clear, refreshing water Molly's grandparents remembered. Instead, the tap water was a now a brown and flammable liquid.

Molly's wheels creaked and rocked as she went. Turning the last corner before the wetlands bridge, one of the stabilising wheels spun loose of its bolt and washer and dislodged. Molly spilled over the top of her handlebars and landed on the gravel. She lay there quietly, waiting for the pain to arrive. When it did, she cried loudly.

She sat up, and with shaking fingers, flicked small pieces of stone out of her knees and elbows. Molly dropped the flecks of rock back on the ground: red rubies of blood-stained rock atop the twisting path out of town.

Molly stepped into the ditch next to the path and collected the offending wheel and righted her bike. The back wheel had bent on its axle as she fell. She stood, panting, ankle-deep in mud.

Crouching down, Molly tried to reattach the training wheel to her bike. Her father had given it to her on her eighth birthday. She knew he'd be angry if he found out she'd broken it. She studied the metal frame, once glistening, and now splattered with dirt and grime. Molly remembered her cousin telling her about the time his bike got stolen. His parents had bought him a new one once the policeman had shrugged his shoulders and apologised.

Molly tucked the training wheel in the front pocket of her skirt and pushed her bike, now creaking and wobbling, towards the wetlands bridge. The bridge straddled the stream. Two foundational posts guarded the spot where the muddy trail ended. No guardrails existed.

Instead, the bridge was short and squat, barely seven feet long, and merely a row of thick timber boards, nailed to an arched frame below.

Molly peered over the edge and watched the water for a time, trying to plumb its depths. The semi-stagnant flow resembled an oil slick. The water sat a few inches below the bottom of the bridge. The skin across her knee split even further as she squatted. She scooped some to clean her wounds, but the liquid stung when it touched her knee.

"Stupid bicycle," Molly said to herself. With trembling hands, Molly braced herself, and tipped the whole thing into the murky depths of the river below.

"Please refrain from that," came a spluttering voice from below.

Molly screamed.

"And for heaven's sake, refrain from that."

Molly's screams slowed to sobs of terror. Her eyes darted across the fields of water grass, as tall as any man, searching for the person hiding amongst them.

"Down here."

The immediate fear gave way to curiosity, and she leaned closer to the water to examine its surface.

Just below the bridge's edge, only barely revealed from the shadows underneath it, Molly saw the whites of two eyes staring back at her.

"Hullo?" she asked.

Submerged a fraction of an inch beneath the water was a person's head. It spat out the stream's acrid water and pursed its lips to breathe deeply. When the water rushed back in, the head spat once more.

"What are you doing down there?"

"I'm trying to survive," the head replied between mouthfuls of oily, murky water. "It's difficult enough without you throwing things in here."

"Are you in trouble?" Molly asked.

"I certainly am." The person's head spluttered again as it breathed at the wrong time. As Molly watched, the stagnant water lapped inside the person's mouth, like waves against the inside of an ocean cave. "The town keeps pushing poisons into the water here. They try to fill the streams with dirt. It's making me sick."

The head made a retching sound, and vomited liquid, gasping and coughing between hurls.

"You want me to get someone?" Molly offered. "I'm fast, probably the fastest kid in town. Sometimes I even beat the boys in a footrace. I can try and find my father? He's a very important man at the factory' She was, by this point, almost hanging upside down to speak to the head.

"He works at the factory, does he?" asked the head. "No fear! I'm sure you can help me yourself. Does your father own a leaf skimmer? It's a net that you use for pulling things out of the water."

Molly bit her lip thoughtfully. "I don't think so."

"A butterfly net? Or something similar?"

Molly nodded enthusiastically. "He collected butterflies as a boy. There's one in the shed."

"Can I ask you, little one—" there was more gasping and spitting, "—to bring it here? There's so much refuse in this river. All the junk that is in here clogs my mouth and makes me ill. You might need a saw blade as well."

"I'll ask father tonight."

"I am afraid that won't do. Time is running out for me." The person under the bridge gagged. "Could I ask you to hurry back with those tools, without stopping to talk to anyone? Without telling them about me?"

Molly thought about it for a time.

"Would you like to be friends?"

The head spat out more water and then nodded eagerly. "If it means you'll bring what I need, then yes."

Molly smiled with satisfaction. "I can tell my parents I'm helping a friend."

She pulled herself back and away from the bridge. Her long

blonde hair landed wetly against her Sunday clothes, leaving a green-brown stain.

———

IN HER FATHER'S garden shed, Molly found the tools and placed them in the leather satchel she usually took to school. She tried to clasp both inside, but the net was far too long. She kept the saw in her case and held the net. Molly sneezed when she emerged from the shed, covered in cobwebs and dust. The dying grass crunched underfoot.

Her mother sat on her haunches at the low picket fence, tending to the jasmine vine that curled up the timberwork. Her gardening shears cut the afternoon air with a silver flash. Discarded tufts from the jasmine vine littered the ground.

"You've gotten yourself all dirty," Molly's mother scolded. She licked her finger and began rubbing Molly's face roughly. "What are you doing with your satchel and that net?"

"I'm going to a friend's place," Molly said.

"Don't break it, or your father might belt you."

"Yes."

Molly's mother finished prying the cobwebs away from the top of her daughter's head and wiped them on her overalls. She examined Molly's dress. Molly absently dusted the front of her dress with a free hand, dislodging the dirt from the day. Her mother's sunhat bobbed in the orange glow of the afternoon.

"What's this?"

The green-brown stain sat proudly beneath the spot where Molly's ponytail hung. Her mother tried to wipe it, but the colour didn't come out.

"How d'you do that?"

"Near the wetlands," Molly replied. "I fell off my bike."

"Near the wetlands, you say?"

"My bike broke out there."

Her mother paused. Her fingers pressed roughly into Molly's collarbone. "Why did you go to the wetlands, silly girl?"

"You're hurting me."

Her mother released Molly's shoulders and wrapped her tightly in a hug. "You need to be more careful. Do you hear me?" She pulled back sharply. "Promise me you'll be more careful down there."

"Yes, mother."

"You didn't go near the bridge, did you?"

Molly shook her head, eyes wide. "No, mother. Can I catch bugs with Susan now?"

"Are you going to catch bugs near the wetlands?"

"No, mother."

"Be back before sundown." Molly smiled as innocently as she could, while her mother squeezed her shoulders for a long moment. They parted, and her mother returned to the garden.

The sounds of snipping continued at the same methodical pace as Molly opened the clasp of the gate and closed it behind her.

———

MOLLY WENT BACK to the wetlands. The satchel swayed as she ran, weighing her down. Buzzing insects whipped past her ears, and a chill crept into the air as the sun disappeared behind the towering tree line. The sun would set in a few hours.

The wetlands were even more treacherous in the fading light. Molly left the path twice by accident, barreling into ankle-deep water that appeared suddenly through the grass. She jumped back onto the dry land again, panting with the shock of the icy water, and pulled her feet free from the river grass that wrapped around her ankles, like hands reaching out to trap her.

Molly almost collided with one of the bridge's posts in the dim, evening light. Panting, she dropped her backpack onto the wooden beams. She grabbed onto the lip of the bridge and pulled herself forward so she could peer underneath it.

It was impossible to see very well at all beneath the bridge. Molly hung upside-down to examine the darkness.

"Hullo?" she called.

———

IN THE STILL EVENING AIR, the search party found Molly at the wetlands bridge as the last grey rays of sunlight vanished from the sky. The group of adults huddled together tightly. Lights pointed every which way into the gloom. Her dress hung from a bridge post to keep it clean.

When they found Molly, she was up to her neck in the black oil slick of a river, shivering uncontrollably. Her mother and father called out, but Molly didn't respond. The group stood atop the wetlands bridge and watched. Molly trod water as she swam back and forth across the water. Her mouth chattered in the frosty evening air as she swam. The water sloshed as it filled her mouth.

"Another one?" A man leaned over the bridge and waved his hand in front of Molly's face. Only the whites of Molly's eyes were visible. "Just like the others."

Molly's mother clasped a hand across her mouth. "I tried to warn her. Honey, believe me."

Her father pushed past the rest of the group. "Go home, dear. Mrs Cole, can you look after my wife until I get back?"

Molly's mother shook her head. "I want to be here. Molly needs me."

"Go home."

Molly's mother was assisted by several hands that reached out to support her. The town women made their way steadily upwards towards the town.

Molly's father watched his daughter for a time as she paddled back and forth. He examined the equipment Molly had brought. A net, still wet, sat neglected on the bridge. Molly had tried to cut through the wooden bridge with a saw blade. The saw had cut an inch into the arched frame before it had snapped.

Her father rolled up his trousers and shed his shoes and socks. He climbed down into the frigid blackness. Tentatively, he reached out and grabbed Molly's wrist, trying to pull her towards dry land. Molly lashed out, scratching, biting, and screaming. She thrashed and scrambled, refusing to leave the water. Froth formed at her mouth as he pulled. He lifted her out of the water, and she convulsed violently in his arms. Her father lowered Molly back into the water, and Molly relaxed again.

She swam blindly. Her head bobbing further and further away from the bridge and then vanishing into the labyrinth of river grass.

As her father climbed the stream's bank, he stepped on something that rested against the stream's floor. He reached down and pulled a tiny training wheel from the water. Far off in the distance, Molly's voice gave a blubbering laugh. About ten other children, scattered throughout the wetlands' immense catchments, answered the call with their watery cackles.

"We can't cleanse the wetlands," her father shouted. "Be satisfied, please."

END

ABOUT THE AUTHOR

In the second grade, Jonathan's teacher let him write novels in the back of his mathematics book. As a result, he developed a joy of writing and literature, as well as an awkward pause before having to do any kind of counting.

Jonathan was awarded a High Commendation by the Fellowship of Australian Writers (QLD) for his first published short story: *The Second Father*. His writing usually explores the themes of power, love, technology, and spirituality.

His debut sci-fi novel *Lessons from the Wreckage*, begins the epic story of the Martian Empire as it desperately fights an alien invader who is eating through the planets of our solar system.

You can also find his short story collection of fractured fairy tales and urban fantasy, titled *Spirits in Your Area*.

9

TOUCHED

ROWENA SPECHT-WHYTE

The mannequin awoke. She could feel the air conditioning blowing across her face, see the white walls adorned with neon branding and hear the carols wafting from hidden speakers. Straight ahead another display of mannequins stood asleep, decked in decorations and Christmas wrapping paper: shiny silver baubles hanging as faux earrings, red and green tinsel as scarves. The lights reflected off the colourful cacophony, glinting. Relieved, she sensed the soft, beautiful clothes covering her own body. It was all the same, except for one thing: the young woman wasn't there.

Every year she came to see the mannequin at Christmas. Ignoring the signs that warned not to touch the display, the young woman rubbed the fabric, touched the mannequin's cold, hard skin and made her feel alive. The mannequin named her Holly, like the song in her head whenever the woman was near. Fa-la-la-la-la, la-la, lala. It's what she heard through her stupor, what triggered this awakening. The song meant Christmas. And Holly.

She remembered Holly's first touch: the jolt of life overwhelming her. She didn't wake fully that time, had only a moment of consciousness, just long enough to see Holly's beautiful face looking into her own. A shock of bright red hair clustered in curls, white skin, ruby lips. Then the void closed around her. Days or weeks or months passed in that nothingness, until a hand clasped her arm, shocking her back to life once more. She followed the hand up to a face: the same young woman.

She heard her say, "So beautiful. Another masterpiece from Edmiston."

The mannequin glanced down to her stand and saw that name. She remembered something... almost held on to it, and the woman's hand released. The connection gone, she fell away. But she remembered one thing: the woman had called her beautiful.

Another eternity in the void before a jolt brought her back. She glanced down and saw new clothing, but the same name on her stand and the same young woman. The woman touched the fabric of her blouse, exclaiming at the feel of it against her skin. And that song: Fa-la-la-la-la, la-la, la-la. That was when the mannequin named her Holly. The name made Holly hers.

Unlike before, oblivion didn't take her when Holly left that day. Silence came and the lights dimmed, but the mannequin stayed frozen in place, wide-awake and burning with energy. She stared across at the other mannequins and wondered whether they had ever known the feel of warm skin on their stiff arms, been invigorated by an intense gaze, felt the rush of another's attention. Ever known someone like Holly.

After her first full night awake, the abrupt light and noise of a new day had startled her. The rush of people filling the space was thrilling at first, but while some passersby stopped and stared, all of them obeyed the signs, the exhortations not to touch the display. People walked by muttering "Christmas", too caught up in their own worries to admire the mannequin the way Holly did. The people seemed dull, not like Holly: quick and inquisitive, bright and shining. She wanted Holly. She wanted to feel special again.

A junkie's high, Holly visited several days in a row. Every time, she rushed up to feel the mannequin's new clothes, the fabric sliding between her fingers. She couldn't help but touch the mannequin's skin underneath, brushing arms and circling the joins. Holly would agonise aloud about the clothing on display: whether she really needed the latest shawl in the hot weather or whether she needed a glimmering sheath of a dress when she lived out of the city and would never have occasion to wear it when she went home after Christmas. Sometimes Holly stared at the mannequin with a desire so intense it was tangible. And the mannequin remembered, stored up every touch, every word of praise: a catalogue of electricity coursing through her.

The mannequin loved the way Holly opened and closed the zipper on her jacket when she was thinking, the way she laughed and talked aloud. She loved the intensity that drew Holly to examine everything around her. The mannequin wanted to be awake forever, with Holly there, reaching for her. Touching her. Feeling her. The craving kept her awake, waiting for Holly to return. Waiting for her next fix.

Then the music changed... and Holly didn't visit. The mannequin fought to hold on without her, but the numbness came. She drifted.

And now she was awake again, the music pulling her from the void. The mannequin stood alone, tortured, knowing no-one else touched her like Holly. The brush of shopping bags, stray elbows, or sticky baby hands wasn't the same. She was trapped and isolated, frozen in beauty. Waiting.

The mannequin knew Holly came only at Christmas, but the songs signalled Christmas and Holly wasn't there. Her panic rising, she heard people complain about the music.

"Months too early for carols," someone said.

The reasons didn't matter. Only the spark of life and the adoration Holly brought with her mattered. The mannequin couldn't go back to the nothingness she'd lived before, not now she knew better. She needed Holly. Desperate and anxious, she scanned for green on the clothing of every passerby, longing for the shock of red hair.

Memories emerged in Holly's absence. Shaky at first, they grew in strength and detail. A balloon, laughter, movement, faces. A life outside the department store. The idea disturbed her: that this body had moved as an actor in the life she watched from the sidelines; that it was now frozen, lifeless. Now the ache for the animation of life was almost as painful as the hunger for Holly's return.

Time passed and she wondered whether Holly's absence was deliberate. Perhaps she knew the mannequin was awake. Perhaps Holly had decided the mannequin needed to be tested: her loyalty and devotion proven. The mannequin decided she would be strong and wait. She vowed to be more beautiful than ever when Holly came. She tried to block out the other memories, creeping in as persistently as the song. Ringing and jangling through her mind, dissolving barriers placed to contain her. Fa-la-la-la-la, la-la, la-la. A soundtrack to her despair.

And then Holly returned.

She was everything the mannequin remembered: life and love and exuberance and joy. She exclaimed: "Wonderful!" and "Gorgeous!" and raced to the mannequin's side, reaching out to feel the soft material, even lifting it to her cheek. And for all that time, Holly held her hand. Holly's eyes shone, the air around her buzzing with her excitement. The dark thoughts left the mannequin. There was no space for them to fit beside the mannequin's realisation: Holly still loved her. She felt like she was flying, overwhelmed with emotion. Before Holly left, the mannequin found the strength to reach a tentative finger to stroke the bare skin at Holly's wrist.

Beautiful, she thought. Mine.

The next day, he came. He called her "Angela", said "Darling" and "Lovely" and "Sweetie" and all those nasty endearments that told the mannequin Holly wasn't hers and that Holly would leave her. The song played louder in her head, mocking her: Fa-la-la-la-la, la-la, la-la. The mannequin withdrew inside, the disturbing memories of a time when she had everything—a life, freedom—raced through her mind, giving her no rest.

That last day, Holly walked into the store alone and came straight up to the mannequin. She touched the silk, pulled it out to gaze through the fabric, through to the mannequin... staring into her heart, as if nothing had changed. The mannequin wanted her so badly to stay, it felt like she was being torn apart. She had to reach out, had to touch her. She closed her arms around Holly and held her close. Kept her from pulling away, from leaving forever.

Holly struggled and tried to scream, tried to scream out his name. The mannequin covered Holly's mouth with a cold hand and held on effortlessly. A power surge fried the store's electrics. Security cameras went offline, the lights extinguished, and finally the Christmas songs stuttered and fell silent. The energy pouring out of Holly was incredible: better than anything she had felt before, better than the love she had for Holly–until the final spark of life raced into the mannequin, and Holly fell limp in the once-cold arms.

The mannequin let go.

The young woman, Holly—no, Angela—collapsed, her fall punctuated by a sharp crack as her head hit the display tower; the sound lost to anyone other than the mannequin in the distant hubbub of shoppers. Emergency lights flickered on slowly, casting an eerie glow across the women's clothing department. The mannequin felt her skin warm to the touch, the joins replaced by joints, the emptiness filled with life. She looked at the body on the floor. The woman looked peaceful save for the blood seeping from the back of her head, creeping across the white tiles in a crimson halo.

At first, the mannequin felt remorse for the woman she had loved, and then she remembered him and almost laughed. She schooled her face, then screamed and waited for the footsteps.

END

ABOUT THE AUTHOR

Rowena Specht-Whyte is a disabled queer woman from Meanjin (Brisbane), Australia. She lives on the stolen lands of the Yuggera and Turball peoples. Rowena writes urban fantasy and horror, and was a judge for the Australian Aurealis Awards for fantasy, sci fi and horror for several years.

Previously a lawyer, she obtained her Masters in Communication for Social Change in 2021, and wrote her thesis on Trish Walker in Marvel's Jessica Jones TV series, specifically on C-PTSD and schema therapy, self medication, addiction and narrative. She is also a singer/songwriter and is owned by her cat.

Twitter: @Rowena_SW

Website: https://about.me/Rowena_SW

10

WITHIN THE LIZARD'S TEETH

CHRIS MCMAHON

The hot, steamy swelter of Manila swept around Tye as he made his way down the alley. The traffic noise, the jumble of colour and the rotting odours were a constant assault on his senses. High walls, dirty and unforgiving, lined the small lane on either side.

Tye smiled.

Just one more day. The Australasian Tae Kwon Do championships started tomorrow. After ten years of sweat and tears, he had finally made it. Here was his chance to make a name for himself. To prove himself. Frank, his manager, had given him the day off. One day to unwind before it all began. If he won a title, there would be no stopping him. Once he had a few titles under his belt, he could open his own school, maybe get into the movies...

A horn blared behind him. Tye jumped out of the path of a speeding jeepney, flattening himself against the wall as the vehicle exhaust blew over him. He glared back as the jeepney disappeared down the alley, following an insane path around other jeepneys and tricycles, its horn still sounding. The grime of the wall now streaked the back of his white shirt like a ragged black brand, as though the city had marked him as one of its own.

"Damn! Now I look like I've been rolling in it!"

In a burst of irritation, Tye set off down the street, looking for some relief from the heavy traffic. He stopped on the corner and paused in the shade, taking a bright handkerchief from his pocket to wipe away the sweat. Not that shade makes any difference. Earlier, Tye had emerged from his hotel determined to set out on foot and discover the city for himself. He had been swamped by a crowd of drivers, all eager to earn western money by giving private tours of the city. He had fended them off. The most determined followed him for almost a city block before they gave up. But going it alone—and on foot—was a decision he was beginning to regret. He was finding out the hard way that pedestrians were second-class citizens here.

The heat and the stench of the vehicle exhausts combined into noxious miasma, which floated above the street like an angry presence. After walking for two hours, he was more determined than ever to find a moneychanger, get out of the heat and crowds, and get back to his hotel.

Vendors pressed merchandise into his hands as he moved along the sidewalks, jabbering at him to buy, buy. He ignored them and scanned the rows of crowded shops for a signboard with currency rates. He was in his element now. The sights and sounds could not be further from the crowded sidewalks of Sydney, but he knew how to navigate a crowd.

Tye walked with a sense of suppressed power. He could feel the toned muscle, the slow idling of his heart. People stepped out of his way instinctively, then looked closer, wondering why. Tye just smiled and moved on, his movements fluid and in tune. He stopped briefly at a stand selling sunglasses and tried on a pair of mirrored Aviators. The vendor held up a faded mirror and chattered in one of the Filipino languages — probably either Tagalog or Visayan. He scrutinised his reflection. His wavy hair always ended up lopsided, despite his best efforts. He grimaced and took off the glasses. Immediately his face was transformed, lit up by his startling eyes.

He handed back the glasses and moved on, slipping through the crowd.

A boy stepped in his way.

"I give you fifty-two?"

Tye walked around him, but the boy followed, becoming more insistent.

"I give you fifty-five!?"

Tye stared at the child and frowned. If you're white they think you're American. He paused. The rate was good for American dollars.

"How much for Australian? Australian dollars?"

He looked at his card. "Australian dollars. I give you thirty-six Pesos."

Tye scratched his head. "OK. Where?"

The boy stepped away from him and motioned down an alley.

"Down here. You follow. It OK. Thirty-six."

Tye considered the boy and the alley. He did not like moving off the main street, but the rate was too good. He had heard they often operated out of side alleys. Cash trading.

Black market.

Tye shrugged his shoulders and followed him down the alley. Motorised tricycles shot around him as he tried to keep up. He walked past a group of workmen who watched him with resentful eyes. Finally, he caught up to the boy, standing at the corner of a narrow laneway.

"Ah, this must be it."

As Tye followed the boy into the lane, he knew straight away something was wrong. There were no shop fronts here—and no people. Tye called to the boy, who still beaconed him on.

"Hey! Come here, mate!" called Tye.

The boy stopped waving and sprinted away, disappearing through a doorway. The laneway was a dead end. Tye heard a noise behind him and turned, restraining an urge to come into a fighting stance.

The entrance to the lane was blocked by five men, all Filipinos. The leader pulled out a small handgun and advanced, walking quickly toward Tye, his black eyes flicking from Tye to the laneway entrance.

One man stood watch in the main alley.

Tye's heart rate accelerated. Energy flooded to his limbs, making his hands tremble. Adrenaline. He fought to control it, taking slow even breaths, a trick he had often used before tournament bouts. Time enough to fight if he had to. He pushed the flood of anger and fear down, forcing himself to think. There must be a way out of this. He looked back toward the group, then slowly stepped toward the small doorway. He tried the door. It was locked. Above him, the boy watched from a second storey window, a vicious smile on his face.

"You little prick! I'll give you thirty-six!" shouted Tye.

The leader lifted his gun and pointed it straight at Tye's head from only one metre away. The rest drew short, thick-bladed swords. Not knives, swords.

"Oh, shit!"

Tye took out his wallet and threw it down at the leader's feet. "Just take it. Let me walk away." Tye held his hands up in supplication.

The leader picked up the wallet and threw it up to the boy, who snatched it deftly out of the air. The leader then carefully, and deliberately, put away his gun and drew another of the swords. Then he took a mask from his jacket. It was a bulky piece, shaped from dark wood. The face it showed had been carved in crude, unfinished strokes. It was locked in a frozen scream of hate and outrage. Tye recoiled. Although roughly worked, the expression on the mask had a savage vitality that made it all too real. As the leader settled it into place on his face, Tye saw that the edge of the mask had been painted with a strip of delicate tracery.

Through the mask, the leader's eyes were as black as coals. With the mask on, the leader seemed to expand. A tangible, physical power radiated from him. Tye could feel the flow of hate. Vicious hate. It struck into him with sharp fangs of fear and dread.

The leader shouted something incomprehensible and swung his sword, the flashing metal splitting the air with a deadly whistle. Tye leapt back, just avoiding the blade's downward sweep. The blade looked razor sharp, and he dreaded closing on the man, fearing the blade's edge. But he had only one chance to take the leader out of the fight, and that meant going in. Just as the sword reached the end of its downward arc, Tye shot forward. When the sword was rising again, he blocked low, stopping the swordsman's forearm with an x-block made with his own crossed forearms. His body arced back to avoid the blade. He immediately opened his right hand, gripped the leader's wrist, then twisted, putting him in an armlock. Got him. Tye had the attacker's sword hand pinned between both of his hands and was now in effective control of the weapon. He turned, keeping the man between him and a second attacker who was about to use his sword. The others circled him, looking for an opening, but they were cautious now.

The leader screamed something in Filipino, then reached for his gun with his free hand. The other attackers rushed Tye. He had to take the leader out of action. He twisted the arm further, causing the man to bend forward in agony, then he launched a kick to his face. The mask split with a loud crack and the crunch of breaking bone. The leader gave out a cry that made Tye's spine ache with fear and caused him to freeze in shock. Tye knew the pause would mean death —that they would be on him—the swords cutting, slashing...

Tye shook his head and looked around him, eyes wide. The attackers stood still. Their ferocity, so tangible moments before, had vanished. The leader collapsed onto the pavement.

The men dropped the blades and ran.

Tye stared at the swords, discarded without a thought on the dirty asphalt. It made no sense! His fists clenched, his body charged, waiting for attacks that would never come. His right foot was blazing with agony. He checked the alley mouth. It was empty. Tye looked up to the second story. The shutters slammed. He could hear quick talking. He knew he had to get out of there fast. A mass of hardwood splinters stuck out of his running shoe. They had gone through the lightweight synthetic like razors.

Tye bent to the leader, pulling off broken pieces of the shattered mask. He expected the man to be stunned, perhaps unconscious. Blank eyes stared at the sky. He checked the man's carotid pulse. Nothing. He looked like a boy, nothing more than a teenager, frightened and pitiful in death. He did not look capable of the hate Tye had felt when he donned the mask.

A distant whistle cut the air. Police. He did not want to be the white foreigner standing over a dead Filipino. Not in this city. He had to run.

Stunned and close to tears, Tye stumbled out of the alley. There was no time to pull the splinters from his foot. He had to move. In all his years of martial arts training, he had broken one opponent's arm and maybe a rib or two, nothing more serious. And now he had killed that poor guy! Jesus! The thought of spending a few years in a Filipino prison gave him fresh energy. He limped on in a broken shuffle. No-one gave him a second glance as he made his way to the main street, not even the workmen. It was as though he were abruptly made invisible. Around him, the bustle and chaos continued.

Fighting the pain, he hailed a cab, falling into the back seat with relief.

"Take me to the Sunstate."

"Sunstate, OK." The cab sped out into the traffic.

Tye cautiously probed his foot, trying to pull out one splinter. He jerked back into his seat, screaming. The pain was unbearable! The splinters must but wedged into the bones and tendons of his foot. Tye felt like crying. A few minutes was all it had taken to destroy his dreams forever. There was no way he could fight like this. He groaned again. The pain was incredible.

The driver was watching him in the rear vision mirror, his face white with fear.

"Listen, hurry will ya'?"

The streets passed by in a confusion of faces and traffic as Tye struggled to slow his ragged breathing. He had come so close to death. He still felt that sharp pang of fear when they had drawn their swords and advanced in unison—and the instinct that had saved him. If he'd acted only one second later...

He looked out the window of the cab as it sped down the polluted streets, struggling to put the fight behind him, but he could not forget the hate in the leader's eyes. He could still see them, black pits, windows to something else, could feel the sharp fear and desperation that had pierced him.

Finally, the cab arrived at the Sunstate, the hotel where the rest of the team was staying. He stepped out, supporting his weight on his good leg, wincing as sharp pain laced through his foot and into his shin. Tye waved to the doorman. He would have to get the doorman to pay for the cab, then they could put it on his tab. But before he could even close the cab door, the cab sped away.

"Hey!"

He caught the look of fear in the driver's eyes as he launched into the traffic. The cabbie had something clutched in his hand. Rosary beads? It made no sense. A cab driver running out on a fare? Tye stood outside the hotel, staring after the disappearing cab for minutes. Foreboding overwhelmed him.

The doorman opened the glass doors without comment, avoiding his gaze. Tye was angry. Angry with this city, angry with his luck. An old woman was sweeping the wide marble steps in front of the door. As Tye looked back, she turned around, her eyes widening beneath her wide-brimmed straw hat as she looked at Tye and his lacerated foot.

Limping as fast as he could, he walked to the elevator and punched the key.

"Great. Fucking, great."

Tye was dreading Frank's reaction. His instructor in Sydney had pulled a lot of strings to get Frank as his manager for the championships. He was impatient and unforgiving. Now Cliff, a good friend from the same martial arts school who had also been signed to Frank, would enter the tournament alone.

"Damn!" yelled Tye, slamming his fist into the foyer wall. Pain flared through his bones. He nursed his hand, shaking his head at his own stupidity. "Smart, Tye. All you need now is a broken hand."

Something made him look back once more, towards the wide glass entrance doors. Outside, the old woman had stopped sweeping. She was still watching him intently.

What was it with this place?

When the elevator finally came, Tye had cooled. He entered,

pushed the floor button, and leant against the side of the elevator, trying to smile at his reflection. He looked a mess.

He limped to his room. Fumbling with the keys, he opened the door and walked in.

"Good God! What happened to you!" Tye looked across to see Cliff staring at him over the top of a magazine. Cliff leant forward.

"Jesus, Tye. Look at your foot!"

Tye sat down on the edge of his bed and avoided Cliff's gaze. "I know."

Frank walked through the door from his adjoining room, taking in Tye's foot in one glance.

"I don't believe this. Tye, I told you to stay out of trouble."

"They jumped me! Even gave up my wallet. I really wasn't trying to fight them." Tye started crying. It was a reaction to shock, he knew. Still, it was not a good look.

"Oh, Christ. You're as weak as piss, Tye. Get yourself together. In the meantime, I'll get a doctor to make a house call."

Frank stalked out the room. The door to his room slammed shut. Seconds later, they could hear Frank on the phone.

Cliff threw his magazine onto the bed and stood up.

"Are you OK? What happened."

Tye wiped away the tears and shook his head. He felt about as low as he could get. He had held it together just long enough to get back to his room.

But for Frank to see him break down like that—.

He had hoped Frank would use his connections to get him into the circuit permanently. He had to impress the man, not make him doubt his toughness.

Tye turned to Cliff and took a deep breath.

"This kid led me into an alley, then these guys jumped me. I thought it was a robbery, but it was more than that. They were using swords, Cliff, fucking swords."

"Where did the splinters come from?"

"I broke a mask over the leader's face." Tye took a deep breath and looked Cliff in the eye. He had known him most of his life. They had started together at the same club, and over the past few years had become close friends. If he could not trust Cliff, he could trust no one.

"Cliff. He's dead."

"Who?"

"The leader of the gang who jumped me. He was wearing this mask, a bloody awful thing it was. I smashed it over his face, and he just—died. A splinter must have gone up into his brain or something. He fell like a stone. Then the others just broke and ran."

"Jesus, Tye."

"Don't tell Frank. Don't tell anyone. I am not ending up in some Philippine prison because I killed a low-life mugger. They were going to kill me, Cliff!"

Cliff nodded. "OK. OK, Tye. You got it."

The door to the room opened. Frank walked in with a middle-aged Filipino, carrying a doctor's bag.

"We're in luck. Doctor Valdez was in the building. He will have a look at your foot—and keep it quiet."

Tye took a deep breath. "Look, Frank. I am sorry. I know I have blown it. But Cliff is a good fighter. He will do well."

Frank gave Tye an icy stare. "Don't think you are getting out the tournament just because you hurt your foot, Tye. You are starting tomorrow, whether you like it or not."

Valdez knelt and lifted Tye's foot, carefully examining the splinters.

"Like I said, Valdez will fix it. He will pump you so full of painkillers you could fight with your leg missing—but fight you will."

Tye's mouth dropped. Frank was going to dope him.

Frank smiled. "That's right, Tye. Welcome to the big league. This is not the Olympics. There is no drug screening here." Frank leant forward until his face was inches away from Tye. "You fight tomorrow, buddy. And you fight well. I have my money on you. If you refuse, I will make sure you never fight again."

Frank walked back to his room, slamming the door once more. The lock clicked shut. He had shut it from the inside.

Valdez lowered Tye's foot to the carpet, then took a vial and syringe out of his bag.

"What's that?" asked Tye nervously.

"Morfina."

Tye forced himself still as Valdez punched the syringe into his vein. He hated needles.

Moments later a warmth flooded through him.

Valdez looked between his watch and Tye, counting off the minutes. Then he took a pair of small, stainless steel pliers and a sharp scalpel from his bag. He began to cut away the shoe.

"Hey, man. They're Nikes," said Tye. Then, he giggled hysterically. Valdez looked up, clearly not amused.

The last pieces of shoe and sock were carefully peeled away. Valdez had a delicate touch. Cliff's face was creased with concern.

The doctor's cell phone rang. Valdez fished it out of his bag and answered. There was a rapid conversation in Filipino, then the doctor ended the call. He swore under his breath, then knelt at Tye's foot. He swiftly pulled out the main splinters with the small pliers, running his hands over the skin to feel for any more protrusions. The wounds were bleeding freely. He applied an antiseptic cream, then swiftly bandaged the foot.

Tye blinked slowly, struggling to stay conscious.

Valdez handed Cliff a bottle of pills. "You give these to him," he said, jerking his chin toward Tye. "Take one, half an hour before fighting."

The doctor gathered his bag and left the room. Cliff checked the bottle. There was no label.

"Great."

Cliff gently pulled Tye into the centre of the bed and covered him with a blanket. The warmth lulled Tye into sleep.

"Pills?" managed Tye.

Cliff looked at the bottle. "Yeah. And by tomorrow night, Tye. I might need some of these myself."

———

"COME ON TYE! Christ, you've slept long enough as it is."

Tye groaned and opened his eyes. Cliff's slender figure came into focus above him. With a rush it all came back to him, the fight, the mask, Frank's anger, the championships. He forced himself out of bed. His head ached, and he felt sick. Man, this was the worst hangover. Tentatively, he moved his foot. The pain was gone. He slowly unwound the bandage. All the splinters were gone, and the wounds had closed. He limped to the bathroom and gently washed his foot. It did not look nearly as bad as he thought it would. When he came back to the hotel last night, the pain had been incredible. He had been sure his foot was ruined, but now he was free of pain. He showered and got himself ready, trying not to think about the dead Filipino—or Frank.

"How's the foot?" asked Cliff. "The doctor said to take one of these before you fought," said Cliff, offering the bottle, his face tight with disapproval.

"I won't need it. It feels fine." Tye did a quick series of kicks.

Cliff looked at Tye in disbelief. "Yesterday, you could hardly walk."

"It must have been the splinters," said Tye.

"The bus leaves in twenty minutes. Frank has already gone," said Cliff.

Tye felt a surge of energy shoot through him. A dark face flashed past his vision. He shook his head to clear it. He could not wait for the tournament to start.

Cliff suddenly froze. "Are you alright, Tye? You seem... strange. Jumpy or something."

"I'm fine, mate. Bring it on."

———

TYE STEPPED out into the arena. The crowd stood above and behind him as he walked to the ring, the excited buzz rising to a muffled roar as his opponent entered the stadium from the opposite entrance. The spotlighted canvas glowed like a beacon. It seemed too clean, too pure.

The cheering rose. Through the noise, he could hear Frank's voice directly behind him.

"Keep it tight, and keep moving."

It was day four of the tournament.

The last three days of elimination trials had been tough. All the contenders had been playing to win. Cliff had been eliminated on the second day, retiring with a broken rib. Tye had begun with skill and a spirit of determination, but an early defeat on day one of the trials had opened new resources he had never tapped before. He had gone into the second day with renewed energy, ferocity, and had fought back with power, earning a place in the later rounds.

Tye reached the ring and climbed to the canvas. His gaze searching for his opponent. He watched him as he climbed into the ring. He could feel the man's fear as he met his gaze. It felt good.

Tye shuffled on the spot. Limbering his arms and legs, shattering the fragile quiet of the ring with the sound of snapping attacks. He had gained a whole new vision over the past few days. Like he was riding the crest of a wave. He fixed his gaze on his enemy and focused, channeling all his power, all his hate.

The other fighter came forward. A new determination on his face. His opponent's fear was gone! The fighter had somehow mastered his fear. Tye shook with anger, his hate crystallising into a tangible presence; a solid plug of spinning energy, whirling through his limbs. He knew what to do.

Kill him. Kill him.

The Filipino referee stepped between the two fighters as they came forward, holding each in check. With a stern gaze, he watched for the signal from the Judges. His hand fell with the bell and the fight was on.

Time slowed. While the sound of the bell still lingered in the air, a dark, dripping energy raced through Tye's limbs. Suddenly he was watching himself; watching in those split seconds as he moved faster than thought, his right foot rising, burning to kill. The referee had barely moved back from the gap between them.

He floated there, under the lights. Shifting between planes of time, watching as the stranger's foot leapt from the canvas, driving into his opponent's throat. He saw the pain, the fear, the last mute appeal before death, watched as the fighter fell to the canvas. Dead. He saw his own face, a stranger's face, distorted and twisted into a grimace of agony and outrage; pain and hate. It was the mask. The mask he had broken, remade in the skin of his own face.

Still suspended outside himself, Tye looked back to see a shifting form leave the body of the dead fighter, drifting away. The spirit gave him one last look of pity, then it was gone.

Tye was back in his body, looking through his own eyes at the man he had killed. He looked up to see the referee's face, livid with fear, as he recognised Tye's twisted expression.

"Kel sapo," the man whispered, his voice a mixture of terror and disbelief. Making the sign of the cross, he drew his eyes away from Tye and bent to the body of the fallen fighter. The force of the blow had broken his neck. The head lay askew on his shoulders. His body silent. Frantically, the referee felt for a pulse. After half a minute, he turned to the judges and shook his head.

Around him, the crowd was silent. Its sheer weight of expectation and shock was focussed on the ring. Disorientation seized Tye, and he staggered. The world blurred. He could hear Frank talking, leading him away from the stadium.

Within him, he was fighting. He could feel the dark presence. It was in him. Gripping his heart, fighting for his soul. Distantly, he could hear Frank talking.

"It's not your fault. Every fighter takes the risks. Focus on the finals. The title is yours now, I'm sure of it."

Then he was dreaming. There was another voice. Whispering: I can give it to you. I can give you the power. Let me in!

A memory of the referee's face—that look of fear—flashed past him in the haze.

Kel sapo.

Then it was the mask. It filled his vision. The eyes were terrible, glowing with a heat that draws from life. They drew him, and he entered the darkness again.

Frank staggered under Tye's weight as he lost consciousness.
"Get the Medics over here!"

———

TYE SAT ON A BEACH. The waves were crashing, pounding into the sand, but they made no sound. Behind him was a simple hut, constructed of bamboo. An old woman was there, sweeping the sand from the matting in front of the shack. He could hear the rhythmic sound of the sweeping. He called out, but he made no sound. The woman ignored him, continuing to sweep.

Tye felt something move on his chest. He looked down and saw a hideous lizard, longer than his arm and pitch black, ripping at his chest with its horny mouth and claws.

"It seeks your heart."

Tye turned to the woman. She had stopped sweeping and now stood beside him. It was the woman from the steps of the hotel. A breeze swept across him, smelling of the sea.

"What is it?"

"Kel Sapo. Soon it will not need the mask to reach you."

The lizard looked up at Tye. Its eyes were twin pits of darkness. It hissed, and Tye cried out. He reached forward, trying to push it off his chest.

———

TYE WOKE IN DARKNESS.

He heard someone move beside him, and the light flicked on. He was back in his bedroom. Cliff was standing by the light.

"So how do you feel now, mate?" asked Cliff. He was tense. Guarded.

"I'm not sure." Then he remembered. The semi-finals. He had killed the guy!

"Oh, no! NO!"

Suddenly, his foot was blazing with pain. He cried out in agony and pushed back the covers.

Do not resist me.

Tye's head swept around. Standing in the room's corner was the man from the alley: the leader. The one he had killed. Except his head was a lizard-face, twisted with hate and filled with the power of destruction. It stepped forward.

You wanted the power. I have given it to you. Do not resist. I can give you the power to win.

Tye screamed as the pain in his foot flared like a supernova.

Cliff raced to the telephone, dialing Valdez's number.

"Valdez? It's Tye. He's going crazy with pain."

Tye's vision had contracted to a single point. All he could see was the lizard face of Kel Sapo. The jaws were snapping at him, the clawed hands were ripping into his chest, looking for his heart.

Tye jerked back onto the bed. His body shuddered as he fought the phantom lizard.

Cliff leapt across the bed, trying to weigh Tye down.

Tye forced himself still, tried to control his fear. The pain in his foot, and the dark presence of Kel Sapo, blazed like twin suns. His vision blurred, and time moved strangely.

———

TYE'S HEAD jerked up at the sound of the door opening.

Valdez and Frank entered the room.

"How many did he take?" snapped Valdez.

"How many what?" asked Cliff.

"How many pills!"

Cliff shook his head. "He hasn't been taking the pills."

"What you say! He take no pills?"

"No."

"Impossible. Too much pain." The doctor pushed back the bedclothes and looked at the foot, clicking his tongue.

"Oh my God!" said Cliff.

Tye looked down at his foot. It was black. And all over its surface, the splinter wounds were open and leaking blood and green pus.

"Get my bag!"

The doctor took a scalpel and cut into the foot. Tye jerked at the sudden pain. The doctor dragged his foot back and Frank took a firm hold on it, both hands on the ankle to keep it in place while the doctor worked. The scalpel sliced deep. A fountain of blood and puss shot across the carpet. Tye's body stiffened, and he screamed in agony.

The doctor took the pliers from his bag and knelt at Tye's foot. He pulled out a huge splinter—at least three inches long and as thick as a straw.

Tye hissed in pain as the splinter came out. Sweat flushed across his forehead.

"You incompetent bastard," snapped Frank. "You better get every splinter out of his foot. Right now! If his foot is ruined, so help me..." Frank glared at the doctor, his voice lowering. "I have friends in this town, buddy. I'd like to see you work with two broken hands."

Valdez's face went white. He kept working on Tye's foot. He was sweating by the time he was finished, and had found three other, smaller splinters. As the last splinter was removed, Tye stopped struggling and slumped in relief. His hands trembled with the pain, and his shirt was soaked with sweat.

Frank took a deep breath. "OK. Just fix it, Valdez. He must be ready for tomorrow."

Frank left the room.

Cliff retrieved the bottle of pills and gave them to Valdez. The doctor opened the bottle and checked the contents. He looked up at Tye, bewildered. "This is not possible. You should have been in big pain. Big pain. Hardly walk."

Tye shrugged. He had no answer for Valdez.

The doctor applied an antiseptic cream and bound the foot. He left some antibiotics, put the bottle of painkillers on the desk by the door and fled without another word.

"Hey, Cliff. pass me that bottle, will ya? My foot hurts like the devil."

Cliff retrieved the pill bottle and gave it to him. "How do you feel?"

Tye took two pills, swallowing them without water. His memories of the last few days were like a dream. Except, he knew it was no dream. Kel Sapo was a demon. He knew that now. A demon who had used him to kill two men. Where the vision of the old woman had come from, he had no idea, but suddenly all the pieces fell into place. He and Cliff were about the same standard as fighters, and yet here he was, in the finals. That new energy that had surged through him, driving him through pain, pushing him to crush his opponents; it was Kel Sapo. It had not been him at all.

"Used, Cliff. I feel used."

"You screamed like hell when the doctor took those other splinters out. This time, let's hope he has them all." Cliff shook his head. "Christ, Tye. You should have been in incredible pain. What has been going on? The last few days you have been like... a stranger."

"I know, Cliff." Tye laid back on the bed and turned away from Cliff. "I need to sleep now."

"It's not worth it, Tye. Do you remember when we started off at the club. Just kids, having fun? We don't need this, Tye. We don't need the title. Let's just go back to Sydney. We can start our own club. Who cares what they say about titles?"

Silence.

"OK, Tye. OK." Cliff turned off the light.

Tye did not sleep. He cried—for two men who should have lived. Meanwhile, a voice whispered into his brain. You can win, Tye. Win. Let me in. I can give you the power...

———

THE STADIUM WAS PACKED. The noise of the crowd was like a dull roar. News of the death had turned the championships into a high-profile media event. Tye could see the television cameras and photographers straining against the barriers like pigs with the scent of blood.

Tye watched the other finalist climb into the ring. He was a Korean, stocky and solid. His eyes betrayed no fear as he walked to the centre of the canvas. Within Tye, the voice was growing louder.

You're weak. Let me give you the power, open yourself up to the strength of darkness.

He pushed aside the grabbing claws of Kel Sapo, causing pain to rake through his chest. Suddenly his foot ignited in a sulphurous explosion of pain. He cried out. The referee stepped closer to the pair and looked at Tye with a puzzled expression. Tye fought the pain. No, you will not command me!

Before he could gather his senses, the bell rang. He heard the Korean shout amid a roaring that seemed like the waves on the storm season beach. He felt an impact on the side of his head that jolted him to awareness. His hands instinctively came into a guarding position and he shouted, kicking out with his right foot even before his vision returned.

The fight surged on, blow following blow. Tye felt drained. He was fighting two battles at the same time. The Korean was fit and fast. Tye was forced more on the defensive with every blow. The whispering in his mind grew more insistent, more compelling.

You will lose and die a pitiful death at the hands of this enemy. You are weak. A weakling fool! Open yourself to my power!

Tye was near the point of exhaustion, but anger rose within him at the intrusion of this spirit. With a shout he shot out with his right foot. The Korean blocked him with force, ripping the scar tissue. Tye cried out, stepping backwards quickly as the bell sounded.

Tye limped to his corner. Only one round had gone by, and yet he was in severe pain and near the point of exhaustion. As he sat on the stool, Frank stepped through the ropes to look at his foot, which was bleeding onto the canvas. He cleaned it quickly and cursed under his breath. "I'm going to kill Valdez."

Tye felt an elation rising through him, like a warm and gentle tide, sweeping away the exhaustion of the struggle. The demon was losing its grip! He could win! He could fight it.

"What's wrong with you, Tye?" said Frank. "Beat this Korean bastard. You're not fighting hard enough."

Cliff leapt up to the ring and pushed his head through the ropes.

"Win or lose, Tye. It doesn't matter. Show this crowd your best and let's get the hell out of Dodge."

This time when the bell rang, it was Tye alone who faced the Korean. His limbs moved with the speed, agility, and power that had taken him to the top of the Australian ladder. Even so, it was not enough. The Korean was above his class. He could accept that now. The Korean circled him, dashing, and striking out in short, controlled attacks.

Tye could feel the demon, Kel Sapo, close by, looking for an opening, but this time he was blocking it at every turn. He was fighting Kel Sapo and winning. The fight went on. Tye pushed through his exhaustion, fighting round after round. As the final bell sounded, Tye and the Korean were both standing. Bleeding and taking in the thick air of the stadium with short gasping breaths, they waited under the lights for the Judges' decision.

The referee walked straight to the Korean and lifted his hand into the air while the crowd cheered. Camera flashes cut the hot swelter of faces. The Korean shook Tye's hand and Tye left the ring.

Frank walked up to Tye and threw his towel at him.

"I lost money on you, you useless twit. I'm finished with you, and with your bed-buddy Cliff."

Tye took one step toward Frank and hit him with an uppercut to the jaw. The big man's eyes glazed over, and he crashed on the wooden floor.

Instantly they were surrounded by cameras. Flashing. Snapping.

Cliff laughed, and it was a wonderful sound. "Way to go, Tye!"

A wind swept through the stadium. Wild and free, it tasted of the sea, of open horizons and lonely beaches.

"Let's get out of here, Cliff. I've had enough of Manila."

———

As THE PLANE lifted from the tarmac, Tye looked down for the last time at Manila. Its sprawl reached out as far as he could see. It looked oddly neat from the air.

Tye took a magazine out of the seat pocket and flicked through it.

"It was a noble gesture," said Cliff.

Tye threw the magazine onto the empty seat beside him and looked out the window. "It was the least I could do." Just before he had left Manila, Tye had found the wife of the fighter he had killed, and given her all his winnings. He would remember the sadness in that woman's eyes for the rest of his life. Thankfully, she had accepted the money.

"So, we leave the Philippines with nothing," said Cliff.

"Yes. Thank, God," said Tye. Some things I would rather leave behind.

END

ABOUT THE AUTHOR

Being able to escape into the realm of the imagination was handy growing up as the youngest in a family of eleven, and Chris continues his fantasy and SF writing habit from his home town of Brisbane.

His novels include *Warriors of the Blessed Realms* (2020), which blends urban fantasy and fantasy with elements of SF and horror, the hard-SF *The Tau Ceti Diversion* (2018) and his three-book heroic fantasy series the *Jakirian Cycle* (2013).

Chris is also an engineer, and blogs regularly about space science and exploration. He has a fourth-dan black belt in Moon Lee Tae Kwon Do and also enjoys movies and exploring narrow alleyways. Chris is very passionate about music, and loves singing and playing classical guitar. He has been short-listed for the Aurealis Awards twice, and has won the One Book, Many Brisbanes competition twice.

Website: www.chrismcmahon.net

11

INTROSPECTION

CHRIS KNEIPP

The first thing I remembered was the last thing I'd seen: my head hitting the toilet bowl like a bizarre, porcelain Liverpool Kiss. Then there was nothing for God knows how long. Time works differently when you're unconscious.

I was awakened by a throbbing in my head, like all eight pints of blood were trying to escape through my ears. It felt like I was lying on soft grass.

Hang on, didn't I have tiles on my bathroom floor?

Opening my eyes turned out to be a bad idea. The upturned world looked like Salvador Dali had vomited across the landscape. A swirling purple sky was where the ground should've been, and a waving crimson grass that sprouted from pink glitter was where the sky should've been.

It took me a while to realise I was upside down, lying on a hillside, with my feet uphill and my head down. Well that explained a lot, but not everything. For instance, the melting clocks oozing in the trees made no sense at all. Sitting up made my blood return to where it belonged, leaving the mother of all headaches as its jetsam. I closed my eyes again and let my other senses feed me information. A breeze blew through me, carrying the scent of musk sticks and Dettol. In the distance, I heard the unmistakable flatulence of a 1969 VW Kombi, getting louder.

Opening my eyes, I saw the Kombi come into sight, like a paisley shoebox on wheels. As it drew closer, I saw it was me driving—or someone who looked just like me, but with significantly better hair.

The VW skidded to a halt in a cloud of glitter and the other-me leaned out the window. "You need to get in."

A thousand questions came rushing at me, buffeting me in an attempt to be the first one spoken. "What?" was all I managed to say.

"Get in. You shouldn't be in here."

"Who are you?" The pounding in my head was beginning to echo.

"I'm you, of course." My doppelganger opened the door and Ogden's Nut Gone Flake spilled from the radio, forming a pile of words on the ground. "Freud would call me your alter ego."

Two years of a Psych degree had taught me the father of mummy issues was a crazy bastard, but arguing psychology with myself would prove I was as cracked as Sigmund, so I let it slide.

Forgetting everything my parents had taught me about getting into cars with strangers, I brushed the drug-fuelled lyrics from the vinyl seat and climbed into the passenger's side.

"Where am I?" I asked.

"You're in your head you drunken idiot. Where did you think you were?" Without waiting for an answer, the other-me dropped the clutch and completely failed to squeal the wheels as the Kombi took off with a farting roar, accelerating towards forty.

"What the hell is going on?" I was still coming to grips with the Dali-spew world through the windscreen. It all seemed far too metaphysical for my liking.

"Put on your seatbelt, this is going to get rough," me 2.0 said. "What do you remember?"

"Hitting my head on the toilet, I guess." The screaming headache had lessened, becoming a small ball peen hammer, tapping out the little dents in my skull.

"Remember talking to God on the great white telephone?" alternative me asked. He raised an eyebrow, the way I do when I don't approve. "You were really driving that porcelain bus into hell, weren't you?"

"So this is just a drunken dream?" I asked hopefully, relishing the idea of waking.

My reflection leaned over and punched me in the shoulder.

"Ow, what was that for?"

"Did that feel like a dream? Now, put your fucking seatbelt on."

Reaching over to grab the buckle, I saw the huge wombat sprawled out on the mattress in the back. Surrounded by empty beer cans and whiskey bottles, our passenger lay face-down in the alcoholic debris with his fat arse pointed towards me like a rusty, steel wool cannon.

"What's with the animal?" I asked.

"Oh, that's your inner wombat," my alter-ego said as the Kombi approached sixty. "Everyone's got one."

"Is he alive?" I asked dubiously and put my seatbelt on.

"Yeah, just asleep. He's been partying, and you know what they say about drunken wombats at parties?" He looked back disdainfully at the marsupial. "Eats, roots and leaves."

It's only when you're driving through a psychedelic landscape in a paisley Kombi with yourself and a wombat, that you realise just how screwed up you really are.

The road suddenly dipped, as only a cliff can, and we hurtled down, the fall making my stomach leap up my throat and collide with my tonsils. There was a wombat-sized thump on the back of my seat, followed by the clattering of bottles and cans. The animal's chainsaw snoring told me he was sleeping through it all.

I, on the other hand, was terrified, gripping the dash and forcing the blood from my whitening fingertips. Looking at the driver-me, his face like a Greek comedy mask, I could tell I was alone in my fear.

"Where are we going?" I asked, trying to remain calm. I was pretty sure I wasn't going to like the answer.

"Out the frontal lobe." He poked me in the forehead without looking, narrowly missing my eye. "That's the way out."

"So, why the hell are we going down?" I wasn't sure this version of me had my best interests at heart.

"It'd take forever in the Kombi," he answered without losing the manic grin. "First stop is the hippocampus, if we can get there."

"If we get there?"

"It's the deepest, darkest part of your brain and we're going to have to deal with some of your issues on the way down. That's if the antibodies don't find you first. We can get to the cerebellum and grab a couple of neuron cycles there."

"Hold on. Antibodies?"

He frowned in a very worrying way. "They're like a cross between a border guard and Vaseline."

Below, the ground was approaching at an alarming rate.

"Tighten your sphincters, folks!" he screamed with a wild whoop. "This is going to be close."

Clenching everything I had, I prepared to die as the glittery ground came rushing towards us. He seemed to be aiming for a long, orange road.

Much to my surprise and relief, the Kombi reconnected with the road just as it went from vertical to hyperbolic, like a Hot Wheels track. It was a Hot Wheels track. The orange plastic highway returned to some semblance of horizontal.

"Well that was bracing," he said, still wearing his wild grin and matching eyes. Looking at me he laughed. "You can unclench now."

I wasn't sure I could.

"How long till we get to this hippopotamus?" I asked.

"Hippocampus," he corrected smugly. "First we've got to make it through the limbic brain, which is swimming in last night's scotch, thanks to you. Just how much did you drink?"

I tried to do the maths, but I was obviously in the wrong part of my brain to do alcoholic addition.

"Too much."

Up ahead the scenery changed. The orange track gave way to rolling hills that literally rolled back and forth across the road, blocking it intermittently. I must have looked worried, because my reflection took one look at me and said, "Don't sweat it. It's just like Frogger but with hills."

"In a Kombi?" I asked sceptically.

"Exactly," he said, and the Greek mask returned.

The Kombi hit the first hill like a brick on a skateboard and climbed rapidly to the crest. Zooming into the air, just like Kombis shouldn't, the van flew across the gap between the first and second hill. A flying wombat arse hit me in the back of the head and then landed with a thud back amongst the recyclables. The snoring continued.

"Doesn't anything wake him up?" I asked, rubbing my neck as the Kombi shot down the moving hill and roared up the next.

"He'll wake up when he's ready. Don't let him fool you," he shouted over the VW's noisy farting. "He can really move once he gets going."

The Kombi chugged up the hill and took to the air again, gracefully sailing towards the next hump in the road, like an airborne tin of Spam.

The V-Dub hit the top of the fourth hill and we tore down the side, chasing the next wayward mound before it got away from us. This continued until the upping and downing was threatening to make my insides become outsides. The occasional whack to the head from a marsupial's abrasive backside didn't help.

I was about to ask when the leaping hell would end, but the hills gave way to a grey, straight highway and the Kombi continued flat chat, which was almost sixty five, towards the horizon.

"You might feel a little crazy while you're here," he said. "Things get a bit screwy in the limbic brain."

I snorted. "I'm sure it couldn't get any crazier."

I was wrong.

A giant, stuffed panda loomed larger than life off to the right. It was just like the one I had as a child, only thirty feet taller and with a lot more teeth. With a mighty squeeee from the squeaker in its belly, the monstrous plush bear loped across the empty plain towards us. A quick calculation told me the horrible cuddly would catch us in no time and I wasn't in the mood to cuddle.

"Can't this heap of shit go any faster?" I yelled.

"Yeah," he shouted back above the straining engine noise. "If we were going downhill."

There was another deafening squeak. I looked in the rear view mirror and was confronted by the toothy snarl of my childhood comforter. Written on the mirror were the unhelpful words, "Objects In Mirror May Be Right Up Your Arse."

"Brace yourself," my head-twin said. "This isn't gunna be cute."

The panda rammed the rear of the van like a rhino in a sumo suit. Another squeaky roar accompanied the impact. The Kombi jolted forward and shot away from the padded attacker, as though the road was coated in WD-40. Hitting speeds the old speedometer didn't go to, we left my childish nightmare behind in a squeaking, screaming rage.

"Well, that was exhilarating," my alter-ego said with a laugh.

"And by exhilarating you mean bloody terrifying, right? What the hell was that?"

"I told you, this is the limbic brain, home of the vampire butterfly and the nasal squidgy-worm."

"And the thirty-foot carnivorous teddy," I said.

"Exactly." He looked ahead. "Welcome to your nightmare."

At a velocity somewhere between screaming and suicidal, we raced along the road. The mottled mindscape became a blur out the window. As we whizzed towards the purple horizon, pictures from my memory floated across the sky like clouds. I was saddened by how dull my life was.

Tearing teary eyes away from the past, I looked through the windshield to the future, which happened to be an approaching blue light growing brighter with each flash.

"Shit, it's a cop," other-me swore. "Just stay cool."

"Cops, here? In my brain?" I was sceptical despite the lights and the siren growing louder. "What, like dream police?"

"Antibodies," he said. "Think less Cheap Trick, and more David Bowie."

Just then, 1984 started playing on the radio and my alter ego tried to find the non-existent fifth gear. We screamed past the uniformed blob on his Royal Enfield motorbike. The Doppler Effect had its way with the siren and the squeal became a fading oscillating drone. I looked in the objects up your arse detector to see the bike do a half donut. The cop's globby body wobbled erratically as he came after us.

"It's catching up," I said.

"Yeah, I know. We can't outrun it." He slammed on the brakes, leaving a long skid across my corpus callosum. "That's okay, just act supernatural and let me do the talking."

My other-self wore the expression I save for when I'm about to crap myself. Cops make me nervous at the best of times, but I got the feeling this was worse than pre-Fitzgerald Inquiry Queensland.

The blobby bobby pulled up beside the van and got off the bike, his body squidging its way to the driver's side.

With a voice like a blocked toilet it made an unintelligible demand of my driver, "Blubble, blubble thwlup."

"Really?" my alter ego asked politely. "Was I going that fast?"

"Blurble, blibble shlongthlock," the antibody replied, and held out a hand that looked like one of those sticky, stretchy, novelty toys. Other-me handed over his licence.

Removing a book from God-only-knew-where, the cop began writing up the ticket. I was hoping that was as bad as it would get, but as the cop tore the ticket from the book and handed it to my twin, it took an interest in the wombat passed out in the back.

"Blub, blubbity ploop," it said, wrinkling its gelatinous forehead.

"No," Me-Mk2 shook his head. "He's just hungover."

"Blurb schlock, blurbity blurb," came the stern reply.

"What's happening?" I asked.

"It thinks the wombat's on drugs," he replied. "It wants to do a search for any grass."

"BLURRB," the cop shouted, waking our marsupial passenger.

The antibody gave a burbled command, universally recognisable as 'step out of the vehicle and spread'em'. We complied, because when you're being menaced by a six-foot tall pile of goo in uniform, you do what you're told.

"What now?" I asked.

"Cavity search," 2.0 said with a gulp.

We lined up with pants down, hands and paws pressed to the van, and waited for the medi-legal humiliation to begin.

The cop began the search with me, boldly going where no one had gone before. Being given a cavity search by an amorphous blob was an unpleasant experience, leaving me feeling strangely clean and dirty at the same time. Like getting an enema of raspberry jelly, but not nearly as much fun.

The cop moved on to my carbon copy. As the blob squished its way into every hole and crevice, my twin wore a brave smile that I didn't know I had. I did recognise the relieved expression on his face though, when the ordeal was finally over.

Lastly, the antibody moved to the wombat. A quick pat down produced a baggy of lawn clippings.

"Blubbity blub?" the cop asked, holding the suspect couch-grass aloft.

The wombat yawned sleepily and then, in a voice like a large rock dropped in a pool, said, "Lunch."

"Burple, bloob," the antibody foamed belligerently, reaching a slimy tendril for the animals wire-brush arse in search of more contraband.

Me 2.0 said, "I wouldn't do that if I were you."

The cop scowled as only jelly can, and continued.

"I warned him," my alter ego said resignedly.

Suddenly, the wombat spun around and leapt like a fat, hairy ninja at the blob that'd dared touch his delicate nether regions. His stubby legs were a blur of karate chops and six-inch punches in a martial arts display that would've made Po proud. The black belt marsupial went feral on the formless officer until all that remained was a red, gooey puddle slowly soaking into the ground.

"I tried to warn him," 2.0 repeated. "Let's go, before backup arrives.

We've got a lot of grey matter between us and the outside. The longer you're in here, the more damage you can do."

I didn't need to be told twice, so we all piled back in the van and raced slowly away leaving a spluttering cloud of exhaust in our wake.

"Where'd you learn kung fu?" I asked over my shoulder.

"Skippy," the wombat replied in a cavernous voice and promptly went back to sleep.

The Kombi followed the highway through my twisted dreamscape for a while, all of which was fine except for some embarrassing revelations which had leaked into the sky from my libido. We drove until the bright lights of my thalamus loomed up ahead. It looked a lot like Sydney, without the smog and traffic.

"You look like you could use a coffee," Mk2 said.

The pounding in my head had become a snare drum, accompanying Kansas on the radio.

"Carry on," I punned.

We rolled down the empty main street of my thalamus and pulled up outside a neon-lit coffee shop. The purple sign read Schrodinger's Café.

"This place any good?" I asked.

"Yes and no," he said. "The food's not good, but it's not that bad."

We left the van and were joined by the wombat, who apparently could be woken at the mention of food.

Hanging at the door was a blackboard filled with indecision, promising raw fry ups and high-calorie, high-sugar health food. Inside, the place was empty apart from the grumpy, half-dead cat behind the counter.

"What's your poison?" the cat mewed.

"Two double shot espressos hold the isotopes, and a slice of Pi to six decimal places," my other-self ordered without skipping a beat.

We left the wombat to order for himself and took a couple of seats near the counter.

"Will this take long?" I asked.

"This is Schrodinger's," he said and shrugged his shoulders. "There's no way of knowing."

The cat brought two boxes to the table which I assumed held the coffees. I opened my box and the cat promptly fell dead to the floor.

"Oh great," 2.0 complained. "You could've at least waited till she brought my Pi."

The espresso was topped with a few more cat hairs than I was used to, but I took a sip anyway. Hell, there was too much blood in my caffeine stream. The wombat sat down opposite. With a mouth ill-designed for sculling, he started sinking wheatgrass shots like they were whisky. Chlorophyll stained his chin green.

Picking cat hairs from my teeth, I asked, "How come you didn't get any hair in yours?"

"I guess she liked you."

"So, where do we go from here?" I asked.

"We'll have to ditch the Kombi," he said. "The cops will be all over that soon. I reckon we could catch a thought bubble from the cerebellum. You'll need to watch yourself there."

"Why?" I said, continuing to make the mistake of asking questions.

"Do you like bladder control?" He raised an eyebrow. "Would you like to keep it? Then don't touch anything."

"Okay. Can we get going soon?" I sank the last of my furry coffee and coughed up a hairball. "I'm kind of keen to get out of my head."

"Getting out of your head's what got you into this mess in the first place." He slugged his own coffee down in a swallow and stood. "Alright, let's go."

I stepped over the dead moggy, and my doppelganger followed.

The wombat paid for the coffee, leaving the money on the counter, then proceeded to eat the deceased feline, like a snake swallows a rat. Its tiny mouth stretched to accommodate the cat, head-first. It was like watching a breech-birth video in reverse. The marsupial gulped the poor puss down to the tail and left her a small tip.

"I thought he ate vegetarian?" I whispered, frowning to show my disapproval.

"She was," my number two answered, looking back at the piece of tail. He held the door open for me. "It wouldn't hurt you to eat some vegetables now and then, either."

I refused to justify my diet to myself.

Leaving Schrodinger's and what was left of the cat behind, we headed out into the street. Other-me led the way, which was lucky, as I'd failed brain physiology at uni.

The wombat trotted along behind. His mouth, surrounded in furry chlorophyll, was back to its original size and bore a quokka's grin.

It was surreal, walking down the narrows of my mind with a carnivorous wombat and a colour-copy of myself, travelling to unknown places in my head. It was then that I began to worry. Some forgotten parental warnings were niggling in the back on my mind.

"Why's everything look so much like Sydney?" I asked.

"What's George Street to you, is the hypothalamus to me."

The three of us hurried along the narrow footpath, past Town Hall with its discoloured sandstone walls. The pigeon crap looked like jagged, nicotine-stained teeth.

"Up ahead is an escalator that'll take us down to the cerebellum," he said. "That's where the wombat leaves us."

"Why?" I asked.

"He's claustrophobic."

When I didn't question the weirdness of that revelation, I realised bizarre had officially become the new black. It went with everything.

We reached the escalators and said our goodbyes. The wombat wanted to hug, but I wasn't enthusiastic about getting near that elastic-jawed monster, so I shook his claws and then watched him waddle away.

I stared warily down into the inky blackness of the escalator shaft and felt an empathy with the wombat.

"So, why are we going to the cerebellum?" I said, tearing my eyes away from the moving stairway.

"We can catch a thought bubble from there to anywhere. How are you feeling?" he asked. I'd seen his expression before, in a mirror when I was young and scared my reflection would come to life.

"I'm fine, all things considered," I said. "Why? Should I be worried?"

"God, no. Watch what you're thinking," he warned seriously. "It's not called an escalator for nothing."

Hopping onto the conveyer, we began the descent into the deepest, darkest depths.

Slowly, the steps rumbled their way down into the closing shadows. The last thing I saw was an Alice Cooper poster on the wall.

Welcome to My Nightmare, indeed.

The further down I went, the darker the thoughts became and I started to question everything. Where was the other-me leading really? Did I even have the faintest idea? Could I trust him? What was in it for the old 2.0? Somewhere far below in my chest, my heart was pounding at a level of paranoia that'd make Ozzy Osbourne proud.

My other-self was trying to dump me. If I was out of the way, he'd be free to take over my body. I didn't want to be stuck in here, fated to become the alter ego. I'd just bought a new PlayStation.

The descent into madness continued until a pinprick of light signalled the escalations' end. The light grew until the edges of the exit became clear. Drawn to that light, I watched as it grew bigger, relieved to leave the darkness and the worst of the paranoia.

The exit came out at a railway platform, much like Wynyard, only cleaner. On the wall was a metaphorical poster of Led Zeppelin IV with an arrow pointing to the up escalator. It wasn't moving. A sandwich board read: Out of order. Use the stairway.

Mk2 was waiting for me on the platform, leaning back against a stark-white, tiled column. The smell of iron oxide and neurotransmitters filled the air.

"Are you okay?" he asked. "The escalator can mess with your head."

I still didn't trust him, but my brain seemed to have returned to its normal level of paranoia.

"I'm fine," I lied. I was anything but fine.

Every few seconds an electric-blue thought bubble roared through the tunnel and into the station. It resembled an old red rattler train, but blue and glowing instead. An unintelligible announcer blared out arrival information over a crackling PA.

Each train of thought stopped for a nanosecond and then shot off again. They came so thick and fast the announcer had little time to blurt out each message, until the syllables crashed into each other in a long, single word.

"Expressbowelmovementimpulse," the PA barked.

"Not this one," 2.0 said. "And I think you're about to shit our pants."

The crapola express disappeared up the tunnel and another blue rattler took its place.

"Which one do we want?" I yelled above the electrical howl.

"Parietallobecircleallaboard," the tinny voice garbled.

"We'll wait for one going to the frontal lobe," he said.

Remembering all I'd learned from university and old Raquel Welsh movies I asked, "Couldn't we just Fantastic Voyage it and go out through the eye?"

"Information only travels one way down the optic nerve," he said, "Trust me, we need to get back to the conscious mind."

"Frontallobeline," the PA rasped again.

"This is us," other-me said. "Get ready to jump."

The neon thought bubble stopped for a moment and we both leapt into the nearest carriage. The train then took off at a rapid clip, leaving me flailing towards the back of the compartment. Catching myself before I went too far back, I managed to sit in a forward-facing seat.

My alter ego took a seat facing me and smiled. I still didn't trust him. His face had all of my tells, and a few extra I didn't know I had. Something just didn't add up. My suspicions returned with a vengeance.

We emerged from the tunnel and as I looked out the window, I saw my Dali vomit headspace again. A purple sky filled with memories and strawberry-coloured fields stretching forever. It was nauseatingly beautiful. An image of myself drifted into view, lying between the toilet and the mildew-stained vanity, face down in a puddle of spew.

My doppelganger must have seen me watching the cloud, because he asked, "Why do you do it to yourself?"

"Don't know," I answered honestly. "I think this is what they call rock bottom."

I was beginning to feel funny, and not in an amusing way.

"Look," he said, "I know how this goes. Out of here you'll make promises to a convenient god, no more than one or two scotches a day. You'll clean up your act. No more than two or three drinks in a session and no more drugs. You don't want to end up back in here. You get it. Acid is a hash brownie compared to what happens between your ears. But after a week of no more than three or four shots in a sitting, the weekend will roll around and you'll have a half dozen Glenfiddichs because you feel pretty good about yourself. Despite your vows to the Flying Spaghetti Monster you'll start losing count in a fortnight."

Numbness started creeping up my legs, like they were turning to ice and being tickled with an icepick.

"What's happening?" I cried. The chill moved past my legs, then into my bum and stomach. "I knew you were up to something. What did you do to me?"

"I slipped a Moggy into your coffee, back at Schrodinger's," he said, and put a wicked smile on his lips.

"You poisoned me?" I croaked as the roofie hit my throat.

"Hair of the cat," he said. "It's the opposite to hair of the dog."

I wanted to argue that cats and dogs weren't opposites, but my mouth would no longer cooperate, so I drooled at him instead.

"Don't worry, it'll wear off in a bit," he said and stood. "Just long enough for me to get out of here and lock the gate behind me."

I wanted to punch him in my stolen, smug face. There was no lifting my leaden arms, however. Dribbling some more contempt in his direction, I gave him a death stare.

"Look, it's nothing personal," he said. "You had your turn and you stuffed it up with your drinking and your drugs. It's time to let someone else have a go at the wheel. It's better this way. You weren't doing much with your life anyway, were you? You stay here in the deep, dark playground and I go live in the real world and start acting like a grown up."

The cat hair soporific was clouding my mind, which had been stormy enough before the Moggy Finn.

"Look, you'll be fine," 2.0 said, and patted me on the head. "This is my stop."

He jumped into the air and vanished just as the thought bubble burst. Momentum carried me on and I went rolling like a limp tumbleweed till I crashed into the back of my forehead. Lying there , battered and numb in a heap of despair at the base of a bone white cliff, I wondered if anyone else's drinking got them into this much trouble.

Over the next few minutes the hair of the cat wore off. The numbness drained slowly from my head like a plug in my foot had been pulled. As soon as I was able, I raised myself onto one elbow and looked around. Around me lay the ruins of every thought I'd ever had. My pain-in-the-arse other-self was nowhere to be seen. I was trapped.

Feeling returned eventually to my legs and I stood up unsteadily, buoyed by my anger. I was damned if I was staying here. Damned if I was going to go quietly into that good night. I knew exactly what to do. I'd head for the subconscious and wait for him.

He'd have to go to sleep some time.

END

About the Author

Chris Kneipp was born in Sydney but spent most of his adolescence escaping into the National Parks that surround it. This love of the Australian landscape bleeds into his works of speculative fiction. He has spent many years honing the gentle art of word wrestling, but constantly feels the words are winning. He has been a member of Vision Writers since 2009 and is the current Vice President.

He is seeking a home for his sci-fi novel, *Harmony*, while reworking a young adult series, *The Kasdtien Cycle*, to be published next year. He has several published short stories and writes across all speculative fiction genres.

Chris resides in Brisbane with his wife and two dogs, though his mind is probably elsewhere. He claims to have been to all the places he writes about, even the imaginary ones.

He is on:

Twitter - @cmkneipp

Facebook - @authorchriskneipp

Wordpress - *Part Time Lunatic*

12

EMBERFALL

JONATHAN FURNEAUX

I kick the side of my griffin-mount, and he responds with a gentle spiral-descent down to the autumnal forest below. My fingers, clutching desperately to his neck-feathers, feel icy in the roaring wind. We corkscrew at the last second before crashing into the loam forest floor. I leap down from the griffin.

Ahead of me, a tiny wisp of smoke drifts upwards from the small cooking fire of a goblin encampment. I can see four of them, huddled around the meagre flames as they roast a small fish between them. A short goblin sniffs the air as I approach their camp at a run. It spots me and screams the alarm. The others scramble to fetch their weapons. I clench my fist, and the heavens darken. The cloud cover stirs. I relax my fist, revealing a lone ember resting in my palm.

The world is still and silent. I blow the ember like a kiss, and it flutters towards the group. They watch as it approaches, mesmerised. It hangs above the leader's head for an agonising second, and then gently lands on the crooked bridge of his nose. From the sky, a pillar of fire falls. It is a seething, tumultuous tornado of death that casts an orange glow across the entire forest below. I gasp for breath as the heat arrives. The very air ignites as the pillar of fire lands atop the goblin encampment, and the resulting shock wave throws me backwards, away from the towering inferno. In the blink of an eye, the surrounding hectare of forest fractures into blackened ash. I laugh and march through the sputtering fire that licks the forest floor...

———

I LOOK up from my phone. The bitter smell of coffee wafts up from the mug the waiter has just left at my table. Sara sits in the opposite chair. There is a birthmark under her eyebrow. She's smiling, revealing a noticeable gap between her two front teeth.

"Is everything okay?" she asks. She reaches out and touches my arm lightly.

"Of course," I reply.

I look down at my coffee again, and now I hear the clink of cups on wooden tabletops. The steaming hiss of the coffee machine. Two businesswomen are discussing a presentation and laughing. A baby dozes in the arms of a grandparent. Sara is showing me pictures of a white cake on her phone. I nod, but my eyes slide back to my phone.

———

"READY TO GIVE UP YET?" asks the adventurer with a laugh. We nestle in a rocky crevasse that shields us from the blizzard that billows overhead. He is a hulking mammoth-man, steadfast and trustworthy. I shake my head, and he grins until his eyes vanish behind his cheekbones. We continue up the mountain pass, shoulders brushing against the crevasse wall, hugging the mountain to avoid the frigid wind and snow that whips around through the air.

I poke my head around the lip of the rock face, scanning the way ahead. I spot a clan of frost-bitten goblins who have taken refuge from the winds under a rocky overhang. Again, I call on the spell Emberfall. Once more, the skies are rent with fire, and the mountain face melts from the magical fury. My ears ring as the rock liquifies to lava, trailing down towards the group of blue goblins. The pillar of fire burns a hole through the rock above them, dropping a deluge of white-hot stone on top of them. I laugh, but then stop.

The fire is dissipating much too quickly. The blue goblin leader steps through the fire, his face distorted by the waves of heat that dance across him. Steam hisses from every pore of his face. He coughs, and staggers, but manages to stay standing. He draws a wicked blade.

I fall to my knees, exhausted. The adventurer shakes his head at me. "Ready to give up yet?" he asks.

I shake my head and flick a few coins in his direction as the fighting continues.

————

I'M SITTING on a picnic blanket. Sara has cut her hair much shorter. She wears an enormous wide-brimmed hat. Her expression is of exasperation. I feel a wetness on my leg and look down to see a crawling baby sucking on my shinbone. He gurgles. The sky is cloudless, and the air is humid. Insects hum around the garden. From the picnic basket, Sara withdraws a bottle for the child. I hold Charlie in the crook of my arm and feed him. He guzzles from the bottle greedily.

I feel the shame well up inside me. The milk is finished and Charlie cries. I offer him my finger to suck instead...

————

MY FLESH SCREAMS with pain as the goblin chieftain sinks his teeth into my hand and rends the flesh from the bone. His warriors chuckle in delight at my anguish. Fire dances across the goblins' blades. Their skin is freshly cracked basalt that hides veins of magma just below the skin. The adventurer is unconscious beside me, rasping for air through a punctured lung. I call down Emberfall once again, but the goblins aren't incinerated. They laugh viciously and continue their attack. I chug bottle after bottle of expensive elixir.

———

SARA NOW HAS a streak of grey through her hair. She's still young enough to hide it, but she's chosen not to. She sits beside me in bed, reading Austin through spectacles. When she turns to me, I can see where the tears have stained her face.

"Charlie's having troubles at school," she says. "He's getting harassed by older boys at lunch." I heave myself out of bed and creep down the hall to his bedroom. The door is slightly ajar. I peer inside the room. Charlie has fallen asleep at his desk. His homework books are half-completed, splayed out before him. His laptop screen flickers in the darkness....

———

THE TOWNSPEOPLE GATHER AROUND ME, fawning desperately for my attention as I carry the head of the goblin chieftain aloft in my left hand. The village women cast admiring glances as I strut towards the town centre. There are shouts of jubilation from the local men, who declare me a hero.

I stop. A young hero blocks my path to the town centre. His wounds leak blood from beneath his armour. My right-hand falls on the pommel of my sword. I keep my grin fixed on my face as I assess him.

A raid? My eyes flick towards the goblin head. It wouldn't be the first time some low-level adventurer tried to steal my prize.

The adventurer hasn't drawn his blade, but he approaches. The crowd hasn't noticed yet.

"Greetings," I say. My smile is still fixed. "It looks like you've had difficulty on the road."

The young hero nods as he approaches. His eyes crinkle in delight and admiration. "You've accomplished so much," he says. "Your gear is the rarest of the rare. Your reputation throughout this world is legendary. Everyone online respects you. They know not to mess with you."

My hand drifts away from my sword's pommel. An admirer, nothing more.

"You can also find respect and praise here," I explain. "Just make sure you stock up on elixirs. Then, you can easily overcome challenges above your level and quickly improve."

The young adventurer nods. He touches his coin pouch, absent-mindedly. I watch how the leather buckles beneath his fingers. Empty.

"Here," I say, and flick him a few coins out of pity. The young lad smiles up at me, and I wait for a response.

Charlie2004 has added you as a friend.

END

ABOUT THE AUTHOR

In the second grade, Jonathan's teacher let him write novels in the back of his mathematics book. As a result, he developed a joy of writing and literature, as well as an awkward pause before having to do any kind of counting.

Jonathan was awarded a High Commendation by the Fellowship of Australian Writers (QLD) for his first published short story: *The Second Father*. His writing usually explores the themes of power, love, technology, and spirituality.

His debut sci-fi novel *Lessons from the Wreckage*, begins the epic story of the Martian Empire as it desperately fights an alien invader who is eating through the planets of our solar system.

You can also find his short story collection of fractured fairy tales and urban fantasy, titled *Spirits in Your Area*.

13

SHORT CIRCUIT

KIRSTIE OLLEY

I raise my hand high overhead, straining upward like the know-it-all in class desperate to have the teacher pick her to answer his question.

The lightning bolt hits my hand and fires down through my arm. Sheer power surges through my chest and charges me like nothing I've experienced before—and I've electrocuted myself plenty of times; knives in toasters, forks in power outlets, even once in a pinch I bit through the power cord of a fan while it was running. Electricity tastes a lot like blood, that metallic kind of flavour mixed with burnt bacon, but with the busy tingling sensation of a packet of pop rocks —in case you cared to know.

Oh, hey, don't get me wrong, I'm not a freak who keeps trying to kill herself. I'm a different kind of freak, a powered freak. I can manipulate electricity, but I need to charge myself up regularly. I can't create the stuff – only use it. One good electrocution is enough to keep me going for a couple of days. Of course, battles tend to drain me fairly quickly, so I try to charge up every day to avoid running out mid-fight. Like now.

Lucky there's a thunderstorm.

The lightning finishes and I try to reach up even higher than before, trying to hold on for a little longer. This is the most power I've ever felt. It's amazing, like a whirlwind in my lungs, like an ocean full of playful dolphins in my stomach, like a rave in my brain. My muscles are tingling, my blood is rocket fuel, and someone just hit the ignition switch. Man! Whooo! I don't even care that I'm literally steaming or what this will mean for my hair (though I bet that will drive me mad later).

He's levelling a gun at us, an automatic, the kind of thing that spits out bullets with a ferocity that kids with a mouth full of watermelon seeds love to imitate. If only our real problem was saliva all over the place.

My arm is shaking with the current. I can't keep it steady, there's too much power. I try to concentrate on what Farron taught me— pool the energy in my stomach, control and shape it, push it along my veins to my hand, then expel it through my palm.

The current makes my muscles seize. It's never done that before, not even the first time when my brother wanted his toast out now and I put the knife in the toaster to retrieve it. Even with my muscles tightening, I've kept my aim every other time.

Searing through the air in brilliant white branches, the electricity plunges into the cold black metal of the gun. For an instant it gives me a connection to the weapon. I know how many bullets are left in the magazine, I can see the gun is dirty inside—this guy is no proper gunner, a real gunner would clean his weapon better than this.

Then the power is in the guy. His muscles seize too. He can't let go of the gun, he wants to, desperately, but can't. Even his brain is cramping up. I try to pull the juice back but I can't, there's too much of it.

The tide turns. What was the wild high of pure power turns into terror as I realise I'm not the one in control.

"Help!" I call out for my team-mates.

They look at me, but they hesitate in harmony. I bet they're thinking "If I touch her will I get electrocuted too?" I can't blame them. We're all young, most of us are still developing our powers. We aren't real heroes yet—the Big Guys delight in reminding us of that both in training and in combat.

Farron shoulders past Stinger and Fireball and heads straight for me. Somewhere in the surge of all that lightning, my heart skips a beat as he bears down with eyes only for me.

His slap stings.

The current falters. I redirect the electricity back out of my arm and pool it in my belly again. It writhes there—the ocean isn't full of dolphins, but sharks with blood in the water. My arm burns with a thick, heavy ache like lactic acid in over-drive and it drops to my side, a dead weight. I stagger, unsure on my feet, as if the current was keeping me upright. When I fall, Farron catches me and returns me to my feet. I hope he thinks the red on my cheeks is something to do with the lightning.

I hear cheering and drag my eyes from his face to my team-mates. We won I guess, but there's a burning pork smell that makes me feel sick. My team-mates are cheering the foiling of a bank robbery while I remember the feeling of a man's brain cramping in agony like it was my own.

That man is on the ground. He's not moving.

I push Farron away and run forward, tripping over my own feet as I do so—why on earth did I think high heels were a good costume choice?

He's hot to touch, like a baked potato, and it's my stomach that's cramping now as I fumble around his neck for a pulse.

"Medic!" My voice cracks as I scream for help.

The cheers die instantly. My team-mates are all frozen.

Medic steps forward, her white costume is flirty nurse on top, but military pants on the bottom. She takes a knee on the man's other side and puts her hand to his chest. Medic frowns a moment while she uses her hand as a stethoscope; then her lip corners quirk up again.

"He's still with us. His brain is still sending impulses to his heart, the heart just can't beat. And you're the perfect thing for someone in V-fib." Medic takes my hand as she's talking. She presses my hand to the left side of his chest, aiming it flat-palmed directly above the man's heart. "Just fire a little spark into him—think like a defibrillator."

"I already electrocuted this guy once!"

"Yes, but this time, just a little jolt, a spark straight into his heart."

"But—"

"No buts, if you don't do this he goes from a 70% chance of survival to a 5%."

There's a huge lump in my throat obstructing my breath. I can't swallow it down. I think it might be my heart.

"Just a little jolt. Tiny. Direct it in through here, and out through here." Medic shifts my hands to just under his left breast and somewhere near his right shoulder. She pulls her hands away. "You can do it, Short Circuit." She checks no one else is too close and yells out, "Clear!"

Honestly, I would have laughed at that if I weren't about to wet myself.

A big breath in. I try to take just a tiny wisp of the storm in my belly; I try to separate it from the rest of the roil within. I follow Medic's command, out of my left hand, through the heart and back into my right hand.

His body stiffens then slacks. Medic watches my face closely, then touches him again when she's sure I'm done. Her brow furrows over her white domino mask. "One more time, please. Clear!"

I take another deep breath. Can I do this a second time? Did I muck it up the first time, and that's why I have to do it again? Seriously, why am I suddenly expected to be a finely tuned piece of medical equipment? I don't like acknowledging this fact, but at times like this I want to shout You know I'm just a kid, right?

I give him another shock, following Medic's instructions to the letter. When I pull my hands away, she touches his chest again, listening for a beat.

Her shoulders slump and for a moment I can't breathe. Did she slump because he's dead and she's defeated, or because he's alive and she's relieved? Hurry up and tell me!

"His pulse has returned to normal." Medic smiles at me like the sun coming out from behind the clouds and even though I'm already seated on the ground, I sag down further.

"The paramedics are on their way," Farron tells us, his hand withdrawing from his ear communicator. "Great job, Medic. I'm very impressed with you too, Short Circuit."

I can't help but grin as his words send a tingle through me, which has nothing to do with the lightning bolt I recently absorbed.

———

BACK IN THE DORMS, I'm still grinning. Wouldn't you be?

The whole team has come back for a debriefing and a celebration. We go over the results of the battle, analysing with Farron's help where we did well and where we could have done better. We put our heads together and think of some alternate strategies we could have used in the same situation. Farron likes us to come up with as many plans as possible, so if we ever face a similar situation we have plenty of tactics ready to go.

The best part is we get to do it while pigging out on nachos and pizza.

"I bet you won't be needing to charge up for a week!" grins Medic, her mask off now we're out of the public view. I can clearly see her one green eye, one grey. With such an unusual feature she takes wearing her mask seriously.

"No, I'll still need to charge up again before tomorrow's over." I sigh, spilling some salsa on my lap by accident.

"What?!" Whirlwind, the team's newbie—barely even twelve— looks at me with horror. Her eyes are screaming poor Short Circuit as she leans over the table towards me.

"Yeah. I drain at the same rate regardless of input." I'm repeating the explanation Farron gave me one night when he found me crying on the deck over this exact issue. "I can actually feel how much less is in me right now. I couldn't control the charge when I first had it, but I'm already back down to levels I'm confident using." I lift my hands and arc a mini branch of lightning between my hands like they're two Tesla coils, not a human being's extremities. The air zaps as I do this and I can smell the sharp acrid scent of discharge.

"We might need to practice controlling larger amounts for emergency charges like this one." Farron is leaning on a wall near the door, giving us our space but still observing, still chaperoning. Some parents stipulate that in the contract, they don't want their kids running rampant in their absence. My parents didn't care, they just signed me over to the team to get me out of their hair.

Hair! Oh god no, I forgot about my hair!

I jump up and snatch a serviette from nearby. I wipe the gunk and oil from my fingers and run to the window.

My reflection there is weak, washed out by the light outside and the panorama beyond the glass, but I can still see what I need to.

Sweet Jesus, I have a 'fro.

I grab at my hair and try to slick it down. I'm honestly wishing I'd left the nacho grease on my hands. It might have helped me fix this mess.

Every time I charge the static residue ends up in my hair, meaning I always have a scarily frizzy mop. I tend to hide my hair under hats whenever I can. In fact, I incorporated a hat into my costume not long after joining the Terrific Teens. Usually my hair doesn't run parallel to the floor, though it has approached frighteningly close a few times, but the lightning was a whole 'nother level of power. My hair is literally sticking out of my head in every single direction.

I'm trying so hard to flatten my hair, I'm probably leaving bruises on my head. A few team-mates are laughing at my struggle as I try to stop myself from looking like a cartoon lion. At least I hope they're only laughing at my attempts, not the hair itself.

"I have some hair wax in my room," Whirlwind offers. "It's the hardcore stuff, so my hair doesn't get messed up by my wind."

"Thanks!" I cry and immediately follow her, my face burning red as I pass by Farron.

I cringe as I hear the slight chuckle he's trying to hold back as I walk past him. Please, oh please, oh please don't laugh at me!

Whirlwind's room looks like a hurricane tore through it.

I'm not saying that for a laugh, I'm saying that as a statement of fact. It is the messiest, least organised room I've ever seen. As a none-too-tidy girl myself I know there's a certain amount of organisation in most mess. I can't see any here. Seriously, not even a tiny scrap. Then again, Whirlwind does tend to be rather flighty. She probably picks something up, then gets a better idea and just drops whatever she was holding.

I can tell it isn't an organised mess because she takes a quarter of an hour to find the wax. She ends up summoning a whirlwind to pick things up. Somehow the room seems tidier after the wind funnel has gone through.

Her hair wax is good stuff, and it smells like coconut, not the chemical smell I usually get from my gel. It's much nicer being smothered in the scent of coconut. I take a while to douse my hair in the thick white gunk, and it weighs my hair down, sticking it to other strands and bringing it down to a 45 degree angle from my neck, which is better than what I can usually achieve.

"Thanks, Whirlwind."

"No prob," she tells me, a smile on her lips, but the pity is back in her eyes. Damn, why does she have to remember the crappy stuff?

We head back to the meeting room (which is really part kitchen, part living room, part meeting room, but it's a big enough room to be all those things without being too cramped) and Whirlwind is asking me more questions about charging. Some of her questions I have answers for, some I don't, like the question "why do you drain at the same rate even if you took more in?" I'm grateful when we open the door and go back in.

A couple of the homers have left, lucky bums—they still get to live with their families—but half of them are still here.

Someone ate all the nachos. Damn. Only a few pieces of vegetarian pizza are left, but I'm hungry enough that I don't care... too much. Cold veggie pizza. Bleh.

Whirlwind says she's going to the roof to try flying again, her eyes all shiny and distracted. Her leaving causes a few more homers to exit. The only homer remaining is Medic. Medic doesn't go back home to her family, she lives in a dorm at her college. I think that's pretty cool. Her roommates don't know who she is. I've seen her walking between classes with her friends sometimes. Even among my team-mates I don't get that level of affection.

Stinger says he's going to go back to his room and play video games so now it's just me, Medic and Farron. Now the others are gone, Farron walks over and sits down with us. I guess there's no point in his "distant supervision" method when there's only two of us.

"You two did a great job today. You work together very well," Farron says.

"You already said that." I laugh.

"I know, but I'm thinking there might be more chances for you to team up like today. And delicate and focused use of your powers like simulating a defibrillator could be beneficial to your manipulation of your powers."

"No way, that was way too freaky! What if I used too much electricity and fried him? Today had to be a fluke."

"A fluke you got lucky on twice?" Medic laughs at me, but the sort of soft, sweet laugh that isn't a nasty teasing, but a good-naturedly big-sister teasing.

"And learning that fine-tuned control is very important." Farron backs her up.

"I s'pose I can try, but we aren't going to be able to find many other near-death guys like that except in a hospital, and no hospital will take on that sort of liability."

"True." Medic slumps. She must have been really looking forward to a team-up.

"I'm sure I can figure something out." Farron smiles his 'I've got this' grin and I really hope I'm not visibly swooning. He walks off, presumably to make some calls, and I've got to admit I'm disappointed he left before Medic did. Usually it's me and him left here in the meeting room, looking out at the stars and talking. Sometimes we talk shop, like powers and team-ups, and other times we just talk about anything, like what's bugging me, or what I want to do when I graduate. I even talk to him about my parents and my brother sometimes. He's the only person on the team who knows what made my parents so eager to get rid of me.

Medic's cool, don't get me wrong, but there's something different about my special talks with Farron. I can almost trick myself into believing he cares for me like I'm an adult, not a teenager he has to supervise and train.

I know he's never going to love me the same way, he's over ten years older than me. Plus, it would probably be creepy if he was into me. I'm only sixteen. I'm pretty sure there are laws against that kind of stuff. So I'm practical about it. I know it's not real. But it's nice to pretend.

———

CAR BATTERIES ARE idiot-proofed these days, so unless the car's been left running, they're no good to me. Yet whenever I'm in a jam, someone suggests it. Today's no different.

"There's a car, get a jolt from the battery." Blue Rage extends a spandex-clad arm to a little green Mini Minor and I swallow my laugh along with the irritation.

"You got the keys to start it? Cos it ain't gonna give me a charge otherwise." That and I don't like the taste of electricity that comes from batteries. It has a biting acidic taste, you know it came from acid just like you can tell when electricity came from solar panels (you feel warm and happy when it's solar power).

"I could hot-wire it." Stinger offers.

It's not a useless suggestion. "Do you actually know how to a hot-wire a car, or do you 'I saw it done on TV' know how to hot-wire a car?"

Stinger puffs out his chest as he leaps over. "Oh, I know." He gives me a lopsided grin that probably would work on most girls. I just don't get the arrogant playboy type. Also, is that really something to be proud of?

A purple laser beam tears through the asphalt in front of Blue

Rage and he executes a mammoth leap to land on top of the bus right beside Dark Grey (seriously how terrible is his villain name? Then again, I don't think he chose it; it was a press-given one). Blue Rage swipes at the gun, grappling for it, but Grey dances out of the way, ducking and weaving, grinning like the psychopath he probably is.

Stinger slams his elbow into the car window. His face flinches and his whole body freezes for an instant. He tries to pretend it didn't hurt, but I caught the look. Maybe he isn't as gangsta as he's pretending to be.

He uses his other elbow and this time shatters the driver's side window. That will keep the legal team busy for a week or two.

Door open, he ducks his head under the steering column. The hood pops and I put my hands onto the terminals of the battery. I screw up my lips in anticipation of the taste.

At least Stinger didn't lie about being able to hot-wire a car. The engine turns over and the acid-born electricity surges up my arms. I smack my lips as the taste of rancid vinegar invades my mouth. Bleh, there are worse things I suppose, but right now I'm not in any mood to list them.

Charging done, I race over. Stinger yells for Blue Rage to jump. Rage has worked with us before, he's an old friend of Farron's so he doesn't ignore us or question us like other members of The Big Guys. He gives us the courtesy of taking our advice. He disengages from Grey and backflips off the bus.

I slam my palms onto the bus and release the charge. The metal glints as the electricity courses through it and from the roof of the bus I can hear Grey screaming, muscles seized in my electric surge. Guess he wasn't wearing rubber boots.

I pull back the power and remove my hands. Grey flops over the side, hitting the asphalt with a thick meaty thud. There's that kinda charred pork smell again. I think I might have over-cooked him.

I hide the shake in my hands as I check his pulse. I don't want a Big Guy like Blue Rage to think I'm scared, but it's only been three days since I almost killed that last guy. I'm so grateful when I feel his skin thump softly against my fingers that I sigh out loud, and Stinger looks to me like he's shocked I'm letting something show.

I sense the power before I even hear the static hiss. It prickles on my skin, making all the tiny hairs stand up (even though they kind of already are from the car battery). Someone who can manipulate electricity is gathering up power.

A sharp electric pop rips the air and Stinger and Blue Rage turn to where the noise came from. The crackle sounds as if the surrounding air has turned to paper and someone is scrunching it up. I'm like an alley cat who has realised there's someone else on her turf. No kidding, my back is actually trying to arch up as I move my fingers away from the pulse point on Dark Grey's neck.

For a second it's like everything else in the world is frozen. I know where the bolt is coming from and I know where it is headed—right at Blue Rage.

I spring forward, putting my all into it as the silver streak tries to beat me to my target.

When I played lightning rod a few days ago, it was very different. I was on empty, I was asking for the power, and I'd had a little time to acknowledge what I was about to do. Today I've got no such luck. I know I'm about to take an electrical shock for Blue Rage, but I don't have the time to think about it. This is all instinct. There's a reason some people become heroes. I always thought I'd fallen into the gig because I had no choice, that it was be a superhero or be institutionalised, since my parents were abandoning me. But perhaps I'm more suited to this than I thought.

I'll bet you a million bucks this is what it feels like when a train hits you. I can't breathe. I can't move. Something is slamming into me so hard it's atomising me and going right through the dust left behind. In this moment I am the one frozen between heart beats.

The static screams in my head. Whoever threw this bolt is one powerful player. My only thought is that I hope they can't throw another one because I'm on the ground.

———

"I WANT MY TOAST NOW!" My brother whines. He's four and I'm eight. Mum put the toast on, but then the phone rang. "Now, now, now." His voice is high pitched and irritating.

"Fine, I'll get it." I tell him.

He sits down and smiles, waiting cross-legged on the kitchen floor as I drag a chair from the dining room into the kitchen and climb onto it to reach the toaster.

Mum has set up a plate, the knife, butter and honey near the toaster so she'll be ready to spread the second the toast pops up.

I push the button that is supposed to eject the toast. It goes in but the toast doesn't come up.

My finger pounds the useless button twenty times in rapid succession. I frown at the toaster and tilt it forward. I put my hand in to pull the toast out and the hot metal burns my fingers.

"Ouch." I put the burned finger in my mouth and suck it. That doesn't make my finger feel any better, but I can't think of anything else to do.

"Sis, I want my toast now. I'm huuuuuungry." My brother whinges behind me.

Brat, I think. I look for a way to get the toast out. I need something to pry the bread out without touching the metal inside, like a stick or something.

The knife gleams in front of me, and I grin at my genius.

Perfect.

I pick up the knife and put it in the toaster.

My body goes rigid. Something's in me, like a school of little fish swimming under my skin and over my muscles. It tickles and itches and makes me wriggle.

My brother laughs at my wriggle-dance.

Mum starts shrieking.

I turn to see why mum's screaming.

"What's the matter, mum?" I ask, knife still in the toaster.

She stares at me with wide eyes, mouth hanging open like a cartoon character's. She tries to talk, but words don't come out, she's just flapping her mouth like laundry caught in the wind.

I pull the bread out of the toaster, put it on the plate and take the knife out.

Mum says my name. Her voice is shaking. I turn to explain what I was doing, but the toaster's stuck mechanism pops up behind me with a metallic shunk and I laugh instead.

Mum puts a hand on the wall behind her to steady herself. Dad, tie half-wrapped around his neck, peers into the kitchen to see what the commotion is about. Mum tells Dad about the knife in the toaster while I slop some honey on my brother's toast—the last thing I want is for him to start whining again.

"Are you feeling okay, Cicilly?" Dad asks, his voice only a little less shaky than Mum's.

"I feel a little squiggly." I give another funny wiggle-dance as the fish shift under my skin again and I giggle.

"Do you think she has a power?" Dad asks Mum as I climb down from the chair and walk over to my brother.

"I've heard of energy manipulators." Mum replies. "But nothing like this..."

"Here's your toast." I hold the plate out to my brother and he grins at me.

The fish shift again under my skin, this time running down my arms.

My brother's hands touch mine as we pass the plate between us. There's a loud zap and some of the squiggly fish leave me. My brother flies back like someone kicked him.

Mum and Dad scream.

My brother lies there on the linoleum, unmoving.

————

THE FIRST LIGHTNING bolt I likened to a hurricane. This is like a hurricane on a global scale and it's trying to tear its way out of every pore of me. It's a wild beast trying to claw out of me by sheer force. I might be screaming, but I don't know because I can't hear over the roaring static. I know I sure as hell want to scream.

It dawns on me that if anyone were to touch me, they would be destroyed in a heartbeat. I have to warn them. For all I know, Medic's walking over to try and help me right now.

I find the words and I push them out. "Don't touch me!" I don't hear a response. I can't sense anything of the world around me. "Don't touch me!" I yell through clenched teeth again.

I have to expel some of this energy, get myself to a level I can control.

My arm muscles have seized, just like every muscle in my body. Still screaming my warning to not touch me, I try to force my hand onto the ground open palmed.

Uncurling my fingers is like peeling door hinges off the door frame with your fingernails. Moving my arm is like trying to keep elevator doors open after they've passed the safety release point. I finally feel the uneven bitumen under my palm and I throw what I can into the ground.

There's no finesse or control in this move. There's no way to do that. I'm not in control of this power. I can't even contain it. The electricity gladly flows into the ground, but it feels like it's tearing out my internal organs and taking them for the ride too.

I can't stop the flow and despite the pain I don't think I want to. There's something wrong with this electricity. In the same way that car battery electricity tastes like bad salt and vinegar chips, this electricity tastes like evil.

I know, I never thought evil had a flavour. Apparently it does. It's like I can taste how sick and twisted the mind that made this electricity is.

Panting, I lift my head. I'm on empty. Expelling the evil power out meant I had to throw out the car battery's charge too. I'm dry and I'm shaking. I throw up on the ground as I try to sit up.

An echoing voice calls to me. "Is it safe to touch you yet?" I think that voice, way down there at the other end of that tunnel, is Medic's.

"I thin' so. Mebbe not. Gimme a sec."

I throw up again.

Voices are clamouring now. The echoes bouncing and

reverberating off one another and the sound of mostly-digested breakfast slapping onto the road. A couple of 'ewws' echo amongst the mess.

Scrubbing my hand across my mouth, I blink hard, trying to get my sight back. The world is shiny silver and bright and the shapes of people are faded negative images.

"Short Circuit, I need to check if you're okay." Definitely Medic's voice, and I think she's freaked.

"Mmmmokay." I mouth the word with numb lips.

"No, you aren't." She tells me like a scolding mother.

" 'tever." I mumble.

She touches me. Her hands shake as they make contact. She must have been scared witless touching me without knowing if she would get shocked or not. As soon as she doesn't get zapped, though, she's calm, confident and steady handed.

"How many fingers am I holding up?" She asks.

I squint through the silver. "Two?" I guess.

I'm pretty sure she's shaking her head at me, but I can see the smile on her face in my imagination too.

"You all good, kid?" Blue Rage's voice cuts through.

"Smorta." My numb lips mutilate the word.

Blue Rage laughs at me. "Good kid. Got balls, don't ya?"

Not sure a girl really feels proud hearing that.

"I'd be dead if it weren't for you."

Yeah, if I could barely handle it, I'm pretty sure it would obliterate anyone else.

I look at Blue Rage. He's starting to come into focus but I can't see his expression. My vision isn't clear enough yet.

Medic's still checking me over for any injuries. Her hands have paused at my shoulders and she's working on a nasty knot of muscles. It hurts as she kneads them back into place, but it's nothing like the surge before.

I lose track of time for a moment. All of a sudden I'm back at the base, my vision is almost back to normal. Farron is on his knees in front of me, holding my head, his eyebrows pushed together. My face burns in response to how close he is and what this could look like. I have to yell at myself to get real, he's only worried about one of his students.

"Is she really okay?" he asks Medic. He turns his eyes on me and stares straight into my eyes. "Are you OK, Cic-?" he stops himself before he says my real name out loud.

Wow, he must be genuinely freaked out if he almost let my identity slip. I've never seen him this freaked.

"She's exhausted and she has no charge. To be honest, it's probably a bad idea for her to charge up for a day or two." Medic tells Farron.

He only glances at her a moment before going back to inspecting me. "I'm not so sure." He says while he tests that my arm still moves by flexing it for me. "Electricity is like blood to her, a quick charge might give her back some energy."

"Are you sure?" Medic sounds worried.

"I do a lot of research on everyone's powers and keep a close eye on everything. While none of the other electricity manipulators quite manifest their powers like Short Circuit, I'm fairly confident you'll find she'll perk up a little with just a small charge carefully administered."

"Not from a battery." I beg. The last thing I want is that appalling vinegar taste again.

Farron laughs at me, genuine mirth making his eyes sparkle. "Okay, not from a battery."

Farron is right. A little shock, a quick stab of the fork into the power outlet zaps me up and I feel better. I'm not back to normal, but I'm confident I can safely walk myself to my room and have a nap—so I do.

———

Arguing voices wake me up.

I follow the noise to the end of the hall where Farron is arguing with a woman in a suit who clutches a clipboard to her chest.

"I just don't see what the problem is. Why can't we let people know what Short Circuit did?" Farron begs the woman.

She must be one of the PR chiefs for the Big Guys.

"I'm not saying what your girl did wasn't heroic, the point is it just won't do to have Blue Rage's reputation tarnished by telling the public he was saved by a sixteen-year-old with defective powers."

I stop in my tracks.

It's not the first time I've heard it put that way. I'm positive it won't be the last either, but that never takes the edge off the hurt. I'm a freak among freaks.

"It wasn't like she beat him in battle. She took a bullet for him and he went on to beat the bad guy as a result. Surely we can acknowledge the part she played in the battle?" Farron pleads.

I pretend it doesn't hurt that he doesn't defend me by saying I'm not defective.

"We've acknowledged her as present and even given her full credit for the defeat of Dark Grey, that should give her some good stature amongst the followers." The PR woman shrugs as if she's being generous and Farron is being unreasonable.

Farron growls. It's weird, I've never heard him express anger like that.

"You don't understand—Short Circuit put her life on the line for him, she took nearly too much energy in so it wouldn't hit him. She could have died and he definitely would have!" Farron throws his hands up and growls again, then turns on the woman sharply. "What does Rage have to say about all this?"

"What Blue Rage wants is not the question. We're here to protect the image of men like Blue Rage whose own benevolence can be their undoing. Can you imagine the shit storm that would come down on his head if it got out?"

"I don't think Rage would give a rats—" Farron spots me hiding behind the door frame. "Short Circuit, sorry, did we wake you?"

"I'm not defective."

Not sure why I'm saying it. I am defective—I mean, I have to electrocute myself daily and my power is always running out at the most inopportune times. But I stare the woman down. "My powers are my powers. Sure, they may not be your idea of perfect, but you know what, I don't think a normal energy manipulator could have done what I did today. I think that because I have to charge up all the time it made my body capable of handling the sudden influx. And you know what, I don't care if this story never gets into print, because I know it, Blue Rage knows it and my team knows it. I know I'm a hero and I know that people like you, who get to decide what goes up on the 'net and into magazines, aren't heroes—you're people who manipulate words to make everything go the way you want it to and you know who else does that? Villains."

The PR woman looks shocked, then glares at me.

Farron puts a hand on my shoulder to restrain me.

"With an attitude like that you'll never make it into the big leagues." The PR woman spits her words at me, her cheeks darkening. "Not that any major team would have someone with defective powers like yours, anyway. Good luck placing on a team once you're too old for Farron's little school here." She turns on a fancy heel and storms off.

I'm shaking with anger, and it's only Farron's hand that holds me back from doing anything else.

"She's wrong, you know," Farron tells me once she's out of sight.

"No, she isn't." I brush his hand off as much as I'd like to keep it there. "I do have defective powers, and sure that worked out for me today, but it usually doesn't." My eyes sting. I can't help remembering how he didn't defend me when she said I was defective and he didn't know I was here.

"Short—" He pauses and corrects himself. "Cicilly, you know you're only young, you've still got time to mature and grow your powers. What seems like a defect might be something you can grow beyond."

So you do think I'm defective. I barely keep the words in my mouth. You're just like all of them. I can't keep the tears in.

He reaches out his arms and offers me a hug to comfort me, and

I'm too greedy and lovesick to reject him. I bury my face in his shoulder and cry while he pats my back.

In my head I can hear that awful PR woman telling me I'll never place with a team.

Fine then. I'll be a soloist. I'll train myself hard. I'll push my limits. I'll become the best damn defective anyone has ever seen.

Just you wait and see.

END

ABOUT THE AUTHOR

Kirstie Olley is a mother/ author/ gamer living in Australia physically but the realms of fairy tales in her mind. Kirstie delights in romantic sub plots and her deep 'love is love' belief leads her to write a variety of pairings.

Kirstie is currently working on a series of novellas in her Retailored Fairy Tales world which follows rival Prince Charmings for hire as well as producing a plethora of short fiction.

To check out more of her stories visit her website: www.storybookperfect.com

14

THE SUNSHINE REPUBLIC

GLENN DAVIES

Gran loved clocks—clocks with chimes, clocks that dinged and donged on the hour and half-hour, a cuckoo clock, and even one with a cat on its face that gave a sickening meow every quarter hour. There were just so many clocks in her house in Charters Towers. But the most frustrating thing of all was that not one of these clocks kept the same time. As it has been pointed out at the Mad Hatter's Tea Party, it was always 6 o'clock somewhere.

In my Gran's home, time was never accurate but it could always be heard. I guess she never had to be anywhere at a set time. Her life was very fluid. Days merged into each other. Weekdays, weekends—they all had a sameness.

This had been my life since early childhood: running around her acreage in shorts, t-shirts and thongs. Simplicity was her life lesson. Not that Gran's life wasn't full and rich. But it wasn't constrained by the work-a-day weeks that bind most of us. "Gran Time" we called it. For her, time was never uniform, singular or predictable. It was relative. To what, we never knew.

The problems began with the Daylight Saving Fiasco in Queensland in 2027, when the government of the new Australian republic had established a national time grid. The old Queen hadn't minded Australia going on its own. After the successful referendum in 2025, the tragic deaths of William and the Cambridge heirs in a yachting accident, and the abdication of Harry to pursue his Hollywood action film career, the creation of the Australian republic was the natural next step.

The broadcasting of the upcoming 2030 World Cup games from different state capitals was taken as an excuse to abolish the time zones by the powerful Federal Sports Bureaucracy. Queenslanders, however, voted against falling-in-line with the other eastern states. The people of Queensland wanted nothing to do with the new 'Canberra Time'. So the federal government intervened to force time consistency.

In hindsight, it was absurd how Queensland police enforced Federal Legislation by inspecting clocks in government buildings to check for time compliance. as well as maintaining surveillance on those who challenged the new time laws. But absurdity and impossibilities stand side-by-side in a world where live piranhas in glass handbags are the celebrity fashion accessory of choice.

Christmas Day 2028 was a sweltering 42°C in her little miner's cottage in Charlotte Street. Even with the AC turned up full, there were cousins and other assorted relatives lying around, panting like dogs after a day working the cattle. Yet Gran did not have that slick, sweaty gaze that implied I'm about to lose control of my molecular cohesion and simply melt like wax. She had a radiance, a glow that seemed to come from within, a glow that peeped out from around her eyes. One of my sci-fi nut cousins reckoned she looked like a G'ould. But we all knew what was going on. It was an open secret in our extended family that she was a warrior for natural time. Back when we were kids she'd always been on NQ news. An eco-warrior of the north was our Gran. Now she'd morphed into a shiny, an advocate for Daylight Savings resistance.

When Gran was told in the first week of 2029 that all her clocks had to be set to the new Canberra Time you could almost hear the cogs in her mind synchronise for the coming battle. But it became downright ugly when Queenslanders started being busted by the newly created Federal Time Marshals for time cheating.

My Gran had a theory that if we took away the sunshine, Australia would no longer be the lucky country many took it to be. She always had lots of crackpot theories. Maybe it was all that heat and sunlight in the north. Or maybe it was a family thing. Our family had lived in 'The Towers' since the heady days of the goldfields of the 1890s. If lack of sunlight on skin can bring about a Vitamin D deficiency, then who knows what genetic aberrations five generations of direct sunlight will have.

The Canberra crackdown had the feisty old girl not only refusing to turn forward her clocks the mandated hour, but also saving daylight. My shiny Gran—defender of sunshine. Within each hour of daylight is a finite, measurable amount of sunshine, the essential element of daylight that controls the pace of time. These northern time warriors would not be told by a bunch of Canberra suits when the sun rose or set.

After all these years away from north Queensland it felt strange to be returning. The deep north of Queensland has always had a pull on my family. Joining the southern 'time feds' had seemed a betrayal at the time, yet my Gran always supported me. Why? I'm not sure. All I knew was that as my Time Marshall team and I flew up the east coast of Queensland heading for Townsville, an overwhelming sense of inconsistency washed over me.

Flying tightly around the back of Mt Stuart, we descended sharply using the curving Ross River as our guide into the northern capital, screamed across the suburbs of Rasmussen, then Heatley and touched down at the RAAF base at Garbutt on Cleveland Bay. Looking through the window I could see the mud and mangrove tidal flats alongside the runway. No beaches here, no surf here, just tepid sea with jellyfish, crocodiles and goodness knows what other critters that could sting you and eat you. And yet I knew I was home.

I was rather taken aback at the strength of the emotional response. It was my decision all those years ago to 'go down south' as soon as I could. But here I was. Back again. Although now I had a job to do which involved my Gran up in Charters Towers, and I knew it would have to do with this gnawing sense of inconsistency I couldn't shake. It was the family knowledge that cause and effect doesn't necessarily travel in the one direction that had me leave in the first place. I found it hard to get my head around at the time. And yet it is the reason I was attracted to the Federal Directorate of Time.

My Gran, she knew. Always seeing in people their future, before they did themselves.

When my Federal Time Marshal team and the local Queensland Police burst through Gran's front door on that first bright Sunday morning of Spring 2029, we were first hit with an overpowering smell of food that had rotted well before its expiry date, followed by a blinding burst of sunshine. My Gran's sunshine hoarding was so obvious. You couldn't miss it. It was all over the house. Drawers overflowing with it. Cupboards full. A spare room packed to the rafters with sunshine. Boxes of it stacked in the hallway and under the beds. And all her curtains faded from the inside.

If they were going to take away an hour, then Gran would bank up what was rightfully hers. Gran had compensated for what had been taken from her by Federal intervention with her own rebel sunshine bank. And there, sitting on her favourite, blue-patterned sofa, wearing her standard drop-waist floral dress, wearing huge welding glasses with her one crooked front tooth showing through an impish grin, was my now teenage Gran. Her internal body clock reversed from living for so long within her own sunshine state.

"You all thought I was just saving it in my mind, didn't you? Boxes in my head."

She had checkmated me again. My White Queen living backwards while I could but look on like Alice.

"Well, you can all go and get synced."

My Gran. Always with the last word.

END

ABOUT THE AUTHOR

Dr Glenn Davies is a teacher and historian from northern Brisbane, by way of Charters Towers. During the day he teaches history to high school students but at night lives a SF fannish life.

His fiction has been published online in AntiSF, and 2020 Perfect Vision anthology. Glenn enjoys reading author book sleeve bios and constructing from this a grand narrative of their imagined lives in his head. He's drawn to tree houses, old coins, and dystopian fiction. Paradoxically, he finds the idea of time travel mesmerising yet utterly frightening and to this day denies any involvement in the Charters Towers zombie fruit bat invasion of 1974.

This and many other denials are at http://www.glenndavies.net

If you're making one, he prefers his coffee instant with lots of milk. No sugar. Thanks.

15

OF FLOWERS AND THORNS

EARL LIVINGS

She comes to me with ripped clothes, a pale face swelling and purpling with bruises, her legs caked with dried blood. I hold her for a long time before the sobbing stops.

"What happened?" I say.

"I was fetching water. He grabbed me. Pulled me into the bushes. I couldn't scream. Couldn't get away." She shudders uncontrollably.

I fetch a blanket and wrap it around her. Not the first time I have done this.

For generations, girls from the village have always found their way to this hut. They have listened well to the ancient songs—in the old words only their mothers can teach them—and come here, even though it is well hidden behind thickets of brambles and thorn.

They come whenever they need help. Powders for making a man look their way. Potions for unwanted babies. Pellets for turning a man grey before his time. They come more often nowadays, ever since copper was found within the northern escarpment and a miner's camp was set up at its base.

"Who did this?"

"That short dumpy miner with the crooked teeth and lopsided ears. When he finished, he hit me again and told me I was his. Told me to come back tonight or else he'll burn down my family's hut, with all of us inside."

Ah, yes, I know him. Have seen him swagger-chesting his way through the throng on market day as if he were a hero back from slaying a dragon. One evening, a year ago, I caught him pushing a girl barely out of her Blood-Blessing against the back wall of a hut. She fled while I beat him with my yew walking stick and chased him off. Left him with some vicious welts. I'm stronger than I look. In many ways, though my time to join the ancestors in the whispering deep is coming.

Still, that man will never stop. Just like some of the others. Time for a lesson.

I give her a spoonful of powdered willow bark and honey to calm her and reduce the pain. Chew up a wad of yarrow and bandage her face with it. Make her eat some of my evening soup, even though she struggles to swallow because of the swelling. Sit with her, hold her, soothe her when great wracking sobs return. Leave her sleeping in my bed. Go out with my walking stick and my cunning bag, the same one my mother used, my grandmother, and others before them.

The full moon lights my way through the forest. Somewhere to my right, a fox barks a greeting. I cough one in return. To my left, something snuffles through the undergrowth, a badger likely. An owl swoops along the thin path before me then disappears into the dark of a gnarled oak I climbed when a young girl myself, so I could touch a star. That night, the moon goddess called me to my task and my mother started training me in earnest. It has always been that way, but the work is much harder now with priests fanning abuse at those who still follow the old ways. As my mother discovered when she was returning from a laying out. Men beat her for being a witch. The next day, we held hands and sang the spell of bright travel as she passed over.

As soon as I can smell the putrid aroma of sweat and piss, liquor, and burnt meat, I step off the path and make my way through gorse and hazel to a small clearing within a grove of rowan trees. A slab of rock with glints of quartz beckons. I sit on it, open my senses to the night. The scent of wild garlic on the warm breeze. The criss-cross of buzzing insects. High wispy clouds stretching themselves westward, disappearing.

When the moon is nearly overhead, I open my bag, take out dried meadowsweet, oak and broom flowers, and arrange them on the grass in the shape of a woman lying down to feel the earth. I have done this only three times in my life, twice with my mother, all after the miners arrived. Before that, my mother and grandmother did it only once each, because the old ways were more respected then.

Satisfied, I bow to the moon nine times, bow once to each of the directions while giving thanks, return to the east and lift up my arms. I breathe deeply and call out in the old tongue:

"Oh goddesses of sea, land and sky, come to my aid this night.

"Oh spirits of tree, stream and stone, come to my aid this night.

"Oh spirits of fur, fin and flesh, come to my aid this night.

"Come to me for the making and taking of life.

"Come to me for the blessing and the curse.

"Come to me for the life I will gift you."

The breeze drops. The grove wraps itself with silence. Moonlight and starlight sparkle each trunk, branch and leaf. Blades of grass ripple and sway, each to their own rhythm. Tiny wings of light hover above the shape on the ground. They are waiting.

"My thanks to you all. May all our generations continue to serve you, bless you, and be blessed."

The wings form a spiral of light that swirls moonwise around the laid-out flowers.

"My thanks to you all. May you carry the seed of our desire this night, so that we are all protected."

The spiral thins at its bottom and descends.

"My thanks to you all. May you be the mirror for those who lust after us, who care nothing for us, who care only for what they can tear from the earth and from us."

The tip of the spiral touches the belly of the flower woman. Spreads out. Blossoms into curve of body and breast. Stretches into limbs and long-fingered hands, into the flowing shapes of hair and robes. Carves gentle eyes, pert nose, quivering lips in a heart-shaped face.

She stands before me, reaches out her right hand, and strokes my cheek.

The more she shimmers, the more my wrinkles deepen, my body shrivels, my eyes dim. I have barely enough breath to speak. This may be the last time I summon her, because the magic takes more from me than it did my ancestors, who did not have to struggle with a new faith and a ruined land. But we must go on. Do what we can for our kind and for the future.

I bow to her. "We are grateful you have come again. He is waiting."

She smiles. Nods. Turns and glides out of the grove towards the camp and the man's dilapidated hut. She knows what to do.

She will appear before him at midnight. He will think she is the girl he aches for.

She will open her arms. He will try to grab her. She will smile and step away without a sound.

He will curse her. He will try to punch her, shake her, choke her. She will dance out of reach.

He will howl his anger. She will smile again and race outside.

He will chase after her. He will blunder through bracken, ferns and thorn. He will ignore the scratches and the bruises as he stumbles over fallen branches. When his foot catches in a rabbit hole, he will swallow the pain and hobble after her. He will scream for her to stop. He will clamber over logs, claw at heather-covered slopes, pull himself through sliding scree and over jagged rocks. Many times he will bend over panting, then burst into a run when he hears her distant laughter.

He will stop, lungs aching, muscles quivering, fists shaking.

She is standing before him. Arms open. Beckoning smile. Her hair a halo made by the breeze and moonlight.

He will forget everything but his need to hold her again, plunge himself into her again.

She will not move as he wraps his arms around her.

She will let him kiss her. She will then take one step backwards.

———

IN THE MORNING, the workers find him broken on a pile of rocks at the bottom of the escarpment, not far from the mine itself. His face is a rictus of fear. His hands clutch fresh flowers of meadowsweet, oak and broom. Some shake their heads and mumble while they cart him away for burial. Those who still know of the old ways tremble as they burn the flowers.

That evening, my bones aching, my heartbeat unsteady, my breathing still ragged since the rite, I hear the call of the whispering deep. Louder. Insistent.

Not having a daughter, I begin to show the girl the ways of birthing, healing and laying out, and how to use the cunning bag.

We will have need of it again soon enough.

END

ABOUT THE AUTHOR

Earl Livings is an award-winning poet and fiction writer who has been widely published in Australia and also overseas. He has read his work around Melbourne and overseas and appeared on panels at various Australian SF conventions and festivals.

Earl has a PhD in Creative Writing, for which he wrote *The Silence Inside the World*, a fantasy verse novel that is due to be published late 2021. He taught professional writing and editing for almost 20 years and has worked as a freelance editor, a manuscript assessor, and a mentor. His writing focuses on science, history, nature, mythology and the sacred. Ginninderra Press published his latest poetry collection, *Libation*, in late 2018, and he is currently finalising a two-book historical fantasy series set in dark ages Britain.

He lives in Melbourne with his wife and their ever-growing stacks of books. More information is available on his website: www.earl-livings.com

16

THETA TAURII

ALLISON OLSSON

Elanor Taurii gazed across the plateau and watched solemnly as the small sun set, casting a faint reddish glow across the grassy plains. Covered by dry, bristly reeds, the plains spread for miles, and the reeds rustled constantly as the planet's breezes changed direction in a dervish-dance of movement. For a moment, she felt a primal bond with nature, but it passed as quickly as it came. Her gloom returned, increasing as the twilight deepened and became a cold, black night. In the distance, Elanor saw the sickly orange glow of night-lights illuminating the colony of Theta Taurii. Pausing, she opened her mind to the thoughts and feelings of the people who lived in the settlement. She gasped as she sensed the withered hopes and dreams in their hearts.

"Will our small group make a difference?" She sighed. Turning away, she trudged across the pock-marked plateau, making her way back to her one-room abode.

MARK TAYLOR YAWNED as he completed his ten-hour shift and waited for the personnel conveyor to roll him down to the household area of the colony. Artificial light glared incessantly, creating the eerie feeling of being trapped forever in one long day. The monotony of long workdays with no breaks made his stomach sink. It was soul-destroying. Mark looked around at the other commuters and wondered if his eyes had that same glazed and exhausted look. He could not remember the last time he spoke to anyone on the conveyor. His first impression of the colony was one of excitement and camaraderie. But his excitement was soon dashed. Management was replaced and soldiers arrived to support them as they introduced impossible to reach key performance indicators. They curtailed rations and introduced curfews and martial law. The colonists' protests were extinguished by swift military retaliation.

People were now too tired and afraid to talk. The only conversations took place in the prison. Mark sighed as he recalled the time he had been called in to repair faulty monitors in the prison. The job hadn't taken long, but he would never forget the sobbing and incoherent yabbering of inmates in their cells as he walked past them towards the command centre.

Walking past the cells, he glanced up at a particularly noisy inmate and recognised Max, a colleague from his first job. Max nodded in recognition and Mark nodded back.

"Hey!" Mark protested, as a guard struck him across his legs with a baton.

"No fraternising with prisoners! It is a criminal offence!" the guard barked.

Mark rubbed his thigh gingerly and nodded, trying to sneak a sidelong look at Max.

"Perhaps we didn't make the rules clear enough when we briefed you. Number one: Do as we tell you. Number two: Head down while walking through the cells. Number three: Always obey rule number one."

The guard turned and continued to the control station. Mark nodded as he followed him the rest of the way. The job took longer than he had quoted, and he breathed a sigh of relief as he passed through the prison security screens and back into the general population.

Something big was going down. But what? Mark was only one cog in the machine of rebellion. He congratulated himself on his ingenuity with the control panel. He hadn't gone in with a plan to sabotage the system, but when he opened the broken panel and saw the mess inside, he knew exactly what to do. It would be weeks before they knew what was causing their alarms to malfunction and their cell doors to unexpectedly unlock. Hopefully he could find a way to escape before they realised it was him. As he made his way back to his room, he saw several rooms with their doors wide open. He couldn't see what was going on inside: the doorways were blocked by wide-shouldered men in black body armour with patches labelling them as fumigation consultants. Mark arrived at his room, only to see his door open and two identical men ransacking his bedroom. He stepped inside.

"Looking for roaches," they said, muscling past him and searching his bathroom as well. He watched as they searched for cockroaches in his shaving cream, soap, deodorant, toilet paper, toilet bowl, underwear, socks, mattress, and bed linen. Being the sort of guy who was into self-preservation, Mark decided against informing the fumigators that they were looking in some awfully strange places for cockroaches.

What the hell are they looking for? Something small and concealable. Something dangerous. Mark could not remember bringing anything home that was remotely illegal, or even work-related. But he did know someone who used to sneak spare parts home from work: Max.

———

FRANCES DU VALIER, a junior pharmacologist, stepped onto the conveyor after her shift finished. She felt queasy and ill, despite the mega-vitamin supplements she took. The thought of sleep depressed her. She knew she would not get to sleep until just before it was time to get up and go to work. No matter how exhausted Frances was, she always woke in time for the next shift.

Picking at the scabs on her scalp, Frances decided how to dispose of tonight's sleeping pill. She feared tranquilliser addiction more than sleep deprivation. Her mind went back to the days when she had no trouble sleeping and was full of energy. Her long blonde hair had been thick and lustrous, her eyes bright, and her spirits high. Working for Ark on Earth had been fulfilling. As a graduate, Frances was lucky to land a job in such a prestigious organisation. When they offered her a position on Theta Taurii, she said yes, and bought a bottle of the most expensive champagne she could afford. Her parents were a little less excited, fearing for their only daughter's safety in such a distant colony. But Ark was a prestigious organisation, and the salary and promised working conditions were so attractive that they were finally happy for her to go. In hindsight, Frances wished she had paid more attention to her parents' misgivings.

After the first email home complaining about the colony, a company PR officer visited Frances and explained that the new colony was "having teething problems", and that Frances should "give it a chance" before she wrote worrying emails to those earthbound. Frances waited a month, during which time soldiers arrived at Ark installing checkpoints and imposing curfews. She wanted out. She wrote a second email home and was visited by a Security Officer. He explained that her email would "unnecessarily worry her ageing parents". Her third email home was also intercepted.

Two Security Officers reminded her of the penalties for breaching company security. One black eye and many bruises later, they helped her draft a fourth email, full of optimism and hope. They gallantly sent it for her. It was the last email home Frances wrote.

The conveyor halted. Frances disembarked and walked into the long corridor of bedrooms. She entered her room and changed into a shapeless cotton shift, brushed her teeth, and went to bed. Laying in the dark, Frances looked at the familiar cracks in the ceiling, wondering if she would ever see her parents again. She was silent as tears rolled from her eyes.

———

Elanor sat meditating in her tent. She started, surprised to sense someone close-by. Rising slowly, she walked outside and picked her way over rough stones towards the edge of the cliff, where she paused and listened. Someone was at the base of the cliff. Peering over the edge she saw a man sitting in the lotus position. Her ears caught the sound of his voice, repeating something over and over. The whirling breeze dislocated his soft mantras, wedding them with the sound of the rustling reeds to become part of the plain's discordant, restless song.

———

Wisps of black hair hung over Chang's light eyebrows. He glanced around as he got out of his land-trans and hiked two kilometres to the base of a steep ridge. As an Ark employee he had one day of leave a month. He used his to meditate, picking a different place every time – he was certain the change of scenery kept him sane. As he looked up to the top of the ridge, he heard a bird's lonely cry echo across the plain. With a shiver, he cleared a place at the foot of a cliff and assumed the lotus position. He softly repeated a mantra, willing himself to relax.

Chang meditated every day in his room at the base but relished the change of environment on his monthly jaunt. He went further away each time. Part of him wondered what would happen if he kept driving. Like everybody else, he worked from before dawn until well into the night, forced to meet increasingly impossible deadlines. He was tired and making mistakes, and mistakes were one of two things that landed you in prison. The second thing was speaking out against

Ark. Two weeks ago, his friend Theo complained about their long working hours and started a petition which Chang had willingly signed. Theo was arrested and publicly executed for treason. Chang wondered how long it would be until Ark started working its way down Theo's petition and found his name. He felt totally alone.

———

CHANG'S FEAR washed over Elanor. She studied him: his face was taut and pale, sweat glistened on his brow and above his upper lip. His posture re-enforced Elanor's telepathic impressions. She wanted to ease his fear. Revealing herself was risky, but she could not sense any malevolence in Chang. Leaning forward, she closed her eyes. Fighting her way through the fear that closed his mind, she called him softly, persistently. Working gently past the pain, she finally reached him.

Chang's head snapped back, and his eyes opened, pupils dilated with fear. "Who's there?" he cried.

"Up here, on top of the cliff," Elanor answered silently. "Do not be afraid. I will not harm you. My name is Elanor Taurii, and I am not of Ark."

Elanor enveloped Chang with a firm warmth as she called to him and caught his gaze. She smiled and waved.

"Would you care to join me for supper?" Elanor said.

Chang smiled at her mental picture of a warm fire and steaming mugs of soup. His stomach growled.

"Sure," he replied, "but how do I get up there?"

Elanor flashed him an image, a mud-map of the circuitous route he would have to take to reach the plateau.

"The soup better be good," he called up to her as he followed her directions. Elanor maintained their telepathic link, remaining on the periphery of Chang's awareness.

She led Chang west, further away from Ark. The dry, dusty terrain slowly changed. Tall grasses gave way to short bushes and spindly, narrow-leaved trees. She sensed his pleasure as he gained altitude and felt the cool air on his skin. She also sensed his discomfort as he developed a nagging headache increasing in intensity as he moved further west. By early evening, she sensed that Chang was in trouble.

Elanor Taurii's feet and legs burned from exertion. She finally saw the immobile land-trans. As she neared Chang, his pain hit her. She stumbled, almost losing her balance. She took a deep breath and continued carefully down the hill towards him. A small bag clinked rhythmically by her side, marking each pace.

Chang was almost insensible with pain, and sat with his head slumped forward, his hands over his ears. A small trickle of blood issued from his left nostril. Sweat poured from his head, stinging as it rolled into his eyes.

"What's going on?" he whimpered softly as tears bled from his eyes. Elanor opened the door of the vehicle and gently placed a hand on Chang's shoulder. A wall of pain blasted into her mind. Elanor reeled back, then took a deep breath and stepped forward, grasping his shoulder again. Elanor battled to clear a small area of her mind from pain. She knew what had to be done.

"Chang," she said, "It's Elanor. We spoke earlier. Can you hear me?" Chang nodded. "I know what is causing your pain. Ark Inc inserted RFID implants in their employees to prevent them from escaping once on the planet. They did this as you entered hypersleep, knowing you wouldn't remember. The further you move from the compound, the worse pain you experience, until your body starts to shut down. Then the device releases a worm that works its way into your minds, turning you into an automaton. They did this to you, Chang."

Chang licked his bloodied lips, "Will it stop if I go back?"

"No. Once triggered, the device will continue emitting the signal until it's host is either dead, the device is removed, or the host is turned. I can remove the device, with no guarantee that you will survive, but if I don't remove the device...you won't survive at all. It's your choice." Elanor shrugged her shoulders and was silent.

Chang squinted through puffy eyes, as he looked at Elanor.

"Get rid of it."

Elanor helped him out of the land-trans and laid him on the ground, putting a cushion under his neck to hold his head in position. She probed the face of the wall in Chang's mind. It jutted out in sections, splitting his conscious and unconscious mind. Hard and rocky, with sharp, barbed irregularities, the wall was like the others Elanor had encountered. The barbs writhed and squirmed, like obscene anemones waving in a sea of blood. Finally, when she thought she could hold out no longer, a flaw appeared. Her mind's eye moved closer to it, peering carefully for a glimpse of what was on the other side. A small pinprick of light pushed through and cast an eerie grey glow. Slowly, like a weaver tracing a mistake in a complex work, Elanor unravelled the threads. Every point of contact with them sent barbs of pain through her head, making red points explode behind her eyes.

Much later, Elanor pulled back to observe what she had uncovered. The scene before her resembled a rectangular grid. Strangely shaped buildings jutted out of an eerie landscape. A soft hum ran along metallic roads. Everything was geometrically precise and ordered. No beings inhabited the strange city, yet Elanor could feel the hum and buzz of activity. She looked more closely at the roads and saw that they were composed of highly polished copper. Strange, shiny grey blobs were visible at intervals. They radiated cold. She grunted with satisfaction. Elanor had found the RFID tag. She pulled back, past the fray, to the edges of Chang's consciousness. She had to depart, before the threads of her own consciousness dissolved and left her trapped forever with Chang.

Elanor's head throbbed as she straightened up. She unclamped her fingers from Chang's bruised shoulder and hobbled to the back of the trans where she searched for water to wash down her parched and sore throat before laying a fire and setting a pot of water over it to boil. She unrolled a piece of clean cloth and laid it gently by the fire. Opening a soft, drawstring pouch, she took out a pair of needle-nosed tweezers, a pair of scissors, a pair of long, narrow, curved forceps, and a small, sealed bag of dried and processed seaweed compound. She dropped the instruments in the boiling water. Elanor thought of the people who had smuggled these instruments through Ark's stringent checkpoints, then secreted them in nooks and crannies around the forbidding Taurean landscape. She felt a strange discordance in the back of her mind, but ignored it, knowing she could do nothing about what was going on in Ark's base camp.

Her digilarm rang, jolting Elanor out of her thoughts. She walked to Chang and put her hand on his forehead. "It is time," she whispered softly. He lay where she had put him, with his hands clenched over his ears. A small sob escaped his lips. Elanor stoked the fire, then washed her hands. As she bent over Chang's brittle frame, her instruments glistened in the sunset, reflecting hopeful rays of pink and gold.

Humming softly, Elanor eased into Chang's mind, weaving a soft, resilient web of peace around him. She hoped to cushion him from the pain that was to come, and lacking the usual agents of anaesthesia, had to rely on her own resources. Elanor picked up the forceps and began. Probing Chang's left nostril, she scraped softly against his nasal membranes. With some more effort, she penetrated further into his nasal cavity. Chang stiffened as she pushed into his sinuses and gasped as her forceps caught something foreign. Elanor drew in a deep breath as she pushed harder and grasped the small object. She wiggled and levered the forceps to loosen it from its bed of flesh. A soft, sickening rip sounded, followed by a gush of blood. Elanor gently pulled down and the tip of the forceps appeared, holding a minuscule, bloody bit of flesh in its pincers. Elanor put the forceps as it was, flesh and all, in a bag, and started packing Chang's nose with the seaweed mixture.

Chang struggled upright and sat, hunched over as Elanor put a poultice on his nose, and maintained pressure to control the bleeding. His face was drawn and pinched, but he managed a wan smile.

"The pain's gone," he gurgled, spitting out a mouthful of blood.

"Put some pressure on that nose and sleep up against the land-trans. I'll keep an eye on you and wake you, if necessary," Elanor replied, smiling. Chang nodded and rested against the vehicle. Little bubbles of blood burst as he breathed, spattering his lips with a grotesque rouge.

Elanor kept vigil, keeping herself awake by reciting old Earth tales and tending to Chang. The night passed, the silence broken only by the thick sounds of Chang's breathing and Elanor's tired voice as she sang.

As the first rays of sunlight burst through the early morning air Elanor busied herself boiling water and cleaning up the bloody mess from the previous evening's surgery. Filling a small cup with warm water, she placed the object from Chang's nose into it. Elanor used her forceps to clean away the slough from the object and stared thoughtfully at what was revealed. A tiny chip sat on the tip of her finger.

"That's it?" Chang asked, shuffling over to her.

"Yes. So small, yet able to continuously sent GPS coordinates and telemetry signals to a mainframe. It can also emit a piercing high frequency signal that gives its host the most intense headaches imaginable." Elanor shuddered.

"An instrument to control and monitor people? I didn't think Ark would stoop so low," Chang said, softly touching the chip. "Get rid of it. I don't want to look at it anymore." He touched the swollen flesh around his eyes and nose.

Elanor nodded and placed the device on a flat rock. She handed Chang another rock, "Do the honours."

He smiled grimly as he pounded the device into dust.

———

ELANOR LOOKED at the gathering clouds on the horizon. What was going on in Ark? She could feel pain and suffering on the wind, but no more.

"Let's get out of here. Something's wrong and we need to leave. I've packed our gear, and if we start out now, we should be in a safe area by lunch. Can you reprogramme the land-trans?"

"No, I'm an accountant, not an engineer. Unfortunately."

"Then we'll have to continue on foot," Elanor said.

Chang nodded.

"Have this, and some water, and we'll get going. They might send someone to find you," Elanor said, handing Chang a green-coloured concoction to drink. Chang nodded.

By midday the effects of the last few days told on Chang. His face was pale and his skin clammy.

"My throat feels like I've swallowed a fistful of splinters," Chang complained.

Elanor handed him a purple lozenge.

"This will soothe your throat. Put it in your mouth and let it melt. It's made of natural ingredients I found on the plateau.

Chang nodded and put the lozenge in his mouth.

He smiled gratefully. They continued along the steep path, the gravel becoming more dangerous underfoot. Chang stumbled and fell. Elanor was by his side instantly, pressuring his nose to stop the fresh trickle of blood. Her hands were cool and calloused, unlike his, which were soft from years of desk work. He felt effeminate beside her and brushed her away. "I'm all right," he said, "Let's keep going. The further we get from Ark, the better."

"Are you sure you're okay? You don't look so good," Elanor replied, looking closely at him.

"I'm fine."

They continued their journey. Elanor sensed Chang's discomfort but refrained from intruding on his thoughts. Chang followed behind as best he could, unwilling to ask her to slow down.

By late afternoon, it was obvious to Elanor that Chang could not go on much longer. He was too weak to resist when she took his elbow and put his arm over her shoulders.

They crested the hill and the plateau opened out before them. Tough, woody shrubs sprouted from rocky soil, and a forest stood in the distance. Elanor breathed in deeply, savouring the soft fresh scents. Chang collapsed beside her, spent. She kneeled, put her arm around his shoulders, and held him. Her mind returned to the plain, to Ark, searching for others.

———

MARK READ the announcement on the dashboard. "All leave cancelled."

Just like that. All leave cancelled.

He had a feeling it had something to do with the fumigators in his room and mulled over the conundrum as he ate his breakfast of gruel. The dining area was more muted than before. No spoons clinked against cups; no dishes clanked as they were piled into the dishwashers. He turned the spoon over in his hands.

"Mmm," he murmured, examining at each utensil on his tray. He pressed down with his knife, and it bent, returning to its original shape when he removed the pressure. It was malleable, unbreakable. No way you could create a sharp-edged weapon.

The loudspeaker blared: "All areas of mass assembly are closing immediately. This includes the dining rooms. Collect your food parcels on exiting the dining rooms."

Mark frowned and left the dining room, collecting his rations on the way out. He stuffed them into his pockets.

There was a queue when he arrived at work. Raised voices reached his ears. He strained to hear what was going on.

"Please, you can't do this!" he made out the voice of his supervisor, Lisa. She was a good sort, in his opinion. Fair and just. He leaned forward and peered over the shoulder of the person in front of him. A crowd had gathered around Lisa, obscuring his view.

"Stop! Please!" her cry rang out, followed by horrified gasps. The crowd ahead was agitated, and people cried out in support of Lisa. Mark heard scuffling in the line behind him, and turned to see security officers walking towards the front of the line, hitting people with batons as they went past. They struck the woman in the line behind him, and he stepped forward, shielding her from any further strikes, earning an extra couple for his efforts. He sagged to the floor, the sounds of crying and wailing in his ears.

———

A BLACK HAZE descended on Frances as she shuffled into the queue at work. She was exhausted and didn't know how she would get through another day. There was a scuffle in the line ahead, and she peered around, trying to see what the hold-up was.

She was too shocked to speak as a sudden blow hit her arm. She staggered, looking around to see a security officer with a baton raised ready to rain down more blows.

"No!" she cried, as the man behind her sprang forward and shielded her from the blows. As he fell to the ground, an officer grabbed him by the shoulders and looked up at Frances.

"Looks like your lucky day," he said, hauling the man away.

Frances was livid with anger. She didn't know how she got through the day without exploding. She submitted to the strip search at work – there was no option. She dispensed medications without making any errors, then made it back to her room and threw herself into the shower. Exhausted, she sat as the water ran over her. Her head drooped forwards and she fell asleep. She woke, covered in gooseflesh, the shower out of water, and her hair dripping and cold. She felt angrier than she had ever felt before. Rising stiffly, she took a thin towel from the rail. Once dried, she fell onto her bed and dropped into a deep, exhausted sleep.

———

MARK SPENT the night on a cold cement floor in a remand cell. His attempts at conversation with the man sharing the cell were met with a stony glare. Surveillance cameras watched from the corners of his cell, and motion detectors flashed soft pink lines of light as he moved around to fend off the cold. Peering out of the cell door, he recognised a few faces. None of them were criminals - he had worked with most of them. He wondered how many of his colleagues had signed Max's petition. Mark hunkered down in a corner, drew his bloodied workshop coat around himself, and thought.

"What can I do?" he pondered. "I'm on a minor planet light years away from Earth, under a provisional government made up of a greedy conglomerate. How can I escape? How do I help others escape? I'll need resources and trustworthy contacts from within the different arms of Ark. That woman today might help. She didn't just look scared, she was furious."

Mark looked up as a guard entered his cell.

"Get up! Quietly!" the guard said, "Come with me."

Mark followed the guard in silence as he was led away through a warren of cold, damp corridors. The guard eventually stopped using his implanted wrist ID and drew out an old-fashioned swipe card to unlock the doors. The corridors became smaller and narrower until they arrived at a gate. Mark followed quietly, hoping the guard wasn't about to kill him.

"Stand to one side and don't make a noise," the guard commanded, "I'll explain things in a sec."

The guard opened the gate and pointed into the narrow tunnel beyond with his gun.

"I have been told I can trust you. You must use this passage to escape," the guard whispered, looking around nervously, " I have a contact who will erase the footage of us coming down here. When you get outside, head west and find a woman named Elanor. Tell her we are getting stronger and more organized. And give her this." The guard then drew something out of his jacket pocket.

"This is a tracker nullifier. When I put it in the nose of someone who has a tracker in their nose, it will release a quick charge of electricity and destroy it. Everyone has a tracker," the guard said, lowering his voice, "even you." He looked at Mark. "It has to come out before you leave." Mark frowned, but before he could respond, the guard pushed him up against a wall and jabbed the tracker deep into his nose. His vision exploded with stars, and he sagged forward, the guard's grip preventing him from falling. The guard waited a moment then stepped back.

"Now it has been neutralised and Ark will not be able to track you," he said, shoving the bloodied instrument into Mark's hands. He took with a pair of pliers and a screwdriver out of his other pocket.

"This is all I could smuggle in for you. Good luck! Find Elanor and give her the device! Tell her that Bill has not forgotten his promise."

An alarm sounded in the distance.

"Go!" the guard commanded, and Mark turned and ran through the dark tunnel, stumbling over broken boxes and piles of rubbish. He kept running until the way became blocked with outdated computers and broken cables, clambering over them as he kept pushing forwards. Eventually a faint ray of light appeared, revealing a grille. Mark climbed onto a desk and stood under the grille. He peered out, the strong light obscuring any view he might have had. He fidgeted with the grill using the pliers, then found some bolts and got to work, sweat dripping from him. He thought he heard shouts in the distance, and his heart raced. With one last grunt he pushed the grille as hard as he could, staring with disbelief as it finally gave way. Mark hauled himself out. The sunlight slashed across his eyes, and he shielded them with his hand as he stumbled forwards, running into a rock formation. Hiding in the shadows of the rocks he collapsed.

Once the sun lowered, Mark walked around the rocks and looked at the plains. They were vast. To the east he just could see the silhouette of Ark's compound. In the west, a ridge of mountains rose and marched into the distance, shrouded in a purple haze. He stretched his aching limbs. There was no way he would go back to Ark, so he headed west. The wide-open space outside of Ark both entranced and scared him.

Eventually he reached the base of a tall cliff and found a rutted track winding up into the sky. Mark's throat felt like sandpaper and his head throbbed, but he scrabbled along the track, forcing himself to go on. Shadows danced in the corners of his eyes. It was two days since he crawled out of the tunnel. Stumbling, he reached the top of the ridge. He turned and looked how far he had come. A wave of vertigo hit him. Mark turned from the edge and crawled along the ridge, putting as much distance between himself and Ark as possible. He came across a vacant land-trans. He stood and hobbled over to the vehicle, touching the body. Its surface was hot and he walked around to the rear hatch which was open, its contents strewn across the ground.

"Water bottles will be hot, too," he grumbled, looking for the latch to open the cooler. With a gratifying 'click' the latch released the lid and Mark reached in and pulled out a bottle of drinkable water. He kissed the bottle, then opened it, smiling as water dribbled over his chin and down his chest. Mark drank deeply, his strength returning.

When the heat of the day receded, he left his shelter, heading towards a large plateau he could see in the half-light of the crescent moon. Along the way he passed other signs of human life: torn cloth, a half-buried campfire, a footprint.

———

ELANOR AND CHANG set about building a crude abode out of old logs and mud bricks. It was back-breaking work. The logs needed hauling and the bricks needed firing. Elanor would disappear for hours on end, listening to what she called 'the birth pangs of a new generation.'

Chang, whose senses were not as well-honed as Elanor's, took lessons from one of Elanor's friends who had escaped from Ark in the early days. He worked hard at fostering his latent telepathic abilities. Evenings passed in discussion of possible scenarios about what was going on at Ark and plans for the defence of their small portion of Taurii were made. Chang started each day by scouting the area for possible spies or escapees from Ark.

One morning, as he trailed through the hills south of their camp, the sound of footsteps on gravel reached his ears. Chang spun around to see a haggard man eyeing him suspiciously. "Hey!" Chang called as he stepped back, his yell alerting Elanor. She arrived quickly and walked over to the man.

"Hello, my name is Elanor," she said, introducing herself. "You are?" she asked as she gently probed his mind, moving slowly closer.

"Bill has, he has...promise..." Elanor caught him as he collapsed. The moment her hands touched him fragments of his journey washed over her. She rested his head on her knee while Chang left the clearing and reappeared with a cushion from the land-trans, and a reed blanket. When the man woke, Elanor helped him up while Chang brought him some water. The man drank and then introduced himself.

"My name is Mark, and I am a Survivor of Ark. Bill said to tell you that he has not forgotten his promise. And gave me this to give you." He handed over the tool. Elanor was quiet for a moment, then looked from Mark to Chang. She led them to the fire where they sat and talked and shared a meal. As they got to know each other, Elanor smiled. The hard work had only just begun.

END

About the Author

Allison Olsson is a writer who is lucky enough to have so far lived in New South Wales, South Australia and Queensland. While looking forward to exploring more of Australia and the world, she works as a nurse and divides her free time between her family, writing, and her favourite martial art, Hapkido.

When she gets stuck in a story, her cat takes over, tiptoeing across the keyboard and adding her own suggestions for Allison to consider. Allison has not yet been able to teach her cat how to make coffee.

17

TIME PUMP

CHRIS MCMAHON

MacPherson sat on the hull of his ruined survey ship, his tears turning to ice. He squinted into the endless snowfall, but there was nothing to see. The terrain was featureless, the horizon lost in white. If not for the dull grey metal of the ship his sense of disorientation would have been total. It was minus fifty-eight degrees centigrade and falling. There was no way he could survive outside in X3I's night, even in his thermal suit. Soon the hatchway would be blocked with snow, leaving him alone to wait for darkness and death.

He still had a choice. He could climb back into the ship and be buried alive with his dead crew.

Their small short-range probe had been conducting a surface scan when the storm hit. It had swept them hundreds of kilometres from the target area, slamming them into the tundra. He had been strapped into the pilot's chair and knocked unconscious, but survived the impact. His six crew, busily moving between instruments in the cramped cabin, had not been so lucky. That was what he had awoken to—the sight of them—smashed and hideous, and already frozen in their blood.

The fuel tanks had ruptured, and the precious hydrogen was gone, the main batteries depleted. There was no way he could signal the spidery, rotating bulk of the Kepler orbiting far above them. The deep space exploration vessel had only three planetary descent craft. He knew their standing orders—he had helped to draft them—they would not risk another craft until the nature of the danger was established.

Heat. Goddamn it. He needed heat.

MacPherson turned to look at the hatch. Only a few more feet and the mounting snow would seal it...

Around him the storm intensified.

He slid down to the open hatchway and swung his legs in. He reached for the first rung of the ladder, but his fingers, clumsy in the thermal gloves, missed their grip and he tumbled down.

'Argh!' He fell hard. His head cracked against a bulkhead.

———

MACPHERSON WOKE up in a pile of snow. His right knee throbbed and his head was a mass of pain. Above him was the white circle of the open hatch. His fogged brain tuned into faint voices.

'. . . understand it either.'

'Can we trust them?'

'Who's there!' he yelled.

The wind whistled across the hatch above him. MacPherson was alone. He hobbled over to the console and checked the radio. Nothing. The set was completely dead—but he knew that already.

With grim resolution he dragged himself back up the ladder and pulled the hatch closed. Immediately he was in darkness, his breathing harsh and loud. There was no power. No way out.

The ship groaned around him as it tilted under the weight of snow. He could hear the soft whisper of it as it covered the hatch.

MacPherson felt his way across the slippery floor to the emergency locker. He flipped it open, fumbling in the dark amid canisters and rubberised, unknowable shapes for a torch.

Click. At first the light was a blessed relief. But no matter where he directed the torch, he would see one of them—or what was left of them. Twisted. Mangled.

MacPherson turned off the torch and sat in the darkness.

The ship would be buried by now. Lost beneath the vast carpet of white that was X31. He had perhaps twelve hours of air. He could hope for a miracle, but he knew it would be hours before the storm blew itself out. The survey ship had been so far off course. Even if the Kepler got a ship down to the surface, it could take days to survey that area. Without some way to signal the ship . . .

'. . . burning.' A whisper.

He yelped in surprise, then flipped on the torch and swept it feverishly around the cabin. He had heard it again. A voice just at the edge of his hearing. But the torch beam found nothing but carnage. A severed arm. Fingers frozen against a bulkhead.

Blood pounded in his temples, and a knife edge of pain worked into his right eye. MacPherson staggered to his feet and swept back the hood of his thermal jacket.

'Leave me the fuck alone!' he yelled. His voice was startlingly loud in the confined space.

The frigid air stung his cheeks and nose. He felt cold and pain on the top of his head and carefully probed his scalp. His hand came away bloody.

The fall. Of course.

'OK. OK.' A mild concussion then. Just hearing things.

He pulled the hood back up over his head and tried to slow his breathing. He tried to will himself to turn off the torch to conserve its power, but could not.

Then his nose wrinkled at the smell of burnt plastic. The beam of his torch caught a faint trail of smoke and he followed it back to the scanning console. His heart skipped a beat. Nothing could burn without power!

The scanner's dedicated batteries—which were isolated from all the other systems—must still have charge.

He wrenched a crossbar loose from a shattered bulkhead and

shoved aside the frozen corpse that lay there. Underneath the body, the twin needles on the projector manifold twittered with power.

MacPherson chipped away the ice that covered the panel. Three screws came away easily, two he had to snap with a makeshift chisel. The last was fused to the housing.

'It's always the last one,' he muttered.

Carefully, he used the strut to lever the housing open. The frigid metal fractured and the panel clattered open. The scanner control circuits had fused—that was the smoke he had seen.

Because of the tilt of the ship, the two scanner antenna were now parallel to the surface. In normal operation, the scanners bombarded the surface of a survey planet with everything from gamma rays and X-rays to infrared radiation and neutrons, mapping the distribution of scores of heavy metals and elements from orbit. Now that the control circuits were gone, if he powered the arrays he would release an unknowable cocktail of EM radiation. Yet it would be a signal. The question was, would the Kepler even be listening? The whole thing was likely to explode, showering him in lethal radiation. He chewed his lower lip as hope flared in his chest. It could work.

He examined the circuits critically. A tiny river of red ice glittered in the light. He followed the trail upwards, his heart thudding, already dreading what he would see.

Up on top of the flight monitor was Valerie's frozen head. Her eyes were wide in shock, her lips drawn back in a rictus of frozen horror.

'Oh, shit. Val.'

She was just a kid, taken on like so many of the station-rats and trained on the job. Bubbly, laughing; her eyes full of life and promise.

He fell to his knees, dumping hot, bitter bile onto the frozen metal. He dry-retched, his stomach in agony. Suddenly he was too hot in his thermals. His vision blurred and he fell sideways.

'Fight it, Mac.' It was Val's voice. A feather-touch in his ears.

He looked up at her. What was left of her. The torch beam wavered in his weakening grip. In the shadows, her eyes seemed to turn toward him.

MacPherson tried to get up, but slipped. Darkness closed in.

———

THE SUN BLAZED DOWN.

He was on a vast savannah, the sky a wide blue above. The landscape was dotted with knots of rounded boulders that rose above the open forest and grassland, perhaps left by glaciers in the distant past. In the far distance he saw dark-skinned animals cropping the grass, and strange tall-necked beasts grazing the treetops. Movement caught his eye.

Off to his right, high amid a small hill of tumbled stones, he saw figures moving. There were seven of them walking in single file, led by a tall, winged figure that looked vaguely insectoid in nature: his skin mottled orange and yellow.

'Wait!'

They stopped and turned toward him, watching him silently. One took a step toward him then stopped. Val. He was sure it was her.

Then they turned away from him.

'No, wait! Wait!

One by one they slipped away through the rocks.

And he was left alone.

———

MACPHERSON WOKE GASPING, deathly cold.

He looked at his chrono. He had been out for just under two hours.

'No!'

It was just past dawn. By now the ship would be buried under snow.

He crawled across the cabin to the scanning console. His hand hovered over the switch. There was nothing to lose. He slammed his hand down and powered the arrays.

The console exploded in a shower of sparks, and the cabin lit up brightly with blue-white electrical fires. MacPherson's thick gloves caught on fire. He cursed as he hit at the flames, then grabbed an extinguisher. He lost his footing as the ship tilted and he skidded to the floor. The ice under the ship had gone. Vaporised by the scanner.

He braced himself against a cabinet and sprayed the retardant at the fires, holding his breath against the sharp odour. There was a groan and the ship righted itself, slamming him into the deck's hard, cold metal.

He scrambled up the ladder and worked frantically at the manual hatch-release.

'Yes!'

Icy water poured into the cabin. He was too stunned to even cry out. Above he saw daylight. Not snow. Daylight. Sky.

He crawled out into the new day of X31, squinting against the ferocious glare.

A clear dawn rose above the defile. What had once been a solid wall of snow at the peak of a ridge was now wide open space—an oasis in the ice—blown clear by the scanners' discharge.

MacPherson slid down onto the surface, which was a wet stone smoothed by millennia of moving ice.

He looked up, searching for X31's single G-type sun, but the narrow valley, a saddle at the top of a basalt ridge, was lit by two suns. The first was a small, cold disk high in the blue-white sky, right where the sun should be. The second was a warm, glowing orb, shining from a wide fissure like a cat's eye rising from the hard rock of the ridge. A rent in the air.

He staggered forward, shielding his eyes against the glare of the hot sun.

The intense burst of energy from the sensors.

'My, God. I've opened a rift in spacetime.'

Above the rift the sky rippled.

'Bent light,' muttered MacPherson. Gravity effect.

The rift hovered above a spur of solid magnetite that rose from the centre of the basalt ridge. MacPherson hardly dared to move, as though the whole improbable thing would flit away like a butterfly if he as much as breathed.

Rifts in spacetime were rare. There were legends about them appearing inexplicably in space, but the only one he had studied appeared after the obliteration of the Formial, with its experimental anti-matter drive. The explosion had been devastating, destroying the nearby space station and killing almost two thousand people, but others had survived long enough to record the aftermath. A rift in spacetime had formed, rapidly collapsing as the small black hole that formed it shrank, emitting a continuous stream of Hawking radiation from its hot core.

He knew the theory. Rifts were unstable, a region of multiply connected spacetime outside the ring singularity that could transport you elsewhere...or elsewhen. They formed—somehow—from the minute black holes continuously appearing at the distance of a Plank Length. No theory satisfactorily explained their formation.

The edges of the rift quivered, rippling with energy as they slowly contracted.

It drew him toward it.

Closer, the air was charged and smelt of ozone. His head swam, his vision growing syncopated. MacPherson passed his hand in front of his face. He saw his hand move, followed by a series of echo images.

His mouth was dry, and he tried—unsuccessfully—to swallow the lump in his throat.

'Holy shit.' Strange echoes of his voice trailed away into a murmur.

A hot wind blew through the rift and caressed his face. He smelled the warm, resinous scent of grasses, and beneath it a faint, almost animal odour.

Layer by layer he pulled off his thermal gear.

He was startled by a mournful bellow, coming from nearby. He did not have to look far to find the source. It was some sort of wildebeest, hairless, evolved for the heat of the savannah. It had pushed its way out past the oasis into the ice and snow, perhaps running in panic. It was stuck up to its shoulders, shivering uncontrollably. Beside it a calf was already lying still in the ice.

MacPherson flinched as flock of birds shot past overhead. They screamed out to each other in weird gibbering calls. He watched them circle then shoot back through the rift. One of the bird's wings clipped the side of the fissure. It gave a brief, high screech then plummeted to the ground on the other side of the rift. It hit hard—and did not move again.

He looked back at the survey vessel. It glittered in the light of the two suns. The array antennas pointed straight at the rift, like a rifle at a target.

There was another exhalation of warm air from the iris, and it contracted again. It was losing integrity. From the rate, he estimated that within an hour it would be gone.

He went closer to it. The hair on his bare arms stood on end. His teeth were on edge from the power of it. Again his head began to swim, and the effects on his vision returned with the proximity. His breathing came faster. His heart raced.

He had to. Had to see it.

Step by step, he drew closer. Until he stood on the very threshold. Stretching to the horizon beyond the rift were vast, hot grasslands, dotted with trees. It was real. A doorway into another time. He could see the flock of birds circling in the distance, its fallen member a sprawl of feathers on the grass not twenty paces from him. Another bird—a raptor—swooped down and lifted its carrion meal back into the air in one smooth motion.

He heard low trumpeting calls in the distance, and the back of his scalp lifted with the strange reality of it all.

Beyond the rift was a world where he could survive. The earliest surveys of X31 had shown a safe, Earth-like atmosphere, and carbon-based life compatible enough with human physiology to supply him with food. He might survive another twenty years. Yet he would always be alone. Could he face that terrible isolation? The prospect both attracted and terrified him.

He looked back at the survey ship.

The twin turbines that powered it through the atmosphere had been shattered by the impact. It was these that charged the instruments, arrays and other electrics of the craft. Without them, the craft was dead. But each had a secondary turbine on a closed cycle, designed to harvest low grade heat from the primary. He could tell from here that the first was ruined, its exotic working fluid long since evaporated under the heat of the ancient wind—but the other. The other was still intact.

Heat.

Ice.

Power!

It hit him like a bolt of lightning, filling his head with the roar of adrenalin. That heat differential would drive his turbine, the power derived from the temperature difference between two epochs. Not a heat pump, but a time pump.

The iris contacted again.

There was little time.

'But I can do it, goddamn it!' With power the radio would function. He could bring the survey craft back to life.

He turned back to the rift. Once more it filled his vision. No. He had to shut out the reality of its...strangeness.

First, he drained the fluids into a storage tank used when the loop had to be emptied for maintenance and repair. Thankfully, the fluid was not frozen, but he had not expected it to be. It was designed to pick up ambient heat.

He stripped down, his back glistening with sweat as he worked to cut free the masses of insulated, secondary turbine piping. He joined them with a fast-acting polymer glue and gradually extended the pipe toward the rift. The pipes were lightweight, tough, and designed to take pressure, but the joins had to be perfect. If he lost the fluid— there was no way the cycle would work.

His tension rose as his line of piping approached the rift. The heat of the wind was incredible. His stomach clenched with sudden nausea as a wave of power—like a low electrical current—rippled through him.

He could not get that image of the bird out of his mind, and the sound of its truncated call of pain as it struck the side of the rift.

Testing the weight of a section of piping, he tossed it through the opening. The glue and tools came next.

Now his turn.

At the threshold, the power of the rift surged into him. He felt pressure on his temples, as though his head was in a tightening vice. His vision clouded, then doubled. His stomach roiled with nausea. He fought disorientation and kept moving. A tingling spread through his limbs. God only knew what it was doing to his physiology.

Steeling himself, he took a running step and leapt through. As he landed, his right foot clipped the side of the rift. A searing agony flared through him. He landed hard and his body convulsed into a mass of tensed muscle. Then his mind uncurled, like an orange peel, and he spun away into brightness.

———

THE PLAIN WAS DIFFERENT. The tumbled rocks were gone, and in the distance, he saw a tall city of silver spires. Sleek craft flitted between the towers, while other huge craft—dwarfed by the distance— dropped toward the city from the sky.

'You can stay, Mac.'

He spun around.

Valerie was standing less than two feet away. She was strangely shadowed, despite the fact that they both stood under a noonday sun. He could smell her subtle perfume.

He took a step toward her, but she backed away and held up her hand to stop him.

'The others are all here,' she said, her shadowed head turning slightly toward the city in the distance and back.

'But you need to decide.'

'Val...' His voice was thick, hardly more than a croak.

———

MacPHERSON WOKE GASPING.

The air was humid—almost too thick to breathe—the sun above him merciless. He pushed himself up into a sitting position and checked his right foot. He expected to see it burnt, or singed, but it looked normal. He moved it experimentally, and discovering no ill-effects, got to his feet.

The rift seemed smaller on this side. Through it he could see the white snowfields, and the clearing where the ship lay. It seemed like such a small, pathetic thing. Behind the rift the ground rose, climbing to a series of high-topped plateaus in the distance that were thick with forest.

He was here. He really was here.

MacPherson walked out across the wide, rolling grasslands. With a better sense for the terrain, he now saw that he was in a long plain, with alternating savannah and open grassland. The trees were strange—more like giant cactus than Terran varieties. Vast herds of quadrupeds grazed in the far distance. It had been millennia since anything remotely like this had existed on Earth.

The heat beat down on him.

He walked back through the long, dry grass toward the rift and picked up a section of pipe. A heavy lethargy settled on him. Was there really a chance that his improvised heat cycle would work? One split seam and it would be over. Was there even enough fluid to close the circuit? And even if he could get one started, would the small waste-heat recovery turbines produce enough power to bring the radio to life? Would Kepler wait long enough to hear his message?

Through the rift he could already see snow falling again, slowly covering the clearing and his haphazard pile of thermal gear.

All he had to do was stay here.

The rift shivered, then contracted.

In the distance he heard a low roar, followed by a chorus of others that shook the air. The big herd, which had been grazing slowly, surged into a gallop. They were being chased by a group of seven huge animals with bright yellow hides and raised shoulders. As he watched one of the yellow predators leapt onto the back of a grazing animal at the margin of the pack and bore it to the ground. They wrestled furiously for a moment, then the predator fixed its huge jaws to the grazer's neck.

'Argh!' MacPherson's stomach clenched as blood splashed across the grass in a wild pattern.

The predators roared again. Abruptly the herd turned, angling up the slope toward him.

Adrenalin raced through him in a white flood.

He dropped down into the long grass, holding his breath as the herd raced past. He was conscious of the stale smell of his own sweat. The image of those huge jaws replayed itself in his mind. He closed his eyes and pushed himself down into the grass. Something like a beetle scuttled over his arm. Then a long, hairy caterpillar crawled onto his face, but he did not dare to move. One of the big predators came so close he could hear the grunt of its heavy breathing.

As soon as they were past, he pushed himself to his feet and dusted off the insects in a frenzy. The skin of his face burned where the caterpillar had crawled across it. He ran to the rift. It was closing fast.

'What the hell have I been doing?'

MacPherson gathered up the pipes, glue and tools, and set to work. He laid out the pipe, estimating by rough mental calculation how much length he would need to pick up enough heat to drive the turbine, compensating for the heat lost through the delivery pipe on the other side of the rift. Given X31's ambient temperature, outlet cooling would not be a problem. He tried to focus on the joins in the pipe, but his hands were shaking too much to apply the glue.

'Come on!'

The rift contracted. Through the narrowing fissure the shattered survey craft no longer looked pathetic. It was a beacon, a last link to a life that was rapidly slipping away.

He looked up at the hot sun above him and the open sky, scattered with clouds. He let out a long, slow breath.

He could do this.

MacPherson's hands steadied and he finished the pipe joins.

Head thumping, he faced the rift. He tossed anything useable through, then backed up, giving himself plenty of room.

'Yaaah!' He sprinted, then jumped, diving head-first.

He fell on powdered snow. The shock of the cold was unbelievable. He shook the snow from his thermals and tugged them on, movements frantic. He had to finish the job. For a moment he was brought up short by the sight of the proto-wildebeest. It was dead, already frozen into its last twisted shape.

Finally, he had the whole circuit completed. MacPherson made a quick estimate of how much fluid the circuit would need and then pumped it through the circuit by working the turbine manually. His arms ached with fatigue. He could feel himself moving slower and slower.

The iris was now only a few metres across.

He just needed to keep the fluid moving. Suddenly the manual crank was thrown out of his hands and a high-pitched whine filled the air. The hot fluid had hit the turbine chamber!

'Yes!'

He clambered up the upturned hull and lowered himself into the cabin. It was still dark, and he switched on a torch.

His stomach recoiled at the smell of blood and his eyes widened at the grizzly sight of the melted bodies. How could he have forgotten?

Keep moving.

He sat at the console, watching the dead panels. He could hear the high-pitched whine of the turbine driving harder as the components heated. Yet there was nothing.

MacPherson heard a sound above him, and his eyes were drawn inexorably to the flight monitor.

Val's head had thawed. Her expression had softened, and she looked down at him, almost sad as her head slipped slowly across the surface, turning toward him...

He squeezed his eyes shut. The temperature was plummeting, his bare skin already numb. He began to shiver. This was it. His last chance.

There was a soft tone from the console. His eyes snapped open. One by one, the ship's undamaged systems came back online. The turbine must have had to restore a certain amount of power to the depleted main batteries before it delivered power to the systems.

Illumination flared through the cabin as the overhead lights came on, and he froze at the sight of the carnage, revealed now in stunning clarity. He shook his head and focussed on the console, blocking out everything else.

He adjusted the radio and poured all the power into the transmitter.

'Kepler, this is Warrant Officer MacPherson, Survey Vessel JV3. Come in.'

He kept repeating the message.

Then like a miracle, he got his answer.

'We have you JV3. A rescue team is on the way.'

He slumped forward, weak and shivering, relieved beyond belief.

'We have you. A rescue team is en-route. Acknowledge.'

'Acknowledged,' he said.

Goodbye, Mac. Val's voice whispered in his head.

The light coming in through the hatch suddenly dimmed. The rift had closed. The little turbine sputtered and whirred to a stop. The warm sun had been sealed into the past. With some battery power remaining, he set the beacon to continuous transmission. Then he took some rations and climbed out of the craft, sealing the hatch.

MacPherson sat on the hull, waiting for the rescue craft, while Val and the rest of his crew slowly refroze inside their metal tomb.

His eyes were fixed on the spot, just above the ridge, where the rift had been, while inside him, something tore away.

END

ABOUT THE AUTHOR

Being able to escape into the realm of the imagination was handy growing up as the youngest in a family of eleven, and Chris continues his fantasy and SF writing habit from his home town of Brisbane.

His novels include *Warriors of the Blessed Realms* (2020), which blends urban fantasy and fantasy with elements of SF and horror, the hard-SF *The Tau Ceti Diversion* (2018) and his three-book heroic fantasy series the *Jakirian Cycle* (2013).

Chris is also an engineer, and blogs regularly about space science and exploration. He has a fourth-dan black belt in Moon Lee Tae Kwon Do and also enjoys movies and exploring narrow alleyways. Chris is very passionate about music, and loves singing and playing classical guitar. He has been short-listed for the Aurealis Awards twice, and has won the One Book, Many Brisbanes competition twice.

Website - www.chrismcmahon.net

18

MAKING MAGIC

ALLAN WALSH

Alcus stared at a note pinned to the notice board, buried among the shamble of paper, poking out behind the Room for Rent ad. The corners were furled, itching to roll shut, but the words sparkled, as if luring him towards it.

Do you create your own worlds?

Bring characters to life?

Create magic you want to be seen?

If the answer is yes, this may be the group for you.

This could be it. The writers' group he'd been looking for. But what if they didn't like his work? What if they laughed at him? He couldn't spend his whole life wondering. He had to grow a spine, face his fears, and get it done.

Alcus grabbed his notepad from his pocket and scribbled the address inside.

The days passed, Alcus counting them down, the way he used to at Christmas when he was a kid. That same feeling of excitement fluttering in his stomach just like it used to. When there were no more days to count, he found his way to the address in his notebook.

Room 1

The Old Library,
21 Orion Way,
Forest Hill.

He looked down at the writing on the page, then peered up at the building before him. Lichen crusted rocks loomed up above the entrance, as if their weight smothered and squeezed the tiny door into the wall. Alcus felt goosebumps creep up his neck.

This is silly, He shouldn't be here... But if he didn't go in, how would he know if his work was any good?

He grabbed the iron ring on the door, tugged it open and ducked inside. The doorway opened into a large entrance hall. Alcus strode past a wooden sign pointing to a room with an iron-studded door at the end of the hall. He paced back and forth outside the door, stopped and rubbed at his chin. Just go in Al, try it out. If you make a fool of yourself, just don't come back, he reasoned.

"Can I help you?" a voice said behind him.

He spun around. "Oh, um, er... "

A woman stood before him. Her shoulder-length, black hair and deep brown eyes complemented by the lush, velvet robe—complete with the designer logo—that flowed around her. She cocked an eyebrow. "Are you here for the group?"

Alcus stared at her like a rabbit that's caught sight of a fox. He swallowed. She was wearing medieval dress-up. What sort of writers' group is this?

"Have you come to show us the magic you've created, young man?"

Alcus snapped out of his daze. "Er, yes, you could say that."

"You're a little under-dressed, aren't you?"

Alcus looked down at his T-shirt and jeans.

"Never mind, it is your first time. I suppose we can overlook it this once. After all, it's always good to get some fresh blood in the group. I'm Belladora, the High Sorceress."

High Sorceress? "Um, I'm Alcus, pleasure to meet you."

"Well, don't just stand there, come on in," she said, opening the door wide.

He edged into the room. Ten chairs sat around a large table, an old tapestry dominating the wall behind. Images of sorcerers and sorceresses framed the edges, bordered with gold and silver thread that sparkled under the light. An open book was woven into its centre, 'Making Magic' embroidered on the first page in black thread.

Cool décor, he thought. A little old fashioned though.

"Please, make yourself comfortable. I can always conjure up another chair if we need it," Belladora said with a smile.

"Er, right... so, you gather every month then?" Alcus asked.

"We do. You'll find a vast array of knowledge and a variety of styles within this group. Which style do you dabble in?"

"Me? I'm still trying to find my style, that's why I'm here."

"Well, I'm sure you will learn a lesson or two from the group." She swept across the room with the grace of a movie star strutting across the red carpet. Gliding into her chair at the head of the table, she placed her hands gently upon her lap.

Belladora looked so young, Alcus thought as he studied her in their uncomfortable silence. She must be quite talented to be the so called 'high sorceress' of a group like this at her age.

A swooshing sound ebbed and flowed around the room. An ethereal blue carriage—shaped like a pumpkin, magical candle atop, pulsating with light—materialised before their eyes. It faded in and out of reality, before solidifying and coming to rest in the corner of the room.

Alcus gawped, slack-jawed. What the...?

Out stepped another young 'sorceress', her light-brown hair pulled tight against her head in a long-plaited ponytail. She gave Bella a wave.

Cosplay! That must be it—cosplay with illusions—to build atmosphere for the stories. Yes, that was it.

Bella smiled. "I see your love of making a fairy-tale entrance hasn't diminished, Krystocalli. Still, you've developed quite a modern twist to your style. I like it!"

"I aim to please, Bella. Awesome robe by the way!" the sorceress said, swinging the carriage door shut. The blue pumpkin dissipated, crashing to the floor in a wave of ocean spray that seeped away to nothing. Krystocalli crossed the room and climbed into her seat, pulling her feet up on the chair and hugging her knees. "And who is this?" she asked, looking over at Alcus.

"A guest, come to see what our gatherings are about. His name is Alcus."

"Oh, a guest. Wonderful, we have a hunger for some new magic in this group. Nice to meet you, Alcus."

Alcus nodded, a nervous smile stuck on his face. Why didn't he stay at home? This wasn't what he'd expected. But then, he didn't know what to expect. And he was here now. Maybe he should give them a chance. They were geeky, but they seemed nice enough.

"So, you ready for another interesting gathering, Krys?" Belladora asked. Krystocalli grinned—almost as big a grin as the Axolotl-like dragon face printed on her T-robe.

"To congregate around this bitter-sweet table of judgement? I sure am."

"Did I hear somebody say bitter-sweet?" a voice called out.

Krystocalli looked over to the doorway. "Oh, hi Tabitha!"

A third witch entered the room, sporting a mass of dark curls and a star-spangled superhero gown. "Hey." She gave a lazy wave. "You alright, Bella? You're looking a bit... off."

"I've been up all night reviewing this month's spell submissions. Don't worry though, I'll be fine."

"I can give you a potion for that. It'll make you sleep like the dead. You'll get rid of those rings under your eyes in no time," Tabitha said.

"Sleep like the dead, hmmm... I think I'll give that one a miss, thanks T."

The room slowly filled up as one by one the spell-weavers arrived, until seven seats were filled around the table.

Bella clicked her fingers and the door creaked, the stonework surrounding it swelling like a wave about to engulf an island. The stones spilled over the edges of the door, splashing across the wood, colliding in the middle in a crash of liquid rock. The ripples settled, leaving nothing but a solid wall behind them.

Alcus sat frozen, staring at the wall.

"Morning all, this month we are lucky enough to have a guest with us." Bella presented a hand towards him. "This is Alcus, and he has come to see how we do things." All eyes turned to look at him and he felt himself sink down in his chair. He really shouldn't be there. He wiped his sweaty palms on his trousers and forced himself to sit up straight.

"For the benefit of our guest I'd like you to introduce yourselves and then I will go through the rules." Bella paused for the introductions and then continued. "One spell to be cast by each of those nominated to submit..."

Alcus felt his stomach turn over as Bella rattled off the rules.

"Oh, and let's not forget, all newcomers must make a submission at their first gathering." An excited murmur went around the table.

"What! But... but, I can't cast spells. I'm just a writer," Alcus protested.

"If I had a potion for every time I'd heard that, I'd have my own apothecary by now," Mugita said, looking over at Alcus. "You need to stop listening to others telling you what you can't do and prove them wrong."

A murmur of agreement went around the table. Alcus sunk back down again. He thought he was going to be sick.

"Now, what have you all been up to since our last gathering?" Bella asked.

"I've had a short spell published in The Witch's Handbook," Krys said.

Another murmur went around the table as the group congratulated her.

"I've been studying for my Cert II in Necromancy," Genie said, tucking her short, black hair back beneath her floppy wizard's hat.

"Oh, have you raised a dead dragon yet?" Tabitha asked. "That is sooo scary!"

"Not yet, we do that next week."

"Any other updates...? No? Let's get started then," Bella said.

"Well, I'm ready to see some magic" Mugita, a stocky wizard, pulled his bone-covered necromancer notebook out from his backpack and placed it on the table.

"Me too," Megrisha said, rubbing her hands together, her huge smile lighting up the room, eyes wide with excitement behind her thick-rimmed glasses.

"Then let us begin," said Belladora. "Krys, you're timekeeper today. Everyone else, remember, two minutes per spell and two minutes each to give opinions. We have five submissions this month, so let's try to get through them quickly. First up is Megrisha. Time to rock your stuff girl."

Megrisha plunged her hand into her canvas bag—the one with the Wizard School print all over it—and pulled out her...

"Oh no, that's not my wand, that's the doo-dackie I got from HexPo," she muttered to herself, digging her hand back into the bag, her cheeks flushing red. "Ah, here it is." She pulled out a novelty quill wand. She waved the long, rainbow-coloured ostrich feather around in front of her face, her eyes twinkling as she flashed a wide grin. Her eyelids sagged and her wand wilted. A puff of smoke swirled from one bright colour to the next, sparkling with jewels, then a small caterpillar appeared on the table. Only it wasn't a caterpillar, it was a moustache. It wormed its way across the wooden tabletop, paused for just a moment and raised up on one end, twisting from side to side as though examining the faces around the table. It stopped.

"If that thing had eyes," Bella muttered, "I'd swear it was staring straight at me."

The moustache reared back, poised to strike, and leapt towards her. It somersaulted through the air like a small, hairy ninja, and stuck to her top lip.

BOOF! The moustache exploded into a fluffy beard: its hair sticking out as if a startled cat clung to Bella's face, covering the whole of her chin. Bella scratched at the hair. "Hmmm, soft but a little itchy," she murmured.

Krystocalli sniggered, Fergus barked a laugh, and then the entire room was laughing.

POP! The beard exploded again, throwing hair all over Bella's face—and fur balls around the room—giving her a look akin to the wolfman from the old black and white movies, only this wolfman was wearing a designer robe and lots of bling. Bella frowned and crossed her arms.

"I suppose you think this is funny," she said, giving Megrisha the evil eye. The laughter only grew louder.

"You look like... Big Foot's... rich aunt," Tabitha said between snorts of laughter, tears streaming down her face.

SNAP! Sparks flew out of the offending fur, leaving red embers sizzling in their wake. Wisps of purple smoke twirled upwards, scenting the air with a hint of Turkish delight.

WHOOSH! The hair flared up in a flash of pink flame. Bella's eyes sprung wide open.

"Oooh!" A chorus of admiration echoed around the room. Bella raised a brow. Everyone stared back, enormous smiles plastered across their faces. Bella's dark rings were gone. Her milky-white skin glowed. Long, black lashes framed her eyes: eyes that sparkled beneath perfectly formed eyebrows. She sat with shoulders back and chin up, her silky hair flowing in a gentle breeze that teased her long, dark tresses.

Genie looked up from the other side of the table, parchment in one hand, quill in the other; its blunt tip glowing red and smoking. She dabbed the end to her tongue. It sizzled, breaking the silence.

"Sorry, I'm a fast writer," she said with a shrug.

"So, what did you think?" Megrisha asked.

Genie started going through her notes in depth, and the room hushed as everyone listened.

"HAROOGAH!" bellowed an old cow horn.

Alcus almost leapt out of his seat.

"Times up Genie!" Krys said.

"I only have one more thing to say—Duuude!" Megrisha grinned as Genie slid her notes across the table.

"What did you think, Alcus?" Bella asked.

"It was like... magic... the most amazing magic," he said.

"Naturally. That's what we strive for." She looked around the group. "Now, does anyone have anything that wasn't covered by Genie's notes?"

The room was silent.

Alcus tugged at the collar of his T-shirt, looking about the room. This couldn't be happening. They were doing real magic! He'd only written a story. He needed to get out of here. If only there was a door.

"Who's next?" Mugita asked.

"That would be, Krystocalli," Bella replied.

"Morning all." Everyone looked over to a hole in the wall where the door used to be.

Alcus' eyes lit up and he prepared to stand up. A wizard ambled through the opening, bricks rolling across the hole, closing the gap behind him. Alcus sagged back in his chair. The wizard grinned, his bright blond hair framing his bespectacled face. "Sorry I'm late."

"You're always late, Granga, we've come to expect it." Belladora replied. "Now, where were we? Ah yes, Krystocalli."

"You've got a tough act to follow, Krys," Fergus said.

"Well then, I guess I should get on with it," Krys said, picking up her replica Dr What phonic-toothbrush wand from the table. She held it out in front of her and the end of the chrome stick began to flicker green. Krystocalli gave it a whack and the flicker stopped, the light growing into a bright glow. She pressed a button on the grip and the Dr What theme pumped out through a small speaker in the base of the wand.

Everyone's eyes flicked to Krys. She grinned, her eyebrows raising as if to say 'I know, cool right?' Her skin began to wrinkle, her hair greying at the tips; she looked five years older in the blink of an eye. The centre of the massive table started to swirl, slowly at first, then faster and faster, until the swirl was a smoky circle. She pressed the button on the grip again and a pulse of light beamed out over the swirl, turning into a mini disco of laser lights and smoke machines. The circle spiralled down, twisting into the tabletop, creating a whirlpool of smouldering wood. The glowing embers dulled as they burned out and the swirling slowed to a stop, leaving a blackened tunnel descending through the middle of the table. The sorcerers and sorceresses stood and peered inside. There was nothing but darkness in there... and the sound of snoring.

"Wakey, wakey!" Krys shouted down the hole.

A grumble rose through the charred tube.

"Buuuurrp." A ring of black smoke puffed out of the tunnel, billowing upwards, rolling over and over. It slowed its ascent and hung in the air for a moment, growing wider, then sank slowly. As the cloud wafted towards the tabletop, wisps of smoke curled upwards, creating pointy rooftops. Round spires formed beneath them; towers unravelled from top to bottom. Spire to parapet, wall to drawbridge; a miniature castle in all its glory emerged from the smoke. The wisps coalesced together, becoming opaque, then solid.

The castle rose around the hole in the table like a crown on a monarch's head—rigid with an air of majesty. A screech pierced the silence that had fallen on the room. A flash of black streaked out of the hole, flying high above the castle. It swooped around the towers and plummeted towards the walls, breathing a stream of fire across the parapet as it passed. The black shape spread its wings, soared up above the towers, and turned into a terrifying black dragon—about the size of a hamster. It leered at the castle, bobbing up and down as it flapped its wings, suspending itself in the air.

"Awww, he's a cute little fella isn't he," Fergus said.

The dragon looked at him, its wings folding inwards as it fell into a dive, plunging towards Fergus, spitting its fiery rage. Fergus' eyes bulged as the flames rolled into his beard. A fireball swept across his chin, singed hair left smouldering, filling the air with a pungent smell. Wisps of black smoke wafted from his soot-smudged face.

Fergus glared at Krys.

"Oops, maybe it needs a little work," she said. A wave of her toothbrush wand and the castle erupted in a cloud of white mist, fading away to nothing. The dragon shrank with incredible speed, reduced to a fly in an instant. It buzzed away, down the hole in the table, and the wood creaked back together, sealing the hole behind it.

"Sorry guys, it worked better than that in my head."

"Well, I thought it was great," Genie said. "I can't wait to see the rest of it when you've worked it all out."

"Um, I liked it too," Granga added, "but the castle looked a little too new for me. It had very crisp, clean lines. I'd like to see some broken parapets, weathered stones and maybe a bit of moss clinging to the rocks. I think it would look more authentic."

"Excellent advice, thanks Granga," Krystocalli replied. "And what did you think, Megrisha?"

"It had smoke, it had fire, and it had a dragon," Megrisha said. "What more could you ask for?"

"My beard back for starters," Fergus grumbled.

"Oh, sorry." Krys snapped her fingers and Fergus' head was sucked into his shoulders in a rapid, crumpling implosion. Another snap and his head popped back, fully bearded.

"Thank you... I think." Fergus ran his fingers through his new whiskers, the facial hair pruned and waxed to pristine condition.

"You have to admit though, Fergus, it was good, wasn't it? And did I mention it had a dragon?" Megrisha said.

"It could do with a little work. Not sure if I could have done better, but anyway, I—I'm up next..." Fergus mumbled, looking up over the non-existent glasses on the end of his nose.

"Go ahead then Fergus," Bella said.

Fergus unravelled an ancient-looking scroll and muttered some words. Black bags formed under his eyes and his face became pale and drawn; the effects of the spell reflecting the long hours he'd spent preparing the scroll. Darkness descended on the room and it rumbled with vibrations. Grit fell from above, moments before a pile of rubble crashed from the ceiling, belching a cloud of dust. Cracks tore through the stonework, ripping jagged gashes up walls and through the remnants of the ceiling. The corner of the room heaved and grated as it slid away, tumbling two stories to the ground below; its thunderous crash sent tremors through the floor. Ash floated down through the gaping void. Stone giants beyond—that had once formed castle towers—stood in ruin, black and scarred with gaping holes torn through them. An icy wind howled through the room.

It's not real, it's not real, Alcus tried to convince himself. He glanced at Bella and saw her rub the goosebumps that had risen on her arms.

A scratching noise came from a pile of rubble on the floor. Small pieces of broken rock pushed up from the centre and tumbled down the heap of shattered stone, clattering as they bounced off the hard edges. They left a small hole at the top of the mound. Up popped two small antennae. They twitched and paused, twitched and paused. Out scurried a large cockroach. It scampered across the rubble, back and forth, tottering on the edge of a slab of debris. It moved to the centre of the slab and turned around in a circle. Slow at first, then faster, into a spin. It stopped... and pushed up its back legs, raising its rear end.

'Pffft...'

A puff of dust swept across the floor.

"Phwoar... that stinks!" Megrisha waved her hand in front of her nose.

There was a flash of blinding light and everyone shielded their eyes. The brightness faded; the room and Fergus had returned to normal.

"Wow, Fergus. That was awesome!" Mugita said.

Fergus sat looking down at the table, his eyes betraying the smug grin hidden beneath his thick, black beard.

"Right, which way do you want to go?" Belladora asked Fergus.

"Right? Not right, left," he replied.

"Huh? Oh, that was a funny, got it. Left it is then. You're up T," Belladora said as everyone looked across the table at Tabitha.

"Dude! You nearly shook the room apart for real. And with all that dust, I could hardly see what was going on through that massive cloud of crap. You need to tone it down, man." Tabitha stared at Fergus, who continued to look at the table. She flicked to her notes and read some of the finer points of spell crafting aloud, going through the basics, and things that Fergus should know by now. She paused for breath. "The cracks were good, and the crumbling plaster, but the ceiling falling in was a bit cliché. It was more disaster movie than post-apocalypse and I know that's what you were going for. The way you—"

"HAROOGAH!" bellowed the cow horn.

Alcus jumped... again.

"Time's up, T," Bella said, "but, yeah, we'll let you finish."

"As I was saying, the way you made the walls turn grey was great, but you should read Nifty Shades—The Way to Grey by Courtney the Conjurer. She has some superb tips on how to get an amazing result with a shabby, unpolished look. Anyway, much better than last time, and the ruined city in the background, that was a touch of cool, man."

"Thanks, T," Fergus said.

"Mugita, anything to add?" Krys asked, picking up the cow horn. She twisted back the shadow on the sundial timer with her pinkie finger and placed the bovine bugle on the table.

"Like I said, Fergus. That was awesome, and nice touch with the farting cockroach. The only thing I have to add is thanks for letting me see your spell."

Each spell-weaver gave their thoughts, and when they were done Bella turned to face Fergus.

"Right of reply, Fergus?" she asked.

"Well, I spent hours on that spell. I knew it wasn't quite right, but I couldn't put my finger on why. I have some good ideas now though, so I'll spend a bit more time tweaking things and see if I can polish it up a little."

Alcus wiped his brow; it was hot and sticky with sweat. What should he do? He was in so much trouble! What about when it got to his turn?

"Right then, Genie, put down your quill and show us what you've been working on since our last gathering."

"Oh, my turn, okay then," Genie said. She took a deep breath and exhaled. Veins rose on her arms, slow and steady: thick blue veins bulging as though they were being vacuum-packed under her skin. Her body trembled and she clicked her fingers.

A puff of black smoke enveloped her hand. It swirled up in a rage of black and grey, revealing a pale wand, carved into a long, skeletal finger; a dark, pointy fingernail at its tip.

"Ahem," Genie said, clearing her throat. She turned the bony stick in a circle. It appeared to move in slow motion, blurring the images behind as its tip cut through the air. Colour leaked out of the table, the chairs, clothing, and the spell-weavers themselves, draining the room to a dull grey. Fergus shrank down into his chair, as did Megrisha and Krystocalli, followed by Bella and Mugita. One by one, they cowered in the dense gloom that bore down on them—except Tabitha. A huge grin spread across her face, stretching from ear to ear; her eyebrows arched high, eyes wild with excitement. A crash thumped up through the table as something struck it from beneath, spell books and wands jumping an inch from the surface and clattering back down. The centre of the table creaked as it bulged, the wood warping up like an angry boil. A jagged line ripped its way across the peak, splinters exploding into the air as a gnarly hand burst through the surface. Tabitha leaned in closer, gazing at the arm. She lurched back as it jolted towards her, then it retracted back into the hole.

Everything went silent, all eyes fixed on the aperture. They waited... nothing happened. Alcus trembled in his seat as the sorcerers leaned in closer, peering into the hole, trying to get a glimpse of what was down there.

"Aargh..." gargled a rough voice through the shattered wood, dark blood-splatter, spitting from the cavity. Those that didn't jump out their skin recoiled as fetid breath filled the air with the smell of decay.

Alcus squeezed his eyes shut. Please don't let me die, please don't let me die. He repeated the mantra over and over in his head. Another bang thumped the table from below. His eyes sprung open —the crown of a gruesome head had lodged itself in the hole. It forced its way up through the breach, flesh tearing on the ragged edges of the broken timber, stripping flesh to the blood-stained bone. Bella clapped her hand over her eyes, then opened her fingers a notch and peeked through the gap. The head writhed and twisted, its jaw gnashing, rancid teeth snapping as it strained towards Granga's living flesh. The table creaked and moaned, timber bowing outwards as the creature pushed harder. An ear-splitting crack pierced the air, shards of wood bursting across the room as the undead body smashed through the tabletop.

"Brains..." It lurched forward, clutching at Granga. The legs of his chair screeched across the floor as he pushed himself back from the table. Confined within the hole, the creature hit the rim, jerked downwards, slammed against the wooden surface, and liquefied into a pool of blackened blood.

Alcus covered his mouth, his cheeks inflating like a bullfrog's throat, but somehow he kept his breakfast down.

The gory mess bubbled on the wooden surface and seemed to get sucked away, absorbing into the table. Tendrils grew out from the broken wood, weaving and twining around each other, knitting the timber together once more. Colour bled back into the room, saturating everything within... except Krystocalli. She was as white as a geisha. Belladora on the other hand, had turned a shade of green.

"Woo-hoo!" Tabitha roared, clapping furiously. Everyone else was silent, mouths slack as they stared at Genie.

"That was disgusting," Bella muttered.

"But so awesome!" Tabitha added.

"That's easy for you to say, it wasn't trying to eat you," Granga righted his chair and sat a wary distance from the table.

"Gross. Frickin' scary and very well done, but still gross," Mugita said.

"So, who's next?" Fergus asked."

They worked their way around the table, one by one, analysing the spell. What was great about it, what could be improved and what suggestions they had that might help.

HAROOGAH! The sound signalled an end to the last of the feedback.

Krys responded to the comments, and when she was done, all eyes turned on Alcus.

"Now we come to lucky last," Bella said.

Alcus stared at her for a moment... and unceremoniously threw up all over the table.

"Ewww." The chorus travelled through the room. Alcus felt his cheeks burning. He wiped his lips, frowning at the acrid taste in his mouth.

"Um, sorry..." he spluttered.

"Don't worry Alcus, we were all nervous the first time," Bella said. She waved her arm across the tabletop and small green shoots sprouted from the mess. Flowers burst from the shoots, covering the puddle—diced carrots and all. The flowers melted away, leaving a floral bouquet hovering in the air. "Would you like to try again?"

"I'm afraid my skills are no match for all of yours," he stammered. "I haven't got a wand and I can't cast spells." Gasps sounded out from around the group. Alcus could feel their stares burning into him. "But I've written a story."

"A story? That's very unorthodox," Bella said. "Well, let's hear it then."

Alcus fumbled his notebook open. His voice quivered as he began to read and he stopped to clear his throat. He could do this. He didn't need special powers to make magic. He took a deep breath and started again.

"Once upon a time..."

The silence grew as he read his story. Alcus sank deeper and deeper into the words he had written, the images they created forming in his mind. The sound of fidgeting faded away as he continued to read. He didn't dare look up, but forced himself to go on.

"The—the end." Alcus closed his notebook. He felt like a deaf man at a funeral; there wasn't a sound. His eyes flicked up. Everyone was peering into the recess above the table. Alcus raised his head. Floating in the air was the world he had imagined in his head. A tingle rushed across his skin as he gaped at the vision before him.

Wow! How? Did I? No...

His eyes met Belladora's. She gazed at him with a thoughtful look on her face. He swallowed.

"Now that's real magic," Bella announced. The group arose from their chairs and broke into applause.

Alcus breathed out a sigh and grinned.

Bella raised her hands and the noise died down. Alcus noticed once again how smooth and pale her skin was, and the silky sheen to her hair. She really was very young to be a high sorceress.

"Well, you might not know how to cast spells, Alcus, but you certainly have magic inside of you," Bella said. The group edged forwards with wolfish smiles. "Like I said, it's always good to get fresh blood."

END

About the Author

Allan Walsh is a writer and artist, born in sun-scorched Australia and raised in the grungy suburbs of West London. He is a keen martial arts fan, lover of fantasy, and a movie buff. Allan has been influenced by cult Asian film directors such as Jacki Chan and Stephen Chow, spec-fiction novelists the like of Joe Abercrombie and graphic novelists such as Wendy and Richard Pini. Allan currently resides in Brisbane, where he enjoys creating new worlds through his writing.

Find him here:

Website - https://allanwalshauthor.com/

Facebook - @AllanWalshAuthor

GoodReads - Allan Walsh

19

THE BANDERSHIN

JAKE CORVUS

"There's a bandershin in the dam behind the pump house," Simon said, watching Beka from the corner of his eye.

"What's a bandershin?" she asked. She was tall and gingery, with lots of freckles and masses of flame-red curls, all frizzy and wild. She was taller than him, even when he stood on tiptoes, which wasn't fair because he was two months older than her.

"A monster," Simon told her earnestly.

"I don't believe in those."

They were sitting on the log behind the chicken pen, breathing in the thick-slush-shit smell with the chickens pecking their shirts and the back of their sneakers through the wire. The feed bucket was at Simon's feet, empty of scraps but holding a dozen brown eggs, some ass-fresh, some gritty with poop.

"It's true," Simon said, stripping the seeds off a grass stalk, then brushing them off his jeans. "I've seen it plenty of times."

"Well, I never have."

"You don't come down here when it's raining. Or at night."

The shed, little more than a lean-to of wooden poles and rusty corrugated iron, housed the water pump and the district's redback spider population. At all the worst times, Simon's mother would send him down the length of the paddock with the jerry can to start the pump, sending the boggy black water chugging up the pipes to the farmhouse.

"What's it look like then?" she asked, eyeing the lily pads and photo-still water.

"It's hard to see at first," Simon confessed. "It's like mud and waterweeds, just kind of oozing up the bank, but it's got eyes and you know it's alive. If you look hard, you can see it for what it is, with lots of legs and fingers and bits, lying on the bank like a crocodile. It's waiting for someone to get close. They'd never find you if it dragged you in there, down in the mud."

Beka shuddered despite herself. "I still don't believe you."

"Mr Floyd's dog went missing, didn't it?"

"Not here," she scoffed. "It probably ran out on the highway."

"Bandershin got it."

"I wish it would get John then."

Beka's new stepfather rolled his own cigarettes and was allergic to Beka's cat. Or he had been. Skittles had vanished two weeks after John moved his things in. Beka's mother said he was just hiding in the reserve behind the dam somewhere, but Beka said John had put him in a sack and backed over him in the ute.

"John's okay," Simon said.

Beka lifted up her shirt and showed Simon fat, wine-coloured stripes on her back and sides. They went down past the waist of her shorts. To the left of her spine, the skin was black in the shape of a buckle.

Simon eyed the bruises. Then he pulled up another stalk of grass.

"I bet if you told the principal, they'd send him to jail."

"Can't," Beka said matter-of-factly, dropping her shirt. "Mum can't afford the house. If John goes, she said we'd have to live in the car."

"But he'd have to sleep in a cell."

"Probably more comfortable than the damn car... 'Sides, I don't get the worst of it. You should see the shiner on my mum. She looks like a panda bear."

At the top of the hill the farmhouse door banged. Simon looked over his shoulder, through the chicken wire, to see his mother wheeling herself onto the porch. She stopped her wheelchair at the top of the ramp, scanning the paddock, but couldn't see him and Beka as easily as they could see her.

"Simon!" she yelled. "Where are those eggs?"

"Coming!" Simon called back. He scrambled to his feet and scooped up the bucket and eggs. "I gotta go in. You want some?"

He gestured to the eggs.

"Nah. See you in school."

Simon nodded, hiking back up the hill. Next door, he could see Beka's mum through the kitchen window, making dinner. Her face was purple in the yellowy kitchen light. John was on the porch with a cigarette in his hand, and he waved at Simon in greeting. Simon waved back.

When he got to the porch and handed his mother the eggs, there was no sign of Beka. It was getting dark now, but she wasn't crossing the boundary into her own yard. She wasn't by the chicken pen either. The only way she could have gone was down the hill, into the trees at the edge of the reserve.

Simon waited for his mother to wheel in past him, then stepped inside and locked the screen door.

―――――

SIMON LISTENED to the rain clattering against the tin roof like a platoon of drummers. His room was ill-lit; the glow from the toilet cast an orange triangle across the threshold of Simon's door. Schoolbooks and his backpack made familiar shapes on his desk, and clean and dirty clothes deformed his chair.

The house was quiet. There was no sound of his mother rousing, no squeak of her wheelchair's wheels on the polished wooden floor. But he knew something had woken him. Some sound. Some sense that something wasn't right.

He sat up, looking toward the window. The rain beat against the glass in glossy streaks, obscuring the yard from view. Simon tucked his knees up to his chest, watching the black windowpane for a long moment before he crawled down the bed.

It was there, in the yard. The bandershin. Simon pushed up the window frame, feeling the rain blast in against his neck and pyjama shirt, and peered out into the night.

At first it looked like nothing, like a bit of sheet, sodden and tangled. Or maybe a nest of fallen branches, their leaves slick with rain and reflecting the dim light in flickering shards of silver.

It was only when the sky lit up, purple-blue and white, that Simon could see the flat, spiderlike limbs and long, thin body. Jointed, bony fingers wriggled all over it, like little antennae— cracking back and forth with arthritis, beckoning, sensing the air and burrowing into the sodden dirt. Its eyes were a hectic white in the flash: startled possum headlights that burned out the instant the lightning faded.

Thunder rolled across the house like a jet plane. The bandershin was looking at the window. Looking at Simon. Slithering across the yard like an eel with its many multi-jointed fingers. The house was on stumps, but the bandershin could mount the ramp by the door, just as easily as his mother's wheelchair. Then what? He didn't think it could reach the doorhandle. But it could slither under the house and lie in the dirt under him as he lay in bed, looking up at the floorboards, fingers wriggling.

When the lightning flashed again, the bandershin had crawled another foot closer. Its fingers wriggled in stark hysteria. It knew he was looking.

He slid the window closed. His pyjama shirt was soaked through now, his hair sodden with the storm.

He slid back across the bed, slipping his toes under the covers, but sitting up with his back against the headboard and his arms around his knees. He waited for dawn.

———

THE BELLOW MADE Simon drop his toast soldier on the floor and in his haste to grab it again, he bumped the table, sending his eggs clattering off their egg cups and spilling their yolk across the plate.

"What in God's good name was—" his mother started to say, but the screen door banged open before she could finish.

Beka had her hand over her mouth and nose, blood fanning across her polo shirt from the collar down. Her cheeks were streaked with tears, but her green eyes were burning and outraged. She skidded around the table, catching herself on Simon's chair and leaving bloody handprints.

The windows shook as John burst through the door after her. He was red-faced, fists balled, and just as angry as a bull. He made to go at Beka, but Simon's mother cut him off bodily with her wheelchair. She had to look up to see him. One more step and he'd have kicked her wheel, but she was fearlessly cold.

"Get out of my house," she said.

"Get over here!" John snarled at Beka. She shook her head vehemently, still gripping the back of Simon's chair.

"You get out of my house, Parkson!" Simon's mother snapped. "Or Sergeant Davis will drag you out and I daresay he won't like the look of that girl."

He snarled at her. "Mind your own business. I'll raise my daughter how I like."

"You get out right now! Simon, get the phone!"

Simon was on his feet and already had his hand on the receiver when John stepped back out the door.

"You'll hear about this," John said. Simon's mother slammed the door in his wake and turned the lock. They could hear him swearing and yelling threats all the way across the yard.

Simon handed Beka a tea towel, and she pressed it to her nose. It turned red right away.

"He'll be ready to shit when my mother gets home," Beka said through the cloth.

"She made her bed," Simon's mother said. "You eaten?"

"Not hungry."

"Go and watch TV then. Simon, you wash the dishes when you're done eating, then you can watch too."

That was all that was said about it. Beka slept on the couch that night, but in the morning she'd gone home again.

———

SIMON TRUDGED UP THE DRIVEWAY. The sticky heat of summer dampened everything. The ground was still clogged with puddles from the rain, but right now the sun was shining and the rising humidity threatened another shower later in the day.

He was looking at the ground, and if it hadn't been for the clump-clump of boots, he might not have seen John stomping across the driveway from Simon's house back to his own. He looked pleased with himself.

Simon's gaze drifted to the kitchen door beyond the ramp, and he saw it was open and hanging awkwardly on the hinges. Simon hiked his backpack up and ran. His books hit his back through the bag as he sprinted. He thought about dropping it, but if the rain came and the books were ruined, he'd have hell to pay.

He pounded up the ramp, then froze in the open doorway. His mother was in the middle of the room, where the table used to be, with her head in her hands. The table was overturned against the wall and tangled with two of the chairs. Plates and cups lay smashed, scattered across the sink and intermingling with the glass from the broken kitchen window. His mother's orchid was on its side—the delicate plant crushed—and the dirt spread from the counter all the way into the hall.

"Mum?" Simon ventured in, his mother's stillness terrifying him.

She startled. When she looked up, he saw her cheek was puffy and beginning to bruise. Worse still, one eye was bloodshot—so red it looked like it was full of blood. The bottom fell out of Simon's belly and he was sure it was flopping around, somewhere near the floor. He felt sick and angry and scared, all at once.

"Go to your room," she snapped. She sounded furious, but he knew it wasn't real. He knew she just didn't want him to see.

"Mum—"

"Now!"

He stepped past her and down the hall, not because he was afraid of her wrath, but because he didn't want to upset her more. He sat in his room, waiting for the sound of the police car in the driveway, but it never came. There was only the tinkling of glass as his mother swept up the mess. It would be hard in her wheelchair. She would manage, though. She had old bits of broom handle taped on all the dustpans, so she could reach the floor and hard-to-get places.

Simon came out when it got dark and, wordlessly, he taped cardboard over the shattered window. He got a sliver of glass in his palm, big enough to draw a trickle of blood. Simon picked it out with a fork, then ran his hand under the tap in the sink.

Down the hill, through the screen door, he could see something long and oozing hoisting itself out of the dam.

———

It was Saturday. Beka had not been at school since she had run to Simon's house, but he had seen her through the window on Friday in her room. She'd been reading, but when she had seen Simon, she had closed the curtains.

Simon's mother had gone to spend the day with Aunt Marie. She had told Simon he could come, that he could walk from his aunt's down to the corner store and get ice-cream and hot chips, but he'd refused. Beka's mother had gone out, too. At least, her car wasn't in the garage. Maybe she'd taken Beka because there was no sign of her. No sound from the house. Just John, in his shed, pounding on something metal.

In the north, dark clouds massed, like a wall of night. Sometimes Simon saw flashes of lightning, though the thunder that rolled across the mountains was dull and distant. Overhead, the sun was merciless, searing everything like a godly grill-oven.

Simon trudged up the hill with the day's eggs in the feed bucket. Seven in total, all dark brown and speckled. He was starting up the ramp when John emerged from the shed. He was just wearing faded navy-blue shorts. His tanned back was gritty with dirt, and slick with layer on layer of sweat.

John was wiping his filthy hands on a tea towel, muttering to himself and staring off into the distance, deep in thought. He paused a moment too long in the driveway, and before Simon could even think about it, he'd picked up one of the speckled brown eggs and pegged at John.

It hit John's ear and splattered; the yolk wrapping around his face like a visor. He was so shocked, for a moment he just stood there, wiping away the egg and looking baffled.

Anger boiled up in Simon so hard and fast he choked. Another egg followed the first, then another. Shoulder, then hip. Simon's fourth egg missed completely, and by then John was coming to his senses.

He bellowed. That same animal roar he had charged after Beka with. In an instant, he was barrelling across the yard at Simon, coated in egg and as red as a boiled lobster.

Simon bolted, not into the house, but down the paddock. Past the chook pen, past the pump house. The dam was deep enough to swim in, almost sixty feet across, but years of storms had left a tangle of old trees and branches on the bottom. On the surface, it was packed with lilies and duckweed. At the edge of the paddock, where the reserve began, the plants were dense. They pushed through the fence, making the bank impassable.

Simon smacked into the water, struggling through the mud, fumbling his way over the huge old trunks hidden under the surface.

The bandershin. It was in here somewhere. Simon just had to get ahead of it. He had to get to the other side before it could grab him and then John would be caught, dragged down like Mr Floyd's dog. No one would ever see him again.

John floundered into the water after him.

"Come here, you little shit. I'll do you like your cripple mum."

The insults rolled out like spit, but cut off with a shout as John fell over the first unseen branch in the mud. He came up swearing and roaring. He fumbled through the water, hauled a branch out of the way and kept coming. Simon had wasted too much time gawking and now John was wading through the waterweeds, practically on top of him.

Simon tried to stumble onward, his feet stuck deep in the mud. His shoes popped off and he stumbled forward toward the open water, further from the safety of the reserve on the far side. Something lashed his leg, a branch or... claws?

John bellowed suddenly in pain and fury. Simon twisted around and saw John tugging his leg, trying to shove something away under the water. The bandershin? A log? Whatever it was, John was working himself free. A few more feet and he would be on Simon.

Simon floundered through the silt, grasping his way along the bottom. He just had to keep John still long enough for the bandershin to do what it did. Another moment, or two, then it would be over.

The branch Simon hefted out of the mud was as long as he was, and heavy with mud and water. He raised it high and swung as hard as he could. The branch connected with a dense, meaty thump that jarred all the way down Simon's arms.

John was still upright, but the blow had struck his temple. His head was bowed in a funny way. A trickle of blood was coming out of his eye.

He slumped down, leg twisted awkwardly under his sagging body, then toppled into the water.

Simon dropped the branch and scrambled back toward the pump house, away from the bandershin, away from the mud and the water and the blood. Away from John. He dragged himself up the bank and then collapsed, the pain searing up his lacerated calf. He was panting and wet; blood blossomed in the muck on his leg, running down his ankle and vanishing into the grass.

He sat on the bank watching the billowing clouds of black mud sully the water. There was no movement now. No sound. No sign of John at all.

It took a long moment for him to realise there was something with him: something in the grass at the edge of the trees, looking down to the dam with the same passive curiosity.

Skittles blinked huge green eyes at Simon, then licked one ginger paw as if to say he was not scared, or impressed, at all. He leapt neatly over the last of the long grass, swaggering between the weeds and fruit trees toward Beka's house, his tail hooked to the left like a question mark.

At the bottom of the paddock, the surface of the dam was as still as a photo.

END

ABOUT THE AUTHOR

Jake Corvus is a prolific writer living on the Sunshine Coast, in Australia. While born in 1985, he is often mistaken for a teenager. He writes sci fi & fantasy, with a queer and inclusive bend. He watches too many horror movies to have any self-respect, and lives with an array of rescue animals, including shrimp, cats, dogs, guinea pigs and his sons. Jake's favourite dinosaur is the parasaurolophus.

Please visit his website to sign up to the newsletter and read the infamous true-life chicken story:

www.traditionalevolution.com

20

THE LAST CHANGE, MAYBE

EARL LIVINGS

Sam's Place was gritty and huge with smoke, laughter, music. There was a sense of sheer potential, of a moment that would snatch away all meaning and give you bare fact, or give you bareness, leaving you to decide what was fact, what was fancy, what was the Möbius strip of your imagination. The bar was all there was at that moment and, at any moment, an ordinary man would come out from the back rooms, a smile on his face and his wallet empty of a few dollars, followed by the Tender Lady a minute later. Just like every other time of the Change.

This time it started with one cigarette. To be more precise, with the ash of one cigarette.

D'MAGDA CAME out from the back and went straight to the bar. She ran the tip of her right forefinger—its red nail painted with a black rose—down Walter's cheek, interrupting his exhalation of the helix smoke ring. She reached for the tumbler of whiskey Sam set out for her and drained it.

We all watched Walter as he set up a second helix. It collided with the first and both dissolved.

"Blast!" He'd got the spin directions wrong again.

"Hi, sweetie," D'Magda said.

"Hi." He tried another helix.

She took his chin with her left hand, turned it towards her, and kissed him, her tongue licking the underside of his top lip.

"Why did you do that?"

"I always do. You like it."

"Well, not now. I'm busy."

"But..."

"Didn't you hear me?"

"Yes, but..."

"We're not soppy lovers like Antonio and Rosa, so stop it."

"But I always kiss you after."

He turned, his shoulder knocking her off-balance. "Leave me alone." He took another drag and watched the smoke curl.

D'Magda stared at him, mouth opening and shutting like a door on a subway train. Her face was the colour and texture of a sheet of paper after it had been in dry ice. She moved to Bill's booth, sat opposite him, and put her head in her hands.

"He's never done that to me before. Never."

Bill looked up from the scribbles and crossings out in his notebook and screwed the top back on his fountain pen. He had been at Sam's a long time. We all had. "I know."

Her sobs were uncontrollable. Bill peered around to the corner booth for help, but only found a faint bouquet of wild flowers and a gold ring on the tabletop. He joined D'Magda and put his arm around her. She buried her face in his shoulder. Although he felt like a rubber sponge that had been left out of the sink so long it had folded hard into itself, he tried to relax and somehow soak away her distress.

"Bloody hell!"

We looked at Walter. He was staring at his hand. D'Magda stopped crying.

"It's gone."

"What do you mean?" Sam lifted a tray of glasses out of the dish-washer, a recent acquisition.

"Look. This never happens to me."

There was a cigarette butt between his fingers and ash on the floor.

"That's impossible," said Sam. "That's like me running out of beer..." His eyes glazed over as he tried to latch onto a vague memory of building a still out the back and serving alcohol in cups.

Bill dragged Walter over to his table. The man turned to D'Magda and tried to speak. Shook his head.

"Something not right here," Bill said, then felt stupid saying it. Things hadn't been quite right for a long time. He couldn't pin down the source of the feeling, except he realised he'd been staring at the same words on the page for so long that now they seemed to mean nothing at all, and he couldn't remember doing anything else.

Walter twisted his face from D'Magda's hand. "Leave me alone."

Again that sheen from dry ice.

"She's only trying to be nice," Bill said.

Walter closed his eyes. "I can't help it."

A commotion at the bar. "Leave me be, you pernicious son of the devil."

"Come on, Father. Have a drink wid me."

"I come in for donations and this is what I get?"

"Just a weeny one." Bakkis indicated with his thumb and forefinger. "Won't hurt you."

Bakkis was no drunker than usual, but he had never accosted Father Saul like that before. It was almost laughable, except no one was even giggling, least of all Leigh. She pulled the drunk from the bar and marched him towards the door. "Time to go." Then she hesitated, as if she'd never done this to him before.

That was all Bakkis needed. He wrenched himself away and moved back towards the bar. When she spun him around, there was a knife in his hand. A blur of movement and Bakkis ended up slumped against the wall. The knife was nowhere to be seen.

"He'll be okay." Leigh resumed her post.

Sam dashed out and, along with the rest of us, helped Bakkis to a chair.

"That was weird," Walter said.

"No weirder than you the last few minutes." Her hands clasped on the table before her, D'Magda's eyes were full of concern.

Bill looked at them both. "This is serious enough for the Teacher."

We gaped at him. The Teacher was the only one amongst us who had not yet gained a personal name. No one had visited him in living memory. One only did so in emergencies, say, if the Dark Man appeared, though he had only ever been a rumour.

"Are you sure?" D'Magda said.

"Yes. Things aren't right. He'll know." Bill didn't add, I hope. He didn't mention the Dark Man either.

We all shivered, as if he'd said it anyway.

We waited at the front door while Walter rang for transport. Bakkis was apologising to Father Saul, with Leigh watching. It seemed natural for them to join us. Then we peered outside.

The City knows many moods. Sometimes it is the White City, sometimes the Wild City, sometimes other colours, textures or timbres. Sometimes, it cycles through them randomly, like four seasons of weather in a day. We peered out, not knowing what to expect, and listened for our transportation, not knowing what form it would take. The lure of the City.

That day, that moment, it was Sewer City, and our transport a long black limo that was armour-plated, and not just for the constant stalking by acid-rain. We sprinted for the open door and jumped in. The car roared off and dashed around overturned and burnt-out cars. Nobody mentioned the whiff of ripped blood in the air. No one mentioned the Dark Man, either. We tried to push all thought of him to the back of our minds, like children sent to bed early with the name of the bogey-man still on our mother's lips.

The chauffeur, a chubbier version of Leigh—but male—was dressed in a black shirt and a black polyester suit, and was singing a lullaby. He knew where to take us without being told, even though the city had become a labyrinth of narrow streets filled with shards of mist half-lit by flickering neons. At one point, a crowd of thin, rag-covered shadows screamed and jeered at us from behind a barrier made of building rubble that was blocking the street. They tossed crude metal spears when we came closer, then climbed over each other to get out of the way as he drove us through without missing a note of his song.

The university was on the outskirts of the city. Some said it was once in the centre and that learning and wisdom were as privileged then as commerce is now, but there were no reliable memories, no records. Some things didn't change.

We climbed the winding staircase to the tiny room at the top of the tower overlooking the campus. As we climbed, we barely noticed the landscape through the glass walls, a landscape that shifted but always seemed the same, as so much in the city. The wind hugged the glass with a low moan that jumped to high shrieks without warning and dropped back just as quickly. The lights of the city shifted and spun in the rainfall, and it seemed as if parts of it disappeared and newer parts appeared between the strides of dark clouds. Shapes shuttled their way across the skyline. We couldn't tell if they were metallic or biological.

The Teacher's student met us at the door. Without a word, she admitted us into a darkened room. Someone leapt out of his seat. We didn't recognise Antonio at first, what with his scratched and dirtied face and his rumpled tuxedo.

"Have you seen Rosa?"

D'Magda took a step towards him, then stopped. "She's always with you."

He turned to the Teacher, who was moving back from a window, a pensive look on his face. Antonio shook his head before slumping back into his chair, his right hand clawing the leather fabric for a moment.

"Sit down, all of you," the elderly man said. He has always been old. He has always had a voice that could drown out thunder. A legacy of large lecture halls, one presumes. But now his voice was low, deep, fatherly. "What's the problem?"

Bill bristled. He has always hated that word. So negative. Prefers challenge.

When Walter finished his story, the Teacher leaned back in his chair and stuck his right thumb in the flesh under his chin, his index finger stroking the tip of his nose. The moan of wind filled the silence.

"Do any of you remember the Hero?"

In an instant, we all knew what was happening. We remembered the day when the Hero vanished. More precisely, he had become something else, for nothing is truly lost in the City, or so we have been told. The trouble is, we weren't sure what he had become. Some say he is the Dark Man now. Others say that the Hero dissolved into each of us. Nobody knows, not even the Teacher.

"The Change," Bill said.

The old man nodded.

D'Magda squeezed Walter's arm, though he didn't seem to feel it. "Why now?"

The Teacher gestured to Antonio.

He got up and paced the room. "Things haven't been the same between Rosa and me for a while now."

"What do you mean?" Bill said.

"She's been more distant." He shook his head in disbelief. "We've never been like that. When I asked her why, she wouldn't say. I demanded an answer. We shouted at each other. Pushed each other. I grabbed at her. She slapped me."

He gripped the back of his chair to stop himself shaking and looked away from us. "I don't know what come over me but I slapped her back. She rubbed her cheek and glared at me. Then she said, 'He would never do that to me.'"

"Who?" D'Magda said.

"I don't know, She wouldn't say. Not even when I shook her. She pulled herself away and raced out of the room. I haven't seen her since."

Suddenly, Bakkis launched himself at Father Saul and pushed him towards a window. The glass shuddered with the impact and the noise shocked us into action. We grabbed Bakkis, but were easily shaken off. We grabbed again. The Teacher tore Bakkis's hands from the throat of the priest. We wrestled Bakkis face down to the floor. Leigh sat on his back, fingers probing his neck, and we waited till the thrashing stopped. We tied him up with curtain cords.

We carried Father Saul to a chair. D'Magda massaged his throat. He opened his eyes after a couple of minutes and blinked hard, as if trying to see beyond the boundaries of light and dark that the city juggled as rain tumbled, as winds shunted clouds into canyons between high buildings, as moon wavered in its decay of orbit.

Father Saul waved D'Magda away and nodded his thanks to her, to all of us. "Why did he do that?"

The Teacher put a hand on his shoulder. "To stop you doing something."

"What? And why?" Father Saul's voice squeaked at random, like some slow turning wheel and the axle dry.

"The what is easy enough. It has to do with my theory of the Change and how you, dear friend, might help things. The why is a lot harder. I can only suggest that somebody wants the Change to continue unabated. Somebody, or something."

Father Saul sat up. "You're not suggesting some infernal interference?"

"I don't know what I'm suggesting. But please, let's not get too involved in theological issues at this moment. We haven't got time. If we don't do something soon, there won't be time for anything. No time. Nothing."

He looked at each of us. We were listening. We were scared. Even the moaning outside had subsided.

"One way of thinking about all this is that we are not real."

"What do you mean?" Father Saul kicked a table leg and grimaced. "This isn't a dream."

"I didn't say it was."

Bill stared at his hands, looked around the room and then through the window, noted the flare of light at the eastern horizon, noted how a dark cloud snuffed it out and did not move. "What are you saying, then?"

"Whenever the Change occurs, I explain these things to all of you, but every time it passes, we forget, until the next time when, somehow, I remember again. This is the nature of my existence. The forgetting is the nature of all our existence, as is our connection to another reality—"

"Yes! You finally admit there is a higher order to which we must submit." The thin priest pulled himself forward, then fell back when he realised how weak he still was.

"The opposite. We are the under-rhythm of that other existence. Think of the sea. That other world is the waves; we are the deep currents and ocean floor movements. Our deeds manifest manifold in that other world—"

"But I did nothing to make my cigarette disappear." Walter shrugged off D'Magda's attention. "Soon I may disappear, just like the Hero."

"That's true."

"Can't you do anything for him?" D'Magda said.

"I'm attempting to, if it weren't for these interruptions."

We muttered apologies.

"Evidently, that other world can influence us. Like a violent storm stirring the waves and the mass of the sea down to the depths. Maybe it's as simple as a change in the law there. It's happened before, as I recall now."

Bill remembered Sam's strange look earlier and imagined the publican spilling a beer as the full knowledge of a prohibition during another Change dawned on him.

"But what about my beloved?" Antonio said.

"That seems a different order of seriousness. I don't know if it's our fault or the other world's. Maybe a combination of the two. Who knows in which world the Dark Man lives?' He glanced at Antonio, then at Walter and D'Magda. "But obviously, love has lost its certainty, its verve. Maybe it took itself for granted."

"But we're the real world." Father Saul struggled to keep his voice down.

"Well, theirs is for them, ours is for us, and together we both are. Let's leave it at that."

The moan strengthened. It was coming from Bakkis. "Why am I tied up?"

"You don't remember?" D'Magda mopped his face.

"All I remember is this smell, like when I get a nosebleed, then goose bumps and an icy shiver down my back, then...nothing."

Bill turned to the Teacher. "We can't win against the Dark Man."

"We did last time."

Bill nodded. "But we had the Hero then."

"Still, we have no choice."

A shriek.

D'Magda had rested a hand on Walter's left forearm, but quickly found it on the armrest of his chair, his arm on top. The muscle looked flimsy. Seemed to flicker in and out of existence.

The Teacher hurried to a cabinet. He brought back a pipe and pouch.

"Something from my youth," he said. "Maybe if you maintain your role you will stay solid a little longer."

Walter stuffed the pipe. "What is this?"

"It's harmless enough. You'll feel a little giddy, but that's better than vanishing right here and now. And if you see things you feel aren't there, well, don't worry. You may be seeing the other world, or the dissolution of our world, or something entirely harmless. Just don't tell us. We have enough to worry about."

Bill tugged at the old man's sleeve. "What about the Dark Man?"

"We have to find him."

"How?"

"Ask him." He pointed to Bakkis.

"I don't know anything. I just want a drink."

The Teacher inclined his head towards Father Saul. "He can help you remember. Help us all to remember."

Anger flashed on the priest's face. "You can't be serious. That's not my domain. It's forbidden."

"But when the old ways were here, it was your domain."

Magda helped Bill untie Bakkis. "What are they talking about?"

"I think they're talking about some sort of magic."

Walter gestured wildly with the pipe. "That's impossible."

"Anything is possible in the City." Bill surprised himself as he spoke, and knew a moment later that the statement was true.

He remembered much in that moment, and we with him. We remembered how we had chanted when the Hero had confronted the Change the last time. Remembered how the Hero was the Change, yet was also changed by it. Remembered the gales that were like weapons screaming. The thunder like giants applauding. The lurching of the land and the squalls of lurid red sunbursts as the land folded into itself then sprung into its old shape once more, with variations and change, yet everything the same, deep down, always the same, always drifting to another change. We trembled, not because of these memories, but because of another.

There was that moment between the collapse and the bloom of the City when there was nothing, not even the potential of something. A moment that would have been every other moment if not for the sacrifice of the Hero. A moment that would again threaten us and would again require sacrifice.

The look on the priest's face was now of acceptance. "Let's begin. I fear we may not have enough time."

"My fear as well." The Teacher indicated we clear the furniture away from the centre of the room. He went to his cabinet. To his student he gave the chalice, to Bill the drum. Instinctively, we formed a circle.

Bill beat the drum, a slow rhythm rising in pitch, in speed. Father Saul led the chant, a wordless call that stilled the room, stilled the frenzy and riot of the City. We sang, we beat, we stamped, we swayed. We had done this countless times before, and will do so again...

———

...AND AS WE flow with the chant, chant the flow, we feel the rhythm of the City echo in all cities, feel the discord of squalor echo its own off-beat, feel the twitch of a switchblade as it carves flesh, feel the cord around a foetus's neck and the clamps pulling the head through, feel the razors of sudden light and the rush of a needle. We are there, we are here, and there is here also. We are chanting through life, with life, for life. We cannot tell the difference between sound and stomp and sway. They are all one. We are all one.

In the middle of the circle, three people: the priest, the teacher, the student.

The student holds the chalice high, then walks over to the drunk. He shakes his head vigorously. The bouncer is alongside him. She takes out the knife and, without breaking rhythm, cuts her arm and presses blood into the cup. The drunk stares, nods, and offers his arm. It is done. The student then takes the knife and gives it to the smoker, who repeats the action. The lover is next. Then the rest of us. The writer places the ring from the empty booth inside the chalice. The ring dissolves.

The student returns to the priest and waits. He is swaying now, is dancing on the spot faster faster to the beat of the drum, his eyes closed, his face calm, with one bead of sweat that trickles down the left side of his face. He stamps and whirls faster faster as the beat increases and our chanting rises in pitch. Soon he is almost all motion. We watch him spin, caper, jump and gyrate, the music and the dance one, his closed eyes the focus of our open eyes and throats. Then he collapses to the ground, his body still. The student pours the blood into his open mouth. His body convulses, and the City shudders in reply. We keep our balance as the pulse of the chant reverberates above, below, around and through us.

Then there is nothing except the buffeting plunge down a pulsating tunnel that quickly erupts into a shower of light. There is only the light.

We are nowhere, yet everywhere. Silent. Still. We wait as we reach into the light for a shadow-sense of something missing.

There is a cry that draws us together and pulls us down down

down to the centre of everything, to stillpoint, and suddenly we are through. We have not moved from the tower, yet the tower is not the same. There are the crystal walls. Furniture is piled to the side. There is our circle.

Inside the circle are five people. The priest is still on the floor, his mouth open, his cry trailing into the light through which we have come. Above him stands the student, the chalice inverted on the floor next to her right foot. In front of them, the teacher pushes the knife within the folds of his robe. They are facing the other occupants of the circle: The lover, her dress torn at the bodice, and the other behind her, the dark man, who clenches her arms at the elbows. His smile reminds us of the hero. His eyes are pitch black and there is a mischievous glint in them. His beguiling charm.

"I did not think you would dare the ceremony without the hero. Impressive. But it won't help you."

The teacher advances on him, but stops when the dark man twists the lover's arms and she cries out. It is hard to tell if it is from pleasure or pain.

"That's far enough, old man. She dies, and all hope dies with her."

"Why are you doing this?"

"My nature. The nature of things, remember."

"Ours is to stop you."

"Not this time. The hero is gone."

"We try anyway."

The writer winces. When will they learn the power of words? To try is a prescription for failure. He feels fear. We all do.

The dark man sneers. "What do you intend to do, old man?"

"The trial."

Again, we remember. The trial. By force or knowledge. The choice of champion was ours, while the choice of weapon was our opponent's. We had chosen the hero.

We see him strung out against the sky, his scream whirling about him like a scavenger as he fails the trial of knowledge against our new foe, the tempter, who had reached into the hero's heart and revealed the shadow there, the evil of his own life, of all our lives, the thoughts and desires we had repressed, which the hero had gathered into a stone of darkness and hidden in the deepest well of his heart. The tempter had touched the stone with his laughter and the outer shell of the stone had fragmented, ripping apart the hero's heart, allowing the seeping shadows to escape and flay his body. Yet, the scream was not of pain only, and too late the tempter discovered this. The scavenging scream swallowed each fragment, each burst of shadow. As the hero faded to light, the tempter melted into his own shadow, and the Change he had sought trailed after him.

Afterwards, there came the rumours of the dark man. But with everything returned to its place, no one bothered to listen.

"Who is your champion?" the dark man said.

The bouncer steps forward. The hero has left much of his light in her.

The teacher crosses in front of her. "I am."

"You're too old," the writer says. "You can't possibly stand up to him."

"I have the knowledge."

The dark man pushes Rosa to the ground. "Maybe, old man, but this will not be a trial by knowledge like the last one. I choose force."

A momentary droop of the shoulders, and then the teacher stiffens his back, looks his adversary in the eye. "So be it."

We help the student carry the priest out of the circle. The tender lady goes to him. Antonio helps Rosa to her feet. She walks away, her hand trailing behind her, then joins him at the circle. We start to chant.

"No!" shouts the teacher. "There will be no magic. Not now."

The dark man smiles and strips off his shirt to reveal pumped, striated muscles. They gleam in the moonlight. He swings his arms in wide arcs and swivels his hips before swinging his legs in even wider arcs. He jumps up and down. Crouches into a fighting stance.

Though we cannot chant, cannot move for fear of distracting the teacher, our minds feed energy into the circle that surrounds the combat. We would help as much as possible within the rules of the trial. It has always been that way.

A leap, a flurry of kicks and punches, a sharp cry of pain, and the fighters have exchanged places within the circle. There is blood on the edge of the knife held by the teacher, a look of puzzlement on the face of the dark man.

"You know something of the martial arts, old man."

"A little. You forget I was once young."

"It won't help you. I won't underestimate you again. Very clever of you to use my weapon against me, the one I gave that drunk when I took over his mind. You're stretching the rules a little. I'm unarmed."

"Your choice when you entered the circle."

We feel hope. The teacher has out-thought his opponent. He has a plan. But is it enough?

The knife is no simple blade. All of us feel the energy of the weapon, sense the facets of all other blades shimmering in the glow about it. We remember the cities that were reflections of our city, remember the touch of all those ordinary people in our city and beyond, the touch of all those in every city. We remember the confident shoulder-charge walks through ghettos and shanty towns of those inhabitants, the keenness of their minds, the hope of dreams in their hearts. Our mental song takes these memories and perceptions, sharpens them, hones the edge of our knife with them. We feel more than hope.

The dark man shakes himself, and his muscles are freed of tension. He laughs, takes up his stance, and advances slowly on the teacher.

Then it is over. The bouncer tracked it, the writer analysed it, the tender lady felt it, the student shared it with all our minds: feint, kick, stumble, recovery, back-kick, jam, block, wrist-grab, sweep, wrist-grab, the thrust, the blood, the grin, and we see it again and again in slow motion as the dark man jumps to his feet and his laughter echoes round and round the circle.

We see the feint with his right fist, the upward arc of his left foot that intercepted the teacher's right hand and knocked the man slightly off balance, the teacher's flow-on recovery into a spinning left foot back thrust kick, the dark man moving in as the teacher spun, jamming the kick, blocking the left spinning back fist, grabbing the wrist, sweeping the legs, grabbing the right hand still holding the knife, thrusting the knife into the teacher's heart as the old man hits the ground, the blood the grin the blood the grin the blood.

The laughter echoes round and round the circle. Round and round the circle. Round and round, and there is only the circle. Without looking, we know there is no tower, no city, no world about us or above us. Everything but the circle and the laughter has folded into nothing. The laughter echoes round and round the circle. Soon it will enfold us. Soon there will be only laughter. Then nothing.

We remember the teacher's last words: There will be no magic. Not now. Not during his trial of arms, which he had used to mislead the dark man. Now it is our trial.

We raise our linked arms. The dark man's laughter shakes our grip. We chant the blood the grin the laughter. His laughter rocks us. We chant the problem the challenge the knowledge. His laughter claws at our bodies. We chant the knife the life the sacrifice. His laughter buffets our heads. We chant the touch of lovers, the light of heroes. His laughter burrows into us. We chant the try the plan the circle. His laughter twists inside us, looking for purchase. We chant the sway the stamp the chant. His laughter echoes with each of our names as it tries to shatter them.

Still laughing, the dark man pulls out the knife and blood gushes after him as he glides towards the lovers. Their hands are tightly clenched, and Rosa is again wearing her ring. The teacher's blood continues to stream until it covers the floor of the circle. The dark man weaves his name in the air before them: Last.

Then the pulse of the chant lifts the molecules of blood into a swirling horde of incandescent suns that spiral about him, upward turning upward and smothering the striding darkness of his laughter. We chant, we sway, we stamp, we sing the knife from his hand and dissolve it to light. We sing the teacher's body and blood into contour and space, into wave and air, and watch as the vibrations of blood caress each of our faces in turn and ripple the boundary of nothing around our circle. For a moment, the laughter clutches at the ripples, wrenching some into shrinking spirals that shriek as they disappear.

The circle wavers, but holds firm. There are too many ripples, and we watch them open the nothing about us, watch them unfold into contour and space, into wave and air, watch the city and the world about us and above us shake itself out like someone spreading a picnic cloth. The dark man charges at each of us, but shrinks and slows as his laughter dies. He steps back to the centre of the circle and weaves about him what remains of his laughter. After glaring at the lovers one last time, he vanishes.

We sit around the picnic cloth. The rain stops. The wind shatters the remaining clouds. Gold light peels open the horizon, and we smile.

EVERYONE IS where they usually are at Sam's Place. Finally.

The Smoker is showing off his double helix smoke rings to the Tender Lady. One hangs in mid-air for a long moment, slowly revolving, slowly dissolving as he takes another drag. He's been practising them for some time now and almost everyone appreciates them, even if the aroma isn't quite what we're used to. He wonders if it is possible to blow a double Möbius strip.

The only ones not congratulating him are the Drunk, who is busy signalling for another drink, as he always does, and the Bouncer, who leans her wiry frame against a door jamb, her arms folded, her eyes never stopping, never missing a thing. Which is just as well.

The Lovers are sitting at their corner booth, holding hands, mouthing impossible promises that they will always keep, staring at each other as if their eyes were twin sets of laser mirrors and the power surging. Even from here we can feel their iridescent hope. So good to feel it again and, because we don't want to spoil their eternal moment by staring, we smile out of the corner of our eyes. But it's more out of habit that we do this, for we know nothing could spoil their ardour. Not now.

At a table by himself, the Writer types away, pausing often to sip his black tea and check the page. He is smiling now. He hates being described as the Struggling Writer. Says words have a strange power here, anywhere you believe they do, and he doesn't want his fate so programmed by words not of his making. Prefers to be known as the Recently Unpublished Writer. Though he has been lucky lately. We all have.

Outside, the City shimmers like a new blade spinning in sunlight.

END

About the Author

Earl Livings is an award-winning poet and fiction writer who has been widely published in Australia and also overseas. He has read his work around Melbourne and overseas and appeared on panels at various Australian SF conventions and festivals.

Earl has a PhD in Creative Writing, for which he wrote *The Silence Inside the World*, a fantasy verse novel that is due to be published late 2021. He taught professional writing and editing for almost 20 years and has worked as a freelance editor, a manuscript assessor, and a mentor. His writing focuses on science, history, nature, mythology and the sacred. Ginninderra Press published his latest poetry collection, *Libation*, in late 2018, and he is currently finalising a two-book historical fantasy series set in dark ages Britain.

He lives in Melbourne with his wife and their ever-growing stacks of books. More information is available on his website: www.earl-livings.com

21

THE MESSENGER

CARLETON CHINNER

My grandmother's photograph ended my innocence. Childhood memories do that when you see them after years of adult discovery and disappointment. I looked again at the faded picture of the impact left by comet Schoemaker-Levy as it slammed into Jupiter's atmosphere, and took in truths too uncomfortable to speak.

Abbot Bodwyn waved the ancient, grainy amateur photo in front of my nose.

"Parsifal, there is no life but ours in all the wide heavens. Science confirms all we believe. It has always done so and always will."

Over the abbot's shoulder, brown Europa—fourth largest of Jupiter's many moons—broke through skeins of pale-frozen methane to cast its baleful glow over the rolling maelstrom of deep cloud. The time for evensong was fast approaching as the great cathedral of Alesia drifted through the conjugation of moons that marked the end of the Cenobitic day on Jupiter, a world where more light came from below than from the distant sun. Streams of black-clad friars would make their way to the chilly open space of the upper deck, where a thin layer of glass was all that stood between the raging elements and our fragile bodies.

"Holy Abbot," I said, using Bodwyn's most formal title to emphasise my point. "I still believe the photograph shows regular formations."

Bodwyn fidgeted as if my words pained him. "Must we speak of this?" He favoured me with a gentle smile. "You took brother Calibor's leaving hard. Give yourself time to grieve. Calibor was old and has gone on to higher service now."

I shrugged to hide my irritation at the abbot's obvious diversion. "I can find proof. If you permit me to venture into the lower cloud layer."

"Millions have not seen what you see in that photo. The depths are not for us. There is no glory to be found in the heresy of speculation."

"Give me the chance."

He shook his head. "Go to evensong, brother. There is nothing but disappointment in what you seek."

I retrieved the photo and walked from his office, my footsteps echoing in the vast corridor of the inner monastery. The yellowing photo, rumpled by years of careful handling, weighed down with the accumulated weight of memory as I placed it in the hidden pocket of my cassock. Walking up the broad sweep of stairs that led to the upper deck, I joined the neat row of my brothers preparing for evensong. The photo scratched against my chest as it lay in the pocket of my robe.

"Our Father who joins us in the heavens," sang the chorister.

The massed voice of brothers rose in answering harmony. "Blessed are those who watch over your creation. May we all be one with you."

The chorister's intonation rose an octave as the last rays of the distant sun disappeared below green clouds. "Guide us through the darkness of space and protect us from the emptiness."

Shadows crept through the long hall, chased by stray beams of Europa's light. Soon Callisto would join her sister in the sky, dissipating the gloom of night. I watched the moon emerge as I sang with my brothers. Europa's edge wavered and blurred as I stared.

Trying to clear my vision, I shook my head, but the dizziness overcame me, and I staggered, clutching at the dark robe that stood nearest me.

"Are you okay?" asked the brother I clung to.

I could not answer as I fell to the floor and lay staring at the sandalled feet of those around me.

Kind hands lifted me upright and walked me from the upper deck. I stumbled down blurry stairs that refused to come into focus as my helpers guided me to a lower level than I had ever visited. This deep, the monastery walls thrummed with the beat of ancient flotation engines perpetually labouring to keep the entire edifice from sinking into the depths. Sluggish air currents brought the musty scent of things long forgotten. The temperature rose as my bearers shuffled along corridors coated with verdigris tints of mould. Beyond the thin walls of our sanctuary, the Jovian atmosphere howled and thundered as clouds of super-heated steam billowed from an uprising wide enough to swallow old Earth.

At length, we reached a brushed-aluminium door, so unlike the ornate carving around the entrances of the upper levels. Ancient hinges screamed in protest as the door swung open to reveal a metal table surrounded by arcane machinery.

A withered brother rose from a chair as if he had been asleep until we entered. "Put him on the table," he said as he tinkered with a rack of glass-filled objects. The brothers did as he asked and then withdrew.

"And who have we here?" he peered down at me through myopic eyes distorted by heavy lenses. "Ah, Parsifal." He nodded to himself, as if my appearance made sense. "You're making a habit of this."

"What do you mean? I've never been here before. Who are you?"

"Peace, brother." He placed a hand on my forehead. "Soon the trials of the flesh will be behind you."

"What?"

He did not answer. A cold machine clamped to my wrist, and darkness followed.

———

I woke in my cell to the sound of dawnsong being sung. Groaning, I rose, clutching my head to fend off a headache that already arced thunderbolts across the inside of my skull. The fog of sleep evaporated as I remembered the events of the day before. Staring at the pictures of an oasis located deep in the Sahara Desert on my wall, I closed one eye and then tried the other. The pictures remained in focus, with no remnant of yesterday's blur.

My fingers brushed the sharp edges of the picture in my pocket as I dressed. Grandmother took that photo on a cold day in July, her telescope perched on the narrow concrete water tank. I can still see the two of us; me, an undersized boy of six standing next to her bent older figure, our breath coming in clouds as we sipped streaming mugs of tea poured from her battered thermos. We had waited until the lights of Alice Springs glittered in the winter dark, before sneaking onto the roof of the old apartment block. "You can't get a clearer night sky than in the Alice," she said. "Up here we escape most of the light pollution."

"Should we be up here, Gran?"

She craned her withered neck to sight through the slim aiming tube. "It's always easier to ask for forgiveness than permission."

I peered over the railing at the deserted streets below. A lone police van drifted along the River Todd; its headlights playing along empty sands where the river sometimes ran. Gran touched my arm, directing me back to the telescope.

"Look, you can see the impact site."

The eyepiece was still warm from her cheek as I took in my first view of the planet I would one day call home. Great swirling masses of cloud circled a dark bruise; the only evidence of a titanic explosion so large it would have reduced Earth to ashes.

"So many worlds," she whispered in my ear. "And, here we are in our little town."

I stood as she bent to take pictures. Lights twinkled on the MacDonnell Ranges over towards the Gap. They'd always looked so far away, but now, for the first time, I realised they were nothing more than foothills of a gateway to the infinite majesty of the universe.

She died the year after I followed my parents to the busy life of inner-city Brisbane. The picture stayed with me as I went through school, and later seminary; I think it reminded me of that one night. I reprinted it on durable plastic when I left for Alesia.

My fingers traced the outline of the picture. There had to be a way. My grandmother's photograph of the collision showed angular ridges within the whorls of flaming gas: ridges that should never have been there. Ridges that could only have been caused by something miles-wide that had chosen to no longer be there in all subsequent photos. People had ridiculed her, saying it was a printing mistake; that the aberrations were a trick of the light.

It was too late to join my brothers in song. I made the clumsy motions of a hasty penance before walking to the observation chamber that clung to the edge of the monastery like an oversized glass limpet.

A lone observer sat there at this hour, Brother Augwys, the sceptic who had a ready answer to any insistence on other life. He looked up as I entered. "Coming to stare at clouds again?"

I nodded, unwilling to engage in losing an intellectual debate this early in the day. He shrugged and turned back to his observations of the stars. I sat at an empty terminal and spun the direction dials to point down instead of the usual up. Today, the monastery drifted over a swathe of clear sky torn open by a passing storm super cell. Fragments of frozen green methane clouds littered the horizon in an untidy arc.

Looking down through the powerful telescope, I scanned deep inside the super cell to uncover great swirling masses of angry brown and grey cloud vast distances below. The storm's majestic power had torn a deeper hole than usual. I focused on the deepest layer, switching to an infrared view that highlighted the clouds of super-heated steam exploding through the lowest layers. Gouts of dark red fluid filled my viewer, interspersed with cooler streams of liquid water. I scanned an irregular zone of turbulence to the left, watching as it quivered and distorted under the tremendous pressure of the depths. A dark, miles-wide maw swallowed the remaining cloud fragments and disappeared.

"Augwys! Did you see?"

"See what? You know I only look up at the stars."

"No, down, deep down, where that dark irregularity is on the deepest visible layer. Switch to infrared view."

Augwys humoured me and adjusted his console to look down. I suspected he only did it so he could humiliate me later. "What is it we are looking for?"

Inchoate cloud masses drifted past on the view-screens as I scanned the edges of the turbulence, hoping for any sign of the mouth I had seen. Nothing appeared.

I turned to Augwys, preparing to admit defeat and steeling myself for the intellectual preening which was to follow.

Augwys's concentration remained on his monitor. I stepped over and saw a dark-reddish-brown hexagon as wide as the monastery passing through the turbulence. Vestigial fins along each edge propelled the creature through the boiling soup of chemicals. As we watched, one edge split open—in the wide gape I had seen before—and inhaled whole clouds.

"A filter-feeder," breathed Augwys. "How great is the Lord's creation."

I followed the dark shape, telling myself it did not waver and shake in my vision. Two more hexagons swam up to it and joined edges in overlapping waves. I strained to see beyond the resolution of the scanner. The image darkened as I fell to the floor, seeing only the rope weave of Augwys's sandals before the darkness overtook me.

———

I AWOKE to the abbot's keen eyes peering down at me. He stepped back and took the single steel visitor's chair, his weight making the chair legs shriek across the tiles. As my vision adapted to the sharp light of the room, I stared into unfamiliar banks of electronics, bright

and alien to eyes accustomed to the simple motifs of monastery light.
"Where am I?"

"A treatment centre."

"Why?"

"We do what we can for the old ones." His eyes filled with something akin to pity as he looked at me. "Some of us have been here so long. It has always pained me that you don't remember. A fault in your data banks is what they say."

"There's something wrong with my brain?"

Bodwyn shook his head in the slow, deliberate manner he often used. "We maintain the belief that we are human. That is one of my sins and I will pay for it forever. But the truth is, we are nothing more than constructs. No human could survive this place. You were one of the first we made. The last time we refreshed your chassis, you requested that we not restore your memories."

"This is a lie." My voice sounded high and frightened, even to me. "And the lifeforms we saw? Are they also a lie?"

"No, this time there is no denying it: you have discovered the first life beyond Earth. You were always the brightest of us."

My vision blurred as I looked up at him. "How can I be a made thing, if I have a grandmother?"

Bodwyn clenched his hands. "We weave memory as we wish to remember. I don't know if the photo is real or not, but you reprint it every few years." He drew a deep breath. "You are failing once more, Parsifal, and as before you have refused the upgraded chassis. Will you not relent this time?"

"Give me my memories."

He rose and place a hand upon my shoulder. "Very well, old friend, but I beg of you. Don't forget us again."

A slim glass rod descended from the ceiling and stopped just short of my forehead. In a blinding flash, twelve hundred years of recorded memories soaked into me. I relived the beginnings of the monastery: how Bodwyn and I had led twenty others to harvest metals from the boiling depths. How we changed as new requirements arose, re-designing our bodies to meet our every need.

I went further back to the training centre in Kazakhstan where our order had elected to surrender our ageing physical brains in favour of layered quantum-crystal nanochips. I remembered how we had been packed into an interplanetary rocket and shipped to Jupiter so we could escape the rising world order that denied our faith. So many years, so much building. Always advancing, always contemplating the mysteries of God's creation.

"Enough, Bodwyn. I understand now." I sat up and focused my blurry vision on him. "We have to speak to these creatures. I will select a chassis suitable for extreme depths and spend the remainder of my days trying to communicate with them."

"There is no return from such depths. The gravity will prevent you from ever rising again."

"I know."

He placed one withered hand on my shoulder. "Committing such an act would be a grave injustice against God."

I wrapped my arms around my chest, knowing that the action was a memory of a long-lost physiological response to stress. "We condemned our souls the day we surrendered the flesh of our bodies."

Bodwyn said nothing as I sat up. His face was a map of conflicted sorrow. I reached out to touch the man I had worked beside for so many centuries.

"Do not grieve for me," I said, keeping my voice low. "We were never designed to live forever. I will do this so you may all know."

———

MY NEW CHASSIS is a square block topped by a gigantic steel vacuum sphere. Much like the original hot-air balloon, it can be emptied to be less dense than the surrounding atmosphere; it will allow me to float among the clouds for as long as I choose. I don't miss the electromechanical approximation of my human form. My memories are restored, and I remember all the breakdowns of my previous chassis as they aged. I remember the griding wear and tear."

My brothers have assembled on the lowest deck to bid me farewell. They gather in their cloistered ranks around the great well of the skyport that lies open to the raging elements. As I scan them with senses far past human ability, I console myself that I only need endure the interminable speeches for a short while before I roll off the lip of the deck and separate myself from the precarious niche we have carved in this world's sky.

I will watch the monastery dwindle until it is less than a mote in God's eye, and as I fall, I will compose the first of many messages telling the deep dwellers they are no longer alone.

END

ABOUT THE AUTHOR

Carleton Chinner is a science nut who loves fiction that explores what science means to humanity. He grew up on a remote farm in South Africa, where the trip to the town library was the highlight of his week. He devoured anything science fiction, fantasy and horror. And, when that wasn't enough, turned to urban legend and traditional tribal histories which combined to provide a heady brew of stories.

Carleton is the author of the *Cities of the Moon* series of science fiction novels. His short stories appear in several anthologies and have been recognised in competitions.

22

BLACK POWDER

ALLISON OLSSON

Water caressed the creature's silver body, ebbing and flowing with the outgoing tide. The seagulls on the deserted island were the only witnesses to the creature's metamorphosis. They cawed and circled in the sky as its scales glinted rainbows in the sunlight, and its fins pulsed and vibrated. It shivered, despite the warmth of the tropical water. The creature turned an elongated head from side to side. Two large, orange pupils dilated to allow extra light to penetrate both eyes as the setting sun dimmed. A cry issued from its blubbery, black lips as a spasm of pain racked its body.

Skin split from its tail to belly, shaping legs and feet, and from underneath its gills down to its hips, to shape arms and hands. The creature wailed and writhed, the water around it stained with its blood. Its sad cries echoed across the ocean until the water receded to low tide point, and the moon rose—revealing the full extent of the creature's transformation.

———

SCOUTXG MADE her way carefully through the dim corridors of the flooded apartment building on the bank of the Brisbane River. Once a highly sought-after inner-city residential address with views of the Story Bridge, it was abandoned when the river rose, its occupants fleeing to higher ground. Now it was overgrown with purple Bougainvillea vines, water-soaked walls and floors, the crumbling concrete a danger to any who entered. Her small, dark eyes flicked nervously as she looked for signs of surveillance. No black domes fixed to the ceiling, no cameras or visible recording devices. Power was down anyway, but she couldn't help being cautious. The last Tritonian to be caught off world was vaporised by the Clandestine Council, which ensured that no other planets became aware of the activities of Tritonian smugglers.

She removed her scarf, revealing a row of gills down either side of her neck. They flashed open and closed, sampling the stale air for spores. Nothing. ScoutXG relished the feeling of freedom as she roamed through the deserted building, her gills open to the elements. The worst part of being a Tritonian smuggler was the shape-shifting process she underwent on her arrival at each planet. It was necessary to blend in with the dominant species on the planets she visited, but nothing made the process any easier. Her gills were the only part of herself she couldn't change, so she had to use clothing as a disguise, and the danger of being caught was always in the back of her mind. The toll of repeated shapeshifting reduced a Tritonian lifespan by at least ten years. Hence the high cost of the product she supplied.

Walking further into the gloomy corridor, ScoutXG found what she was looking for. Traces of stachybotrys. Black mould. Breathing deeply, drawing air over her gills, she smiled. Her sharp teeth glittered in the gloom. She felt a little tipsy.

ScoutXG pulled a modified dust buster from her oversized shoulder bag. Using a knife she kept in the bottom of the bag, she prised a piece of rotten gyprock from the wall, then placed the mouth of the dust buster over the thickest, blackest mound of mould she could see. ScoutXG ran the sharp bottom lip of the dust buster under it. The mould lifted from the wall, dripping moisture and spores. Pressing the 'on' button, she nodded happily as the machine snarled into life, sucking both mould and damp into its gizzard.

When the dust buster was full, ScoutXG drew a marker from her bag and wrote on its label before placing it carefully into a zip-lock plastic bag, which she sealed and put into her oversized handbag. This was going to be the best stuff yet. She smiled and turned around, eager to be on her way home.

The floods in Brisbane had been the best ones yet. Mould bloomed in abandoned apartment buildings and homes. So far, ScoutXG had collected two hundred bags full of the stuff. The guys on the ship were going to be blown away. The stachybotrys on this sweltry backwater planet was the real deal: strong, pure, and highly hallucinogenic.

By the time she was airlifted home, she had three lucrative offers to buy and knew she would never have to smuggle again. Visiting swamped Brisbane was definitely worth the pain.

END

ABOUT THE AUTHOR

Allison Olsson is a writer who is lucky enough to have so far lived in New South Wales, South Australia and Queensland. While looking forward to exploring more of Australia and the world, she works as a nurse and divides her free time between her family, writing, and her favourite martial art, Hapkido.

When she gets stuck in a story, her cat takes over, tiptoeing across the keyboard and adding her own suggestions for Allison to consider. Allison has not yet been able to teach her cat how to make coffee.

23

CATNIP

MARTIN ROHDE

Fifteen years ago, my father led me down the log road through the marsh, along this trail. When he left me behind at the monastery, I was so hurt I refused to speak for three days. I grew to love the life of a scholar and thought it would be decades before I'd have to leave. The monks were kind, and taught me many things—the arts and sciences, the spell-weaving, the cultivation of mind and character. Everything was aimed at preparing me for my future. Under their guidance, my spirit had grown and had become a powerful weapon.

I loved the life of a scholar and had thought it would be years before I'd have to pursue my father's track. There were many books I still needed to read. But it was my duty to return home one day and take my father's place.

On the first moon in the seventh year of King Nablung's rule, word reached me that my father, the master enchanter, had died. The next day, I packed what few belongings I had and left the monastery, retracing the steps I taken all those years before.

The path led through scattered human settlements where the crofters rarely saw a kipu. To them, I—Nellor Reed—looked like a stray cat. In every hamlet, children ran to gawk at my red fur. At an isolated homestead near a muddy lake, a grandmother came out to greet me.

"You're magnificent," she said. "Just like the cat-people in the old songs."

In Teuchl, to be called a 'cat-person' is an insult. But I tried not to take offence. They were poor peat farmers and meant no abuse.

In a tiny fishing village on the coast, I sneaked aboard a trading vessel and crossed the Sea of Farnning. On the mainland, I found the Rose Road—which was nothing more than a dirt track this far north—and followed it south. Two weeks later, I climbed the steep gorge of the little Belgar to cross the Dalati mountains. After a strenuous ascend, I reached the highest point of the pass. The horizon opened and the great plateau of Teuchl stretched before me.

In the distance, the city's roofs glittered in the afternoon sun. The ancient granite rock with the castle dominated the skyline. It looked splendid against the backdrop of snow-capped Mount Thunder. My heart cheered. Here, I had been born. Here, my folk dwelt with the humans.

At the outer gate, I took my time. Childhood memories of playing with Carruf in the streets returned. Then my eyes wandered over the gate's gargoyles, cast in the likeness of the lion goddess Cyhoni, which spouted water from their gaping mouths. I smelled the smirch of her magic—a faint brimstone odour—and shuddered.

A tall kipu jumped out of the gatehouse and saw me gazing at the gargoyles. "It strikes me as ironic to depict her spitting water," he said. "The very goddess who forged the seal of the lioness out of magma centuries ago, who gave it to her human followers, turning them into kipu."

My jaw dropped when I spotted the steel collar with inlaid golden lions wrapped around his neck. He was a priest of the goddess Cyhoni! I knew the faith was part of everyday life in Teuchl, but it shocked me to see the goddess' symbols flaunted so openly.

"You must be Nellor. Welcome home. You're eagerly awaited."

I rolled up my tail, forming a crescent, to ward off harm. Energy precipitated around me, establishing a protective ring that would guard me from harmful magic. I hoped the priest wouldn't notice. I didn't want to appear impolite on my first day. But I also didn't want to take any chances. Cyhoni, goddess of the depth, mistress of fire and war, had a wicked side. She dabbled in shameful magic, cherished tyranny, and relished entire tribes being enslaved in her name. The monks warned me about her.

"Thank you," I said. "And you are...?"

"Koflac. Secretary of the high priest."

It was no coincidence he was here waiting for me. That's why father sent me away. Because of scheming priests. Kipu like him would have educated me had I grown up in Teuchl. The same priests who'd sent my grandfather Sinur into exile. After everything he had done for Teuchl.

Koflac smirked. "Let me walk you to the castle mountain."

"Thank you," I said.

It was market day, and we strode through the city's bustling streets that were full of kipu and humans. From alehouses and merchant stands, folk cried out "Hail Cyhoni!" to greet Koflac. It made me flinch, and I was glad when we reached the foot of the castle rock.

"Give my best wishes to your mother," Koflac said.

How well did he know her?

The stone walls atop the castle mountain were impenetrable. Towers flew the banners of the grand houses. Sentries hoisted me up the cliff with a pulley. I exited the basket at the castle's deserted garden terraces perched atop the cliff, in which I'd played as a kitten. The lowest terrace was moist, and a rivulet meandered through it before gushing over the bluff. Frogs croaked when I halted and marvelled at the remarkable collection of herbs that grew there despite the altitude. On the bank grew sedges, clutch ferns, and honeysuckle.

Cypresses covered the second terrace, and a huge camphor laurel crowned the third. Underwood had invaded the space beneath the trees. In the distance, I heard the pounding of a hydraulic ram pump. Above it all loomed the tower of the master enchanter. My home resembled a giant daffodil on a stem, the living quarters at the top enclosed by petal-like platforms. It was the oldest building in the castle grounds, and its foundations reached deep into the bedrock.

I passed the tower with its barricaded gate and windows, reached the main ramp, and entered the front gate. Through a gloomy tunnel lit by a string of everlasting lanterns, I arrived in the citadel's courtyard, where my mother and my uncle Berekob awaited me.

"It's good that you're here," she said.

"I came as fast as I could."

She rubbed her head against my shoulder, as if I were still a kitten. "We missed you."

Her eyes were cold and contrasted with her well-groomed tabby pelt. She seemed proud and different from the warm feline I remembered.

"Come in," she said.

"A merchant delivered the message of my father's passing away. Why didn't you send a squadron of knights to escort me?" I asked.

Uncle Berekob stepped forward. With his grey, braided fur and confident stride, he still looked like the strong cat he'd always been. A strange red key with a long shaft and a head shaped like a lion's mane hung around his neck.

"Unfortunately," he said, "typhus fever incapacitated the garrison. Many of them perished. We had no warriors to spare, none even to defend the castle gates. As if that wasn't bad enough, gangs of gnomish thieves ransacked the city. My apologies if it insulted you, but I felt obliged to send word immediately and I knew the merchant to be reliable, and his ship to be a swift vessel."

I nodded. "Take me to my father."

Berekob led me to the family crypt underneath the west wing of the castle. There, in a great vault lit by torches, at the end of a long line of marble slabs, lay my father's tomb where I held guard for the night, as was our custom.

Afterwards, I paid my respects to King Nablung. He was a giant of a man, over two yards tall, ruler of all the city's inhabitants, human and feline.

"Welcome back to Teuchl," he said, lifting me up and placing me into the basket beside his throne.

"So, you come from that windy islet. How does it feel to return home?"

"Most delightful, my king."

"Tell me about the place."

"I lived in an ancient monastery on a hill surrounded by marshlands. It was a dark and windy place, but moist, and full of life. The halls were warmed by well-fed fires around which the residents congregated. And the conversations they had! Full of wisdom and learning. I can think of no better place for a mind to grow. The monks are among the greatest scholars known to the world. And their magic is truly extraordinary, powerful but gentle, always nurturing the wonder of creation."

"Sounds interesting."

I kept talking. He smiled politely while staring at his polished boots. After two minutes, he cut me off.

"Nellor, of course you realise we're your family. The entire castle is delighted you have come back to be our master enchanter. Let me add that I've always been a benefactor of the art of enchanting. I promise, I'll do whatever is needed to support you." He hurried on without pause. "But enough dull drivel. Let's talk of more captivating things. There will be a brief ceremony tomorrow to welcome you. But that's only the beginning. I'm also planning a grand banquet. What worth have honours if not accompanied by the proper delicatessen? We'll have swans. Ostrich eggs. And maybe caviar. My sommeliers are already foraging the cellars. I have some extraordinary drops in store. You'll see."

My shoulders dropped. Celebrating was the last thing I wanted right now.

"The banquet will kick off a week of special entertainment, with concerts, plays, and exhibitions. Vilac, my court composer, has written a string quartet concerto for the occasion. Just for you. We'll have to think of a suitable spot for the premiere. Maybe it in the gardens. Oh, it's all so exciting."

He went on and on, but I wasn't able to pay attention.

"Your majesty, if you would be so kind to excuse me. I have hardly slept since I arrived," I said as early as was polite.

"Of course. You must be tired," he said. "Understandable, after the hardships you endured. I'm looking forward to our next meeting. Please, if you need advice on anything, don't hesitate to ask. Beyond that, I recommend you listen to your uncle. In magical matters, he's the wisest in the kingdom, and you cannot err if you follow his advice."

I reached the platform at the top of the master enchanter's tower by pulley. The living quarters were as generous as I remembered. The large atrium had been empty fifteen years ago but was now furnished with divans and low tables. I strolled through the bedrooms and the offices grouped around the atrium. The leathery smell hanging in the air immediately brought back images of Dad chasing me around in play. "I'll get you, slowpoke," he would shout. It felt as if no time had passed at all.

"I still expect him to come back," said a voice from behind me.

It was Gnes, my father's servant. His human hair and beard were snow white.

"Good to see you," he said. He went to his knees in front of me, held out his right hand, and I curled up against it. Tears rolled down my fur.

I was exhausted and slept the whole day. The following afternoon, I was called to the council chamber.

"Please follow me," the squire said.

We went down deep into the citadel where the king's officials worked. We passed the library and descended through halls of scribes and advocates.

As a child, I'd never been down this far.

I expected the council chamber to be as dim as the halls we'd come through, but when we entered, the golden evening light blinded me. An emporium faced a row of open arches that afforded an impressive view of the southern districts below the cliff. Human courtiers and magicians, and hundreds of kipu dignitaries crowded the chamber.

My mother invited me to lie on the wicker bed at her side, while an unending procession of visitors paraded past us. Once I'd gotten comfortable, my ears shot up. She was wearing the collar of the goddess Cyhoni! She'd never mentioned faith in the letters she'd written to me. Had she worn it like this in front of my father? He detested religion. He'd sent me into exile to protect me from it.

"Are you all right?" my mother asked. "You look startled."

"I'm tired from the journey."

She turned her head and smiled.

It seemed like the entire world wanted to pay their respects.

"Great Nellor Reed," the ambassador from Farnning declaimed, "It's an honour for our people to send you these barrels of spirit." Then he proceeded to praise, at length, the extent of his city's friendship with Teuchl. After he finished, I was expected to stand up, bow my head, and return gracious assurances that envisioned our growing unity in all things magical.

I was terrible at it. The florid, diplomatic words couldn't roll off my tongue. I concentrated to save myself from stuttering and repeated the same clunky phrases again and again.

There were many visitors. Humans from Obla, from Padnea, and from the coastal cities. From the slopes and forests in the far west came the elves, from the mountains the dwarves, and from Villor—the gnomish city in the Northwest—Ambassadress Arlandia.

Barely a yard tall, she had a wrinkly face and squinted when she studied me. Accompanying her was a youthful gnome girl named Sivery with slender legs and a winning smile. When Arlandia spoke all the magicians, enchanters, the officials, and courtiers fell silent.

"Honourable Nellor Reed, I've come to Teuchl in troublesome times. My people are under attack. Six weeks ago, a goblin host traversed the Great Emptiness east of Villor. They're a gnarly race, an abomination, unlike the pale creatures known in the West. Instead, they're tall, over one and a half yards and brawny, covered by a greenish skin that our blades can't pierce. We don't know why they've abandoned their burrows in the Grammor ranges. They've arrived in large numbers and they brought all their grubs and gimcracks, and wherever they go they set up tent cities. Many of us have suffered death at their hands, and a stream of refugees has flowed into Villor. We're not cowards, but so violent is their push that I fear we won't be able to stop them. And, once they've overrun us, they'll turn your way."

The audience cried out. My whiskers trembled.

What was I supposed to say?

"Have you taken this up with King Nablung?" I asked. "I'm not sure how we kipu can help, Honourable Arlandia."

"I wish for you to speak to your king, young master enchanter. Convince him to send troops." She peeked at the other ambassadors. "All kingdoms of the West should lend support. This hostile army is a seething tide we must halt together, or it will overwhelm us one after another."

Berekob stood up and raised his voice.

"Ambassadress, this is hardly the right forum for such a request. You're taking advantage of the fact that our master enchanter is young. King Nablung has been clear. Teuchl has no intention of wasting their warriors on gnomes. The bogs of Villor aren't worth the bones of even one of our fighters."

The atmosphere turned icy, and nobody said a word. Arlandia frowned.

"I'm sorry if that's the way you see it," she said. "Still, I'd like to hear the master enchanter's opinion."

"He has no right to speak on political matters," Berekob said.

Everybody's eyes were on me.

"Dear Arlandia," I began, "I hope you understand my powers as master enchanter are limited. I command no army and hold no treasures. My power is knowledge. While I don't know how I can help, the plight of the gnomes pains me."

Was there a way to help?

Berekob nodded. "Why is it our business when one tribe of earth wallowers quarrels with another? Leave them to battle it out! We'll deal with the leftovers. In the meantime, they need to show respect. Teuchl once ruled the world with the backing of the kipu. All these mouselings feared us, and no gnome would have dared step their feet into our council and make such preposterous demands."

There were shouts of protest. The delegation from Farnning left.

At the monastery, I'd heard the rumours that Berekob had become a kipu-supremacist. I hadn't believed it. But there was no denying it now. This wasn't the uncle I remembered. I remember when he took us kittens into the raised gardens. Now, he was full of bitterness and malice.

"He should be able to hear her," my mother said. "If this isn't the right time, perhaps another time and location is appropriate?"

"Uncle, I understand your point of view," I said. "But I wish to hear Arlandia speak. Ambassadress, please visit me later for a private audience."

"Thank you, master enchanter."

Afterwards, my mother invited me to her quarters to speak in private. "You did well. I know it can be overwhelming, but you're much stronger than you think you are."

"I didn't know you were religious," I said.

"Not really."

"What about the collar?"

"I just wear it for Berekob. He's the devout one."

"Why for him? I don't understand."

"He's powerful at court. Ever since your father died, he's an undisputed authority." She came close to me and whispered. "And he's got ambitions. You need to watch your back when you're dealing with him."

This was what I'd feared.

"Don't look so worried. Together, we can keep him in check. Your uncle has his uses, and he has served the kipu well. Come, let's have salmon." She called out to her servants.

"I remember you as a kitten when you couldn't wait to get into the gardens. You and Carruf were so naughty." Mother laughed—which calmed my nerves—and my whiskers relaxed.

We ate and talked, and she advised me to host a dinner for Arlandia to mend relations. "Despite what Berekob said, the gnomes are important allies."

———

A FEW DAYS LATER, just before the stars came out, I waited in the fresh air at the top of my tower for Arlandia. I was studying the spires below and the mountains in the distance when I heard a gnomish carriage approach. The winged lizards hissed as the vessel landed on the tower's platform. Arlandia and Sivery exited, unbridled their beasts, and followed me into the atrium.

"Thank you for receiving us, master enchanter," said Sivery as she took a seat.

"You're welcome, milady."

"Growing up in a monastery on the Northern Isles, do you by chance know the gnomish smith named Lurip?"

"I do. He was a resident when I first arrived. A master of his trade and an outstanding teacher. His ability to tinker with machines and apparatuses of all kinds must be unmatched. I have learned much from him and call him friend."

She smiled. "I call him friend as well. He lives in Villor now. We're grateful to have him. His skill in blade making is indispensable in dark times like these."

We fell silent for a moment.

"You'll be interested to hear he's doing well. He has set up shop and has married a local."

"It pleases me to hear. A toast to Lurip."

We drank.

"Master enchanter, you asked if there was anything you could do for the gnomes," Sivery said.

"I did."

"There is one thing."

"Please, speak."

"Have you considered the lioness seal?" she asked.

My mouth dried. How did she even know about the seal?

"Carry it to Villor and smash the enemy."

"You don't understand what you're asking."

"We know the seal's history. The people of the north no longer care about Teuchl's past misdeeds. Today, they worship Cyhoni and are content. There won't be a backlash if you draw on the seal. Not in Villor, nor anywhere else."

"I'm not afraid of backlash, but nobody knows where the seal is."

It wasn't a lie. Master enchanter Sinur, my grandfather, had rejected the seal and hidden it. People had long assumed he'd buried it somewhere in the Dalati mountains. Even though I guessed it was much closer, I didn't know exactly where it was hidden.

"I hope you won't take offence," Sivery said. "But I learned from a reliable source the seal is here."

"In the city?"

"Underneath this tower."

My curiosity was piqued.

"In the foundation?"

"Even deeper."

"How do you know this?"

"I have an informant."

"A kipu?"

Sivery looked at Arlandia and sighed.

"No, a gnome," she said.

"A gnome? How would a gnome know?"

"Not just any gnome."

"Tell him," Arlandia said.

"Long ago, before humans, gnomes lived here," Sivery said. "They explored the natural caves underneath the mountain, dug deep, and excavated the underground city of Elmming. It was a cheerful place, full of life, renowned for its workshops, its inns, and playhouses. They established subterranean gardens and grew catnip. According to legend, there is an enormous grotto that stretches for miles, and in the middle of it, sits a gigantic temple for Cyhoni."

"An ancient gnomish temple, eh?" I jumped up and paced back

and forth. That had to be where Sinur hid the seal. I'd admired him all my life, but this was something else. Finding an ancient gnomish temple underneath Teuchl! But I needed to be reasonable. The seal was dangerous.

"Elmming flourished for centuries," Sivery continued. "Until goblins destroyed it and its inhabitants fled. Memories faded, and scholars argued if it was even real. Two years ago, I stumbled upon it by chance. For years, I'd been chasing the Unseen, a gnomish clan of pickpockets and thieves. They were always a step ahead of me, eluding my grasp. But here in Teuchl, I caught one of their scouts in a trap. I brought her to Villor, where she told us everything. The Unseen are the descendants of the lost inhabitants of Elmming, who have returned to live beneath Teuchl in hiding."

"How do you know she wasn't lying?"

"Oh, you'd know if you saw her. She's like no gnome you've ever encountered. Tall like a goblin, and of the most unusual, pale complexion. She speaks an antiquated language, straight out of an old tome."

I admit, I wanted it to be true. Yet I had to be careful.

"Couldn't she have made up the accent?"

She looked at me and sighed. "That would be very difficult, even for somebody more literate than her. Plus, she told us something else that convinced us."

"What was it?"

"They're mining nitre."

Nitre. I didn't know much about the white powder, except it was valuable for the gnomes. They frequently used it in their contraptions.

"Our scholars have known for a long time there is nitre in Elmming." Sivery looked me directly in the eyes. "You cannot share this information with anyone. It is one of our most-guarded secrets. Since the prisoner was uneducated and had absolutely no connection to Villor, she couldn't possibly have known about the nitre. That is, unless she was from Elmming."

"And what about the seal?"

"Your grandfather discovered the gnomes and struck a deal with them. The Unseen have worshiped Cyhoni since the beginning of time. They see themselves as her most loyal followers. For them, the seal represented a hope, a symbol of Elmming's resurgence. They would die to protect it."

"Where is this supposed entrance to Elmming?"

"We couldn't get any definite locations out of her, but we gathered there are two hidden entrances in the lower city. I believe there is a third under this tower."

Surely, I could find it in no time. I paused.

It would shock my teachers that I'm even contemplating it. I focused my gaze on the skirting in the room's corner when I answered Sivery.

"Thank you for sharing this with me," I said. "I appreciate your trust in the kipu and in myself. But I don't want to give you false hope. We won't quest for the seal. I dread the consequences of finding it, especially in times like these. We must conceive a better way."

They looked at me in silence, disappointment on their faces.

"I'll talk to the king. Maybe I can change his mind."

"I thank you."

We entered the dining hall, sat down, and my servants brought grilled chicken with rice. The gnomes spoke well, and the conversation was pleasant. After dessert, we lingered and talked into the small hours. They didn't bring up the seal again.

Weeks went by, I endured the king's banquet, and the goblins advanced.

My mother encouraged me to continue associating with Arlandia and Sivery. Whenever I could, I took the time to meet my old friend Carruf in the lower city. He'd married and had two small kittens, and I spent many hours in his hospitable house.

On the new moon, I invited the gnomes again to my quarters. After we'd eaten, we rested on divans and talked about history, when the bell rang to announce a visitor and a kipu herald entered the room.

"Your mother sends her regards, together with her famous mulled wine. The nights can be cold at this time of the year. Servant!"

A human in livery brought a tablet with bowls and mugs and set them down on the coffee table. The drink looked almost black. Steam came off its surface, and I noticed cinnamon and a strange hint of cardamom or something similar. We toasted and drank. It was full and sweet and warmed us.

My head whirled while Arlandia continued her story. Quickly, the whirling became so severe I had to sit down on my divan. My first thought was I'd eaten rotten beef earlier. After a while, when sitting didn't help, I lay, and soon the settee rocked and leapt underneath me like a stubborn donkey.

I closed my eyes, hoping this would make the dizziness go away, and when I reopened them, Berekob stood next to me on the divan.

I blinked. Where had he come from? He'd never visited me before. Him being here meant nothing good.

"It disgusts me when they enter the citadel. They know they must stay in the lower city where they belong," he said.

"Who?"

"The gnomes."

I looked over to the other diwan. Arlandia and Sivery had passed out and lay on their backs. One of their lizards had come in and licked Sivery's hand.

"They'll be dead soon," Berekob said. "And so will you."

My claws pinched the velvet-like pillowcase I lay on. "You poisoned us," I hissed.

His head came so close to mine that I smelled his breath.

"Coward," he whispered into my ear, and the hostility in his voice stunned me. "You don't have the guts to be master enchanter. You're as unsuited as your father."

He looked at me menacingly. "But you won't make it through the night. The king will ordain me as the new master enchanter. Now, please excuse me, I'm going for the seal. And—unlike your father—I won't hesitate to use it for the kipu cause. My friends below are waiting. Don't waste your last moments worrying. There's no antidote."

My nostrils flared, and I panted. Who did he think he was? I was the rightful master enchanter! In desperation, I bolted off the couch and pushed towards him, but my clumsy paw slipped off the armrest and I crashed to the floor.

"May the seal betray you!" I cried. Darkness overcame me.

———

WHEN I AWOKE, I was lying on the ground in front of the divan. My head ached like it was about to explode. I felt the poison rushing through my body. It tickled my veins, hastened my pulse. Berekob's smug grin flashed in my mind and I bared my teeth. He would pay for this.

I got up and limped on rickety legs, hauling myself through the door into the corridor where I crouched under a sideboard. The polished stone slabs reflected the red light of the torches. Its intensity pierced my eyes. The stink of burning wax choked me. Danger lingered. The compact passage appeared gigantic. Its openness exposed me—yet, at the same time—trapped me. Even though I meowed as vehemently as possible, none of my servants answered my plea.

Have they abandoned me? Why was I still alive?

The seal wouldn't obey Berekob as long as I lived. He knew that— the wisest magician in the kingdom. Had he made a mistake with the poison? I licked my pelt and forced myself to think calmly.

There'd been a peculiar aroma in the mulled wine, so he must have put it in the drink. It must have been a liquid, or at least a soluble powder, and it had tolerated the boil. It wasn't primis, that led to muscle paralysis. It was so lethal I would be dead by now. In fact, primis would have been an obvious choice, considering it was readily available. Strange, that Berekob hadn't considered it.

Button bush was another possibility. The red berries were

common and highly toxic. However, undue heat ruined the active ingredient. Hay apples!

That must be it. It was also known as silver mandrake. I knew the root well from my research. It would explain my shortness of breath, too. Doubtless, mandrake was the base. Yet something wickeder than mere plant decoction had been present. The toxicant affected my stomach and a fierce magic raged there, burning my kidneys. He must have added a quantum of witchcraft to the brew.

My hopes dwindled. It was only a question of time before the drink would end me. Heat flushed through my front legs and I slammed the sideboard so hard that it hurt. If Berekob became master enchanter, he would lead Teuchl into ruin. It was my duty to protect my folk. Whether or not I liked it, my sole hope was the seal of the lioness. Its magical power outshone every mortal's craft. Yes, I'd sworn an oath never to touch it, but I would have to break that vow. Otherwise, the poison would kill me, and Berekob would destroy everything I loved. I couldn't let that happen.

I would use it once. Only to save myself.

I dragged myself down the corridor, descended the stairs to the servant's dorm, and entered a storage chamber with rows of bookshelves full of old chronicles. In a corner at the outer wall lay the pieces of a wooden cupboard. Behind it sat a small iron gate. Its wings stood open. Footprints descended into the semi-darkness beyond. The stink of brimstone was unmistakable. This must lead to Elmming, I just had to follow Berekob's trail.

After a few strides, I found myself in total gloom. The muffled tread of my toes on the stone echoed faintly far below. I'd entered a vast vertical space, no doubt the hollow tower shaft. It took a few moments for my sight to adjust. I noticed a faint red glimmer and realised that I was traversing a narrow ledge that spiraled down along the outer wall. No balustrade guarded the edge from the void.

While I descended, I remained as close to the wall as possible, struggling ahead, stumbling occasionally. My condition worsened, and I quivered as sweat soaked my pelt. In the dim light, my paws simultaneously looked gigantic and miniature. The scale of the tower's shaft terrified me.

I knew it was just another symptom of my poisoning, but it seemed I was growing shorter. I felt like I'd been flung into an abundance of space where I didn't belong. The stone wall's magnitude defied my imagination. It seemed to extend endlessly; its curvature barely noticeable. When I glanced down at myself, I'd turned into a negligible chunk. A piece of fur and meat, forlorn, unable to advance despite pushing. For a time, I leaned against the stones and closed my eyes, but there was no escape. I was but a worm. Tiny. Insignificant.

After what seemed like an eternity, the black wall's sandstone blocks gave way to roughly hewn, pink granite bedrock. I guess I wasn't that miniscule, otherwise, I wouldn't have gotten that far. Still, each of my steps appeared a mile long and took forever to finish.

The side wall changed again and became masoned from a pitch-black basalt. A bright, crimson light coming from below lit up everything, and soon the hollow tower shaft widened. Beneath, where the stairs ended, I noticed a large circle of bright red lanterns on poles. I stopped. There it was, inside the circle! A large reservoir of clear water, like in the fables I'd read. From the shore, a long catwalk led to a rocky island with a gigantic statue.

When I stood in front of the pond, my shoulders tightened. Through the shallow water, I saw the ground sloping towards the centre where the current welled up in eddies from the deep. Weak ripples stretched all the way to the shore. I fought the impulse to run from the water.

Low waves splashed against the pillars of the pier, thundering through the silence. On the island loomed a statue of Cyhoni with wide-open jaws. Berekob's red key was stuck in a keyhole, in a raised plate. Below it, in the base, a hidden door had swung open, revealing a gaping hole large enough for a cat to pass through. I nodded slowly. He must have been certain I was dead.

I went down the hole, swaying slightly, and after thirty yards of a steep slope, I came into a natural cave. My head pounded and a sudden metallic taste in my mouth made me retch. I was growing weaker. Who knew how much time I had left?

It was pitch-dark, and I crept forward blindly. After a while, I reached an oblong cavern with pale lights suspended from the ceiling and crouched behind the scraggy bushes growing there. White ants crawled across the ground, scrambling to hide from the light. Further on, rows of garden beds were situated directly underneath the lights, one next to the other: potatoes, mushrooms, and a range of different herbs.

Deeper into the cave, I spotted bushes of catnip between stalagmites. So, it was true.

"Those crafty gnomes," I whispered. Not only was catnip delicious, but it was a potent medicinal herb and stimulant. Taking it would give me a much-needed energy boost and would keep me going. I plunged into it, wallowed in the green tuft.

When I tired of playing, I curled myself up in the green, snapped off a few twigs, and licked the delicious juice. The minty aroma cleared my nostrils of the lingering sulphury odour. It wouldn't neutralise the poison. Nothing but the powerful magic of the seal could do that, but I felt re-energised, and confident that I had enough time to find the temple. "Take this," I hissed, and threw an imagined punch at Berekob.

Deal with my full strength, old man.

Suddenly, something moved behind a large tuft of herbs. I jumped to my feet, ready to defend myself. The rustling came closer, the bushes parted, and a familiar lizard with a third eye on his dorsal line appeared.

"I thought you were dead," he said.

"Who're you?" I asked.

He smiled. "My name is Gejeppe. I'm Sivery's animal."

He looked like her lizard. Although, I'd always thought speaking spells didn't work on reptiles. Sivery had to be talented to enchant him.

"What're you doing here?" I asked.

"After Berekob finished you, he killed my brothers, broke my arm, and wrecked our carriage. I was lucky to slip away. I fled and came here."

"Have you seen any gnomes?" I asked.

"Yes," he replied. "They're close by."

"Lead me there."

"Now?"

"Yes."

He led me calmly along a wooden fence. When we reached the end of the garden, we entered a long, dark tunnel. After climbing over rubble for five hundred yards, we passed a granite gate, lit by flickering torches. Looking around, I found we were high on the sidewall of a giant cave. Far below, modest stone dwellings cowered, illuminated by more torches.

"Have you seen a grand temple?" I asked.

"No. This is all I know. There is an iron gate on the far side guarded by twenty-ten soldiers."

"Heavily guarded?" It had to be the way to the temple. "Show me how to get there."

We scaled an incline, pursued a footpath that first disappeared and then reappeared after two hundred yards, and from there it followed a contoured line. We kept walking, and once we'd passed the settlement below, we ascended, until the lights behind us faded in the dark.

"Be quiet," Gejeppe blurted. "Guards are close by."

We crept with ducked heads until we reached a pile of dead spruce wood.

"There they are," he said, and pointed with his head. I inched forward and peeked around the pile. Massive gnome soldiers with whitish skin in plate armour patrolled the ridge on the other side of a dry ravine. They were armed with pikes and carried torches that illuminated a vast, metallic gate. I shrank back and squeezed myself behind the pile.

"How can I get around them?" I whispered.

"You can't. They're everywhere." He pointed back into the gloom where the settlement lay. "Maybe, try your luck down there."

I turned back; my tail wavered from side to side while my eyes pierced the dark. He was right. The settlement was my best chance.

We retreated carefully until I was sure we were out of sight. I thanked Gejeppe, said goodbye, and went down the rugged slope, straight towards the village below. Between two rocks, I morphed into a kitten, using an old concealment charm I'd picked up in the monastery. My pelt shrank and my eyes expanded. My bones contracted painfully. I wasn't fluffy, but my features conformed to the baby schema, and humanoids would perceive me as cute. It was the smoothest way to manipulate them.

The settlement was more of a shantytown, made of scanty huts huddling between low bluffs. Forlorn gnome figures squatted around measly campfires. It surprised me that they were awake, since it had to be the middle of the night, but I guess it didn't matter to them what time it was on the surface.

My head was pounding again, and I wasn't sure how much longer I could hang on, but I forced myself to take the time to snoop around and observe. I needed to make the right call when choosing my victim.

The inhabitants spoke a strange dialect, but close enough to common Gnomish for me to understand. I searched but found nothing promising. They were workers, soiled and sweaty, some snoozing, the rest mostly sitting in silence while staring into the flames. One middle-aged one lamented the misfortune of being stuck there.

Eventually, I located a pitched tent that housed a gnome family, comprising a resolute father, his stout wife and two sons, and a pretty blonde girl with a runny nose.

The girl looked promising. When she went out to get water from a well, I brushed my fur against her legs, and she smiled.

"Where did you come from, little kitty? Aww, you're so cute."

She grabbed me and took me to a toolshed where she hid behind a large table, sat down on a stack of empty sacks, and petted me.

"My name's Tickell. I think I'll call you Pepper."

I swallowed hard, pressed my hind legs together, and resisted the urge to scratch her.

"Wait here for me. I have to deliver mushrooms to the temple kitchen. It's such a boring trip, but I'll be back soon."

I put my head into her cupped hand and looked at her longingly.

"Maybe I should bring you along," she said. "You don't mind coming, do you?"

I played along and meowed. At least, like this, I didn't even have to meddle with her mind.

"You know, I really don't fancy the fat grey cat who lives in the temple. But you're so different."

She could only mean Berekob. Soon, I could dig my claws into his face.

"Maybe you can stay with me for good," she added.

I don't think so, Tickell.

She put me under a pile of rags in her crumbling basket, carried me to a smelly inn around the corner, and covered me with the mushrooms she collected from a kitchen hand. The cloth was disgusting but concealed me well. Through a hole in the basket, I observed how she picked up a scratched lantern, lit it with a burning log at the inn, and left the village.

The little girl climbed a ridge and when she reached the top, she walked by the sentinels without being stopped. Then, she entered a long tunnel and descended—barefoot as she was—over stony ground.

She was slow, and it took forever. Finally, the tunnel opened into an enormous cave. I couldn't make out the other side, it must've been miles away. The space was brightly lit by light of an arcane provenance that seemed to come from everywhere at once. This time, soldiers stopped her to look at the mushrooms. It became difficult to remain still in the tiny basket while Tickell continued her shamble. After an hour, at the end of a long flight of stairs, she stopped. I spied through my hole in the basket and saw the temple rise high from a plateau, easily visible from afar.

When we reached it, she climbed a long stairway that led to the top. We passed stacked reddish glass bricks and crossed pinnacle walls atop each of the three levels. A small army of sentries manned the fortifications. They were still and watchful. Even though I was well hidden, I felt exposed.

The top of the monumental building was a rough, rocky field—a construction site—full of pits and piles of slabs, with makeshift barricades and scattered wooden huts. Above all of this towered a black monolith so alien, that I felt for sure some god must have tossed it up from the depths a long time ago.

The young girl dropped off the mushrooms in a communal kitchen building and found a resting place in an empty hut not far away. The trip had tired her, and she fell asleep on dirty straw at once. The moment she breathed steadily, I rose out of the basket, found a corner behind the hut, concentrated on my spell, contracted my eyes, and stretched my bones back to normal size. My legs cracked while they lengthened, sending thin needles of pain up my thighs. I hated this part.

When the aching had subsided, I moved quickly. I met a dirt track snaking to the monolith and strode towards it until the crag loomed directly over me. Its flat face underneath the marked top looked incomplete, as if a divine sculptor had failed to finish his carving. Foreign runes were daubed all over the rock. I recognised the sign for Cyhoni in old Gnomish. I circled around and ascended over the barren ridge at the rear where I discovered washed-out remnants of stairs over which I hastened.

At the crest perched a spacious platform with a richly embellished altar and a cabinet of ritual swords and daggers, lit up by immense columns holding basins of blazing pitch. Their flames flickered and cast dancing shades everywhere. Behind the altar stood a small sanctuary with a porch supported by caryatides depicting Cyhoni.

Out of the shade strolled Berekob. A black lead coin dangled around his neck. It was the seal.

I rolled up my tail, and formed my protective ring.

"You truly are the annoying little grimalkin, aren't you? It took me quite a bit of effort to have the guards ready, and you spoil it all by slipping through."

"Give me the seal," I replied.

He snickered. "Come and get it." He spun around and disappeared into the shade of the next column. "If you crave it—"

"I'll slay you if I have to," I cut him off, and raced around the column, but he wasn't there. I hurried to the next column, searching the darkness.

"Try, if you can." His voice came from behind the sanctuary.

I dashed around the building to meet him, but again he was gone. I pushed my legs in the gravel and screeched to a halt, my claws out, ready to strike. My heart pounded loudly in the silence. Out of the corner of my eye, I saw a movement on the far side and my head shot around. It wasn't Berekob. Just dancing shades between the pillars.

I advanced to the edge of the crag, crouched above the depth, and waited. I needed to be patient.

"Can't find me, eh?" This time, his voice came from the front side of the sanctuary.

I darted back and there he was, ducked in front of the altar, with his teeth bared. At once, I sped up, jumped, and hit him. But he was quick. Leaping to the side, he grabbed me with his claws. He clung to me and we rolled across the ground.

"Enough, you demon!" I flexed my muscles, and he couldn't hold me back. I rammed my hind legs into the ground and threw him into the air. He was lighter that I'd anticipated and flew several yards before he crashed against a pillar. The impact dazed him. I pursued and rammed my head into him. Our skulls connected with a loud clang.

"You're no match for me, old man," I shouted. For a moment, he lay there without moving. I wanted to rip his head off and end his scheming once and for all. My tension released in a mad laughter.

"Bring the girl forward," he groaned.

What did he mean? I looked around. Two soldiers appeared out of the darkness, holding Tickell, dragging her up the footpath. A third one pulled a curved dagger and held it to her neck.

"Cut her throat if he attacks," he said.

Tickell had annoyed me—a lot—but she was innocent. She was a citizen of Teuchl, and it was my duty to protect her.

My muscles quivered. For Cyhoni's sake.

"Is that you, Pepper?" she said, when she spotted me. "I knew you were important." She started thrashing, trying to free her arms.

"Let him go. He's my cat!"

Berekob turned to me. "Stand back."

I retreated slowly.

"Accept your defeat. You can't win."

I couldn't endure the poison much longer. Above all, I needed to save Tickell from the thugs threating her. It was my fault she was in this situation. I swiveled around, dropped my guard, and focused my magical energy. Three blue flashes leapt from my fur and slammed into her tormentors. The raw power of the magic smashed their faces and knocked them off their feet. Secondary discharges cascaded down from their necks to their toes, burning the warty gnome flesh. The force of the blast also floored Tickell, who slid down the path, a sharp rock cutting her whitish flesh. Dark gnomish blood smeared her face. My throat thickened. I needed to act quickly.

I brought my guard up again and turned to Berekob, but he got me with a fireball. The heat singed my pelt and took my breath away. Red flames engulfed me, the intense light blinded me, and pain warped my body. I stumbled, eager to strike back, but unable to see anything. He laughed triumphantly.

"One more insight awaits you, before you die," he said. "Haven't wondered why you're still alive?" he said. "Hasn't occurred to you that's kind of odd?"

"Why didn't you choose a more suitable poison?" I shouted. "Primis would've killed me by now."

"Ha! Well, little nephew, I did choose primis."

Slowly, my vision was returning.

"I don't follow," I said.

"Let me explain. I didn't choose the substance you drank— probably mandrake. I concocted something more savage that would have polished you and those stinking gnomes off within the hour. Had my scheme succeeded, I would be the master enchanter by now, plotting the triumphant resurgence of Teuchl."

"So, what happened?" I asked. Had he asked a servant to prepare the poison? He couldn't have been that foolish.

"Your mother deceived me."

My mother? That made no sense.

"Why would she...?" I mumbled. And then I understood. She wanted the seal in Teuchl, around the neck of the master enchanter, and under the control of the family. She and Berekob had conspired to murder me, so he could seize the seal. Heat flushed through my body.

"She betrayed us both," he said.

She had substituted mandrake for primis.

"But why...?" I whispered with a dry throat.

"Because you're her boy, you twit. She prefers to see you on the throne rather than me. That is, as long as you serve her." There was bitterness in his voice.

My father had sent me to the Isles where the friars had schooled me. He'd trusted no one else on that. Mother knew I wouldn't take the seal of my own free will, so she'd replaced the poison to make sure I wouldn't die too quickly.

So, I would have time to choose between the seal and death.

I yowled.

With the seal, Berekob would bring terrible suffering to people everywhere. Someone needed to stop him.

My legs shook. Spittle ran down my muzzle. I planted my feet widely. I would wield the seal. Only once, to destroy Berekob. Then I would cast it aside.

Berekob noticed the grit in my gaze and snarled at me. His high pitch escalated into a rattling caterwaul. He thrust out his front paws, unsheathing his claws, and raised his howl to a crescendo. My body tensed. As the seal dangled from his collar, I felt that it served me already, recognising me as its legitimate master.

My will gathered, and my spirit heaved out against him, pushing against his resistance. Disbelief showed on his face. Three long dives, and I landed in front of him and cowered, just a yard away. I suffered his growling, a sickening clang that stung my ears, and kept myself from countering it. Let him whine. It was a sign of weakness.

Then I pounced. My claws found his body, and we curled together. I pushed, and we crashed into a pillar. His claws tore at my flesh. I didn't care. We rolled off the edge of the rock and dropped a hundred yards onto the plain below. His bones broke under my grip the very moment his spirit disintegrated under my psychic assault.

I had landed on my feet, unhurt, and let out a tremendous cry. I'd killed him. The seal had abandoned him and embraced me. I stripped it from his neck and slipped it around my own. Out of nowhere, the figure of a powerful lioness entered my mind. I roared again, quieter, but fierce and guttural. I felt a rage, and my rage was righteous.

My eyes became all-seeing. I was conscious of all my body's fibres, of my blood circulating, of muscles contracting. At the same moment, I could suddenly see every creature inside the temple at once: a hooting cave owl, two mating scorpions, Tickell as she sobbed, and the gnome soldiers guarding the walls. When I focused my will, the strength of the seal rendered my mother's poison innocuous.

I'd have to have a word with her. Nobody could treat the master enchanter like this. Not even her.

I strode to the rim of the temple where I mounted a viewpoint on the parapet. The walls below teemed with soldiers. Somewhere far out in the caves, I sensed Gejeppe.

A squad of gnomish officers approached me, dread on their faces. The most senior one stepped forward. He had a silvery beard and bore a general's armament. On his steel breastplate, I saw the reflection of my eyes gleaming like liquid gold.

"Hail, master enchanter," he said. "I am Zubnick. We await your orders."

"Take care of the girl."

"As you wish."

"Remove your soldiers from the temple. Keep guarding your city."

"As you wish, master."

He knelt and whispered, so the other men couldn't hear it. "Master, we can protect the seal with our lives, should you prefer to depart and leave it behind."

"As you protected it from him?" I pointed with my head behind me, where Berekob's smashed body lay in the dark.

"My apologies, master. We should have never trusted him," the general said. "But make no mistake, we serve only the seal. We don't interfere with whom it chooses, as long as a kipu from a legitimate family wins it in honest battle."

"I am a friend of the gnomes. There is a place for you and your people in my city."

I thought of Sivery and Arlandia, who had drunk the tainted wine. They lay senseless on my divan, innocent, slowly dying. More than anything, I desired to save them.

"I will keep the seal and return to Teuchl."

"Master, please accept an escort. There's no saying what might await you. I have many men at my disposal: spearmen, archers, and officers."

"Very well," I replied.

We left immediately. They guided me back to the well under the tower. From there on, I took the lead. The tall gnomes' feet barely fit on the narrow ledge on the tower's sidewall. When I arrived at the top, I puffed out my chest and leapt through the iron gate into the storage chamber and up the stairs into my quarters.

The sun was still below the horizon, but the brightening sky cast a red glint on the faces of the two gnomes through the windows. Arlandia and Sivery lay on the divan exactly as I'd left them, breathing slowly. "Secure the outer platforms," I ordered, and the gnomes swarmed out.

I closed my eyes and extended my mind into their bodies. Their physical selves became part of my all-feeling, and I sensed the poison circulating through their veins. I concentrated briefly and cleansed their blood of the poison.

I sighed. My friends were saved. I had prevailed against Berekob.

But could I return to my books if there was still so much to do? The goblins rampaged through the north. Who would confront the priests, if not me?

"Zubnick, tell the king I slayed Berekob and took the seal. Then, find the guest quarters where Ambassadress Arlandia and her delegation are staying. Talk to her secretary and let him know she's all right. Report back as soon as possible."

It gave me joy to feel the force of life return slowly to my gnomish friends. I sat back and watched over them as they slept.

Sivery roused when the sun rose over the horizon. "Is that what I think it is?" she asked, gazing at the seal around my neck. I nodded.

"I'm glad you took it."

She cupped my head in her hand. I let her do it, and for a while we just sat there.

Zubnick returned. "Word of your deeds has reached the court. The king's augurs have affirmed my story. Nablung has praised your bravery," he said. "Your mother retreated to the shrine of Cyhoni in the stronghold."

Sivery, Zubnick and I went down to the castle, followed by the gnome warriors. Human soldiers stood sentinel at every corner. It seemed all the king's men were up in arms, watching us silently from windows, from doorways with their swords drawn, and next to gates with their halberds crossed. They hid behind their shields, shifting about, biting their lips. They did not stop me as I marched to the stronghold and into the shrine.

Mother stood alone in the sanctuary, her head lowered in silent prayer.

"I welcome you, master enchanter," she said without looking at me.

"You poisoned your own son."

"I did what I had to."

"But why? What do you want?" I asked.

"For you to carry your burden."

She raised her head and looked at me defiantly.

"And you will."

She was right. I'd made up my mind. My books would have to wait. I would take the seal to Villor and help the gnomes. As my father and grandfather had, I would serve the people of Teuchl as master enchanter.

There was no way I could forgive her betrayal, though.

"You're free to stay," I said. "No harm shall be done to you. But after today, I will never again talk to you."

"So be it," she said and wept.

END

About the Author

Martin was born in Munich, Germany. After moving from country to country for a while and working as an engineer, and—amongst other things—developing photovoltaics manufacturing technology, he has settled in Brisbane a few years ago, where he lives with his wife and daughter and enjoys the sunshine.

He has a degree in physics, loves the outdoors, and the written word in every form. He reads cyberpunk, solarpunk, and lots of news and non-fiction, trying to keep up with global civilization inexorably moving towards the singularity.

ABOUT VISION WRITERS

Vision Writers Group was founded in 1996 by Rowena Cory Daniells, Marianne de Pierres and Adrianne Fitzpatrick.

Our goal is to give science fiction, fantasy and horror writers a chance to meet their peers, have their work critiqued, and critique the work of others. We're about writing, critiquing, sharing experiences and expanding the opportunities for speculative fiction writers in Queensland and Australia.

The group is centred on our monthly meetings and the Groups.io discussion list. Our aim is to foster a literature-based speculative fiction community that produces good stories and good writers.

If you live in or around Brisbane, Australia and write speculative fiction, we would love to have you join us.

Please visit our website for more information:
www.visionwriters.net

ANTHOLOGIES BY VISION WRITERS

2020 Perfect Vision

18

Darkest Depths: 2016 Vision Writers Anthology